Voices from the Hills

Voices from the Hills

EDITED BY *Robert J. Higgs*

CO-PUBLISHED WITH APPALACHIAN CONSORTIUM PRESS

Selected Readings
of Southern Appalachia

AND *Ambrose N. Manning* East Tennessee State University

FREDERICK UNGAR PUBLISHING CO.
NEW YORK

Copyright © 1975 by Frederick Ungar Publishing Co., Inc.
Printed in the United States of America
Designed by Irving Perkins

Co-published with the Appalachian Consortium Press, Boone,
North Carolina 28607

Many selections in this volume are included with the permission of the
copyright owners. The editors are grateful for their cooperation; a full list
of acknowledgments follows the text.

Library of Congress Cataloging in Publication Data
Main entry under title:

Voices from the hills.

    Bibliography: p.
    1. American literature—Southern States.
2. Appalachian Mountains, Southern—Addresses,
essays, lectures.   3. English language in the
United States—Dialects—Appalachian region—Addresses,
essays, lectures.   I. Higgs, Robert J., 1932–
II. Manning, Ambrose N.
PS551.V64   810′.8′0975   75–4949
ISBN 0–8044–2383–0
ISBN 0–8044–6271–2 pbk.

It is worthy notice, that our mountains are not solitary and scattered confusedly over the face of the country; but that they commence at about 150 miles from the sea-coast, are disposed in ridges one behind another, running nearly parallel with the sea-coast, though rather approaching it as they advance north-eastwardly. To the south-west, as the tract of country between the sea-coast and the Mississippi becomes narrower, the mountains converge into a single ridge, which, as it approaches the Gulph of Mexico, subsides into plain country, and gives rise to some of the waters of that gulph, and particularly to a river called the Apalachicola, probably from the Apalachies, an Indian nation formerly residing on it. Hence the mountains giving rise to that river, and seen from its various parts, were called the Apalachian mountains, being in fact the end or termination only of the great ridges passing through the continent. European geographers however extended the name northwardly as far as the mountains extended; some giving it, after their separation into different ridges, to the Blue ridge, others to the North mountain, others to the Alleghaney, others to the Laurel ridge, as may be seen in their different maps. But the fact I believe is, that none of these ridges were ever known by that name to the inhabitants, either native or emigrant, but as they saw them so called in European maps. In the same direction generally are the veins of limestone, coal, and other minerals hitherto discovered: and so range the falls of our great rivers.

—THOMAS JEFFERSON
Notes on the State of Virginia, 1781–82

Contents

Preface   xiii

Introduction   xvii

PART I

I. *Exploration and Early Travels: First Impressions*   3

    A. *The Land and Landscape: A New Eden*   3

JOHN LEDERER   5
The Third and Last Expedition, and Conjectures
of the Land Beyond the Apalataean Mountains

JOHN FONTAINE   8
FROM *The Journal of John Fontaine*

TIMOTHY FLINT   12
The Garden of God FROM *Biographical Memoirs
of Daniel Boone*

JAMES KIRKE PAULDING   19
FROM *Letters from the South*

ANNE NEWPORT ROYALL   21
FROM *Sketches of History, Life, and Manners
in the United States*

B.   *The First Inhabitants: The Noble Naturals*   25

HENRY TIMBERLAKE   27
FROM *Memoirs of Lieut. Henry Timberlake*

ABRAHAM STEINER AND
FREDERICK C. DE SCHWEINITZ   35
Report of the Journey of the Brethren Abraham
Steiner and Frederick C. De Schweinitz to the
Cherokees and the Cumberland Settlements

ANNE NEWPORT ROYALL   42
FROM *Letters from Alabama on Various Subjects*

JOHN G. BURNETT   47
Removal of the Cherokees

C.   *The Mythical Heritage: Poor White and
Hillbilly*   55

WILLIAM BYRD II   57
FROM *The History of the Dividing Line*

ALEXANDER WILSON   59
FROM *American Ornithology*

THOMAS ASHE   61
FROM *Travels in America, Performed in 1806*

JAMES KIRKE PAULDING   64
FROM *Letters from the South*

TIMOTHY FLINT   68
FROM *Recollections of the Last Ten Years*

ANNE NEWPORT ROYALL   72
FROM *Sketches of History, Life, and Manners
in the United States*

II.   *Backwoods Humor: Tall Tale and Tall Talk*   77

DAVID CROCKETT   79
A Bear Hunt

GEORGE WASHINGTON HARRIS   85
Sut Lovingood's Daddy, Acting Horse, 86
Parson John Bullen's Lizards, 92

MARK TWAIN   101
Journalism in Tennessee

III. *Southern Romanticism: The Sublime and the Beautiful*   109

THOMAS JEFFERSON   111
Natural Bridge (FROM *Notes on the State of Virginia*)

WILLIAM GILMORE SIMMS   114
The Travellers (FROM *Charlemont*)

JOHN ESTEN COOKE   118
The Secret of the Mountains

SIDNEY LANIER   121
Friendship in the Hills (FROM *Tiger Lilies*)

DAVID HUNTER STROTHER ("PORTE CRAYON")   127
The Mountains

IV. *Local Color: Realism and Romance*   131

MARY NOAILLES MURFREE (CHARLES EGBERT CRADDOCK)   133
The Dancin' Party at Harrison's Cove (FROM *In the Tennessee Mountains*)

JOHN FOX, JR.   154
Christmas Eve on Lonesome

V. *New Dimensions of Realism: Renaissance in the Hills*   161

ANNE W. ARMSTRONG   163
The Cow in the Corn (FROM *This Day and Time*)

BEULAH ROBERTS CHILDERS   171
Sairy and the Young 'uns

THOMAS WOLFE   190
The Great Schism (FROM *The Hills Beyond*)

SHERWOOD ANDERSON   208
A Jury Case

VI.   *Uses of the Past: The Search for Identity*   217

JESSE STUART   219
Vacation in Hell

MILDRED HAUN   236
Melungeon-Colored

JAMES STILL   252
A Master Time

HARRIETTE ARNOW   263
Adjusting (FROM *The Dollmaker*)

JAMES AGEE   275
Family Ties (FROM *A Death in the Family*)

WILMA DYKEMAN   289
Sins of the Fathers (FROM *Return the Innocent Earth*)

VII.   *Muse of the Mountains: Appalachian Poetry*   303

SIDNEY LANIER   305
Thar's More in the Man Than Thar Is in the Land

DONALD DAVIDSON   308
Sanctuary

JESSE STUART   312
FROM *Man With a Bull-Tongue Plow*, 312
FROM *Album of Destiny*, 313
FROM *Kentucky Is My Land*, 316

LOUISE MCNEILL   318
FROM *Gauley Mountain*, 319
FROM *Paradox Hill*, 322

BILLY EDD WHEELER   325
FROM *Song of a Woods Colt*

LEE PENNINGTON   331
FROM *Scenes from a Southern Road*

JANE STUART   335
FROM *Eyes of the Mole*

DAVID MCCLELLAN 339
FROM *Leaves from the Legend of Luther Lamp*

MARION HODGE 344
Cole's First Song

JIM WAYNE MILLER 347
FROM *Dialogue with a Dead Man*

PART II

Echoes and Reverberations: Essays in Criticism and Culture 355

ROBERT PENN WARREN 357
Some Don'ts for Literary Regionalists

THEODORE ROOSEVELT 365
Sevier, Robertson, and the Watauga
Commonwealth, 1769–1774 (FROM *Winning of the West*)

SAM HOUSTON 374
Opposing the Kansas-Nebraska Bill (FROM *Writings of Sam Houston*)

ARNOLD J. TOYNBEE 383
Scotland, Ulster, and Appalachia (FROM *A Study of History*)

WALTER BLAIR 389
Six Davy Crocketts

EDMUND WILSON 408
"Poisoned!"

RANDALL STEWART 419
Tidewater and Frontier

H. L. MENCKEN 431
The Hills of Zion

JACK WELLER 440
Education (FROM *Yesterday's People*)

xii   *Contents*

JIM WAYNE MILLER   447
A Mirror for Appalachia

EARL F. SCHROCK, JR.   460
An Examination of the Dialect in *This Day and Time*

JAMES ROBERT REESE   474
The Myth of the Southern Appalachian Dialect as a Mirror of the Mountaineer

CRATIS WILLIAMS   493
Who are the Southern Mountaineers?

LOYAL JONES   507
Appalachian Values

HARRY M. CAUDILL   518
O, Appalachia!

Acknowledgments   533

Selected Bibliography   537

Preface

This work attempts to make available to the modern reader some of the best Southern Appalachian literature and criticism. To our knowledge it is the first collection of its kind ever assembled; if it is not, we feel that it is certainly one of the most comprehensive, containing literary selections covering a period of three centuries, and essays on the principal themes reflected in the writing. It is our hope that this broad, literary-cultural approach to the study of Appalachia will prove to be rewarding to teachers, students, and lay readers who wish to know more about this region of America.

Southern Appalachia comprises a territory larger than that of England, Wales, and Scotland combined, and even after a century of exploitation of coal, timber, and other natural resources, remains one of the richest areas on earth. It is also one of the richest in history and literature, both oral and written. For two hundred years it has been the site of one controversy after another: the Revolution, Indian removal, slavery, whiskey-making, religion, dam construction, unionism, welfare, ecology, conservation, and tourism. As the Kentucky writer Harry Caudill has observed, it has been discovered and rediscovered many times; and what is needed today are not additional discoveries and revelations but appreciation of what has already been found and written about.

In editing, we have tried to rely as much as possible on the texts of first editions or facsimiles, making only minor changes in punctuation and spelling in some of the early material for the sake of clarity. The date which appears at the end of each selection is that of the first edition; where two appear, the second refers to that of a later publication upon which the text we used was based.

The completion of this book would not have been possible without the support of a number of people. In particular we wish to express our gratitude to Mr. Borden Mace, Executive Director of the Appalachian Consortium, for his advice and to Dr. Jerry Rust, Director of the Research Advisory Council at East Tennessee State University, for the services of Mrs. Lynn Wilson, graduate assistant, whose help has been virtually indispensable. We are also grateful to Jesse Stuart, who generously contributed his own writing, and encouragement throughout; and to Loyal Jones, Director of the Center for Appalachian Studies, Berea College, for advice and information, especially regarding many fine writers who attended Berea. Although official acknowledgments appear elsewhere, we want to thank all authors, heirs, publishers, and trustees who gave permission to include material. We wish to make special acknowledgment to Dr. Cratis Williams, Dean of the Graduate School, Appalachian State University, for permission to use and quote from his masterful dissertation, *The Southern Mountaineer in Fact and Fiction.* We have referred to this comprehensive study many times as we have to another invaluable source, *Travels in the Early Tennessee Country (1540–1800)* by Samuel Cole Williams. We are indebted to Mrs. Robert R. Miller and Mrs. Gordon Brown for their kind permission to use passages from this work. Another collection of travel literature, Thomas D. Clark's *Travels in the Old South,* has also been of great value. Thanks are due to Dr. John B. Tallent, Chairman of the Department of English at East Tennessee State University, for his encouragement of this project and of Appalachian Studies in general, and to Mr. Hal Smith, Head Librarian, Charles Sherrod Library, and the library staff, for service in many ways. We are especially grateful to Miss Edith Keys, Reference Librarian, for her assistance. We would like to express a hearty and grateful tribute to our wives, Reny Higgs and Mary Manning, who contributed many hours in typing and proofreading. In these capacities we acknowledge, too, the timely aid of our friend Louise Byron, and of Joy Morgan, who also served. This has literally been a group project. While we humbly take responsibility for any shortcomings in the book, any successes it might achieve must be widely shared.

ROBERT J. HIGGS
AMBROSE N. MANNING

East Tennessee State University
Johnson City, Tennessee
1974

Introduction

Perhaps the simplest definition of Southern Appalachian literature is that writing which deals with the inhabitants of the mountain country in the states of Maryland, Virginia, West Virginia, Kentucky, Tennessee, North and South Carolina, Georgia, and Alabama. Traditionally its themes are the Civil War, feuding, moonshining, religious fundamentalism, and the eternal conflict between nature and civilization. Whereas the literature of the Tidewater South has focused upon the relationship between aristocrats, Negroes, and poor whites, that of Southern Appalachia has centered upon the mountaineer, his struggles with himself, nature, and the outside world. From the pages of literally thousands of novels and stories he has emerged as a legendary figure of worldwide renown, and, along with the cowboy, has become a truly indigenous American type. He cannot, however, be categorized or described simply but appears in literature and mass media in a number of roles from hick to hero. In this present volume we seek to illustrate the wide range of images in the hope that the recognition of this diversity will lead to a better understanding of the Southern mountaineer and his native land, both on the part of himself and others.

In our attempt to reveal the complexity of the Appalachian culture, we have drawn upon primary sources covering a period of over three hundred years. Considering our subject, this range of selections is most appropriate, for a distinguishing feature of the native Appalachian is a deep sense of the past, consciously recognized or not. It is, in fact, the very inertia of tradition which has made the mountaineer so wary of change. Once this wariness was the cause of almost immediate criticism, but this is no longer so. In a time when more and more people in and out of Appalachia are questioning the direction of modern life, there is ample justification for taking a close look at traditional mountain resistance to "progress." By the same token it is high time for the region itself to examine at length its own myths and customs to determine to what extent its problems have been self-inflicted. Anyone who contrasts the edenic accounts of the early explorers in the seventeenth and eighteenth centuries with Harry Caudill's brilliant lament, "O, Appalachia!" over three centuries later, has no alternative but to conclude that something has gone wrong. Other than the simple explanation of original sin, in which incidentally most Appalachians believe strongly, there appear to be no clear and simple answers. There are, however, a variety of views, and we have tried to present as many of them as possible. Selections are included on themes ranging from Indian removal and myth-making through language and religious fundamentalism. If the reader can find meaningful and valid relationships between these subjects and others, then we will feel that as far as Appalachia is concerned, we will have succeeded in some degree in the battle against what Leslie Fiedler has called "the endemic disease of our era, the failure to connect."

The plan of this book is comprehensive but simple. Instead of beginning with the tall tale, perhaps the most famous genre of mountain writing, we start with early accounts from explorers, soldiers, missionaries, and tourists, simply because in their diaries, journals, and letters are found the prototypes of all the dominant regional themes. Following the section on early travels are selections from what we feel to be the other significant modes and genres of Appalachian writing: Southern Romanticism, the Tall Tale, Local Color, the Realism of the Twenties and Thirties, and recent fiction which defies classification, except that it reveals on the part of the authors a search for the usable past, a quest for meaning and identity. We have also included an ample serving of Appalachian poetry which, like the fiction, is characterized in content by a sense of the land and a love of nature. In a day when so much poetry seems cerebral and solipsistic, it is refreshing to find verse which speaks of living upon the earth. The purpose of the second part of the book, the essays, is to shed light not only on the literature but upon the history and culture of the region. Further discussion and comment which might be helpful precede each of the sections.

The literary purist might object to our cultural approach, and to help soften any such blows we have included "Some Don'ts for Literary Regionalists" by Robert Penn Warren, which deals effectively with the problem of regional thought. In a project such as ours we are aware of the inherent dangers of provincialism and sociological interpretation of literature, but we are also conscious of what seems to be a greater danger than either, the study of "literature as literature." The inevitable consequence of this approach is myopia and elitism, which as far as Appalachia is concerned, have been evident in the study of Southern literature itself. For the most part, Appalachia has been regarded as a poor but eccentric relation of the rest of the South and in anthologies passed off with a tall tale or two and a story illustrative of local color. While such treatment might be understandable when considering the whole range of Southern letters, the effect is a rather facile dismissal of one of the most complex and fascinating regions of America. The impression, we might add, is one of hurried patronage and academic condescension. Hopefully this book will help to put Appalachian literature in better perspective without engendering any sort of regional cultism.

PART I

I. Exploration and Early Travels: First Impressions

A. The Land and Landscape: A New Eden

Living as we do in the last third of the twentieth century, it is difficult if not impossible to imagine the awesome beauty that the eyes of the first white travelers into the Southern Appalachian mountains beheld. A hunting or hiking trip, or a view from the Blue Ridge Parkway, may provide something of their impressions, but the experience can never be recaptured. Even their attempts to commit to paper what they saw often seem pathetic in light of what they wished to convey, and more than one writer acknowledged the futility of words in capturing the wonder around them. Whether those who left accounts were in the mountains as explorers, hunters, soldiers, missionaries, or tourists, one theme which unites all accounts from the latter part of the seventeenth century through the middle of the nineteenth is that of "God's plenty," not in variety of people but in profuseness of flora and fauna. An acquaintance with the early travel writings of Appalachia will reveal ample cause for the pervasiveness of the myth of Eden in all our literature.

3

JOHN LEDERER

Little is known of John Lederer's background. He was well educated in his native Germany and went to Virginia in 1668. Governor William Berkeley commissioned him to explore the Valley of Virginia Piedmont. Lederer began his three expeditions in March, 1669. On his third journey in 1670, his companions deserted him, and he went on alone with an Indian guide. The deserters went back with tales of his misuse of government funds on the expedition. Upon his return, Lederer found himself ostracized, and moved to Maryland, where he became an American citizen. *The Discoveries of John Lederer*, describing these journeys, was published in London in 1672. The following excerpt is one of the earliest accounts of the natural verdure and beauty of the Southern Appalachians.

The Third and Last Expedition, and Conjectures of the Land Beyond the Apalataean Mountains

The four and twentieth we travelled thorow the *Savanae* among vast herds of Red and Fallow Deer which stood gazing at us; and a little after, we came to the Promontories or Spurs of the *Apalataean*-mountains.

5

These *Savanae* are low grounds at the foot of the *Apala-taeans*, which all Winter, Spring, and part of the Summer, lie under snow or water, when the snow is dissolved, which falls down from the Mountains, commonly about the beginning of June; and then their verdure is wonderful pleasant to the eye, especially of such as travelled through the shade of the vast Forest, come out of a melancholy darkness of a sudden, into a clear and open skie. To heighten the beautie of these parts, the first Springs of most of those great Rivers which run into the *Atlantick* Ocean, or *Chesapeack* Bay, do here break out, and in various branches interlace the flowry Meads, whose luxurious herbage invites numerous herds of Red Deer (for their unusual largeness improperly termed Elks by ignorant people) to feed. The right Elk, though very common in *New Scotland, Canada,* and those Northern parts, is never seen on this side of the Continent: for that which the *Virginians* call Elks, does not at all differ from the Red Deer of *Europe,* but in his dimensions, which are far greater: but yet the Elk in bigness does as far exceed them: their head, or horns, are not very different; but the neck of the Elk is so short, that it hardly separates the head from the shoulders, which is the reason that they cannot feed upon level ground but by falling on their knees, though their heads be a yard-long: therefore they commonly either brouse upon trees, or standing up to the belly in ponds or rivers feed upon the banks: their Cingles or tails are hardly three inches long. I have been told by a *New-England*-Gentleman, that the lips and nostrils of this creature is the most delicious meat he ever tasted. As for the Red Deer we here treat of, I cannot difference the taste of their flesh from those in *Europe.*

The sixth and twentieth of *August* we came to the Mountains, where finding no horse-way up, we alighted, and left our horses with two or three Indians below, whilst we went up afoot. The ascent was so steep, the cold so intense, and we so tired, that having with much ado gained the top of one of the highest, we drank the Kings Health in Brandy, gave the Mountain His name, and agreed to return back again, having no encouragement from that prospect to proceed to a further discovery: since from hence we saw another Mountain, bearing North and by West to us, of a prodigious height: for according to an observation of the distance taken by Col. *Catlet*, it could not be less than fifty leagues from the place we stood upon.

Here I was stung in my sleep by a Mountain-spider; and had not an Indian suckt out the poyson, I had died: for receiving the hurt at the tip of one of my fingers, the venome shot up immediately into my shoulder, and so inflamed my side, that it is not possible to express my torment. The means used by my Physician, was first a small dose of Snake-root-powder, which I took in a little water; and then making a kinde of Plaister of the same, applied it neer to the part affected: when he had done so, he swallowed some by way of Antidote himself, and suckt my fingers end so violently, that I felt the venome retire back from my side into my shoulder, and from thence down my arm; having thus sucked half a score times, and spit as often, I was eased of all my pain, and perfectly recovered. I thought I had been bit by a Rattle-snake, for I saw not what hurt me: but the Indian found by the wound, and the effects of it, that it was given by a Spider, one of which he shewed me the next day: it is not unlike our great blue Spider, onely it is somewhat longer, I suppose the nature of his poyson to be much like that of the *Tarantula*.

I thus being beyond my hopes and expectation restored to my self, we unanimously agreed to return back, seeing no possibility of passing through the Mountains: and finding our Indians with our horses in the place where we left them, we rode homewards without making any further discovery. (1672)

JOHN FONTAINE

John Fontaine was born in 1693 in Taunton, Ireland. As a young man he made several important explorations of the province of Virginia, the most famous being that in 1716 with Governor Spotswood over the Blue Ridge and to the Shenandoah Valley. The purpose of the journey was to explore the Virginia frontier and encourage settlement. The expedition was made widely known in the novel, *The Knights of the Golden Horseshoe*, published in 1845 by William Alexander Caruthers. According to legend, Governor Spotswood bestowed upon some gentlemen of the company a small golden horseshoe inscribed with the Latin motto: *"Sic Juviat Transcendre Montes"* ("How delightful it is to cross the mountains!"). After his travels in America, Fontaine lived in Ireland and Wales and died in 1767. *The Journal of John Fontaine, 1710–1719* was first published in 1838 in *A Tale of The Huguenots*, an autobiography of James Fontaine, John's father.

FROM *The Journal of John Fontaine*

The 4th [of September, 1716]—We had two of our men sick with the measles, and one of our horses poisoned with a rattlesnake. We took the heaviest of our baggage, our tired horses, and the sick men, and made as convenient a lodge for them as we could, and left people to guard them, and hunt for them. We had finished this work by twelve, and so we set out. The sides of the mountains were so full of vines and briers, that we were forced to clear most of the way before us. We crossed one of the small mountains this side of the Appalachian, and from the top of it we had a fine view of the plains below. We were obliged to walk up the most of the way, there being abundance of loose stones on the side of the hill. I killed a large rattlesnake here, and the other people killed three more. We made about four miles, and so we came to the side of James River, where a man may jump over it, and there we pitched our tents. As the people were lighting the fire, there came out of a large log of wood a prodigious snake, which they killed; so this camp was called Rattlesnake Camp, but it was otherwise called Brooks' Camp.

The 5th—A fair day. At nine we were mounted; we were obliged to have axe-men to clear the way in some places. We followed the windings of the top of James River, observing that it came from the very top of the mountains. We killed two rattlesnakes during our ascent. In some places it was very steep, in others, it was so that we could ride up. About one of the clock we got to the top of the mountain; about four miles and a half, and came to the very head spring of James River where it runs no bigger than a man's arm, from under a large stone. We drank King George's health, and all the Royal Family's, at the very top of the Appalachian Mountains. About a musket shot from this spring there is another, which rises and runs down on the other side; it goes westward, and we thought we could go down that way, but we met with such prodigious precipices, that we were obliged to return to the top again. We found some trees which had been formerly marked, I suppose, by the Northern Indians, and following these trees we found a good, safe descent. Several of the company were for returning; but the Governor persuaded them to continue on. About five, we were down on the other side, and continued our way for about seven miles further, until we came to a large river, by the side of which we encamped. We made this day fourteen miles. I, being somewhat more curious than the rest, went on a high rock on top of the mountain, to see fine prospects, and I lost my gun. We saw, when we were over the mountains, the footing of several elks and buffaloes, and their beds. We saw a vine which bore a sort of wild cucumber, and a shrub with a fruit like unto a currant. We eat very good wild grapes. We called this place Spotswood Camp, after our Governor.

The 6th—We crossed the river, which we called Euphrates. It is very deep; the main course of the water is north; it is fourscore yards wide in the narrowest part. We drank some healths on the other side, and returned; after which I went a swimming in it. We could not find any fordable place, except the one by which we crossed, and it was deep in several places. I got some grasshoppers and fished; and another and I, we catched a dish of fish, some perch, and a fish they call chub. The others went a hunting, and killed deer and turkeys. The Governor had graving irons, but could not grave any thing, the stones were so hard. I graved my name on a tree by the river side; and the Governor buried a bottle with a paper inclosed, on which he writ that he took possession of this place in the name and for King George the First of England. We had a good dinner, and after it we got the men together, and loaded all their arms, and we drank the King's health in Champagne, and fired a volley—the Prince's health in Burgundy, and fired a volley, and all the rest of the Royal Family in claret, and a volley. We drank the Governor's health and fired another volley. We had several sorts of liquors, viz., Virginia red wine and white wine, Irish usquebaugh, brandy, shrub, two sorts of rum, champagne, canary, cherry, punch, water, cider, &tc.

I sent two of the Rangers to look for my gun, which I

dropped in the mountains; they found it and brought it to me at night, and I gave them a pistole for their trouble. The highest of the mountains we called it Mount George, and the one we crossed over Mount Spotswood. (1838, 1872)

TIMOTHY FLINT

Born in 1780 in North Reading, Massachusetts, Timothy Flint was educated at Harvard and served for many years as a pastor in the East and a missionary in the West. In 1816 he met Daniel Boone near St. Charles, Missouri, and incorporated his impressions in what was to become, according to Professor James K. Folsome, "the most widely read popular biography of the early nineteenth century," the *Biographical Memoir of Daniel Boone* (1833), later issued under the title *The First White Man in the West* (1856). Flint's depiction of the wonders that greeted the eyes of America's most famous frontier explorer is at once realistic and mythopoeic. The title has been supplied for the portion of the memoir that follows.

The Garden of God

The first of May, 1769, Finley and Boone, with four others, whose names were Stewart, Holden, Mooney, and Cool, and who had pledged themselves to the undertaking, were assembled at the house of Boone, in readiness to commence their journey. It may be imagined that all the neighbors gathered to witness their departure. A rifle, ammunition, and a light knapsack were all the baggage with which they dared encumber themselves. Provisions for a few days were bestowed along with the clothing deemed absolutely necessary for comfort upon the long route. No shame could attach to the manhood and courage of Daniel Boone from the fact that tears were said to have rushed to his eyes, as he kissed his wife and children, before he turned from his door for the last time for months, and perhaps forever. The nature of the pioneer was as gentle and affectionate as it was firm and persevering. He had power, however, to send back the unbidden gush to its source, and forcibly to withdraw his mind from enervating thoughts.

Beside, the natural elasticity of his temperament and the buoyancy of his character came to his aid. The anticipation of new and strange incidents operated to produce in the minds of the travelers, from the commencement of the enterprise, a kind of wild pleasure.

With alert and vigorous steps they pursued a north-west course, and were soon beyond the reach of the most distant view of their homes. This day and night, and the succeeding one, the scenes in view were familiar; but in the course of the four or five that followed, all vestiges of civilized habitancy had disappeared. The route lay through a solitary and trackless wilderness. Before them rose a line of mountains, shooting up against the blue of the horizon, in peaks and elevations of all forms. The slender store of food with which they had set out, was soon exhausted. To obtain a fresh supply was the first and most pressing want. Accordingly, a convenient place was selected, and a camp constructed of logs and branches of trees, to keep out the dew and rain. The whole party joined in this preliminary arrangement. When it was so far completed, as to enable a part to finish it before nightfall, part of the company took their rifles and went in different directions in pursuit of game. They returned in time for supper, with a couple of deer and some wild turkeys. Those, whose business it was to finish the camp, had made a generous fire and acquired keen appetites for the coming feast. The deer were rapidly dressed, so far at least as to furnish a supper of venison. It had not been long finished, and the arrangements for the night made, before the clouds, which had been gathering blackness for some hours, rolled up in immense folds from the point, whence was heard the sudden burst of a furious wind. The lightning darted from all quarters of the heavens. At one moment every object stood forth in a glare of dazzling light. The next the darkness might almost be felt. The rain fell in torrents, in one apparently unbroken sheet from the sky to the earth. The peals of thunder rolled almost unheard amid this deafening rush of waters. The camp of the travelers, erected with reference to the probability of such an occurrence, was placed under the shelter of a huge tree, whose branches ran out laterally, and were of a thickness of foliage to be almost impervious to the rain. To this happy precaution of the woodsmen, they owed their escape from the drenching of the shower. They were not, perhaps, aware of the great danger from lightning, to which their position had exposed them. . . .

During the day they began the ascent of the ridge of the Alleghany, that had for some days bounded their view. The mountainous character of the country, for some miles, before the highest elevations rose to sight, rendered the traveling laborious and slow. Several days were spent in this toilsome progress. Steep summits, impossible to ascend, impeded their advance, compelling them to turn aside, and attain the point above by a circuitous route. Again they were obliged to delay their journey for a day, in order to obtain a fresh supply of provisions. This was readily procured, as all the varieties of game abounded on every side.

The last crags and cliffs of the middle ridges having been scrambled over, on the following morning they stood on the summit of Cumberland Mountain, the farthest western spur of this line of heights. From this point the descent into the

great western valley began. What a scene opened before
them! A feeling of the sublime is inspired in every bosom susceptible of it, by a view from any point of these vast ranges,
of the boundless forest valleys of the Ohio. It is a view more
grand, more heart stirring than that of the ocean. Illimitable
extents of wood, and winding river courses spread before
them like a large map. "Glorious country!" they exclaimed.
Little did Boone dream that in fifty years, immense portions
of it would pass from the domain of the hunter—that it
would contain 4 millions of freemen, and its waters navigated
by nearly two hundred steamboats, sweeping down these
streams that now rolled through the unbroken forests before
them. To them it stood forth an unexplored paradise in the
hunter's imagination.

After a long pause, in thoughts too deep for words, they
began the descent, which was made in a much shorter time
than had been required for the opposite ascent; and the
explorers soon found themselves on the slopes of the subsid-
ing hills. Here the hunter was in his element. To all the party
but Finley, the buffaloes incidentally seen in small numbers
in the valleys were a novel and interesting sight. It had as
yet been impossible to obtain a shot at them, from their distance or position. It may be imagined with what eagerness
Boone sought an opportunity to make his first essay in this
exciting and noble species of hunting.

The first considerable drove came in sight on the afternoon
of the day on which the travelers reached the foot of the
mountains. The day had been one of the most beautiful of
spring. The earth was covered with grass of the freshest
green. The rich foliage of the trees, in its varied shading,
furnished its portion of the loveliness of the surrounding landscape. The light of the declining sun lay full on the scene
of boundless solitude. The party had descended into a deep
glen, which wound through the opening between the highlands, still extending a little in advance of them. They pursued its course until it terminated in a beautiful little plain.

Upon advancing into this, they found themselves in an area of considerable extent, almost circular in form, bounded on one half its circumference by the line of hills, from among which they had just emerged. The other sections of the circle were marked by the fringe of wood that bordered a stream winding from the hills, at a considerable distance above. The buffaloes advanced from the skirt of wood, and the plain was soon filled by the moving mass of these huge animals.

The exploring adventurers perceived themselves in danger of what has more than once happened in similar situations. The prospect seemed to be that they would be trampled under the feet of the reckless and sweeping body, in their outward course.

"They will not turn out for us," said Finley; "and if we do not conduct exactly right, we shall be crushed to death."

The inexperienced adventurers bade him direct them in the emergency. Just as the front of the phalanx was within short rifle distance, he discharged his rifle and brought down one of the bulls, that seemed to be a file leader, by a ball between the horns. The unwieldy animal fell. The mass raised a deafening sort of bellow, and became arrested, as if transfixed to the spot. A momentary confusion of the mass behind ensued. But, borne along by the pressure of the multitudes still in the rear, there was a gradual parting of the herd direct from the front, where the fallen buffalo lay. The disruption once made, the chasm broadened, until when the wings passed the travelers, they were thirty yards from the divisions on either hand. To prevent the masses yet behind from closing their lines, Finley took the rifle of one of his companions, and leveled another. This changed the pace of the animals to a rout. The last masses soon thundered by, and left them gazing in astonishment, not unmixed with joy, in realizing their escape. "Job of Uz," exclaimed Boone, "had not larger droves of cattle than we. In fact, we seem to have had in this instance an abundance to a fault."

As this was an era in their adventures, and an omen of the abundance of the vast regions of forests which they had descried from the summits of the mountains, they halted, made a camp, and skinned the animals, preserving the skins, fat, tongues, and choice pieces. No epicures ever feasted higher than these athletic and hungry hunters, as they sat around their evening fire, and commented upon the ease with which their wants would be supplied in a country thus abounding with such animals. . . .

What struck them with unfailing pleasure was, to observe the soil, in general, of a fertility without example on the other side of the mountains. From an eminence in the vicinity of their station, they could see, as far as vision could extend, the beautiful country of Kentucky. They remarked with astonishment the tall, straight trees, shading the exuberant soil, wholly clear from any other underbrush than the rich canebrakes, the image of verdure and luxuriance, or tall grass and clover. Down the gentle slopes murmured clear limestone brooks. Finley, who had some touch of scripture knowledge, exclaimed in view of this wilderness-paradise, so abundant in game and wild fowls, "This wilderness blossoms as the rose; and these desolate places are as the garden of God."

"Ay," responded Boone; "and who would remain on the sterile pine hills of North Carolina, to hear the screaming of the jay, and now and then bring down a deer too lean to be eaten? This is the land of hunters, where man and beast grow to their full size."

They ranged through various forests, and crossed the numerous streams of the vicinity. By following the paths of the buffaloes, bears, deer, and other animals, they discovered the Salines or *Licks*, where salt is made at the present day. The paths, in approaching the salines, were trodden as hard and smooth, as in the vicinity of the farm-yards of the old settlements. Boone, from the principle which places the best pilot at the helm in a storm, was not slow to learn from innumerable circumstances, which would have passed unnoticed by a less sagacious woodsman, that, although the country was not actually inhabited by Indians, it was not the less a scene of strife and combat for the possession of such rich hunting grounds by a great number of tribes. He discovered that it was a common park to these fierce tribes; and none the less likely to expose them to the dangers of Indian warfare, because it was not claimed or inhabited by any particular tribe. On the contrary, instead of having to encounter a single tribe in possession, he foresaw that the jealousy of all the tribes would be united against the new intruders.

These fearless spirits, who were instinctively imbued with an abhorrence of the Indians, heeded little, however, whether they had to make war on them, or the wild beasts. They felt in its fullest force that indomitable elasticity of character, which causes the possessor, every-where, and in all forms of imagined peril, to feel sufficient to themselves. Hence the lonely adventurers continued fearlessly to explore the beautiful positions for settlements, to cross and name the rivers, and to hunt.

By a happy fatality, through all the summer they met with no Indians, and experienced no impediment in the way of the most successful hunting. During the season, they had collected large quantities of peltries, and meeting with nothing to excite apprehension or alarm, they became constantly more delighted with the country.

So passed their time, until the 22d of December. After this period adventures of the most disastrous character began to crowd upon them. We forthwith commence the narrative of incidents which constitute the general color of Boone's future life. (1833, 1856)

JAMES KIRKE PAULDING

James K. Paulding was born in Putnam County, New York, in 1778. Although he had only four years of education in a log school house, he became a noted writer and public official in national naval affairs, living most of his life in New York City and Washington. In the summer of 1816 he embarked for health reasons on a tour of Virginia and West Virginia, including Richmond, the Alleghenies, and the Shenandoah Valley. He traveled with another bachelor and friend, Oliver Noll, the fictitious "Frank" to whom *Letters from the South* were written. Paulding, like so many writers of the early nineteenth century, was entirely captivated by the majesty of the Appalachian Mountains.

FROM *Letters from the South*
Letter IX

. . . The first view we got of the mountains was from a hill a few miles from Louis court-house. You know I was *raised*, as they say in Virginia, among the mountains of the North, and I never see one that it does not conjure up a hundred pleasing associations. . . . It was just such an evening when we first caught a view of the distant undulating mountain, whose fading blue outline could hardly be distinguished from the blue sky with which it almost seemed to mingle. Between us and the mountain was spread a wide landscape,—shade softening into shade, with such imperceptible gradations, as blended the whole into an indescribable harmony. Over all was spread that rich purple hue, which painters have often attempted to imitate in vain. All that they have been able to do is, to put us in mind of it, and leave the rest to imagination. . . .

We ascended the Blue Ridge at Rockfish Gap, by a winding road, rising so gently as to be almost imperceptible; nor should we have known the height to which we had arrived, had it not been for the gradual expansion of the prospect, which at last became so extensive and magnificent, that I would describe it, if I thought I could communicate any thing of the impression I received. This I hope you will take as a sufficient reason for my declining the task. Nearly on the summit, a little descending to the West, stands an extensive tavern and boardinghouse, where we halted for the night; and where I advise you to stop, if you ever travel this way. The air is delightfully pure, elastic and envigorating;—a spring of the finest water in the world (except the waters of Helicon) bubbles from a rock of freestone close by;—the house is exceedingly comfortable; and the prospect of the long valley to the West, as it gradually faded, and melted, and became lost in the shades of night, was calculated to awaken the soul,—which so often falls fast asleep in the racket of noisy towns. (1817)

ANNE NEWPORT ROYALL

Born in 1769, Anne Royall is one of the most fascinating women in American history. Called by Helen Woodward in *The Bold Women* "America's first hitchhiker," she traveled over much of the country in the early part of the nineteenth century, recording her impressions in letters and sketches, meeting presidents, and defending Masons whenever and wherever they came under attack. She was a well-known Washington, D. C., newspaperwoman in her day, and also the author of one novel, *The Tennessean*, which has been called "the worst American novel of all time." She was one of the first to claim uniqueness for the residents of Southern Appalachia.

While today the word "Appalachia" quite often conjures up an image of polluted streams and denuded hills, Anne Royall presents a picture almost utopian, with the possible exception of incipient commerce made particularly difficult at the time by the general inaccessibility of the region.

FROM *Sketches of History, Life, and Manners in the United States*

When you gain the eastern limit of Cumberland you have an extensive view of East Tennessee, Clinch River, Kingston, and Campbell's Fort: all are present at once, to view. It was truly grand and picturesque. The Fort rises conspicuous above the rest, it being situated on a high hill, descending rapidly at all points. What a scene this for the fancy and pen of a poet! while I have neither leisure nor talents to exhibit it in simple prose.

The Cumberland mountain leaves you on the bank of Clinch River, a beautiful smooth-flowing stream, about 250 yards wide, navigable its whole length, which is a little less than 200 miles. While crossing Clinch (which you do in a boat) you witness another display of the rich and beautiful scenery which abounds in this country. Kingston lies before you—the majestic Tennessee shows itself below, having just joined Clinch river, while Campbell's Fort appears at the same time looking down upon the junction of these noble streams, from its lofty eminence to the right, decorated with fruit trees and shrubberies, like the guardian genius of the place. . . .

East Tennessee resembles the western part of Virginia, being nothing but alternate mountains and rivers. We cross no mountain, however, but the Cumberland, our road following the Holston river, which appears and disappears at intervals. The land on those rivers, however, is fertile, and yields hemp, corn, tobacco, wheat, rye, oats, flax, sweet and Irish potatoes, fruit, such as apples, pears, and peaches, all sorts of garden vegetables, particularly melons, that exceed those of any country I have seen, both in size and flavor. East Tennessee exports flour, indian corn, Irish potatoes, whiskey, bacon, cider, apples, cider-royal, Tennessee-royal, hemp, tobacco, iron, beef, butter, cheese, beeswax, lard, feathers, indian-meal, onions, and great quantities of plank, scantling, and other timber. These articles they exchange mostly for cotton, either in Alabama or New-Orleans, and this they again exchange for merchandise. The merchants have to wagon their goods from Philadelphia, as they cannot ascend the river, without great difficulty. We met a number of those wagons every day, ten and twelve teams together. They were so heavily laden, and the weather so warm that they never travelled more than ten and twelve miles per day. The poor horses I was sorry for them; the skin in many instances being rubbed off with the gears. . . .

I passed the head of Holston, yesterday, after tracing it from the shoals, where it is three miles in width, to a small creek, and finally to its source, which is two small springs, one on each side of the road, in Washington County, Virginia. Tennessee river waters five states, Virginia, North Carolina, Tennessee, Alabama, and Kentucky. (1826)

B. *The First Inhabitants: The Noble Naturals*

Will Rogers—who was of part Cherokee ancestry—
supposedly remarked, when told by a lady that her folks
came over on the *Mayflower*, that his *met* the *Mayflower*. In
that response is contained the attitude of native Americans
toward talk of white discovery and exploration on the North
American continent, and it was with some reluctance that we
included a section on the impressions of the first European-
born inhabitants, as if the natives themselves were being
discovered. The justification for the selections, however, lies
more in what they tell the white man about the history of his
motives than in what they reveal about Cherokee culture of
the time. The term "noble naturals" itself is as reflective of
the white conqueror as of those whose lands were taken.
Few if any ever denied the nobility of spirit of the Cherokee,
and "naturals" was a universal designation for all American
Indians. To the white invader the Indian was indeed a
"natural"—natural man living in a natural world. Both were
sources of endless amazement and both had to be converted
or subdued. In the brief passages on the Cherokee we have
selected, there is contained perhaps the saddest chapter in
the whole Appalachian experience, the gradual subjugation
and final removal from ancestral lands of the first native
Appalachians.

HENRY TIMBERLAKE

A native of Hanover County, Virginia, Lieutenant Henry Timberlake fought in the French and Indian War, and in 1761 was ordered to join the regiment of Colonel William Byrd, III. When peace was made with the Indians in the same year, Timberlake spent the next three months among the Cherokees, observing their life and customs. He accompanied three Indians to England in 1762, married in London, and returned to Virginia in 1763. Still sympathetic to the Indians, he went back to England with several of them in 1764. He died shortly before his *Memoirs* were published in 1765. Timberlake's tolerance and understanding are as significant as his detailed descriptions of Cherokee life.

FROM *Memoirs of Lieut. Henry Timberlake*

The Cherokees are of a middle stature, of an olive colour, tho' generally painted, and their skins stained with gunpowder, pricked into it in very pretty figures. The hair of their head is shaved, tho' many of the old people have it plucked out by the roots, except a patch on the hinder part of the head, about twice the bigness of a crown-piece, which

27

is ornamented with beads, feathers, wampum, stained deers hair, and such like baubles. The ears are slit and stretched to an enormous size, putting the person who undergoes the operation to incredible pain, being unable to lie on either side for near forty days. To remedy this, they generally slit but one at a time; so soon as the patient can bear it, they are wound round with wire to expand them, and are adorned with silver pendants and rings, which they likewise wear at the nose. This custom does not belong originally to the Cherokees, but taken by them from the Shawnese, or other northern nations.

They that can afford it wear a collar of wampum, which are beads cut out of clam-shells, a silver breast-plate, and bracelets on their arms and wrists of the same metal, a bit of cloth over their private parts, a shirt of the English make, a sort of cloth-boots, and mockasons, which are shoes of a make peculiar to the Americans, ornamented with porcupine-quills; a large mantle or match-coat thrown over all compleats their dress at home; but when they go to war they leave their trinkets behind, and the mere necessaries serve them.

The women wear the hair of their head, which is so long that it generally reaches to the middle of their legs, and sometimes to the ground, club'd, and ornamented with ribbons of various colours; but, except their eyebrows, pluck it from all the other parts of the body, especially the looser part of the sex. The rest of their dress is now become very much like the European; and, indeed, that of the men is greatly altered. The old people still remember and praise the ancient days, before they were acquainted with the whites, when they had but little dress, except a bit of skin about their middles, mockasons, a mantle of buffalo skin for the winter, and a lighter one of feathers for the summer. The women, particularly the half-breed, are remarkably well featured; and both men and women are streight and well-built, with small hands and feet.

The warlike arms used by the Cherokees are guns, bows and arrows, darts, scalping-knives, and tommahawkes, which are hatchets; the hammer-part of which being made hollow, and a small hole running from thence along the shank, terminated by a small brass-tube for the mouth, makes a compleat pipe. There are various ways of making these, according to the country or fancy of the purchaser, being all made by the Europeans; some have a long spear at top, and some different conveniences on each side. This is one of their most useful pieces of field-furniture, serving all the offices of hatchet, pipe, and sword; neither are the Indians less expert at throwing it than using it near, but will kill at a considerable distance.

They are of a very gentle and amicable disposition to those they think their friends, but as implacable in their enmity, their revenge being only compleated in the entire destruction of their enemies. They were pretty hospitable to all white strangers, till the Europeans encouraged them to scalp; but the great reward offered has led them often since to commit as great barbarities on us, as they formerly only treated their most inveterate enemies with. They are very hardy, bearing heat, cold, hunger and thirst, in a surprizing manner; and yet no people are given to more excess in eating and drinking, when it is conveniently in their power: the follies, nay mischief, they commit when inebriated, are entirely laid to the liquor; and no one will revenge any injury (murder excepted) received from one who is no more himself: they are not less addicted to gaming than drinking, and will even lose the shirt off their back, rather than give over play, when luck runs against them.

They are extremely proud, despising the lower class of Europeans; and in some athletick diversions I once was present at, they refused to match or hold conference with any but officers.

Here, however, the vulgar notion of the Indians uncommon

activity was contradicted by three officers of the Virginia regiment, the slowest of which could outrun the swiftest of about 700 Indians that were in the place: but had the race exceeded two or three hundred yards, the Indians would then have acquired the advantage, by being able to keep the same pace a long time together; and running being likewise more general among them, a body of them would always greatly exceed an equal number of our troops.

They are particularly careful of the super-annuated, but are not so till of a great age; of which Ostenaco's mother is an instance. Ostenaco is about sixty years of age, and the youngest of four; yet his mother still continues her laborious tasks, and has yet strength enough to carry 200 weight of wood on her back near a couple of miles. I am apt to think some of them, by their own computation, are near 150 years old.

They have many of them a good uncultivated genius, are fond of speaking well, as that paves the way to power in their councils; and I doubt not but the reader will find some beauties in the harangues I have given him, which I assure him are entirely genuine. Their language is not unpleasant, but vastly aspirated, and the accents so many and various, you would often imagine them singing in their common discourse. As the ideas of the Cherokees are so few, I cannot say much for the copiousness of their language.

They seldom turn their eyes on the person they speak of, or address themselves to, and are always suspicious when people's eyes are fixed upon them. They speak so low, except in council, that they are often obliged to repeat what they were saying; yet should a person talk to any of them above their common pitch, they would immediately ask him, if he thought they were deaf? . . .

The Indians, being all soldiers, mechanism can make but little progress; besides this, they labour under the disadvantage of having neither proper tools, or persons to teach the use of those they have: Thus, for want of saws, they are obliged to cut a large tree on each side, with great labour, to make a very clumsy board; whereas a pair of sawyers would divide the same tree into eight or ten in much less time: considering this disadvantage, their modern houses are tolerably well built. A number of thick posts is fixed in the ground, according to the plan and dimensions of the house, which rarely exceeds sixteen feet in breadth, on account of the roofing, but often extend to sixty or seventy in length, beside the little hot-house. Between each of these posts is placed a smaller one, and the whole wattled with twigs like a basket, which is then covered with clay very smooth, and sometimes white-washed. Instead of tiles, they cover them with narrow boards. Some of these houses are two story high, tolerably pretty and capacious; but most of them very inconvenient for want of chimneys, a small hole being all the vent assigned in many for the smoak to get out at. . . .

They have few religious ceremonies, or stated times of general worship: the green corn dance seems to be the principal, which is, as I have been told, performed in a very solemn manner, in a large square before the town-house door: the motion here is very slow, and the song in which they offer thanks to God for the corn he has sent them, far from unpleasing. There is no kind of rites or ceremonies at marriage, courtship and all being, as I have already observed, concluded in half an hour, without any other celebration, and it is as little binding as ceremonious; for though many last till death, especially when there are children, it is common for a person to change three or four times a-year. Notwithstanding this, the Indian women gave lately a proof of fidelity, not to be equalled by politer ladies, bound by all the sacred ties of marriage. . . .

They seldom bury their dead, but throw them into the river; yet if any white man will bury them, he is generally rewarded with a blanket, besides what he takes from the corpse, the dead having commonly their guns, tommahawkes, powder, lead, silver ware, wampum, and a little tobacco, buried with them; and as the persons who bring the corpse to the place of burial, immediately leave it, he is at liberty to dispose of all as he pleases, but must take care never to be found out, as nothing belonging to the dead is to be kept, but every thing at his decease destroyed, except these articles, which are destined to accompany him to the other world. It is reckoned, therefore, the worst of thefts; yet there is no punishment for this, or any other crime, murder excepted, which is more properly revenged than punished.

This custom was probably introduced to prevent avarice, and, by preventing hereditary acquisitions, make merit the sole means of acquiring power, honour, and riches. The inventor, however, had too great a knowledge of the human mind, and our propensity to possess, not to see that a superior passion must intercede; he therefore wisely made it a religious ceremony, that superstition, the strongest passion of the ignorant, might check avarice, and keep it in the bounds he had prescribed. It is not known from whence it came, but it is of great antiquity, and not only general over all North America, but in many parts of Asia. On this account the wives generally have separate property, that no inconveniency may arise from death or separation.

The Indians have a particular method of relieving the poor, which I shall rank among the most laudable of their religious ceremonies, most of the rest consisting purely in the vain ceremonies, and superstitious romances of their conjurors. When any of their people are hungry, as they term it, or in distress, orders are issued out by the headmen for a war-dance, at which all the fighting men and warriors assemble; but here, contrary to all their other dances, one only dances at a time, who, after hopping and capering for near a minute, with a tommahawke in his hand, gives a small hoop, at which signal the music stops till he related the manner of taking his first scalp, and concludes his narration, by throwing on a large skin spread for that purpose, a string of wampum, piece of plate, wire, paint, lead, or any thing he can most conveniently spare; after which the music strikes up, and he proceeds in the same manner through his warlike actions: then another takes his place, and the ceremony lasts till all the warriors and fighting men have related their exploits. The stock thus raised, after paying the musicians, is divided among the poor. The same ceremony is made use of to recompence any extraordinary merit. This is touching vanity in a tender part, and is an admirable method of making even imperfections conduce to the good of society.

Their government, if I may call it government, which has neither laws or power to support it, is a mixed aristocracy and democracy, the chiefs being chose according to their merit in war, or policy at home; these lead the warriors that chuse to go, for there is no laws or compulsion on those that refuse to follow, or punishment to those that forsake their chief: he strives, therefore, to inspire them with a sort of enthusiasm, by the war-song, as the ancient bards did once in Britain. These chiefs, or headmen, likewise compose the assemblies of the nation, into which the war-women are admitted. The reader will not be a little surprised to find the story of Amazons not so great a fable as we imagined, many of the Indian women being as famous in war, as powerful in the council.

The rest of the people are divided into two military classes, warriors and fighting men, which last are the plebeians, who have not distinguished themselves enough to be admitted into the rank of warriors. There are some other honorary titles among them, conferred in reward of great actions; the first of which is Outacity, or Man-killer; and the second Colona, or the Raven. Old warriors likewise, or war-women, who can no longer go to war, but have distinguished themselves in their younger days, have the title of Beloved. This is the only title females can enjoy; but it abundantly recompences them, by the power they acquire by it, which is so great, that they can, by the wave of a swan's wing, deliver a wretch condemned by the council, and already tied to the stake. (1765)

ABRAHAM STEINER AND
FREDERICK C. De SCHWEINITZ

Brother Abraham Steiner was born in Bethlehem, Pennsylvania, in 1758. Educated at Nazareth, he taught at Boys' Day School in Bethlehem before making his first missionary tour to the Indians in Muskingham Valley, Ohio, with the Moravian missionary Rev. Heckewelder in 1789. Feeling called to the mission field, he visited the Cherokees and in 1801 established the first Moravian mission among the Cherokees in Springplace, North Georgia. Ill health forced him to move to Salem, North Carolina, where he was principal of the Salem Academy for ten years, until his death in 1833.

Frederick C. De Schweinitz was also born in Bethlehem, Pennsylvania, in 1744. He visited Wachovia, where Brother Steiner was temporarily living, in 1796, and accompanied Steiner on his journey to the Cherokees in 1799. De Schweinitz is supposed to be the writer of the account below which appears in Samuel Cole Williams' *Early Travels in the Tennessee Country (1540–1800)*. According to Williams he married a German baroness, and administered a Moravian estate near Gnadenfeld until his death. The translation of the report from the German was made for Williams by Rev. W. N. Schwarze, Dean of Moravian College at Bethlehem at about the time of publication of *Early Travels* in 1928.

While the sincerity of Brothers Steiner and De Schweinitz cannot be doubted, they nevertheless were proselytizing not only for Christianity, but—however inadvertently—for a culture that would subjugate the Indians' total way of life.

Report of the Journey of the Brethren Abraham Steiner and Frederick C. De Schweinitz to the Cherokees and the Cumberland Settlements

At all the houses we passed we saw fine corn fields, partly enclosed by low fences. The corn was mostly in corn-sheds, built up on stakes. We saw, also, beans, pumpkins, white cabbage, and some tobacco. The fields as well as much of the uncultivated land were overgrown with rampion. In the afternoon, at 3 o'clock, we reached Tellico Blockhouse again.

In the evening Major Lewis, Agent for the Cherokees, arrived from Southwest Point, and with him his interpreter, Dick Fields* a half-breed, clothed entirely in Indian fashion, with hunting-pouch, girdle, etc., set with corals. This one seems to be a sensible and modest man, speaks a pure English and receives an annual salary of $300.00 from the United States, as interpreter. As he was with us at the inn that evening, Bro. Steiner entered into conversation with him. To the question, how strong his nation might be, he gave as estimate, 3000 warriors; and added that their land extended 300 miles from the east to the west, up to the Muscle Shoals, and southward 200 miles to the Creeks. *Question*: What kind of a nation are the Chickamagas? *Answer*: They are all Cherokees and we know of no difference. There is, indeed, a town here that bears this name, but that is all the difference. *Question*: Is your nation satisfied with the regulations of the government? *Answer*: Yes, quite so. They understand that all

* Fields in later years was one of the Cherokee leaders, active in the aid of John Ross in the troublous days of 1832–1833. [Williams' note.]

arrangements made are well intended and should turn out to their advantage. *Question*: Would any one, who came with the intention of acquainting them with their God and Creator and of instructing them and their children in the Word of God and other useful knowledge, receive permission to live among them, and according to the nature of the circumstances even outside of a Town? *Answer*: Such a person could dwell where and how he pleased; his nation would offer no objection; but this is a matter concerning which the agent must be asked, for without his permission no white could dwell within the nation. Concerning instruction in the Word of God, this would be agreeable, welcome and useful to the nation. Recently, however, Mr. Bullen had travelled through his nation, on his way back from the Chicasaws, and had declared that they were much too evil and malicious a people to be instructed in the Word of God. *Question*: What reason had Mr. Bullen for this? *Answer*: Mr. Bullen came just at the time of their Green Corn Dances, which customarily continue for three or four, sometimes eight days. This dance began on Saturday, and Mr. Bullen admonished them not to dance on Sunday but to hallow it to God. They gave no ear to his admonitions but answered him, that it had been the custom of their fathers, once the dance had begun, to continue it so long until all was at an end; and in this matter they would make no innovations, and so they danced on the Sunday.

The Green Corn Dances are held at the time when the first corn is ripe, and every year in a different town, and when they have been held in all towns, they begin again with the first. For these dances the inhabitants of several towns meet, eat and drink until all provisions in the town have been used up, and then the dance is at an end. In respect to the Christian religion Dick Fields thought that the same could not be introduced until the youth had been instructed in reading, writing and the English language, because otherwise they could have no conception thereof. He was answered: God imparts comprehension and experience, if we ask him to do so. He looks upon the heart and not upon the outward appearance. This we had witnessed among his countrymen of the Delaware Nation, where many of the old people, who understood nothing but their own language, had received the Word of God.

After the counsel of God for our salvation had been explained to him and the gospel story had been briefly related, he was asked, "do you think that your nation would be glad to hear this and believe it?" Whereupon he replied, "I am sure that they will hear it gladly and attentively, but I cannot affirm that they will believe it." As it was very late, and he was tired and sleepy because of his journey today, he took a courteous farewell of us and promised to listen to more tomorrow. . . .

Early in the morning of the 19th, the beloved man of Chota, the old Arcowee, came across the river. He was decked out in all his finery and had a silver medal on his breast, hanging on a ribbon about his neck. On the one side was stamped a head, the symbol of freedom; on the other, a white man and an Indian sitting together under a tree, smoking tobacco, as the sign of friendship. The State of Virginia formerly had such medals struck off. Arcowee came to us at once, in order to talk to us and Mr. Carey was persuaded to act as our interpreter. Bro. Steiner rehearsed again the reasons for our coming hither.

After Bro. Steiner had ceased speaking, Arcowee began and said, "I heard yesterday evening that you were here and that you expected me. I then looked toward heaven and saw my father there. I thought all night long upon what I might hear today; and now, indeed, I hear great words. The Great Father of all breathing things, in the beginning created all men, the white, the red and the black. He placed the red men here toward the going down of the sun and the white men toward the rising of the sun. Then after a great day, long past, the white men came hither in their great canoes and received permission to build a city. This, however, had not sufficed them, but they had gone ever further. This had caused conflicts between the red and the white people that eventually brought on a war. Therein both had been wrong, for the Father who dwells above does not regard this with favor but would have it that all should be brethren. The whites are now called the older brothers and the red the younger. I do not object to this and will call them so, though really the naming should have been reversed, for the red people dwelt here first. The Great Father of all breathing things, who has created all men, has given me, also, the breath of life and can take it again so soon as it him pleases. I am thankful to him, who has up to this time preserved to me the breath of life. But we have all been made of the earth and must all, sooner or later, return to the earth again. The Great Father, who dwells above, sees all, knows all that we speak with one another. He is near, also, at this our meeting and rejoices to see us and hear our words. He beholds our most insignificant actions and has given us much for our profit that we do not regard. One need only look upon the water, without which we could not live. He made it. The fire in the fire-place. What a little thing! yet he has created it for our benefit; and what, especially, would the poor red man do if there were no fire, since they have not as many warm clothes as have the whites. Everywhere there is fire, hidden in a subtle manner, it may be drawn even from the smallest stone; and thus it is with everything else that one sees, all point to the almighty power of God. The whites have, indeed, the advantage; they can make themselves clothes against the cold. The red people can only build the small canoes and cross small waters; the whites, on the other hand, build enormous canoes and cross safely over the greatest waters. They have, too, the great book from which they can learn all things. When the Great Father in the beginning created men, he had a great book; this he first extended to the red men and bade them speak to it (i.e. read it) but they were unable to do so. Then he offered it to the white people with the same command. As soon as they saw it, they were able to speak to the book at once; and thus it has come about that the white people know so much that is not known to the red. The time appears to have come when the red people should learn it, too. When the white people first came to this land they had the great book, wherein is the Word of God, but they did not instruct the red concerning it. I believe, therefore, that you have been inspired of the Great Spirit to be willing to come to us and to teach us. For my part, I will bid you welcome; I am well satisfied and it pleases me very much. My people are now not at home. So soon as they return, I will take counsel with them and, perhaps, soon send you answer. I believe that it will be as agreeable to my people as it is to me. I am delighted that there is thought for the old loved town of Chota. When you came there you could not see my house, so much has the place been overgrown with grass, yet you found it; that rejoices me exceedingly. I am now quite alone. The other loved ones are gone, though they ever desired to maintain peace (therewith he signified allegorically that they had been murdered by the whites). Never, however, will I leave Chota but remain there till I die or perish."

Then he pointed to his medal and said: "I always wear it, in order to think of peace. It was given me by beloved men. I will always maintain peace and never forget the good words of loved men of the United States. I will remember, also, your great words and communicate them to my people." Then he took each of us by the right arm and shook it as a token of friendship.

Bro. Steiner, then, said to him, that our brethren had not sent us to take any of their land or to carry on trade, in order to become rich; but solely because of love to them and to hear whether they would receive the Word of God. He had said quite rightly that God had regard for our most insignificant actions; also that we were made of the earth and should return to the earth. Should we now hear from them that they had a desire to learn to know God and his Word, we would heartily rejoice. He thanked us then, that we had so honored him and his nation as to come such a distance to them. We gave him several tobacco-pipe heads, upon which he said: "When I smoke out of these and the smoke rises upward, I will look after it toward heaven and first think of the Father of all breathing things and then of you and of your words." Then he thanked us again and said, that he hoped we would soon come again and then bring him better pipes. After a while he came to us again, shook us by the right arm, took leave and then went home. (1799, 1928)

ANNE NEWPORT ROYALL

In her letters and sketches, Anne Royall comments upon practically every aspect of American life, and the Indian question is no exception. With her reporter's eye for detail, she reveals the basic incompatibility of the Cherokee culture and that of the white man. The inevitability of complete removal of the Cherokee is implicit within her account.

FROM *Letters from Alabama on Various Subjects*
Letter XXX

Melton's Bluff
January 20th, 1818

Dear Matt,

. . . Hearing eleven boats had arrived about two miles from hence, and had haulted up the river, we set off, as I said before, in a little canoe, to see the Indians, which are on their way to their destination beyond the Mississippi. Government, agreeably to their contract, having completed the boats, the news of the arrival of the Indians had been received with much interest; but being unable to proceed by water, we quit the canoe, and proceeded by land in our wet shoes and hose.

We arrived at the Indian camps about eleven o'clock. There were several encampments at the distance of three hundred yards from each other, containing three hundred Indians. The camps were nothing but some forks of wood driven into the ground, and a stick laid across them, on which hung a pot in which they were boiling meat; I took it to be venison. Around these fires were seated, some on the ground, some on logs, and some on chairs, females of all ages; and all employed, except the old women. There were some very old gray-haired women, and several children at each camp. The children were very pretty; but the grown females were not. I saw but few men. I asked the interpreter where they were: he said they had gone to hunt; some of them had returned, and were skinning and others preparing their game for their journey. But none of them were near the women's department; they kept at a very respectful distance.

I have heard much of the elegant figures of the Indians; true, some nations of Indians are elegantly formed, but such is not the case with the Cherokees. They are low in stature, and there is nothing majestic or dignified about them. They have no expression of countenance. They have a dead eye; but their feet and hands are exceedingly small and beautiful. This is all the beauty I could distinguish about them. No lady that ever I saw has a hand so small or so well turned as these Indian women; and the same may be said of their feet. But, after all, they are ugly lumps of things. They are thick and short. Their hair is jet black, and very coarse. It parts from the crown of the head to its termination on the forehead, as the Dutch women wear theirs, and clubbed up behind with a blue or red ferret. Their colour is that of dark mulattoes. They were all well dressed; at least as well as most white women are, when engaged in their ordinary employment. Some were engaged in sewing, some in cooking, and some in nursing their babies, which were the prettiest little creatures I ever beheld.

Their manner of nursing is singular. They do not hold their

infants in their arms, or on their laps, as our women do; but on their backs, confined in such a manner that they are in no danger of falling, or moving in any direction. This is done by means of a blanket, or a part of one, drawn tight round the infant, leaving its head and arms out. This blanket is fastened round the waist of the mother, and the top I do not know exactly how; but the utmost confidence seems to be reposed in its tenacity, as the mother never touches the child with her hands, or is at any more trouble with it whatever. The little things clasp their arms round the necks of their mothers, which they never move: no crying, nor fretting, nor any apprehension of danger disturbed the serenity of these little philosophers, on our approaching them. I have been told that the mothers suckle them, where they are, by raising the breast up to the child's mouth, which is very probable.

The Indian women appear to sustain no inconvenience from the incumbrance of their children. They went through the different vocations of pounding their corn into meal, carrying wood and water, with the same apparent ease as those that had no children. Seeing several little girls of from ten to twelve years old, I asked the women why they did not make those little girls nurse their little ones. They answered no other way than by shaking their heads, and smiling at my ignorance, no doubt. I went up to one of them, who was pounding corn, took the pestle out of her hand and helped her to pound: she laughed at my awkwardness, and took it out of my hand. She had, sitting by her on a washing-tub, a large tray full of parched corn. This it was that she was pounding into meal; and as she finished each portion, she emptied it into another tray. Every thing about her was neat and clean. The Indian corn was parched to a nice light brown, and looked "very interesting." The meal manufactured from this corn, is not fine, nor do they make it into bread at all, but mix it with common water and drink it. 'Tis rarely that they drink water in any other way. No one, who has never tasted it, would believe what a delicious drink it is.

Having walked about and made a number of inquiries, I sat myself down and made signs to an old Indian woman that I wanted to smoke: she very courteously handed me her pipe. The seat I had chosen was near one of those women, whom I had observed for some time, sedulously engaged with her needle. She was engaged making a family dress, in which she discovered all the skill and industry necessary to accomplish it. Their dresses were made like our ladies, and were put on. They had fine cotton shawls on their shoulders, and many of them had men's hats on their heads; but no bonnets were seen amongst them. They all had good shoes or mockasins on their feet, and some hundreds of beads round their necks; but their broad faces and coarse hair (as coarse as a horses mane) were quite disgusting. There is one elegance, however, which they possess in a superior degree to any civilized people that I am acquainted with; and this is not their beautiful hands and feet, already mentioned, but their walk. No lady, however skilled in the art of dancing, can walk with so much grace and dignity as these Indians, both men and women: and this, I am told, is peculiar to almost all Indians.

Although there were such a number of them, so near together as to be seen from one camp to the other, yet there was the greatest ardor imaginable: not the least noise to be heard. How would so many whites have managed to maintain the good order evinced by these Indians? Even their dogs were not permitted to bark at us. The poor dogs! I felt for them: they were nothing but skin and bone! The same word that we use to encourage our dogs to seize on any thing, or to bark, the Indians use to control theirs, which is *hiss*! One of our party told me that it was *hiska*! which means "be still." The dress of the men was equally as decent and fashionable as that of the women. Many of them had on very neat half-boots, broad cloth coats, and good hats; though some prefer tying their heads up with a handkerchief, as being more convenient to hunt in.

By all that I have said in regard to these Cherokees, you may perceive they are far advanced in civilized arts and manners. This great work was accomplished by the indefatigable labors of the Reverend Gideon Blackburn! And yet, what an aversion they manifest toward our language! I was told that nearly all those that I saw, both understood and could talk good English; but not one word could I get out of them, of any sort. Their inter-communications were carried on by signs. I saw many of the half-breed, as they are called, here; the offspring of a white and an Indian—but they were as unsociable as the others. I was thinking that this would be a good plan to promote their civilization, but the result proves that any plan would not succeed. It is very probable, that the most effectual means have been resorted to by our government to overcome their prejudices. I mean our rifles. (1830)

JOHN G. BURNETT

Autobiographical information on Private John G. Burnett is contained in his birthday story. His life does not appear to be exceptional for a young man growing up in America in the early part of the nineteenth century, but his sensitivity to the treatment of the Cherokee is indeed exceptional as his remarkable reminiscence reveals. The Cherokee removal culminated in the forced march of the Eastern Band to Oklahoma in 1838–39 that has become known in American history as the infamous "Trail of Tears."

Removal of the Cherokees

Children.

This is my birthday December the 11th 1890. I am eighty years old today. I was born at Kings Iron Works in Sullivan County, Tennessee, December the 11th 1810. I grew into manhood fishing in Beaver-Creek and roaming through the forest hunting the deer, the wild boar, and the timber wolf, often spending weeks at a time in the solitary wilderness with no companions but my rifle, hunting knife, and a small hatchet that I carried in my belt in all of my wilderness wanderings.

On these long hunting trips I met and became acquainted with many of the Cherokee Indians, hunting with them by day and sleeping 'round their camp fires by night. I learned to speak their language, and they taught me the arts of trailing and building traps and snares. On one of my long hunts in the fall of 1829 I found a young Cherokee who had been shot by a roving band of hunters and who had eluded his persuers and concealed himself under a shelving rock. Weak from loss of blood the poor creature was unable to walk and almost famished for water. I carried him to a spring, bathed and bandaged the bullet wound, built a shelter out of bark peeled from a dead chestnut tree, nursed and protected him feeding him on chestnuts and roasted deer meat. When he was able to travel I accompanied him to the home of his people and remained so long that I was given up for lost; by this time I had become an expert rifleman, a fairly good archer, and a good trapper and spent most of my time in the forests in quest of game.

The removal of the Cherokee Indians from their life long homes in the year 1838 found me a young man in the prime of life and a private soldier in the American army, being acquainted with many of the Indians and able to fluently speak their language I was sent as interpreter into the Smoky Mountain Country in May 1838 and witnessed the execution of the most brutal order in the History of American Warfare. I saw the helpless Cherokees arrested, dragged from their homes, and driven at the bayonet point into the stockades, and in the chill of a drizzleing rain on an October morning I saw them loadded like cattle or sheep into six hundred and forty five wagons and started toward the West.

One can never forget the sadness and solemnity of that morning. Chief John Ross led in prayer, and when the bugle sounded and the wagons started rolling, many of the children rose to their feet and waved their little hands good-bye to their mountain homes knowing they were leaving them forever. Many of these helpless people did not have blankets, and many of them had been driven from home barefooted. On the morning of November the 17th we encountered a terrifick sleet and snow storm with freezing temperature, and from that day untill we reached the end of the fateful journed on March the 26th 1839, the sufferings of the Cherokees were awful. The trail of the exiles was a trail of death. They had to sleep in the wagons and on the ground without fire, and I have known as many as twenty-two of them to die in one night of pneumonia due to ill treatment, cold and exposure.

Among this number was the beautiful Christain wife of Chief John Ross. This noble hearted woman died a martyr to childhood. Giving her only blanket for the protection of a sick child, she rode thinly clad through a blinding sleet and snow storm, developed pneumonia, and died in the still hours of a bleak winter night with her head resting on Lieutenant Greggs saddle blanket.

I made the long journey to the west with the Cherokees and did all that a private soldier could do to alleviate their sufferings. When on guard duty at night I have many times walked my beat in my blouse in order that some sick child might have the warmth of my overcoat.

I was on guard duty the night Mrs. Ross died. When relieved at midnight, I did not retire but remained around the wagon out of sympathy for Chief Ross, and at daylight was detailed by Captain McClellan to assist in the burial. Like the other unfortunates who died on the journey her uncoffined body was buried in a shallow grave by the roadside far from her native mountain home, and the sorrowing cavalcade moved on.

Being a young man I mingled freely with the young women and girls. I have spent many pleasant hours with them when I was supposed to be under my blankets, and they have many times sung their mountain songs for me, this being all that they could do to repay my kindness. And with all of my associations with Indian girls from October 1829 to

March the 26th 1839, I did not meet one who was a moral prostitute. They are kind and tender hearted and many of them are beautiful.

The only trouble that I had with anybody on the entire journey to the West was with a brutal teamster by the name of Ben McDonal who was useing his whip on an old feeble Cherokee to hasten him into the wagon. The sight of that old and nearly blind creature quivering under the lashes of a bull whip was too much for me. I attempted to stop McDonal and it ended in a personal encounter. He lashed me across the face, the wire tip on his whip cutting a bad gash in my cheek. The little hatchet that I had carried in my hunting days was in my belt and McDonal was carried unconscious from the scene.

I was at once placed under guard but Ensign Henry Bullock and Private Elkanah Millard had both witnessed the encounter. They gave Captain McClellan the facts and I never was brought to trial. Years later I met 2nd Lieutenant Riley and Ensign Bullock at Bristol at John Robersons and Bullock jokingly reminded me that there was a case still pending against me before a court-martial and wanted to know how much longer I was going to have the trial put off? McDonal finally recovered and in the year 1851 was running on a boat out of Memphis Tennessee.

The long painful journey to the West ended March the 26th 1839 with four thousand silent graves reaching from the foot hills of the Smoky Mountains to what is known as Indian territory in the West, and covetousness on the part of the white race was the cause of all that the Cherokees had to suffer.

Ever since Ferdinand DeSoto made his journey through the Indian Country in the year 1540, there had been a tradition of a rich Gold mine somewhere in the Smoky Mountain Country, and I think the tradition was true. At a festival at Echata on Christmas night 1829, I danced and played with

Indian girls who were wearing ornaments around their necks that looked like Gold.

In the year 1828 a little Indian boy living on Ward Creek had sold a Gold nugget to a white trader and that nugget sealed the doom of the Cherokees. In a short time the country was over run with armed brigands claiming to be government agents who paid no attention to the rights of the Indians who were the legal possessors of the country. Crimes were committed that were a disgrace to civilization. Men were shot in cold blood—lands were conficicated. Homes were burned and the inhabitants driven out by these gold hungry brigands.

Chief Junaluska was personally acquainted with President Andrew Jackson. Junaluska had taken five hundred of the flower of his Cherokee Scouts and helped Jackson to win the battle of the Horseshoe leaving thirty three of them dead on the field, and in that battle Junaluska had drove his Tomahawk through the skull of a Creek Warrior when the Creek had Jackson at his mercy.

Chief John Ross sent Junaluska as an envoy to plead with President Jackson for protection for his people, but Jacksons manner was cold and indifferent toward the rugged son of the forest who had saved his life. He met Junaluska, heard his plea, but curtly said, "Sir your audience is ended. There is nothing that I can do for you."

The doom of the Cherokees was sealed. Washington DC had decreed that they must be driven West and their lands given to white men, and in May 1838 an army of four thousand regulars and three thousand volunteer soldiers under Command of General Winfield Scott, marched into the Indian Country and wrote the blackest chapter on the pages of American History.

Men working in the fields were arrested and driven to the stockades. Women were dragged from their homes by soldiers whose language they could not understand. Children were often separated from their parents and driven into the stockades with the Sky for a Blanket and the Earth for a Pillow, and often the old and infirm were prodded with bayonets to hasten them to the stockades. In one home death had come during the night. A little sad faced child had died and was lying on a bear skin couch and some women were preparing the little body for burial. All were arrested and driven out leaving the child in the cabin. I don't know who buried the body.

In another home was a frail mother, apparently a widow, and three small children, one just a baby. When told that she must go, the mother gathered the children at her feet, prayed an humble prayer in her native tongue, patted the old family dog on the head, told the faithful creature good bye, and with her baby strapped on her back and leading a child with each hand started to her exile, but the task was too great for that frail mother, a stroke of heart failure relieved her sufferings. She sunk and died with her baby on her back and her other two children clinging to her hands.

Chief Junaluska who had saved President Jacksons life at the battle of the Horseshoe witnessed this scene, the tears gushed down his cheeks, and lifting his cap he turned his face toward the Heavens and said, "Oh my God, if I had known at the battle of the Horseshoe what I know today, American history would have been differently written."

At this time December 1890 we are too near the removal of the Cherokees for our young people to fully understand the enormity of the crime that was committed against a helpless race. Truth is the facts are being concealed from the young people of today. School children of today do not know that we are living on lands that were taken from a helpless race at the bayonet point to sadisfy the white mans greed for Gold.

Future generations will read and condemn the act, and I do hope posterity will remember that private soldiers like myself and like the four Cherokees who were forced by General Scott to shoot an Indian chief and his children, had to execute the orders of our superiors. We had no choice in the matter. Twenty five years after the removal, it was my privilege to meet a large company of the Cherokees in the uniform of the Confederate Army under Command of Colonel Thomus. They were encamped at Zollicoffer.* I went to see them. Most of them were just boys at the time of the removal, but they instantly recognized me as "the soldier who was good to us." Being able to talk to them in their native language I had an enjoyable day with them. From them I learned that Chief John Ross was still living and ruler of the nation in 1863, and I wonder if he is still living? He was a noble hearted fellow and suffered a lot for his race. At one time he was arrested and thrown into a dirty jail in an effort to break his spirit, but he remained true to his people and led them in prayer when they started to their exile, and his Christian wife sacrificed her life for a little girl who had pneumonia. The Anglo Saxon race would build a towering monument to perpetuate her noble act in giving her only blanket for the comfort of a sick child.

Incidently, the child recovered, but Mrs. Ross is sleeping in an unmarked grave far from her native Smoky Mountain Home.

When Scott invaded the Indian Country, some of the Cherokees fled to caves and dens in the mountains and were never captured, and they are there today. I have long intended going there and trying to find them, but I have put off going from year to year and I am now too feeble to ride that far.

The fleeting years have come and gone and old age has overtaken me. I can truthfully say that neither my rifle nor my knife are stained with Cherokee blood. I can truthfully say that I did my best for them when they certainly did need

* Now Bluff City, Tennessee, between Johnson City and Bristol, Tennessee-Virginia.—Editors

a friend. Twenty five years after the removal I still lived in their memory as "the soldier who was good to us."

However, murder is murder, whether committed by the villian skulking in the dark or by uniformed men stepping to the strains of martial musick. Murder is murder, and somebody must answer. Somebody must explain the streams of blood that flowed in the Indian Country in the summer of 1838. Somebody must explain the four thousand silent graves that mark the trail of the Cherokees to their exile.

I wish I could forget it all, but the picture of those six hundred and forty five wagons lumbering over the frozen ground with their cargo of suffering humanity still lingers in my memory. Let the Historian of a future day tell the sad story with its sighs, its tears, and dieing groans—let the Great Judge of all the Earth weigh our actions and reward us according to our works.

Children thus ends my promised birthday story.

this December—
the 11th 1890—

Private John G. Burnett
Captain McClellans' Company—2nd Regiment
2nd Brigade Cherokee removal 1838–39. (1956)

C. The Mythical Heritage: Poor White and Hillbilly

Owing to the general inaccessibility of the mountains, travel was relatively light in the seventeenth and eighteenth centuries compared to that in the back country all along the Southern frontier; but impressions of outsiders passing through the lower country eventually had an enduring influence on the general concept of the Southern mountaineer. While the mountaineer may be quite different from the Southern poor white, both share a common mythical heritage which in part grew out of the impressions of aristocrats such as William Byrd. The works of Byrd and later observers such as Alexander Wilson and Thomas Ashe portray all the traditional characteristics of the degraded poor white and mountaineer—laziness, slovenliness, and love of whiskey and violence. Then as now there were those— Timothy Flint, for example—who disagreed with these stereotypes.

WILLIAM BYRD II

Born in 1674, William Byrd was educated in England and
Holland. A Virginia aristocrat of the first rank, he was interested in all aspects of life, as is revealed by his fascinating
diaries. His attitude toward the poor white has been representative of many upperclass observers of the South from
the eighteenth century to the present. In fact, Byrd helped to
establish dividing lines between social classes as well as
states.

FROM *The History of the Dividing Line, Between
Virginia and North Carolina as Run in 1728–29*

Surely there is no place in the World where the Inhabitants
live with less Labour than in N Carolina. It approaches
nearer to the Description of Lubberland than any other, by
the great felicity of the Climate, the easiness of raising Provisions, and the Slothfulness of the People.

Indian corn is of so great increase, that a little Pains will
Subsist a very large Family with Bread, and then they may
have meat without any pains at all, by the Help of the Low
Grounds, and the great Variety of Mast that grows on the

High-land. The Men, for their Parts, just like the Indians, impose all the Work upon the poor Women. They make their Wives rise out of their Beds early in the Morning, at the same time that they lye and Snore, till the Sun has risen one-third of his course, and disperst all the unwholesome Damps. Then, after Stretching and Yawning for half an Hour, they light their Pipes, and, under the protection of a cloud of Smoak, venture out into the open Air; tho', if it happens to be never so little cold, they quickly return Shivering into the Chimney corner. When the Weather is mild, they stand leaning with both their arms upon the cornfield fence, and gravely consider whether they had best go and take a Small Heat at the Hough: but generally they find reasons to put it off till another time.

Thus they loiter away their Lives, like Solomon's Sluggard, with their Arms across, and at the Winding up of the Year Scarcely have Bread to Eat.

To speak the Truth, tis a thorough Aversion to Labor that makes People file off to N Carolina, where Plenty and a Warm Sun confirm them in their Disposition to Laziness for their whole lives. (1841; 1866)

ALEXANDER WILSON

Born in Paisley, Scotland, in 1776, Alexander Wilson came to America in 1802, where he later met the naturalist William Bartram, under whose influence Wilson was to achieve fame as an ornithologist. Described by Henry Adams as "grumbling," he reminds one at times of a traveler in a Smollett novel. Wilson's letters in his *American Ornithology* are highly readable and according to historian Thomas D. Clark "of genuine historical value." The excerpt from Wilson's *Ornithology* helps to perpetuate the poor white stereotype originating with William Byrd.

FROM *American Ornithology or Natural History of the United States*

The productions of these parts of North Carolina are hogs, turpentine, tar, and apple brandy. A tumbler of toddy is usually the morning's beverage of the inhabitants, as soon as they get out of bed. So universal is the practice, that the first thing you find them engaged in, after rising, is preparing the brandy *toddy*. You can scarcely meet a man whose lips are not parched and chopped or blistered with drinking this poison. Those who do not drink it, they say, are sure of the ague. I, however, escaped. The pine woods have a singular appearance, every tree being stripped, on one or more sides, of the bark, for six or seven feet up. The turpentine covers these parts in thick masses. I saw the people, in different parts of the woods, mounted on benches, chopping down the sides of the trees; leaving a trough or box in the tree for the turpentine to run into. Of hogs they have immense multitudes; one person will sometimes own five hundred. The leaders have bells round their necks; and every drove knows its particular call, whether it be a conch-shell, or the bawling of a negro, though half a mile off. Their owners will sometimes drive them for four or five days to a market, without once feeding them.

The taverns are the most desolate and beggarly imaginable: bare, bleak, and dirty walls;—one or two old broken chairs, and a bench, form all the furniture. The white females seldom make their appearance; and every thing must be transacted through the medium of negroes. At supper, you sit down to a meal, the very sight of which is sufficient to deaden the most eager appetite. . . . The house itself is raised upon props, four or five feet; and the space below is left open for the hogs, with whose charming vocal performance the wearied traveller is serenaded the whole night long, till he is forced to curse the hogs, the house, and every thing about it. (1828)

THOMAS ASHE

Thomas Ashe was born in Dublin, Ireland, in 1770. According to historian Thomas D. Clark, Ashe became involved in various troubles before coming to America to record his impressions in 1806. His condemnation of Americans was refuted by a number of his contemporaries. Ashe died in 1835, after what Dr. Clark describes as a career of intrigue, misrepresentation, and fraud. To the mythical poor white characteristics of laziness and dirtiness, Ashe helped to add two more: violence and intemperance.

FROM *Travels in America, Performed in 1806*

. . . the quarrel took a smaller circle, confined to two individuals; a Virginian by birth; and a Kentuckyan by adoption. A ring was formed, and the mob demanded whether they proposed to *fight fair*, or to *rough and tumble*. The latter mode was preferred. Perhaps you do not exactly understand the distinction of these terms. Fight fair however is much in the English manner; and here, as there, any thing foul requires interference; but when parties choose to *rough* and *tumble*, neither the populace nor individuals are to intermeddle or hinder either combatant from tearing or rending the other on the ground, or in any other situation. You startle

61

at the words *tear* and *rend*, and again do not understand me. You have heard these terms I allow applied to beasts of prey and to carnivorous animals; and your humanity cannot conceive them applicable to man: it is nevertheless so, and the fact will not permit me the use of any less expressive term. Let me proceed. Bulk and bone were in favor of the Kentuckyan; science and craft in that of the Virginian. The former promised himself victory from his power, the latter from his *science*. Very few rounds had taken place, or fatal blows given, before the Virginian contracted his whole form, drew up his arms to his face, with his hands nearly closed in a concave, by the fingers being bent to the full extension of the flexons, and summoning up all his energy for one act of desperation, pitched himself into the bosom of his opponent. Before the effects of this could be ascertained, the sky was rent by the shouts of the multitude; and I could learn that the Virginian had expressed as much *beauty* and *skill* in his retraction and bound, as if he had been bred in a menagerie, and practised action and attitude among the panthers and wolves. The shock received by the Kentuckyan, and the want of breath, brought him instantly to the ground. The Virginian never lost his hold, like those bats of the south who never quit the subject on which they fasten till they taste blood, he kept his knees in his enemies body; fixing his claws in his hair, and his thumbs on his eyes, gave them an instantaneous start from their sockets. The sufferer roared aloud, but uttered no complaint. The citizens shouted with joy. Doubts were no longer entertained; and bets of three to one were offered on the Virginian. The Kentuckyan not being able to disentangle his adversary from his face, adopted a new mode of warfare; and, in imitation of the serpent which rushes such creatures to death as it proposes for its food, he extended his arms round the Virginian and hugged him into closer contact with his huge body. The latter disliking this, cast loose the hair and convex eyes of his adversary, when both, folded together like bears in an embrace, rolled several turns over each other.

The acclamations increased, and bets run that the Kentuck-yan *"would give out,"* that is, after being mutilated and deprived of his eyes, ears, and nose, he would cry out for mercy and aid. The public were not precisely right. Some daemon interposed for the biggest monster; he got his enemy under him, and in an instant snapt off his nose so close to his face that no manner of projection remained. The little Vir-ginian made one further effort, and fastening on the under lip of his mutilator tore it over the chin. The Kentuckyan at length *gave out,* on which the people carried off their victor, and he preferring triumph to a doctor, who came to circatrize his face, suffered himself to be chaired round the ground as the champ of the times, and the first *rough and tumbler.* The poor wretch, whose eyes were started from their spheres, and whose lip refused its office, returned to the town, to hide his impotence, and get his countenance repaired. . . .

The dinner [in the Kentucky cabin] consisted of a large piece of salt bacon, a dish of homslie, and a turreen of squir-rel broth. I dined entirely on the last dish, which I found incomparably good, and the meat equal to the most delicate chicken. The Kentuckyan ate nothing but bacon, which indeed is the favourite diet of all the inhabitants of the State, and drank nothing but whiskey, which soon made him more than two thirds drunk. In this last practice he is also sup-ported by the public habit. In a country then, where bacon and spirits form the favourite summer repast, it cannot be just to attribute entirely the causes of infirmity to the climate. No people on earth live with less regard to regimen. They eat salt meat three times a day, seldom or never have any vege-table, and drink ardent spirits from morning till night! They have not only an aversion to fresh meat, but a vulgar preju-dice that it is unwholesome. The truth is, their stomachs are depraved by burning liquors, and they have no appetite for anything but what is high-flavoured and strongly impreg-nated with salt. (1808)

JAMES KIRKE PAULDING

Instead of indicting back-country inhabitants in the man-ner of Wilson and Ashe, James Kirke Paulding provides a more objective contrast between the tidewater and frontier cultures. Paulding in effect defends the Virginia mountaineer by showing that his way of life is not necessarily inferior but only different from that of the seaboard.

FROM *Letters from the South*
Letter X

Dear Frank,

. . . The mountain called the Blue Ridge not only forms the natural but the political division of Virginia. I know not whether you have observed it, but all the considerable States, to the South of New-York inclusive, have two little scurvy, distinct, and separate local interests, or rather local feelings, operating most vehemently, in a kind of undertone not much heard abroad, but, like certain domestic accents, exceedingly potent at home. The east and west sections of these States are continually at sixes and sevens, and as the west is generally the most extensive, as well as fruitful, it is gradually getting the upper hand of the other, and removing the seat of power farther into the interior. These distinctions, so far as I have been able to trace them, originated in the struggles of little village politicians striving to become popular, by affecting to be the guardians of the village rights, which they defend most manfully, long before they are attacked. Their wise constituents in time begin to perceive clearly, that they have been very much imposed upon, and in fact made slaves of, by a few people in a distant corner of the state,—and then nothing will do but a convention, to set matters right, and put things topsy-turvy.

This snug little rivalry is beginning to bud vigorously in Virginia. The people of whom I am now writing call those east of the mountain Tuckahoes, and their country Old Virginia. They themselves are the Cohees, and their country New Virginia. The origin of these Indian phrases, I am not able to trace. I understand, however, that in parts of Virginia, east of the Blue Ridge, there is a species of large mushroom growing under ground, and known by the name of Tuckahoe. It may be, that as this part of Virginia was settled while the Indians inhabited the great valley, west of the Blue Ridge, they might have stigmatized the white settlers as Tuckahoes —mushrooms, in allusion to their being upstarts—new comers. If it were only a matter of six or eight hundred years ago, I might go near to prove, that the first settlers were arrant Troglodytes, and were called by the Indians Tuckahoe, because like that notable fungus, they grew under ground. But this, among other matters, I leave to the future antiquarian.

Certain it is, that however these names may have originated, they are now the familiar terms by which people of Old and New Virginia are designated east of the Blue Ridge. It is the old story of Mrs. Farmer Ashfield and Mrs. Planter Grundy. Mrs. Ashfield leads the tone among the Cohees, squints at Mrs. Grundy, the fine lady of the Tuckahoes, because forsooth, and marry come up, my lady gives herself airs, and wears such mighty fine clothes, when she goes to the Springs. Now Goody Ashfield, for her part, don't care for fine things, not she; but then she can't bear to see some people take upon themselves, and pretend to be better than other people. Then Madam Grundy, if the truth must be told, is sometimes apt to turn up her nose, when she sees plain Mrs. Ashfield industriously mending a pair of breeches, the original colour of which is lost in the obscurity of the patches. She *wonders* at her daughter pulling flax, or weaving, or turning a great spinning-wheel that deranges people's nerves sadly. *Wonders*, in a very kind and friendly way, why Farmer Ashfield can think of making such a slave of his daughter, and why, as he can afford it, he don't send her to one of the great boarding-schools in Philadelphia, to get a polish, and learn to despise her vulgar old father and mother. All these wonderments are, of course, wormwood to Mrs. Ashfield, who thereupon pulls Mrs. Grundy to pieces, when she goes away.

As to Squire Grundy and Farmer Ashfield, they have certain smug matters of dispute to themselves. The Farmer insists upon it, at town-meetings and elections, that the Squire enjoys greater political privileges than he does; that the country of Tuckahoe has more representatives in the legislature than it ought to have; that all Squire Grundy's negroes go to the polls, and vote: that the seat of government ought to be removed, that the poor enslaved Cohees may not be toted all the way to Richmond to hear orations, and get justice; and that, finally, the Squire gives himself such airs of superiority, that there is not such thing as getting along with him. On the other hand, Squire Grundy maintains that he pays more taxes than the Farmer; that taxation and representation as naturally go together as whiskey and vagabonds; that not numbers but property ought to be represented; that his negroes are included in the number of voters because they are taxed; and that, finally, the Cohees, not being able to comprehend this, are a set of ignorant blockheads. The Farmer says, "It is a dom lie;" and both parties are more convinced than before. The end of all this will be, that the Cohees will probably at last carry their point, and, in consequence thereof, be just as well off as they were before. (1817)

TIMOTHY FLINT

In the previously excerpted Boone biography and in other works, Flint is a staunch defender of the West, especially against such detractors as Dr. Timothy Dwight. While the backwoodsman may not have the sophistication and manners of his fellow countryman on the Atlantic Coast, he is, according to Flint, no less civilized.

FROM *Recollections of the Last Ten Years*
Letter XVII—St. Charles

The people in the Atlantic states have not yet recovered from the horror, inspired by the term "back-woodsman." This prejudice is particularly strong in New England, and is more or less felt from Maine to Georgia. When I first visited this country, I had my full share, and my family by far too much for their comfort. In approaching the country, I heard a thousand stories of gougings, and robberies, and shooting down with the rifle. I have travelled in these regions thousands of miles under all circumstances of exposure and danger. I have travelled alone, or in company only with such as needed protection, instead of being able to impart it; and this too, in many instances, where I was not known as a minister, or where such knowledge would have had no influence in protecting me. I never have carried the slightest weapon of defence. I scarcely remember to have experienced any thing that resembled insult, or to have felt myself in danger from the people. I have often seen men that had lost an eye. Instances of murder, numerous and horrible in their circumstances, have occurred in my vicinity. But they were such lawless rencounters, as terminate in murder every where, and in which the drunkenness, brutality, and violence were mutual. They were catastrophes, in which quiet and sober men would be in no danger of being involved. When we look round these immense regions, and consider that I have been in settlements three hundred miles from any court of justice, when we look at the position of the men, and the state of things, the wonder is, that so few outrages and murders occur. The gentlemen of the towns, even here, speak often with a certain contempt and horror of the backwoodsmen. I have read, and not without feelings of pain, the bitter representations of the learned and virtuous Dr. Dwight, in speaking of them. He represents these vast regions, as a grand reservoir for the scum of the Atlantic states. He characterizes in the mass the emigrants from New England, as discontented coblers, too proud, too much in debt, too unprincipled, too much puffed up with self-conceit, too strongly impressed that their fancied talents could not find scope in their own country, to stay there. It is true that there are worthless people here, and the most so, it must be confessed, are from New England. It is true there are gamblers, and gougers, and outlaws; but there are fewer of them, than from the nature of things, and the character of the age and the world, we ought to expect. But it is unworthy of the excellent man in question so to designate this people in the mass. The backwoodsman of the west, as I have seen him, is generally an amiable and virtuous man. His general motive for coming here is to be a freeholder, to have plenty of rich land, and to be able to settle his children about him. It is a most virtuous motive. And notwithstanding all that Dr. Dwight and Talleyrand have said to the contrary, I fully believe, that nine in ten of the emigrants have come here with no other motive. You find, in truth, that he has vices and barbarisms, peculiar to his situation. His manners are rough. He wears, it may be, a long beard. He has a great quantity of bear or deer skins wrought into his household establishment, his furniture, and dress. He carries a knife, or a dirk in his bosom, and when in the woods has a rifle on his back, and a pack of dogs at his heels. An Atlantic stranger, transferred directly from one of our cities to his door, would recoil from a rencounter with him. But remember, that his rifle and his dogs are among his chief means of support and profit. Remember, that all his first days here were passed in dread of the savages. Remember, that he still encounters them, still meets bears and panthers. Enter his door, and tell him you are benighted, and wish the shelter of his cabin for the night. The welcome is indeed seemingly ungracious: "I reckon you can stay," or "I suppose we must let you stay." But this apparent ungraciousness is the harbinger of every kindness that he can bestow, and every comfort that his cabin can afford. Good coffee, corn bread and butter, venison, pork, wild and tame fowls are set before you. His wife, timid, silent, reserved, but constantly attentive to your comfort, does not sit at table with you, but like the wives of the patriarchs, stands and attends on you. You are shown to the best bed which the house can offer. When this kind of hospitality has been afforded you as long as you choose to stay, and when you depart, and speak about your bill, you are most commonly told with some slight mark of resentment, that they do not keep tavern. Even the flaxen-haired urchins will turn away from your money.

In all my extensive intercourse with these people, I do not recollect but one instance of positive rudeness and inhospitality. It was on the waters of the Cuivre of the upper Mississippi; and from a man to whom I had presented bibles, who had received the hospitality of my house, who had invited me into his settlement to preach. I turned away indignantly from a cold and reluctant reception here, made my way from the house of this man,—who was a German and comparatively rich,—through deep and dark forests, and amidst the concerts of wolves howling on the neighbouring hills. Providentially, about midnight, I heard the barking of dogs at a distance, made my way to the cabin of a very poor man, who arose at midnight, took me in, provided supper, and gave me a most cordial reception. (1826)

ANNE NEWPORT ROYALL

While James Kirke Paulding noted the distinct differences between the Tuckahoes and the Cohees, Anne Royall made distinctions between the inhabitants of the western states and those of Appalachia. Though she was amazed and perplexed by many of the customs and especially by the language of the mountaineers, Anne Royall rarely resorted to the disparaging tone characteristic of many outsiders; or if she did, she alleviated her views by good humor and sympathy.

FROM *Sketches of History, Life, and Manners in the United States*

On the bosom of this vast mass of mountains are the six counties of Virginia, known by the names of Greenbriar, Monroe, Nicolas, Pocahontas, Giles, and Tazewell, elevated to the clouds, resembling each other in every thing: Greenbriar, however, as she is the mother of the whole, commands most wealth, having the advantage in good land. But with respect to the appearance of the inhabitants, their pursuits and manners, they are alike, and to these we may add Alleghany, also clipped from the wings of Greenbriar. These counties have been erroneously confounded with the western country, whereas there is as much difference between the people of the western states and those, as there are between any two people in the union. The inhabitants of the western states are an enterprising, systematical, industrious people, to which they are stimulated by the fertility of their soil, and numerous navigable rivers. These last are likewise distinguished for energy of mind, politeness of manners, and application to business; whereas the former exhibit a striking contrast to all these traits. These counties, remote from commerce and civilized life, confined to their everlasting hills of freezing cold, all pursuing the same employments, which consist in farming, raising cattle, making whiskey, (and drinking it,) hunting and digging *sang*,* as they say, present a distinct republic of their own, every way different from any people.

Appearance—The young people of both sexes are very fair and beautiful, and many of them well formed: the men are stout, active, and amongst the best marksmen in America. They are, both male and female, extravagantly fond of dress; this, and their beauty, only serves to expose their unpolished manners, and want of education. They have no expression of countenance, nor do they appear to possess much mind. One great proof of this, is, that all places of honor, profit, or trust, are monopolized by strangers. . . .

. . . the most astonishing circumstance which distinguishes this country, and one that has often been remarked, is that it never has produced one tolerable smart man. From Montgomery to Harrison, there never has been reared one man of abilities of any sort, while Kenhawa, inferior as it may be, has produced one of the brightest stars of American genius, I mean Henry Ruffner, L.L.D., a man of profound erudition, who would do honor to any country; he is the son of Col. Ruffner, mentioned in these sketches. I am told he is professor

* Ginseng

of Greek, in Washington college, Va. This cannot be the effect of climate; if it be, how do we account for the opposite result in Switzerland, and other cold countries, which has produced some of the greatest geniuses in the world; nor can it be the effect of education, as genius exists without it. Indeed, West Virginia has dealt out genius with a sparing hand: with the exception of John Breckenridge, I am told she has never produced one man that might be called great.

. . . their dialect sets orthography at defiance, and is with difficulty understood. . . . Some words they have imported, some they have made out and out, some they have swapped for others, and nearly the whole of the English language is so mangled and mutilated by them, that it is hardly known to be such. When they would say *pretence*, they say *lettinon*, which is a word of very extensive use among them. It signifies a jest, and is used to express disapprobation and disguise; "you are just lettinon to rub them spoons—Polly is not mad, she is only lettinon." Blaze they pronounce *bleez*, one they call *waun*, sugar *shugger*; "and is this all it ye got?" handkerchief *hancorchy*, (emphasis on the second syllable;) and "the two ens of it comed loose;" for get out of the way, they say get out of the road: Road is universally used for way; "put them cheers, (chairs) out of the road." But their favorite word of all, is *hate*, by which they mean the word thing; for instance, *nothing*, "not a hate—not waun hate will ye's do:" What did you buy at the stores, ladies? "Not a hate—well you hav'nt a hate here to eat." They have the *hickups*, and corp, (corps) are a *cute* people. Like Shakespear, they make a word when at a loss: *scawm'd* is one of them, which means spotted. They have rock houses and rock chimneys, &c. &c.

It would cure any one of the spleen to take a day or two in the country near the border of this republic.—"Billy, tell Johnny he must bring Sammy home;" if you were to tell them there were no such words, they would put you down as a fool. Their houses are adorned throughout with netting and fringe of coarse cotton, and the *han'tawel*: This last puzzled me much; I thought it meant one exclusively for the hands, but it is distinguished from a spacious one that sticks by the four corners to the wall, near the door or window, (if there be one in the house.) Thus disposed, a looking-glass, of neat device, about four by six inches, is confined in the centre; and by this last, hangs suspended, by one end, a long narrow lucid housewife, with some dozen pockets, consisting of as many different colors. These are grappled by a comb-case, but you would never know it by the name; it is not made of horn at all, but of paste-board, on the outside of which is pasted a bit of painted paper; this comb-case is about the size of a lady's reticule, and differs from it in shape only in this, that the part next the wall terminates in a triangle, by which it is suspended amongst its fellow ornaments. The ingenuity, taste, and pride, of the females, seems to be centered in this group of fineries —meantime you are addressed by the mistress of the family, "I reckon you are a most starved," while she is busied in preparing you something to eat: while this is doing, you are suffering the torments of the ordeal, from the impertinent curiosity of the whole family, in asking, "What may be your name? where are you going? from whence you come? and whether you are married? and have you any children? and whether your father and mother be alive?" At length a small table is drawn into the centre of the same apartment you are in, while the noise produced by it, jars every nerve in your body. This table is covered, (in many instances, with a cloth black with grease and dirt,) ten or a dozen plates, (I'll say nothing of them,) are placed on it, and finally one or two small dishes, on which is piled fried meat, to the height of a modern pyramid, with a hay-stack of sliced bread upon a plate. At one end of the table is another pile of besmeared, becracked, cups and saucers, which seem to maintain their place on the edge of the table by magic. You are now asked to sit down with the man, his wife, and four or six dirty boys and girls, around a table about large enough for two persons; and what's to be done, now? If you offer to touch the pyramid of bread to help any one of the party, great part of it tumbles over the table. But this is unnecessary, for each one reaches over the table with the utmost facility and helps himself; now and then, his sleeve, as black as your hat, coming in contact with the meat and bread, while their faces and noses are enough to set you against eating, forever; and as for the meat, you might as well try to insert your knife into a brick-bat. The coffee, however, and butter are fine, and nothing would affront them more than to offer them pay; meanwhile if you happen to lay any of your clothing where they can get hold of it, if to soil it sends it to perdition it must go there; they take it in their dirty hands again and again, turn it over and over, and when one has besoiled it another one must satisfy his curiosity. If you tell them the most interesting anecdote, they pay no more attention to you than if you were muttering Greek; take up the most amusing book and read to them, it is the same thing, and two-thirds of them would be *afraid* it was not a good book. (1826)

II. *Backwoods Humor: Tall Tale and Tall Talk*

Regardless of the true nature and character of the Southern
mountaineer during the 1820s, he emerged in the following
decades as a distinct comic type, especially as he appeared in
the Tall Tale. Practitioners of this genre seemed to compete
in the game of one-up-manship in the use of language and
imagination. The Crockett sketches help to set the tone for a
heroic age in which men were more than a match for the
wilderness that surrounded them. Thus, whether in fun or in
earnest, characters in yarns of the old Southwest were
invariably larger than life. The genre is generally said to have
begun with A. B. Longstreet's *Georgia Scenes* in 1835, but
by general consent one of the best narrators of this type of
fiction was George Washington Harris, creator of Sut
Lovingood. In addition to the two Lovingood stories, we have
included in the nonfiction section poles of critical opinion on
the meaning and significance of this remarkable East
Tennessee fool. The most famous master of the mode was
Mark Twain, and the selection we have chosen, "Journalism
in Tennessee," illustrates well the uninhibited humor and

gross exaggeration which characterized the best of Southwest humor. Although the Tall Tale had by and large spent its force by the end of the Civil War, it left an important literary legacy as seen in the works of such twentieth-century writers as Thomas Wolfe, William Faulkner, Flannery O'Connor, and Robert Penn Warren.

DAVID CROCKETT

Born in the mountains of East Tennessee in 1786, David Crockett left home at the age of thirteen and appeared twelve years later to fight under Andrew Jackson in the war against the Creeks. Having established a reputation as a great Indian fighter and frontiersman, he entered politics as a justice of the peace in 1816, was elected colonel of his military regiment, and later elected to the Tennessee legislature and to Congress for two terms. He was opposed to Jackson, and his supporters anonymously published many works to enhance his reputation, of which *Sketches and Eccentricities of Colonel David Crockett* (1833) is one. According to James A. Shackford in his biography *David Crockett, the Man and the Legend* (Chapel Hill, 1956), the author of this work was Mathew St. Clair Clarke, Clerk of the House of Representatives. The work was published earlier in the same year under the title *Life and Adventures of Colonel David Crockett of West Tennessee*, apparently with Crockett's knowledge and assistance, the subject's protestations notwithstanding. Defeated in an attempt for reelection in 1835, Crockett became disgusted with politics. He led a group of Tennesseans into the war for the independence of Texas, and died in the Battle of the Alamo in 1836.

Today the legendary Crockett is far more famous than the

historical one. Biographical information is often elusive and contradictory, as Walter Blair illustrates in his essay "Six Davy Crocketts." "A Bear Hunt" (title supplied) from *Sketches and Eccentricities* is a paradigm of the outlandish tales surrounding this "king of the wild frontier."

A Bear Hunt

The following story will be read with interest, both on account of the original ideas which it may present; and likewise, as it will serve to illustrate the character of Colonel Crockett in a new light. I shall give it, as far as my recollection serves me, in the colonel's own language.

"Well, as I have told you, it has been a custom with me ever since I moved to this country, to spend a part of every winter in bear hunting, unless I was engaged in public life. I generally take a tent, pack horses, and a friend 'long with me, and go down to the Shakes, where I camp out and hunt till I get tired, or till I get as much meat as I want. I do this because there is a great deal of game there; and besides, I never see any body but the friend I carry, and I like to hunt in a wilderness, where nobody can disturb me. I could tell you a thousand frolics I've had in these same Shakes; but perhaps the following one will amuse you:

"Sometime in the winter of 1824 or '25, a friend called to see me, to take a bear hunt. I was in the humour, so we got our pack horses, fixed up our tent and provisions, and set out for the Shakes. We arrived there safe, raised our tent, stored away our provisions, and commenced hunting: for several days we were quite successful; our game we brought to the tent, salted it, and packed it away. We had several hunts, and nothing occurred worth telling, save that we killed our game.

"But, one evening as we were coming along, our pack horses

loaded with bear meat, and our dogs trotting lazily after us, old Whirlwind held up his head and looked about; then rubbed his nose agin a bush, and opened. I knew, from the way he sung out, 'twas an old *he* bear. The balance of the dogs buckled in, and off they went right up a hollow. I gave up the horses to my friend, to carry 'em to the tent, which was now about half a mile distant, and set out after the dogs.

"The hollow up which the bear had gone made a bend, and I knew he would follow it; so I run across to head him. The sun was now down; 'twas growing dark mighty fast, and 'twas cold; so I buttoned my jacket close round me, and run on. I hadn't gone fur, before I heard the dogs tack, and they come a tearing right down the hollow. Presently I heard the old bear rattling through the cane, and the dogs coming on like lightning after him. I dashed on; I felt like I had wings, my dogs made such a roaring cry; they rushed by me, and as they did I harked 'em on; they all broke out, and the woods echoed back, and back, to their voices. It seemed to me they fairly flew, for 'twasn't long before they overhauled him, and I could hear 'em fighting not fur before me. I run on, but just before I got there, the old bear made a break and got loose; but the dogs kept close up, and every once in a while they stopped him and had a fight. I tried for my life to git up, but just before I'd get there, he'd break loose. I followed him this way for two or three miles, through briars, cane, *etc.* and he devilled me mightily. Once I thought I had him: I got up in about fifteen or twenty feet, 'twas so dark I couldn't tell the bear from a dog, and I started to go to him; but I found out there was a creek between us. How deep it was I didn't know; but it was dark, and cold, and too late to turn back; so I held my rifle up and walked right in. Before I got across, the old bear got loose and shot for it, right through the cane; I was mighty tired, but I scrambled out and followed on. I knew I was obliged to keep in hearing of my dogs, or git lost.

"Well, I kept on, and once in a while I could hear 'em fighting and baying just before me; then I'd run up, but

before I'd get there, the old bear would git loose. I sometimes thought 'bout giving up and going back; but while I'd
be thinking, they'd begin to fight agin, and I'd run on. I
followed him this way 'bout, as near as I could guess, from
four to five miles, when the old bear couldn't stand it any
longer, and took a tree; and I tell you what, I was mighty
glad of it.

"I went up, but at first it was so dark I could see nothing;
however, after looking about, and gitting the tree between
me and a star, I could see a very dark looking place, and I
raised up old Betsy, and she lightened. Down come the old
bear; but he wasn't much hurt, for of all the fights you ever
did see, that beat all. I had six dogs, and for nearly an hour
they kept rolling and tumbling right at my feet. I couldn't
see any thing but one old white dog I had; but every now
and then the bear made 'em sing out right under me. I had
my knife drawn, to stick him whenever he should seize me;
but after a while, bear, dogs and all, rolled down a precipice
just before me, and I could hear them fighting, like they
were in a hole. I loaded Betsy, laid down, and felt about in
the hole with her till I got her agin the bear, and I fired;
but I didn't kill him, for out of the hole he bounced, and he
and the dogs fought harder than ever. I laid old Betsy down,
and drew my knife; but the bear and dogs just formed a
lump, rolling about; and presently down they all went again
into the hole.

"My dogs now began to sing out mighty often: they were
getting tired, for it had been the hardest fight I ever saw. I
found out how the bear was laying, and I looked for old
Betsy to shoot him again; but I had laid her down somewhere and couldn't find her. I got hold of a stick and began
to punch him; he didn't seem to mind it much, so I thought
I would git down into the crack, and kill him with my knife.

"I considered some time 'bout this; it was ten or eleven
o'clock, and a cold winter night. I was something like thirty
miles from any settlement; there was no living soul near me,

except my friend, who was in the tent, and I didn't know where that was—I knew my bear was in a crack made by the shakes, but how deep it was, and whether I could get out if I got in, were things I couldn't tell. I was sitting down right over the bear, thinking; and every once in a while some of my dogs would sing out, as if they wanted help; so I got up and let myself down in the crack behind the bear. Where I landed was about as deep as I am high; I felt mighty ticklish, and I wished I was out; I couldn't see a thing in the world, but I determined to go through with it. I drew my knife and kept feeling about with my hands and feet till I touched the bear; this I did very gently, then got upon my hands and knees, and inched my left hand up his body, with a knife in my right, till I got pretty fur up, and I plunged it into him; he sunk down and for a moment there was a great struggle; but by the time I scrambled out, every thing was getting quiet, and my dogs, one at a time, come out after me and laid down at my feet. I knew every thing was safe.

"It began now to cloud up: 'twas mighty dark, and as I didn't know the direction of my tent, I determined to stay all night. I took out my flint and steel and raised a little fire; but the wood was so cold and wet it wouldn't burn much. I had sweated so much after the bear, that I began to get very thirsty, and felt like I would die, if I didn't git some water: so, taking a light along, I went to look for the creek I had waded, and as good luck would have it, I found the creek, and got back to my bear. But from having been in a sweat all night, I was now very chilly: it was the middle of winter, and the ground was hard frozen for several inches, but this I had not noticed before: I again set to work to build me a fire, but all I could do couldn't make it burn. The excitement under which I had been labouring had all died away, and I was so cold I felt very much like dying: but a notion struck me to git my bear up out of the crack; so down into it I went, and worked until I got into a sweat again; and just as I would git him up so high, that if I could turn him over once more he'd be out, he'd roll back. I kept working, and resting, and while I was at it, it began to hail mighty fine; but I kept on, and in about three hours I got him out.

"I then came up almost exhausted: my fire had gone out and I laid down, and soon fell asleep; but 'twasn't long before I waked almost frozen. The wind sounded mighty cold as it passed along and I called my dogs, and made 'em lie upon me to keep me warm; but it wouldn't do. I thought I ought to make some exertion to save my life, and I got up, but I don't know why or wherefore, and began to grope about in the dark; the first thing I hit agin was a tree: it felt mighty slick and icy, as I hugged it, and a notion struck me to climb it; so up I started, and I climbed that tree for thirty feet before I came to any limb, and then slipped down. It was awful warm work. How often I climbed it, I never knew; but I was going up and slipping down for three or four hours, and when day first began to break, I was going up that tree. As soon as it was cleverly light, I saw before me a slim sweet gum, so slick, that it looked like every *varmunt* in the woods had been sliding down it for a month. I started off and found my tent, where sat my companion, who had given me up for lost. I had been distant about five miles; and, after resting, I brought my friend to see the bear. I had run more perils than those described; had been all night on the brink of a dreadful chasm, where a slip of a few feet would have brought about instant death. It almost made my head giddy to look at the dangers I had escaped. My friend swore he would not have gone in the crack that night with a wounded bear, for every one in the woods. We had as much meat as we could carry; so we loaded our horses, and set out for home." (1833)

GEORGE WASHINGTON HARRIS

George Washington Harris was born in 1814 in Allegheny City, Pennsylvania. At an early age he was taken by Samuel Bell, his half-brother, to Knoxville, Tennessee, where later he worked at a variety of jobs, including that of captain of the steamboat *Knoxville*. In this capacity he participated in the removal of the Cherokee Indians in 1838, shortly after which he bought a large tract of land in Blount County in the foothills of the Great Smoky Mountains. He began submitting political articles to the *Knoxville Argus* in 1839, and in 1843 he contributed *Sporting Epistles* to William T. Porter's New York *Spirit of the Times*. Later he worked as a silversmith, postmaster, and railroad conductor and became a strong secessionist. His anti-republican and anti-yankee satires appeared in the *Nashville Union and American*. He is most famous for his one book, *Sut Lovingood's Yarns*, which appeared in 1867. In the twentieth century, he has been recognized as one of the most accomplished craftsmen of the old southwest school of humor.

Sut Lovingood's Daddy, Acting Horse

"Hole that ar hoss down tu the yeath." "He's a fixin fur the heavings." "He's a spreadin his tail feathers tu fly. Look out, Laigs, if you aint ready tu go up'ards." "Wo, Shavetail." "Git a fiddil; he's tryin a jig." "Say, Long Laigs, rais'd a power ove co'n didn't yu?" "Taint co'n, hits redpepper."

These and like expressions were addressed to a queer look-ing, long legged, short bodied, small headed, white haired, hog eyed, funny sort of a genius, fresh from some bench-legged Jew's clothing store, mounted on "Tearpoke," a nick tailed, bow necked, long, poor, pale sorrel horse, half dandy, half devil, and enveloped in a perfect net-work of bridle, reins, crupper, martingales, straps, surcingles, and red ferret-ing, who reined up in front of Pat Nash's grocery, among a crowd of mountaineers full of fun, foolery, and mean whisky.

This was SUT LOVINGOOD.

"I say, you durn'd ash cats, jis' keep yer shuts on, will ye? You never seed a rale hoss till I rid up; you's p'raps stole ur owned shod rabbits ur sheep wif borrerd saddils on, but when you tuck the fus' begrudgin look jis' now at this critter, name Tarpoke, yu wer injoyin a sight ove nex' tu the bes' hoss what ever shell'd nubbins ur toted jugs, an' he's es ded as a still wum, poor ole Tickytail!

"Wo! wo! Tarpoke, yu cussed infunel fidgety hide full ove hell fire, can't yu stan' still an listen while I'se a polishin yer karacter off es a mortul hoss tu these yere durned fools?"

Sut's tongue or his spurs brought Tarpoke into something like passable quietude while he continued:

"Say yu, sum ove yu growin hogs made a re-mark jis' now 'bout redpepper. I jis wish tu say in a gineral way that eny wurds cupplin redpepper an Tearpoke tugether am durn'd infurnal lies."

"What killed Tickeytail, Sut?" asked an anxious inquirer after truth.

"Why nuffin, you cussed fool; he jis' died so, standin up et that. Warn't that rale casteel hoss pluck? Yu see, he froze stiff; no, not that adzactly, but starv'd fust, an' froze arterards, so stiff that when dad an' me went tu lay him out an' we push'd him over, he stuck out jis' so (spreading his arms and legs), like ontu a carpenter's bainch, an' we hed tu wait ni ontu seventeen days fur 'em tu thaw afore we cud skin 'im."

"Skin 'im?" interrupted a rat-faced youth, whittling on a corn stalk, "I thot yu wanted tu lay the hoss out."

"The hell yu did! Aint skinin the natral way ove layin out a hoss, I'd like tu no? See a yere, soney, yu tell yer mam tu hev yu sot back jis' bout two years, fur et the rate yu'se a climbin yu stan's a pow'ful chance tu die wif yer shoes on, an' git laid hoss way, yu dus."

The rat-faced youth shut up his knife and subsided.

"Well, thar we wer—dad, an' me (counting on his fingers), an' Sall, an' Jake (fool Jake we calls 'im fur short), an' Jim, an' Phineass, an' Callimy Jane, an' Sharlottyann, an' me, an' Zodiack, an' Cashus Clay, an' Noah Dan Webster, an' the twin gals (Castur and Pollox), an' me, an' Catherin Second, an' Cleopatry Antony, an' Jane Barnum Lind, an' me, an' Benton Bullion, an' the baby what haint nam'd yet, an' me, an' the Prospect, an' mam hersef, all lef in the woods alone, wifout ara hoss tu crup wif."

"Yu'se counted yersef five times, Mister Lovingood," said a tomato-nosed man in ragged overcoat.

"Yas, ole Still-tub, that's jis the perporshun I bears in the famerly fur dam fool, leavin out Dad in course. Yu jis let me alone, an' be a thinkin ove gittin more hoops ontu yu. Yus leakin now; see thar." Ha! ha! from the crowd, and "Stilltub" went into the doggery.

"Warnt that a devil's own mess ove broth fur a 'spectabil white famerly tu be sloshin about in? I be durned ef I didn't feel sorter like stealin a hoss sumtimes, an' I speck I'd a dun hit, but the stealin streak in the Lovingoods, all run tu durned fool, an' the onvartus streak all run tu laigs. Jis look down the side ove this yere hoss mos' tu the groun'. Dus yu see em?

"Well we waited, an' wished, an' rested, an' plan'd, an' wished, an' waited agin, ontil ni ontu strawberry time, hopin sum stray hoss mout cum along; but dorg my cats, ef eny sich good luck ever cums wifin reach ove whar dad is, he's so dod-dratted mean, an' lazy, an' ugly, an' savidge, an' durn fool tu kill.

"Well, one nite he lay awake till cock-crowin a-snortin, an' rollin, an' blowin, an' shufflin, an' scratchin hissef, an' a whisperin at mam a heap, an' at breckfus' I foun' out what hit ment. Says he, 'Sut, I'll tell yu what we'll du: I'll be hoss *mysef*, an' pull the plow whilst yu drives me, an' then the "Ole Quilt" (he ment that fur mam), an' the brats kin plant, an' tend, ur jis let hit alone, es they darn pleze; I aint a carein.'

"So out we went tu the pawpaw thicket, an' peel'd a rite smart chance ove bark, an' mam an' me made geers fur dad, while he sot on the fence a-lookin at us, an' a studyin pow'r-ful. I arterards foun' out, he wer a-studyin how tu play the kar-acter ove a hoss puffectly.

"Well, the geers becum him mitily, an' nuffin wud du 'im but he mus hev a bridil, so I gits a umereller brace—hit's a litil forked piece ove squar wire bout a foot long, like a yung pitch-fork, yu no—an' twisted hit sorter intu a bridil bit snaffil shape. Dad wanted hit made kurb, es he hedn't work'd fur a good while, an' said he mout sorter feel his keepin, an' go tu ravin an' cavortin.

"When we got the bridil fix'd ontu dad, don't yu bleve he sot in tu chompin hit jis like a rale hoss, an' tried tu bite me on the arm (he allers wer a mos' complikated durned ole fool, an' mam sed so when he warnt about). I put on the geers, an' while mam wer a-tyin the belly ban', a-strainin hit pow'rful tite, he drapt ontu his hans, sed 'Whay-a-a' like a mad hoss wud, an' slung his hine laigs at mam's hed. She step'd back a littil an' wer standin wif her arms cross'd a-restin em on her stumick, an' his heel taps cum wifin a inch ove her nose. Sez she, 'Yu plays hoss better nur yu dus husban.' He jis' run backards on all fours, an' kick'd at her agin, an'——an' pawd the groun wif his fis.

"'Lead him off tu the field, Sut, afore he kicks ur bites sumbody,' sez mam. I shoulder'd the gopher plow, an' tuck hole ove the bridil. Dad leaned back sulky, till I sed cluck, cluck, wif my tounge, then he started. When we cum tu the fence I let down the gap, an' hit made dad mad; he wanted tu jump hit on all fours hoss way. Oh geminy! what a durn'd ole fool kin cum tu ef he gins up tu the complaint.

"I hitch'd 'im tu the gopher, a-watchin him pow'ful clost, fur I'd see how quick he cud drap ontu his hans, an' kick, an' away we went, dad leanin forard tu his pullin, an' we made rite peart plowin, fur tu hev a green hoss, an' bark gears; he went over the sprowts an' bushes same as a rale hoss, only he traveled on two laigs. I wer mitily hope up bout co'n; I cud a'mos' see hit a cumin up; but thar's a heap ove whisky spilt twixt the counter an' the mouf, ef hit ain't got but two foot tu travil. 'Bout the time he wer beginin tu break sweat, we cum tu a sassafrack bush, an tu keep up his kar-acter es a hoss, he buljed squar intu an' thru hit, tarin down a ball ho'nets nes' ni ontu es big es a hoss's hed, an' the hole tribe kiver'd 'em es quick es yu cud kiver a sick pup wif a saddil blanket. He lit ontu his hans agin, an kick'd strait up onst, then he rar'd, an' fotch a squeal wus nur ara stud hoss in the State, an' sot in tu strait runnin away jis es natral es yu ever seed any uther skeer'd hoss du. I let go the line an' holler'd, Wo! dad, wo! but yu mout jis' es well say Woa! tu a locomotum, ur Suke cow tu a gal.

"Gewhillitins! how he run: when he cum tu bushes, he'd clar the top ove em wif a squeal, gopher an' all. P'raps he tho't thar mout be anuther settlment ove ball ho'nets thar, an' hit wer safer tu go over than thru, an' quicker dun eny how. Every now an' then he'd fan the side ove his hed, fust wif wun fore laig an' then tuther, then he'd gin hissef a roun-handed slap what soundid like a waggin whip ontu the place whar the breechbands tetches a hoss, a-runnin all the time an' a-kerrin that ar gopher jis 'bout as fas' an' es hi frum the yeath es ever eny gopher wer kerried I'll swar. When he cum tu the fence, he jis tore thru hit, bustin an' scatterin ni ontu seven panils wif lots ove broken rails. Rite yere he lef the gopher, geers, close, clevis, an' swingltress, all mix'd up, an' not wuf a durn. Mos' ove his shut staid ontu the aind ove a rail, an' ni ontu a pint ove ho'nets stop'd thar a stingin all over; hits smell fool'd em. The balance on em, ni ontu a gallun, kep' on wif dad. He seem'd tu run jis adzactly es fas' es a hon'et cud fly; hit wer the titest race I ever seed, fur wun hoss tu git all the whipin. Down thru a saige field they all went, the ho'nets makin hit look like thar wer smoke roun' dad's bald hed, an' he wif nuffin on the green yeath in the way ove close about im, but the bridil, an' ni ontu a yard ove plow line sailin behine, wif a tir'd out ho'net ridin on the pint ove hit. I seed that he wer aimin fur the swimin hole in the krick, whar the bluff am over-twenty five foot pupendicu-ler tu the warter, an' hits ni ontu ten foot deep.

"Well, tu keep up his karacter es a hoss, plum thru, when he got tu the bluff he loped off, ur rather jis' kep on a run-nin. Kerslunge intu the krick he went. I seed the warter fly plum abuv the bluff from whar I wer.

"Now rite thar, boys, he over-did the thing, ef actin hoss tu the scribe wer what he wer arter; fur thars nara hoss ever foaldid durned fool enuf tu lope over eny sich place; a cussed muel mout a dun hit, but dad warn't actin muel, tho' he orter tuck that karacter; hits adzactly sooted tu his dispersi-tion, all but not breedin. I crept up tu the aidge, an' peep'd over. Thar wer dad's bald hed fur all the yeath like a peeled inyin, a bobbin up an' down an' aroun, an' the ho'nets sailin roun tuckey buzzard fashun, an' every onst in a while one, an' sum times ten, wud take a dip at dad's bald head.

He kep' up a rite peart dodgin onder, sumtimes afore they hit em, an' sumtimes arterard, an' the warter wer kivered wif drownded ball ho'nets. Tu look at hit frum the top ove the bluff, hit wer pow'ful inturestin, an' sorter funny; I wer on the bluff myse'f, mine yu.

"Dad cudent see the funny part frum whar he wer, but hit seem'd tu be inturestin tu him frum the 'tenshun he wer payin tu the bisness ove divin an' cussin.

"Sez I, 'Dad, ef yu's dun washin yersef, an hes drunk enuff, less go back tu our plowin, hit will soon be powful hot.' 'Hot —hell!' sez dad; 'hit am hot rite now. Don't (an onder went his hed) yer see (dip) these cussed (dip) infun—(dip) varmints arter me?' (dip) 'What,' sez I, 'them ar hoss flies thar, that's nat'ral, dad; you aint raley fear'd ove them is yu?' 'Hoss flies! h—l an' (dip) durnation!' sez dad, 'theyse rale ginui—(dip) ball ho'nets, (dip) yu infunel ignurant cuss!' (dip) 'Kick em—bite em—paw em—switch em wif yure tail, dad,' sez I. 'Oh! soney, soney, (dip) how I'll sweeten yure— (dip) when these (dip) ho'nets leave yere.' 'Yu'd better du the levin yursef dad,' sez I. 'Leave yere! Sut yu d—n fool! How (dip) kin I, (dip) when they won't (dip) let me stay (dip) atop (dip) the warter even.' 'Well, dad, yu'l hev tu stay thar till nite, an' arter they goes tu roos' yu cum home. I'll hev yer feed in the troft redy; yu won't need eny curyin tu-nite will yu?' 'I wish (dip) I may never (dip) see to-mor-rer, ef I (dip) don't make (dip) hame strings (dip) outer yure hide (dip) when I dus (dip) git outen yere,' sez dad. 'Better say yu wish yu may never see anuther ball ho'net, ef yu ever play hoss agin,' sez I.

"Them words toch dad tu the hart, an' I felt they mus' be my las, knowin dad's onmollified nater. I broke frum them parts, an' sorter cum over yere tu the copper mines. When I got tu the hous', 'Whar's yer dad?' sez mam. 'Oh, he turn'd durn fool, an' run away, busted every thing all tu cussed smash, an's in the swimin hole a divin arter minners. Look out mam, he'll cum home wif a angel's temper; better sen'

fur sum strong man body tu keep him frum huggin yu tu
deth. 'Law sakes!' sez mam; 'I know'd he cudent act hoss fur
ten minutes wifout actin infunel fool, tu save his life.'

"I staid hid out ontil nex' arternoon, an' I seed a feller
a-travelin'. Sez I, 'How de do, mister? What wer agwine on at
the cabin, this side the crick, when yu pass'd thar?' 'Oh,
nuthin much, only a pow'ful fat man wer a lyin in the yard
ontu his belly, wif no shut on, an' a 'oman wer a greasin ove
his shoulders an' arms outen a gourd. A pow'ful curious,
vishus, skeery lookin cuss he is tu b'shure. His head am as
big es a wash pot, an' he hasent the fust durned sign ove
an eye—jist two black slits. Is thar much small pox roun
yere?' 'Small hell!' sez I, 'no sir.' 'Been much fightin in this
neighborhood lately?' 'Nun wuf speakin ove,' sez I. He
scratched his head—'Nur French measils?' 'Not jis clost,' sez
I. 'Well, do yu know what ails that man back thar?' 'Jist gittin
over a vilent attack ove dam fool,' sez I. 'Well, who is he eny
how?' I ris tu my feet, an' straiched out my arm, an' sez I,
'Strainger, that man is my dad.' He looked at my laigs an'
pussonel feeters a moment, an' sez he, 'Yas, dam ef he aint.'

"Now boys, I haint seed dad since, an' I dusent hev much
appertite tu see im fur sum time tu cum. Less all drink!
Yere's luck tu the durned old fool, an' the ho'nets too."
(1854, 1867)

Parson John Bullen's Lizards

AIT ($8) DULLARS REW-ARD.

'TENSHUN BELEVERS AND KONSTABLES! KETCH 'IM! KETCH 'IM!

This kash will be pade in korn, ur uther projuce, tu be
kolected at ur about nex camp-meetin, *ur thararter*, by eny
wun what ketches him, fur the karkus ove a sartin wun SUT
LOVINGOOD, dead ur alive, ur ailin, an' safely giv over tu

the purtectin care ove Parson John Bullin, ur lef' well tied, at Squire Mackjunkins, fur the raisin ove the devil pussonely, an' permiskusly discumfurtin the wimen very powerful, an' skeerin ove folks generly a heap, an' bustin up a promisin, big warm meetin, an' a makin the wickid larf, an' wus, an' wus, insultin ove the passun orful.

    Test,   JEHU WETHERO.

                        Sined by me,

                    JOHN BULLEN, the passun.

I found written copies of the above highly intelligible and vindictive proclamation, stuck up on every blacksmith shop, doggery, and store door, in the Frog Mountain Range. Its blood-thirsty spirit, its style, and above all, its chirography, interested me to the extent of taking one down from a tree for preservation.

In a few days I found Sut in a good crowd in front of Capehart's Doggery, and as he seemed to be about in good tune, I read it to him.

"Yas, George, that ar dockymint am in dead yearnist sar-tin. Them hard shells over thar dus want me the wus kine, powerful bad. *But*, I spect ait dullers won't fetch me, nither wud ait hundred, bekase thar's nun ove 'em fas' enuf tu ketch me, nither is thar hosses by the livin jingo! Say, George, much talk 'bout this fuss up whar yu're been?" For the sake of a joke I said yes, a great deal.

"Jis' es I 'spected, durn 'em, all git drunk, an' skeer thar fool sefs ni ontu deth, an' then lay hit ontu me, a poor inner-sent youf, an' es soun' a belever es they is. Lite, lite, ole feller an' let that roan ove yourn blow a litil, an' I'll 'splain this cussed misfortnit affar: hit hes ruinated my karacter es a pius pusson in the s'ciety roun' yere, an' is a spreadin faster nur meazils. When ever yu hear eny on 'em a spreadin hit, gin hit the dam lie squar, will yu? I haint dun nuffin tu one ove 'em. Hits true, I did sorter frustrate a few lizzards a littil, but they haint members, es I knows on.

"You see, las' year I went tu the big meetin at Rattlesnake Springs, an' wer a sittin in a nice shady place convarsin wif a frien' ove mine, intu the huckil berry thickit, jis' duin nuffin tu nobody an' makin no fuss, when, the fust thing I remembers, I woke up frum a trance what I hed been knocked inter by a four year old hickory-stick, hilt in the paw ove ole Passun Bullin, durn his alligater hide; an' he wer standin a striddil ove me, a foamin at the mouf, a-chompin his teeth— gesterin wif the hickory club—an' a-preachin tu me so you cud a-hearn him a mile, about a sartin sin gineraly, an' my wickedness pussonely; an' mensunin the name ove my frien' loud enuf tu be hearn tu the meetin 'ous. My poor innersent frien' wer dun gone an' I wer glad ove hit, fur I tho't he ment tu kill me rite whar I lay, an' I didn't want her tu see me die."

"Who was she, the friend you speak of Sut?" Sut opened his eyes wide.

"Hu the devil, an' durnashun tole *yu* that hit wer a she?"

"Why, you did, Sut"———

"I *didn't*, durn ef I did. Ole Bullin dun hit, an' I'll hev tu kill him yet, the cussed, infernel ole talebarer!"———

"Well, well, Sut, who was she?"

"Nun ove y-u-r-e b-i-s-n-i-s-s, durn yure littil ankshus picter! I *sees yu* a lickin ove yure lips. I *will* tell you one thing, George; that night, a neighbor gal got a all-fired, overhandid stroppin frum her mam, wif a stirrup leather, an' ole Passun Bullin, hed et supper thar, an' what's wus nur all, that poor innersent, skeer'd gal hed dun her levil bes' a cookin hit fur 'im. She begged him, a trimblin, an' a-cryin not tu tell on her. He et her cookin, he promised her he'd keep dark—an' then went strait an' tole her mam. Warnt that rale low down, wolf mean? The durnd infunel, hiperkritikal, pot-bellied, scaley-hided, whisky-wastin, stinkin ole groun'- hog. He'd a heap better a stole sum *man's* hoss; I'd a tho't more ove 'im. But I paid him plum up fur hit, an' I means tu keep a payin him, ontil one ur tuther, ove our toes pints up tu the roots ove the grass.

"Well, yere's the way I lifted that note ove han'. At the nex big meetin at Rattilsnaik—las' week hit wer—I wer on han' es solemn es a ole hat kivver on collection day. I hed my face draw'd out intu the shape an' perporshun ove a taylwer's sleeve-board, pint down. I hed put on the convicted sinner so pufeckly that an'ole obsarvin she pillar ove the church sed tu a ole he pillar, es I walked up to my bainch:

" 'Law sakes alive, ef thar ain't that *orful* sinner, Sut Lovingood, pearced plum thru; hu's nex?'

"Yu see, by golly, George, I *hed* tu promis the ole tub ove soap-greas tu cum an' hev myself converted, jis' tu keep him frum killin me. An' es I know'd hit wudn't interfare wif the relashun I bore tu the still housis roun' thar, I didn't keer a durn. I jis' wanted tu git *ni* ole Bullin, onst onsuspected, an' this wer the bes' way tu du hit. I tuk a seat on the side steps ove the pulpit, an' kivvered es much ove my straitch'd face es I could wif my han's, tu prove I wer in yearnis. Hit tuck powerful—fur I hearn a sorter thankful kine ove buzzin all over the congregashun. Ole Bullin hissef looked down at me, over his ole copper specks, an' hit sed jis' es plain es a look cud say hit: 'Yu am thar, ar you—durn yu, hits well fur yu that yu cum.' I tho't sorter diffrent frum that. I tho't hit wud a been well fur *yu*, ef I hadent a-cum, but I didn't say hit jis then. Thar wer a monstrus crowd in that grove, fur the weather wer fine, an' b'levers were plenty roun' about Rattilsnaik Springs. Ole Bullin gin out, an' they sung that hyme, yu know:

"Thar will be mournin, mournin yere, an' mournin thar,
On that dredful day tu cum."

"Thinks I, ole hoss, kin hit be possibil enybody hes tole yu what's a gwine tu happin; an' then I tho't that nobody know'd hit but me, and I wer cumforted. He nex tuck hisself a tex pow'fly mixed wif brimstone, an' trim'd wif blue flames, an' then he open'd. He cummenced ontu the sinners; he threaten'd 'em orful, tried tu skeer 'em wif all the wust varmints he cud think ove, an' arter a while he got ontu the idear ove Hell-sarpints, and he dwelt on it sum. He tole 'em how the ole Hell-sarpints wud sarve em if they didn't repent; how cold they'd crawl over thar nakid bodys, an' how like ontu pitch they'd stick tu 'em as they crawled; how they'd rap thar tails roun' thar naiks chokin clost, poke thar tungs up thar noses, an' hiss intu thar years. This wer the way they wer tu sarve men folks. Then he turned ontu the wimmen: tole 'em how they'd quile intu thar buzzims, an' how they wud crawl down onder thar frock-strings, no odds how tite they tied 'em, an' how sum ove the oldes' an' wus ones wud crawl up thar laigs, an' travil *onder* thar garters, no odds how tight they tied *them,* an' when the two armys ove Hell-sarpents met, then——That las' remark *fotch 'em.* Ove all the screamin, an' hollerin, an' loud cryin, I ever hearn, begun all at onst, all over the hole groun' jis' es he hollered out that word 'then.' He kep on a bellerin, but I got so buisy jis' then, that I didn't listen tu him much, fur I saw that my time fur ackshun hed cum. Now you see, George, I'd cotch seven ur eight big pot-bellied lizzards, an' hed 'em in a littil narrer bag, what I had made a-purpus. Thar tails all at the bottim, an' so crowdid fur room that they cudent turn roun'. So when he wer a-ravin ontu his tip-toes, an' a-poundin the pulpit wif his fis'—onbenowenst tu enybody, I ontied my bag ove reptiles, put the mouf ove hit onder the bottim ove his britches-laig, an' sot intu pinchin thar tails. Quick es gunpowder they all tuck up his bar laig, makin a nise like squirrils a-climbin a shell-bark hickory. He stop't preachin rite in the middil ove the word 'damnation,' an' looked fur a moment like he wer a listenin fur sumthin—sorter like a ole sow dus, when she hears yu a whistlin fur the dorgs. The tarifick shape ove his feeters stopp't the shoutin an' screamin; instuntly yu cud hearn a cricket chirp. I gin a long groan, an' hilt my head a-twixt my knees. He gin hisself sum orful open-handed slaps wif fust one han' an' then tuther, about the place whar yu cut the bes' steak outen a beef. Then he'd fetch a vigrus ruff rub whar a hosses tail sprouts; then he'd stomp one foot, then tuther, then bof at onst. Then he run his han' atween his waisbun an' his shut an' reach'd way down, an' roun' wif hit; then he spread his big laigs, an' gin his back a good rattlin rub agin the pulpit, like a hog scratches hisself agin a stump, leanin tu hit pow'ful, an' twitchin, an' squirmin all over, es ef he'd slept in a dorg bed, ur ontu a pisant hill. About this time, one ove my lizzards scared an' hurt by all this poundin' an' feelin, an' scratchin, popp'd out his head frum the pas-sun's shut collar, an' his ole brown naik, an' wer a-surveyin the crowd, when ole Bullin struck at 'im jis' too late, fur he'd dodged back agin. The hell desarvin ole raskil's speech now cum tu 'im, an' sez he, 'Pray fur me brethren an' sis-teren, fur I is a-rastilin wif the great inimy rite now!' an' his voice wer the mos' pitiful, trimblin thing I ever hearn. Sum ove the wimmen fotch a painter yell, an' a young docter, wif ramrod laigs, lean'd toward me monstrus knowin like, an' sez he, 'Clar case ove Delishus Tremenjus.' I nodded my head an' sez I, 'Yas, spechuly the tremenjus part, an' Ise feard hit haint at hits worst.' Ole Bullin's eyes wer a-stickin out like ontu two buckeyes flung agin a mud wall, an' he wer a-cut-tin up more shines nor a cockroach in a hot skillet. Off went the clawhammer coat, an' he flung hit ahine 'im like he wer a-gwine intu a fight; he hed no jackid tu take off, so he unbuttond his galluses, an' vigrusly flung the ainds back over his head. He fotch his shut over-handed a durnd site faster nor I got outen my pasted one, an' then flung hit strait up in the air, like he jis' wanted hit tu keep on up furever; but hit lodged ontu a black-jack, an' I seed one ove my liz-zards wif his tail up, a-racin about all over the ole dirty shut, skared too bad tu jump. Then he gin a sorter shake, an' a stompin kine ove twis', an' he cum outer his britches. He tuck 'em by the bottim ove the laigs, an' swung 'em roun' his head a time ur two, an' then fotch 'em down cherall-up over the frunt ove the pulpit. You cud a hearn the smash a quarter ove a mile! Ni ontu fifteen shorten'd biskits, a boiled chicken, wif hits laigs crossed, a big dubbil-bladed knife, a hunk ove terbacker, a cob-pipe, sum copper ore, lots ove broken glass, a cork, a sprinkil ove whisky, a squirt, an' three lizzards flew permiskusly all over that meetin-groun', outen the upper aind ove them big flax britches. One ove the smartes' ove my lizzards lit head-fust intu the buzzim ove a fat 'oman, es big es a skin'd hoss, an' ni ontu es ugly, who sot thuty yards off, a fannin hersef wif a tucky-tail. Smart tu the las', by golly, he imejuntly commenced runnin down the centre ove her breas'-bone, an' kep on, I speck. She wer jis' boun' tu faint; an' she did hit fust rate—flung the tucky-tail up in the air, grabbed the lap ove her gown, gin hit a big histin an' fallin shake, rolled down the hill, tangled her laigs an' garters in the top ove a huckilberry bush, wif her head in the branch an' jis' lay still. She wer interestin, she wer, ontil a serious-lookin, pale-faced 'oman hung a nankeen ridin skirt over the huckilberry bush. That wer all that wer dun to'ards bringin her too, that I seed. Now ole Bullin hed nuffin left ontu 'em but a par ove heavy, low quarter'd shoes, short woolen socks, an' eel-skin garters tu keep off the cramp. His skeer hed druv him plum crazy, fur he felt roun' in the air, abuv his head, like he wer huntin sumthin in the dark, an' he beller'd out, 'Brethren, brethren, take keer ove yer-selves, the Hell-sarpints *hes got me!*' When this cum out, yu cud a-hearn the screams tu Halifax. He jis' spit in his han's, an' loped over the frunt ove the pulpid *kerdiff!* He lit on top ove, an' rite amung the mos' pius part ove the congregashun. Ole Misses Chaneyberry sot wif her back tu the pulpit, sorter stoopin forrid. He lit a-stradil ove her long naik, a shuttin her up wif a snap, her head atwix her knees, like shuttin up a jack-knife, an' he sot intu gittin away his levil durndest; he went in a heavy lumberin gallop, like a ole fat waggon hoss, skared at a locomotive. When he jumpt a bainch he shook the yeath. The bonnets, an' fans clar'd the way an' jerked most ove the children wif em, an' the rest he scrunched. He open'd a purfeckly clar track tu the woods, ove every livin thing. He weighed ni ontu three hundred, hed a black stripe down his back, like ontu a ole bridil rein, an' his belly wer 'bout the size, an' color ove a beef paunch, an' hit a-swingin out frum side tu side; he leand back frum hit, like a littil feller a-totin a big drum, at a muster, an' I hearn hit plum tu whar I wer. Thar wer cramp-knots on his laigs es big es walnuts, an' mottled splotches on his shins; an' takin him all over, he minded ove a durnd crazy ole elephant, pussessed ove the devil, rared up on hits hind aind, an' jis' *gittin* from sum imijut danger ur tribulashun. He did the loudest, an' skariest, an' fussiest runnin I ever seed, tu be no faster nur hit wer, since dad tried tu outrun the ho'nets.

"Well, he disapear'd in the thicket jis' bustin—an' ove all the noises yu ever hearn, wer made thar on that camp groun': sum wimen screamin—they wer the skeery ones; sum larfin—they wer the wicked ones; sum cryin—they wer the fool ones (sorter my stripe yu know); sum tryin tu git away wif their faces red—they wer the modest ones; sum lookin arter ole Bullin—they wer the curious ones; sum hangin clost tu thar sweethearts—they wer the sweet ones; sum on thar knees wif thar eyes shot, but facin the way the ole mud turtil wer a-runnin—they wer the 'saitful ones; sum duin nuthin—they wer the waitin ones; an' the mos' dangerus ove all ove em by a durnd long site.

"I tuck a big skeer myself arter a few rocks, an' sich like fruit, spattered ontu the pulpit ni ontu my head; an' es the Lovingoods, durn em! knows nuffin but tu run, when they gits skeerd, I jis' put out fur the swamp on the krick. As I started, a black bottil ove bald-face smashed agin a tree furninst me, arter missin the top ove my head 'bout a inch. Sum durn'd fool professor dun this, who hed more zeal nor sence; fur I say that eny man who wud waste a quart ove even mean sperrits, fur the chance ove knockin a poor ornary devil like me down wif the bottil, is a bigger fool nor ole Squire Mackmullen, an' he tried tu shoot hissef wif a onloaded hoe-handle."

"Did they catch you Sut?"

"Ketch thunder! *No sir!* jis' look at these yere laigs! Skeer me, hoss, jis' skeer me, an' then watch me while I stay in site, an' yu'll never ax that fool question agin. Why, durn it, man that's what the ait dullers am fur.

"Ole Barbelly Bullin, es they calls 'im now, never preached ontil yesterday, an' he hadn't the fust durn'd 'oman tu hear 'im; *they hev seed too much ove 'im.* Passuns ginerly hev a pow'ful strong holt on wimen; but, hoss, I tell yu thar ain't meny ove em kin run stark nakid over an' thru a crowd ove three hundred wimen an' not injure thar karacters *sum.* Eny-how, hits a kind ove show they'd ruther see one at a time, an' pick the passun at that. His tex' wer, 'Nakid I cum intu the world, an' nakid I'm a gwine outen hit, ef I'm spard ontil then.' He sed nakidness warnt much ove a sin, purtickerly ove dark nights. That he wer a weak, frail wum ove the dus', an' a heap more sich truck. Then he totch ontu me; sed I wer a livin proof ove the hell-desarvin nater ove man, an' that thar warnt grace enuf in the whole 'sociation tu saften my outside rind; that I wer 'a lost ball' forty years afore I wer born'd, an' the bes' thing they cud du fur the church, wer tu turn out, an' still hunt fur me ontil I wer shot. An' he never said Hell-sarpints onst in the hole preach. I b'leve, George, the durnd fools am at hit.

"Now, I wants yu tu tell ole Barbelly this fur me, ef he'll let me an' Sall alone, I'll let him alone—a-while; an' ef he don't, ef I don't lizzard him agin, I jis' wish I may be dod durnd! *Skeer him if yu ken.*

"Let's go tu the spring an' take a ho'n.

"Say George, didn't that ar Hell-sarpint sermon ove his'n, hev sumthin like a Hell-sarpint aplicashun? Hit looks sorter so tu me." (1857, 1867)

MARK TWAIN

Regarded by many as the greatest of all American writers, Mark Twain was conceived in East Tennessee and born in 1835 in Florida, Missouri. The background of his own family's move west is in part reflected in the early chapters of *The Gilded Age*, which was co-authored with Charles D. Warner, a traveler in Southern Appalachia and a student of the region as well as an important critic and essayist. The frontier influence abounds throughout the work of Twain, especially as seen in his fondness for the Tall Tale, of which "Journalism in Tennessee" is an excellent example. The work originally appeared in a Buffalo, N. Y., newspaper in 1869. A leader in the realistic movement of the nineteenth century, he was called by his friend William D. Howells "the Lincoln of our Literature."

Journalism in Tennessee

The editor of the Memphis *Avalanche* swoops thus mildly down upon a correspondent who posted him as a Radical: "While he was writing the first word, the middle, dotting his i's, crossing his t's, and punching his period, he knew he was concocting a sentence that was saturated with infamy and reeking with falsehood."— *Exchange.*

I was told by the physician that a Southern climate would improve my health, and so I went down to Tennessee and got a berth on the *Morning-Glory and Johnson County Warwhoop* as associate editor. When I went on duty I found the chief editor sitting tilted back in a three-legged chair with his feet on a pine table. There was another pine table in the room and another afflicted chair, and both were half buried under newspapers and scraps and sheets of manuscript. There was a wooden box of sand, sprinkled with cigar-stubs and "old soldiers," and a stove with a door hanging by its upper hinge. The chief editor had a long-tailed black cloth frock-coat on, and white linen pants. His boots were small and neatly blacked. He wore a ruffled shirt, a large seal ring, a standing collar of obsolete pattern, and a checkered neckerchief with the ends hanging down. Date of costume about 1848. He was smoking a cigar, and trying to think of a word, and in pawing his hair he had rumpled his locks a good deal. He was scowling fearfully, and I judged that he was concocting a particularly knotty editorial. He told me to take the exchanges and skim through them and write up the "Spirit of the Tennessee Press," condensing into the article all of their contents that seemed of interest.

I wrote as follows:

"SPIRIT OF THE TENNESSEE PRESS

"The editors of the *Semi-Weekly Earthquake* evidently labor under a misapprehension with regard to the Ballyhack railroad. It is not the object of the company to leave Buzzardville off to the side. On the contrary, they consider it one of the most important points along the line, and consequently can have no desire to slight it. The gentlemen of the *Earthquake* will, of course, take pleasure in making the correction.

"John W. Blossom, Esq., the able editor of the Higginsville *Thunderbolt and Battle-Cry of Freedom,* arrived in the city yesterday. He is stopping at the Van Buren House.

"We observe that our contemporary of the Mud Springs *Morning Howl* has fallen into the error of supposing that the election of Van Werter is not an established fact, but he will have discovered his mistake before this reminder reaches him, no doubt. He was doubtless misled by incomplete election returns.

"It is pleasant to note that the city of Blathersville is endeavoring to contract with some New York gentleman to pave its wellnigh impassable streets with the Nicholson pavement. The *Daily Hurrah* urges the measure with ability, and seems confident of ultimate success."

I passed my manuscript over to the chief editor for acceptance, alteration, or destruction. He glanced at it and his face clouded. He ran his eye down the pages, and his countenance grew portentous. It was easy to see that something was wrong. Presently he sprang up and said:

"Thunder and lightning! Do you suppose I am going to speak of those cattle that way? Do you suppose my subscribers are going to stand such gruel as that? Give me the pen!"

I never saw a pen scrape and scratch its way so viciously, or plough through another man's verbs and adjectives so relentlessly. While he was in the midst of his work, somebody shot at him through the open window, and marred the symmetry of his ear.

"Ah," said he, "that is that scoundrel Smith, of the *Moral Volcano*—he was due yesterday." And he snatched a navy revolver from his belt and fired. Smith dropped, shot in the thigh. The shot spoiled Smith's aim, who was just taking a second chance, and he crippled a stranger. It was me. Merely a finger shot off.

Then the chief editor went on with his erasures and interlineations. Just as he finished them a hand-grenade came down the stove-pipe, and the explosion shivered the stove into a thousand fragments. However, it did no further damage, except that a vagrant piece knocked a couple of my teeth out.

"That stove is utterly ruined," said the chief editor.

I said I believed it was.

"Well, no matter—don't want it this kind of weather. I

know the man that did it. I'll get him. Now, *here* is the way this stuff ought to be written."

I took the manuscript. It was scarred with erasures and interlineations till its mother wouldn't have known it if it had had one. It now read as follows:

"SPIRIT OF THE TENNESSEE PRESS

"The inveterate liars of the *Semi-Weekly Earthquake* are evidently endeavoring to palm off upon a nobel and chivalrous people another of their vile and brutal falsehoods with regard to that most glorious conception of the nineteenth century, the Ballyhack railroad. The idea that Buzzardville was to be left off at one side originated in their own fulsome brains—or rather in the settlings which *they* regard as brains. They had better swallow this lie if they want to save their abandoned reptile carcasses the cowhiding they so richly deserve.

"That ass, Blossom, of the Higginsville *Thunderbolt and Battle-Cry of Freedom,* is down here again sponging at the Van Buren.

"We observe that the besotted black-guard of the Mud Springs *Morning Howl* is giving out, with his usual propensity for lying, that Van Werter is not elected. The heaven-born mission of journalism is to disseminate truth; to eradicate error; to educate, refine, and elevate the tone of public morals and manners, and make all men more gentle, more virtuous, more charitable, and in all ways better, and holier, and happier; and yet this black-hearted scoundrel degrades his great office persistently to the dissemination of falsehood, calumny, vituperation, and vulgarity.

"Blathersville wants a Nicholson pavement—it wants a jail and a poor-house more. The idea of a pavement in a one-horse town composed of two gin-mills, a blacksmith-shop, and that mustard-plaster of a newspaper, the *Daily Hurrah!* The crawling insect, Buckner, who edits the *Hurrah,* is braying about this business with his customary imbecility, and imagining that he is talking sense."

"Now *that* is the way to write—peppery and to the point. Mush-and-milk journalism gives me the fan-tods."

About this time a brick came through the window with a splintering crash, and gave me a considerable of a jolt in the back. I moved out of range—I began to feel in the way.

The chief said: "That was the Colonel, likely. I've been expecting him for two days. He will be up now right away."

He was correct. The Colonel appeared in the door a moment afterwards with a dragoon revolver in his hand.

He said: "Sir, have I the honor of addressing the poltroon who edits this mangy sheet?"

"You have. Be seated, sir. Be careful of the chair, one of its legs is gone. I believe I have the honor of addressing the putrid liar, Colonel Blatherskite Tecumseh?"

"Right, sir. I have a little account to settle with you. If you are at leisure we will begin."

"I have an article on the 'Encouraging Progress of Moral and Intellectual Development in America' to finish, but there is no hurry. Begin."

Both pistols rang out their fierce clamor at the same instant. The chief lost a lock of his hair, and the Colonel's bullet ended its career in the fleshy part of my thigh. The Colonel's left shoulder was clipped a little. They fired again. Both missed their men this time, but I got my share, a shot in the arm. At the third fire both gentlemen were wounded slightly, and I had a knuckle chipped. I then said I believed I would go out and take a walk, as this was a private matter, and I had a delicacy about participating in it further. But both gentlemen begged me to keep my seat, and assured me that I was not in the way.

They then talked about the elections and the crops while they reloaded, and I fell to tying up my wounds. But presently they opened fire again with animation, and every shot took effect—but it is proper to remark that five out of the six fell to my share. The sixth one mortally wounded the Colonel, who remarked, with fine humor, that he would have to say good-morning now, as he had business up-town. He then inquired the way to the undertaker's and left.

The chief turned to me and said: "I am expecting company to dinner, and shall have to get ready. It will be a favor to me if you will read proof and attend to the customers."

I winced a little at the idea of attending to the customers, but I was too bewildered by the fusillade that was still ringing in my ears to think of anything to say.

He continued: "Jones will be here at three—cowhide him. Gillespie will call earlier, perhaps—throw him out of the window. Ferguson will be along about four—kill him. That is all for to-day, I believe. If you have any odd time, you may write a blistering article on the police—give the chief inspector rats. The cow-hides are under the table; weapons in the drawer—ammunition there in the corner—lint and bandages up there in the pigeon-holes. In case of accident, go to Lancet, the surgeon, down-stairs. He advertises—we take it out in trade."

He was gone. I shuddered. At the end of the next three hours I had been through perils so awful that all peace of mind and all cheerfulness were gone from me. Gillespie had called and thrown *me* out of the window. Jones arrived promptly, and when I got ready to do the cow-hiding he took the job off my hands. In an encounter with a stranger, not in the bill of fare, I had lost my scalp. Another stranger, by the name of Thompson, left me a mere wreck and ruin of chaotic rags. And at last, at bay in the corner, and beset by an infuriated mob of editors, blacklegs, politicians, and desperadoes, who raved and swore and flourished their weapons about my head till the air shimmered with glancing flashes of steel, I was in the act of resigning my berth on the paper when the chief arrived, and with him a rabble of charmed and enthusiastic friends. Then ensued a scene of riot and carnage such as no human pen, or steel one either, could describe. People were shot, probed, dismembered, blown up, thrown out of the window. There was a brief tornado of murky blasphemy, with a confused and frantic war-dance glimmering through it, and then all was over. In five minutes there was silence, and the gory chief and I sat alone and surveyed the sanguinary ruin that strewed the floor around us.

He said: "You'll like this place when you get used to it."

I said: "I'll have to get you to excuse me; I think maybe I might write to suit you after a while; as soon as I had had some practice and learned the language I am confident I could. But, to speak the plain truth, that sort of energy of expression has its inconveniences, and a man is liable to interruption. You see that yourself. Vigorous writing is calculated to elevate the public, no doubt, but then I do not like to attract so much attention as it calls forth. I can't write with comfort when I am interrupted so much as I have been to-day. I like this berth well enough, but I don't like to be left here to wait on the customers. The experiences are novel, I grant you, and entertaining, too, after a fashion, but they are not judiciously distributed. A gentleman shoots at you through the window and cripples *me*; a bomb-shell comes down the stove-pipe for your gratification and sends the stove-door down *my* throat; a friend drops in to swap compliments with you, and freckles *me* with bullet-holes till my skin won't hold my principles; you go to dinner, and Jones comes with his cowhide, Gillespie throws me out of the window, Thompson tears all my clothes off, and an entire stranger takes my scalp with the easy freedom of an old acquaintance; and in less than five minutes all the blackguards in the country arrive in their war-paint, and proceed to scare the rest of me to death with their tomahawks. Take it altogether, I never had such a spirited time in all my life as I have had to-day. No; I like you, and I like your calm, unruffled way of explaining things to the customers, but you see I am not used to it. The Southern heart is too impulsive; Southern hospitality is too lavish with the stranger. The paragraphs which I have written to-day, and into whose cold sentences

your masterly hand has infused the fervent spirit of Tennesseean journalism, will wake up another nest of hornets. All that
mob of editors will come—and they will come hungry, too,
and want somebody for breakfast. I shall have to bid you
adieu. I decline to be present at these festivities. I came
South for my health; I will go back on the same errand, and
suddenly. Tennesseean journalism is too stirring for me."

After which we parted with mutual regret, and I took apart-
ments at the hospital. (1869, 1905)

III. *Southern Romanticism: The Sublime and the Beautiful*

Romanticism is extremely difficult to define, but if there is a single concept that can with certainty be associated with the term it is the love of nature. Whereas the spinners of the backwoods yarns rarely if ever spoke of the beauty of nature, the romantic writers were profuse and rhapsodic in their praise. In the works of such writers as William Gilmore Simms, Sidney Lanier, and John Esten Cooke, there appears to be an element of cultism in descriptions of nature designed to create a feeling of sublimation in the reader, that is, a sense of awe and mystery. To a degree the same is true of Thomas Jefferson as he records his impressions of the Appalachian Mountains of Virginia. The formulas were quite similar to those used by English romantics such as Anne Radcliffe and the poet Thomas Gray describing Alpine scenes: precipitous cliffs, misty crags, leaping cataracts, and ineffable splendor and beauty at every turn. The philosophic views of Immanuel Kant and Edmund Burke on the subject of sublimity are also called to mind.

Sut Lovingood pronounces over and over that he has "no soul," but in Sidney Lanier's *Tiger Lilies*, not only do the characters have souls, but, in typical transcendental fashion, so does the physical world. Though one can find brutal characters like Lanier's Gorm Smallin in romantic fiction about the Southern mountains, there is always the stronger suggestion of the idea of the noble savage, as seen for example in the "Porte Crayon" sketch. A recurring romantic motif is the notion of the mountains not as the playground for the fool but the fortress for souls who love liberty. Basically, then, the contrast between the mountaineer of the tall tale and that of romantic prose is that between the world views of Hobbs and Rousseau, between the belief that uncivilized man is essentially bestial and the opposite belief that man in his natural state is basically good. In Appalachian writing there seems an abundance of material to support both claims.

THOMAS JEFFERSON

One of the most remarkable men of all time, Thomas Jefferson was born at Shadwell, Albemarle County, Virginia in 1743. At the age of sixteen he entered William and Mary College where he became a favorite of the social and intellectual leaders of Williamsburg, including Governor Fauquier. Jefferson's rise to fame was enhanced by his talent as a forceful and graceful writer as evident in the Declaration of Independence, and his powers of expression served him well throughout a long and impressive career. Diplomat, president, architect, inventor, archeologist, musician, and educator, he was a product of the neo-classical age. Like all great spirits, however, Jefferson cannot be so easily categorized, for he was also an American romantic as seen in his faith in the common man and his belief in the possibilities of the American West, of which the mountains were a major part. Jefferson's interest in the mountains becomes obvious near the beginning of *Notes on the State of Virginia*, from which the following romantic impressions on Natural Bridge are taken. The notes were compiled in 1781–82 and were first published anonymously in Paris in 1784 in 200 copies at Jefferson's expense. The limited edition was followed by popular printings in England, America, and the Continent. Jefferson died on July 4, 1826.

Natural Bridge

The *Natural Bridge*, the most sublime of nature's works, though not comprehended under the present head, must not be pretermitted. It is on the ascent of a hill, which seems to have been cloven through its length by some great convulsion. The fissure, just at the bridge, is by some admeasurements, 270 feet deep, by others only 205. It is about 45 feet wide at the bottom, and 90 feet at the top; this of course determines the length of the bridge, and its height from the water, its breadth in the middle is about 60 feet, but more at the ends, and the thickness of the mass, at the summit of the arch, about 40 feet. A part of this thickness is constituted by a coat of earth, which gives growth to many large trees. The residue, with the hill on both sides, is one solid rock of limestone.—The arch approaches the semi-elliptical form; but the larger axis of the ellipses, which would be the chord of the arch, is many times longer than the transverse. Though the sides of this bridge are provided in some parts with a parapet of fixed rocks, yet few men have resolution to walk to them, and look over into the abyss. You involuntarily fall on your hands and feet, creep to the parapet and peep over it. Looking down from this height about a minute, gave me a violent head-ache. If the view from the top be painful and intolerable, that from below is delightful in an equal extreme. It is impossible for the emotions arising from the sublime, to be felt beyond what they are here: so beautiful an arch, so elevated, so light, and springing as it were up to heaven! the rapture of the spectator is really indescribable! The fissure continuing narrow, deep, and straight, for a considerable distance above and below the bridge, opens a short but very pleasing view of the North mountain on one side, and Blue ridge on the other, at the distance each of them of about five miles. This bridge is in the County of Rockbridge, to which it has given name, and affords a public and commodious passage over a valley, which cannot be crossed elsewhere for a considerable distance. The stream passing under it is called Cedar-creek. It is a water of James' river, and sufficient in the driest seasons to turn a grist mill, though its fountain is not more than two miles above. (1784, 1825)

WILLIAM GILMORE SIMMS

William Gilmore Simms was born in 1806 in Charleston, South Carolina, where he spent most of his life. Though best known for his novel *The Yemassee* and his revolutionary war romances, Simms was also the author of several border novels dealing with frontier life in the nineteenth century, including *Guy Rivers* (1834), a story of violence in the gold country of the Georgia Hills; *Richard Hurdis: A Tale of Alabama* (1838) based on the activities of the frontier outlaw John A. Murrell; and *Beauchampe, or the Kentucky Tragedy* (1842) which deals with a famous Kentucky murder case known in American literature by the same title as Simms' work (see "Kentucky Tragedy" in *Oxford Companion to American Literature*). The fiction of Simms is in some respects realistic, but it is frequently characterized by an unabashed romanticism as seen in the following passage from his novel *Charlemont*.

The Travellers

Let the traveller stand with us on the top of this rugged eminence, and look down upon the scene below. Around us, the hills gather in groups on every side, a family cluster, each of which wears the same general likeness to that on which we stand, yet there is no monotony in their aspect. The axe has not yet deprived them of a single tree, and they rise up, covered with the honored growth of a thousand summers. But they seem not half so venerable. They wear, in this invigorating season, all the green, fresh features of youth and spring. The leaves cover the rugged limbs which sustain them, with so much ease and grace, as if for the first time they were so green and glossy, and as if the impression should be made more certain and complete, the gusty wind of March has scattered abroad and borne afar, all the yellow garments of the vanished winter. The wild flowers begin to flaunt their blue and crimson draperies about us, as if conscious that they are borne upon the bosom of undecaying beauty; and the spot so marked and hallowed by each charming variety of bud and blossom, would seem to have been a selected dwelling for the queenly Spring herself.

Man, mindful of those tastes and sensibilities which in great part constitute his claim to superiority over the brute, has not been indifferent to the beauties of this place. In the winding hollows of these hills, beginning at our feet, you see the first signs of as lovely a little hamlet as ever promised peace to the weary and the discontent. This is the village of Charlemont.

A dozen snug and smiling cottages seem to have been dropped in this natural cup, as if by a spell of magic. They appear, each of them, to fill a fitted place—not equally distant from, but equally near each other. Though distinguished, each by an individual feature, there is yet no great dissimilarity among them. All are small, and none of them distinguished by architectural pretension. They are now quite as flourishing as when first built, and their number has had no increase since the village was first settled. Speculation has not made it populous and prosperous, by destroying its repose, stifling its charities, and abridging the sedate habits and comforts of its people. The houses, though constructed after the fashion of the country, of heavy and ill-squared logs, roughly hewn, and hastily thrown together, perhaps by unpractised hands, are yet made cheerful by that tidy industry which is always sure to make them comfortable also. Trim hedges that run beside slender white palings, surround and separate them from each other. Sometimes, as you see, festoons of graceful flowers, and waving blossoms, distinguish one dwelling from the rest, declaring its possession of some fair tenant, whose hand and fancy have kept equal progress with habitual industry; at the same time, some of them appear entirely without the little garden of flowers and vegetables, which glimmers and glitters in the rear or front of the greater number.

Such was Charlemont, at the date of our narrative. But the traveller would vainly look, now, to find the place as we describe it. The garden is no longer green with fruits and flowers—the festoons no longer grace the lowly portals—the white palings are down and blackening in the gloomy mould —the roofs have fallen, and silence dwells lonely among the ruins,—the only inhabitant of the place. It has no longer a human occupant.

"Something ails it now—the spot is cursed."

Why this fate has fallen upon so sweet an abiding place— why the villagers should have deserted a spot, so quiet and so beautiful—it does not fall within our present purpose to inquire. It was most probably abandoned—not because of the unfruitfulness of the soil, or the unhealthiness of the climate —for but few places on the bosom of the earth, may be found either more fertile, more beautiful, or more healthful—but in compliance with that feverish restlessness of mood—that sleepless discontent of temper, which, perhaps, more than any other quality, is the moral failing in the character of the Anglo-American. The roving desires of his ancestor, which brought him across the waters, have been transmitted without diminution—nay, with large increase—to the son. The creatures of a new condition of things, and new necessities, our people will follow out their destiny. The restless energies which distinguish them, are, perhaps, the contemplated characteristics which Providence has assigned them, in order that they may the more effectually and soon, bring into the use and occupation of a yet mightier people, the wilderness of that new world in which their fortunes have been cast. Generation is but the pioneer of generation, and the children of millions, more gigantic and powerful than ourselves, shall yet smile to behold, how feeble was the stroke made by our axe upon the towering trees of their inheritance.

It was probably because of this characteristic of our people, that Charlemont came in time to be deserted. The inhabitants were one day surprised with tidings of more attractive regions in yet deeper forests, and grew dissatisfied with their beautiful and secluded valley. Such is the ready access to the American mind, in its excitable state, of novelty and sudden impulse, that there needs but few suggestions to persuade the forester to draw stakes, and remove his tents, where the signs seem to be more numerous of sweeter waters and more prolific fields. For a time, change has the power which nature does not often exercise; and under its freshness, the waters *do* seem sweeter, and the stores of the wilderness, the wild-honey and the locust, *do* seem more abundant to the lip and eye. (1842)

JOHN ESTEN COOKE

Born in Winchester, Virginia, in 1830, John Esten Cooke attended school in Richmond, studied law under his father, and was admitted to the bar in 1851. When the *Southern Literary Messenger* and *Harper's New Monthly Magazine* accepted his work in 1852, he began his career as a prolific and popular writer. His early work, including the novels *Leather Stocking and Silk* (1854) and *The Virginia Comedians* (1854), shows an intimate knowledge of the history of the Valley of Virginia. An ardent secessionist, he served in the Confederacy for the entire Civil War, finally surrendering with Lee. After the war he took up farming and continued writing, primarily about the settlement of Virginia and the importance of farming in the postwar South. "The Secret of the Mountains" is typical of the romantic sensibility of a number of mid-nineteenth century writers. Whereas mountains appear to have a brutalizing effect in the writings of George Washington Harris, they offer, in the eyes of John Esten Cooke, inspiration and hope for all who can read their message.

The Secret of the Mountains

I know not how it is with others but to me all sorrows and heart-sinkings come with far less poignancy amid the fair, calm, silent mountains. They seem to afford the soul that consolation which the ever-surging sea of life, breaking on rugged shores, yearns for in the far southern solitudes, where stretch the golden sands, and the flowery savannahs roll their gentle grassy slopes to the lip of the weary waves. Above the level lowlands, with their broad sail-dotted rivers, their marts of traffic and never-ceasing toil, the mountains seem to breathe a purer atmosphere, and the heart turns to the true in life with less distraction. Like the town-tied carrier pigeon which struggles and beats the lower air for liberty, and being loosed soars steadily towards heaven—more and more steadily moves as it reaches upper air—the soul soars here in a calmer ether, almost above the obscuring clouds of life.

In the long evenings of December, it is true, all this is partially forgotten beside the dying, white-blooded ember, which wafts the restless mind back over the sea that has been past, to its storms, its shipwrecks, its despair. Then, it is true, the whitened brand, which we thought the gray, crumbling ashes had extinguished, burns again upon being moved and blows upon the breath of memory,—and the heart, like a stricken moor-fowl, suddenly droops its wing from the skies and drops to earth, cut down by a thought that flashes through the half-darkness of its gathering oblivion.

But when morning dawns upon the mountains, and the wide valleys are steeped in the shadows of the lofty pines, and nature seems to smile with her large, bright eye upon the world, the heart again revives. Revives in joy and peace with all those roseate recollections and inspiring dreams which beguile us of the ills of life. In the clear golden sunlight sorrow seems to wane and fade, and again we see through a clear and healthful atmosphere the various forms which God has sent to beguile us of the ills of life,—the tranquil hopes, the serious joys, the calm and tender love of woman and of friends; that greatest solace to the poor heart, torn and wounded by the thorns along that path of life it is doomed to tread. Like the image of the river-pine whose outline reflected in the stream is stirred for a moment by some passing 'keel, but settles again serenely in the blue vault of heaven below, the heart again subsides into a calm, happy peace—heaven-born.

The mountain-nations, through all history have ever hoped, and bent their eyes upon the great mist-shrouded future:—in Spain's old Moorish, and in her modern days; in the times of Hassan in Arabia; in Saxon England, and Gaelic Scotland; in Hungary from the times of Saint Stephen; and in Switzerland, which, all mountain, is another name for liberty and hope. The men of Grütli hope still in their mountain cave, meet often to take counsel on the midnight heath; and the Switzer tells you they will one day rise in their old-world might, and shape the destiny of their country.

It is not difficult to explain this hope, give a sufficient reason for those mountain influences; but the heart only could estimate justly the explanation. Unless the enquirer has stood above the lowland, amid the clear, fair sunshine, and felt upon his brow the joyous inspiration of the mountain wind; unless he has forgotten, thus placed, the small, soul-obscuring harassments of life, and felt there, before nature and nature's God, the high, clear, trustful hope of better and brighter things for all, whether his country, or his heart-friends, or himself; unless banishing from his memory all evil thoughts, he has gone thus high up upon the silent peaks and seen the sun climb slowly, or at setting write its hymn of praise in golden letters on the blue heart-moving heavens—I fear it is wholly beyond my power (as it was beyond the power of the helm man seen by Count Armaldoes) to tell him in what lies the *secret of the mountains.* (1852)

SIDNEY LANIER

Born in 1842 in Macon, Georgia, Sidney Lanier was graduated from Oglethorpe University in 1860. His plans to study
in Germany were interrupted by the Civil War. In 1864 he
was captured and imprisoned at Point Lookout, Maryland,
for four months. His experiences as a prisoner of war provide
part of the background for his novel *Tiger Lilies* (1867),
which also has an East Tennessee setting based on Lanier's
summer visits in the 1850s to his grandfather's estate in Mont-
vale Springs. Chapter Two from *Tiger Lilies* illustrates the
young Lanier's preoccupation with German transcendental-
ism. Published in the same year as the *Sut Lovingood Yarns*
and, as Edmund Wilson remarks, dealing with the same general culture, *Tiger Lilies*, like the work of John Esten Cooke
and other romantics, presents an idealized view of Southern
mountain life which still has an appeal for many readers
today. The title for the selection from *Tiger Lilies* has been
supplied.

Friendship in the Hills

> *Theseus.*—"And since we have the vaward of the day,
> My love shall hear the music of my hounds.
> Uncouple in the western valley; let them go!
> We will, fair queen, up to the mountain's top."
> *Midsummer Night's Dream.*

Not far above the junction of the Little Tennessee and Holston rivers, immediately upon the banks of the former stream, occurs a level plat, or "cove," as it is there called, of most romantic beauty. Here the river suddenly ceases its wild leaping down the mountains, and, like a maiden about to be married, pauses to dream upon the alliance it is speedily to form with a mightier stream. On each side the wide expanse of this still river-lake, broad level meadows stretch away some miles down the stream, until the hoydenish river wakes from its dream and again dashes down its narrow channel between the mountains.

The meadows are inclosed by precipitous ridges, behind which succeed higher ridges, and still higher, until the lofty mountains wall in and overshadow them all.

The hills sit here like old dethroned kings, met for consultation: they would be very garrulous, surely, but the exquisite peace of the pastoral scene below them has stilled their life; they have forgotten the ancient anarchy which brought them forth; they dream and dream away, without discussion or endeavor.

On the last day of September 1860, huntsman Dawn leapt out of the east, quickly ran to earth that old fox, Night, and sat down on the top of Smoky Mountain to draw breath a minute. The shine of his silver hunting-gear lit the whole mountain, faintly. Enough, at any rate, to disclose two men who with active steps were pursuing a road which ascends the mountain half way, and which at a distance of two miles from the cove just described diverges from a direct course to the summit, passing on to the Carolina line. The younger of the two, equipped with a light sporting-rifle and accoutrements, walked ahead of his companion, a tall, raw-boned, muscular mountaineer, who with his right hand carried a long slim-barrelled gun, while with his left he endeavored to control the frantic gambols of a brace of deer-hounds whose leash was wrapped round his bony fingers.

"Waal I reckin!" exclaimed the mountaineer, whom the 24,999 may hereafter recognize as Cain Smallin; "and how many bullets, mought ye think, was fired afore he fotch the big un to the yeth?"

"O! Gordon Cumming was a hunter, you know, and all hunters exaggerate a little, perhaps unconsciously. He *says* he fired two hundred balls into the elephant before he fell."

"A master heap o' lead, now, certin, to kill one varmint! But I suppose he got a mortial sight o' ven'zon, an' hide an' truck o' one sort an' another off'n him. I recommember Jim Razor flung fifteen bullet into a ole b'ar on Smoky Mount'n, two year ago come Chris'mas; but hit ai'nt nothin' to your tale. Would'n' I like to see one o' them—what was't you called 'em? I'm forgitful."

"Elephants."

"One o' them elephants a-waddlin' up yan mount'n of a hot summer's day!"

As this idea gained upon the soul of Cain Smallin, he opened his mouth, which was like a pass in the mountains, and a torrent of laughter brawled uproariously through it.

"I hardly think he would make as good time as that deer yonder, that you've frightened half to death with your monstrous cackle. Look, Cain! In with the dogs, man! I'm for the top of the mountain to see the sun rise; but I'll come down directly and follow along, as you drive, to catch any stragglers that may double on you."

With a ringing yell the mountaineer loosed his dogs, and followed after with rapid strides.

"Take my hat," muttered he, "*an'* boots! The boy said he

had'n' seen a deer sence he left here four year ago fur college, an' I raally thought he'd be master keen fur a drive. An'
he a runnin' away f'om the deer, an' hit in full sight, an' the
dogs a'ter it! But them blasted colleges'll ruin any man's son,
I don't care *who* he is!"

Meanwhile, Philip Sterling, the unconscious object of the
mountaineer's commiseration, by dint of much climbing and
leaping over and across obstacles which he seemed to despise
in the wantonness of youthful activity, at length reached the
mountain-top, and stood still upon the highest point of an
immense rock, which lay like an altar upon the very summit.
A morning mist met him, and hung itself in loose blank folds
before him, like the vast stage-curtain of some immeasurable
theatre. But the sun shot a straight ray through the top of
the curtain and, as if hung to this horizontal beam with rings
of mist, it drew itself aside and disclosed the wonderful-
scened stage of the world—a stage (thought Philip Sterling)
whose tricksy harlequins are Death and Chance, and whose
trapdoors are graves—a stage before which sits an orchestra
half composed of angels, whose music would be ravishing
did not the other half, who are devils, continually bray all
manner of discords by playing galops for our tragedies, and
dirges for our farces—a stage whose most thrilling perform-
ances are sad pantomimes, in which a single individual's soul
silently plays all the parts—a queer "Varieties" of the Universe, where rows nightly occur, in which the combatants are
Heaven and Hell.

Airy 24,999 who hover with me round this mountain-top,
ye might almost see these thoughts passing in review in Philip
Sterling's eyes, as he stands dreamily regarding the far scene
below him. Ye do not notice, I am certain, the slender figure,
nor the forehead, nor the mouth, nose, and chin; but the eyes
—Men and Women!—the large, gray, poet's eyes, with a
dream in each and a sparkle behind it—the eager, hungry
eyes, widening their circles to take in more of the morning-

beauties and the morning-purities that sail invisibly about—
these ye will notice!

"From the eyes a path doth lie
To the heart, and is not long;
And thereon travel of thoughts a throng!"

—quoth Hugo von Trimberg. And these eyes of Philip Sterling's go on to say, as plainly as eyes can say: "Thou incomprehensible World, since it is not possible to know thee perfectly, our only refuge is to love thee earnestly, that, so, the
blind heart, by numberless caresses, may learn the truth of
thy vast features by the touch, and may recognize thy true
voice in the many-toned sounds that perplex a soul, and may
run to meet thee at hearing thy step only."

"Yet I know not, O World, whether thou are a wrestler
whom I must throw heavily, or a maiden whom I must woo
lightly. I will see, I will see!" cried Philip Sterling to himself.

(Bless my life, 24,999! How long our arms are when we are
young! Nothing but the whole world will satisfy their clasp;
later in life we learn to give many thanks for one single, faithful, slender waist!)

"And so," continued our younger eager-soul, "I choose to
woo thee; thou shalt be my maiden-love. I swear that thy
voice shall be my Fame, thy red lips my Pleasure, thine eyes
my Diamonds; and I will be true knight to thee, and I will
love thee and serve thee with faithful heart and stainless
sword till death do us part!"

"But what a fool I am," said Philip Sterling aloud, "to be
vowing marriage vows before I'm even accepted, nay, before
I've fairly declared my passion! Hasty, mi-boy! But I wish I
were down in the cities; I'm ready for work, and it's all a
dream and a play up here in the mountains."

One may doubt if Pygmalion, being so utterly in love, was
at all surprised when his statue warmed into life and

embraced him. Philip Sterling, at any rate, making love to this sweet statue of the world, did not start when he heard a step behind him. He turned, and beheld a tall figure, in whose face, albeit mossed like a swamp-oak with beard, beamed a cheerful earnestness that was as like Philip's enthusiasm as a star is like a comet.

" 'Life is too short,' " quoted the stranger, advancing with open hand extended, " 'to be long about the forms of it.' My name's Paul Rübetsahl!"

"And mine is Philip Sterling!"

The two hands met and clasped. Philip had always a *penchant* for the love-at-sight theory, and I know not if Paul Rübetsahl was any more sensible. The two young transcendentalists looked in each other's faces. The frank eyes searched each other a moment, and then turned away, gazing over the valley, along the river dividing the mountains, on, to the far horizon. In this gaze was a sort of triumphal expression; as who should say, "Two friends that have met on a mountain may always claim that as their level, and their souls may always sail out over hills that are hard to climb, over valleys that are tilled with sweat and reaped with Trouble's sickle, over cities whose commerce perplexes religion, over societies whose laws and forms oppress a free spirit; from such a height we may look down and understand, at least not despise, these things."

And with that high egotism of youth whereby we view the world in its relations to us, and not also in our relations to it, and stretch out our eager hands to grasp it, as if it were made for us and not we also for it; in this happy exaltation, each of these two youths cried out in his heart, "Behold! O world, and sun, and stars—behold, at last, two Friends!" (1867)

DAVID HUNTER STROTHER
("PORTE CRAYON")

A valued contributor to *Harper's New Monthly Magazine*, David Hunter Strother was born in Martinsburg, Virginia (now West Virginia), in 1816. He journeyed through Virginia and other parts of the South, compiling and illustrating travel essays which were published under the name of "Porte Crayon." During the Civil War he was on the staff of the Union army, and later served as American Consul-General at Mexico City (1879–1885). His description of the mountains is so impassioned as to be reminiscent of the famous plea for liberty of his fellow Virginian, Patrick Henry. In this view, the mountains, instead of being impediments to progress, are the very symbol of liberty, the natural home for natural men.

The Mountains

"Montani semper liberi" is the motto of a new State, in accordance with the popular and poetic belief that Liberty finds her favorite abode in mountainous countries, although history would seem to teach us that civil liberty has been generally better understood and maintained by the educated and enlightened populations of great commercial cities.

Nevertheless, as man always absorbs and reflects (chameleon-like) somewhat of the local color of his surroundings, we may readily perceive in the sights, sounds, and very smells of this rugged wilderness suggestions of a rude, instinctive independence, and individuality fiercely impatient of external control.

See how the mountains rear their bristling backs against the tyranny of plows and harrows—how their free torrents leap and foam in their rocky channels, shouting defiance to the fetters of dikes and dams, equally scornful of the burdens of commerce and the base drudgery of manufactures!

Here the arrowy trout flashes through transparent waters, leaping for his morning and evening meal, and sleeps at noonday in deep, shadowy pools, unvexed by hooks or nets. The wild turkey displays his green and golden plumage, strutting and gobbling in conceited majesty, unadmired except by silly hens, unscared but by the subtle fox. The red doe, with tender wildness, leads her speckled fawns through forests whose echoes have never been startled by the woodman's axe. From unshorn thickets the brindled wolf glares and watches, still preferring starvation to servitude.

Then how fresh and cooling come the earthy odors from damp beds of moss and springs trickling through fern-shaded rocks! How invigorating the aroma of crushed mint and pennyroyal by the way-side, fragrant hickory buds and spicy walnuts plucked from overhanging boughs! How royally refreshing the smell of cedar woods, hemlocks, and pines! And how balmy sweet the wild grapes blossom—a bouquet for a wood-nymph!

Amidst such surroundings the mountaineer is born and nurtured in poverty and seclusion. He has no set pattern to grow up by, with none of the slop-shops of civilization at hand to furnish him ready-made clothing, manners, or opinions. Rugged paths harden his baby feet; the chase of rabbits and ground-squirrels toughens his boyish sinews. Human nature, family traditions, and some hints from his fellow-denizens of the woods form the basis of his moral education, while his mother makes his breeches.

Simple but strong, uncouth but sincere, the man of the mountains knows nothing of the luxury and refinements of cities, and is equally protected from most of their attendant vices and miseries.

> "A rifle for the red deer's speed,
> A rugged hand to case the seed—
> With these their teeming huts they feed."

Without rivalry, he knows little either of envy or ambition; with nothing, he is rich in the independence arising from few and simple wants. (1872)

IV. *Local Color: Realism and Romance*

The local color writing which swept the country in the years after the Civil War was a subdivision of the realistic movement led by William Dean Howells, Henry James, and Mark Twain. As influential editor of the *Atlantic* and later *Harper's*, Howells published a number of local colorists, including Bret Harte and Mary N. Murfree, and he laid down a definition of the new fiction designed to eliminate the fanciful and incredible. "Realism," he said, "is the truthful treatment of material." Howells admitted that he had found the Sut Lovingood yarns "coarse" and undoubtedly he also found them unrealistic. Over the years, however, this judgment has almost been reversed in the eyes of a number of students of American literature, the tall tales appearing to contain much more "truth" and "realism" than the picturesque stories which came later. Unquestionably, the local colorists sought authenticity in the depiction of various sections of the country before the standardization wrought by material progress and new modes of transportation, but the result was usually some sort of combination of verisimilitude and nostalgia served up with obeisance for the patronizing taste of genteel Northern readers. As far as the Southern mountaineer was concerned, the result of local color was a popularization of stereotypes still strongly entrenched a hundred years later. The tone was set by Mary N. Murfree's *In the Tennessee Mountains.* According to Cratis Williams in his landmark study of the Southern mountaineer, "the year of its publication may be called the *annus mirabilis* in the history of the mountain people in fiction, for 1884 definitely marks the time at which the Southern mountain people had become generally recognized as a people possessing their own idiosyncrasies, and not to be confused with other southern types." Fiction in a similar vein is found in the North Georgia stories of Joel Chandler Harris as well as those of Kentucky feuds by John Fox, Jr.

MARY NOAILLES MURFREE
(CHARLES EGBERT CRADDOCK)

Mary N. Murfree was born in 1850 near Murfreesboro, Tennessee, at Grantland, the family home on the Stone River, which was destroyed in 1862 during the Civil War. At an early age, she was stricken with fever, which resulted in slight lameness for the rest of her life. As a teenager she began annual summer visits to the family cottage at Beersheba Springs in the Cumberland Mountains where she gathered material for her many novels and stories that were to make her famous under the pseudonym of Charles Egbert Craddock. *In the Tennessee Mountains* went through 23 editions in the author's lifetime. She was the author of 25 published works, mostly fiction set in the Southern mountain area. "The Dancin' Party at Harrison's Cove" from *In the Tennessee Mountains* may be considered the touchstone of all local color writing on southern Appalachia.

The Dancin' Party at Harrison's Cove

"Fur ye see, Mis' Darley, them Harrison folks over yander ter the Cove hev determinated on a dancin' party."

The drawling tones fell unheeded on old Mr. Kenyon's ear,

as he sat on the broad hotel piazza on the New Helvetia Springs, and gazed with meditative eyes at the fair August sky. An early moon was riding, clear and full, over this wild spur of the Alleghanies; the stars were few and very faint; even the great Scorpio lurked, vaguely outlined, above the wooded ranges; and the white mist, that filled the long, deep, narrow valley between the parallel lines of the mountains, shimmered with opalescent gleams.

All the world of the watering-place had converged to that focus, the ball-room, and the cool, moonlit piazzas were nearly deserted. The fell determination of the "Harrison folks" to give a dancing party made no impression on the preoccupied old gentleman. Another voice broke his reverie, —a soft, clear, well-modulated voice,—and he started and turned his head as his own name was called, and his niece, Mrs. Darley, came to the window.

"Uncle Ambrose,—are you there? So glad! I was afraid you were down at the summer-house, where I hear the children singing. Do come here a moment, please. This is Mrs. Johns, who brings the Indian peaches to sell,—you know the Indian peaches?"

Mr. Kenyon knew the Indian peaches, the dark crimson fruit streaked with still darker lines, and full of blood-red juice, which he had meditatively munched that very afternoon. Mr. Kenyon knew the Indian peaches right well. He wondered, however, what had brought Mrs. Johns back in so short a time, for although the principal industry of the mountain people about the New Helvetia Springs is selling fruit to the summer sojourners, it is not customary to come twice on the same day, nor to appear at all after nightfall.

Mrs. Darley proceeded to explain.

"Mrs. Johns's husband is ill and wants us to send him some medicine."

Mr. Kenyon rose, threw away the stump of his cigar, and entered the room. "How long has he been ill, Mrs. Johns?" he asked, dismally.

Mr. Kenyon always spoke lugubriously, and he was a dis-
mal-looking old man. Not more cheerful was Mrs. Johns; she
was tall and lank, and with such a face as one never sees
except in these mountains,—elongated, sallow, thin, with
pathetic, deeply sunken eyes, and high cheek-bones, and so
settled an expression of hopeless melancholy that it must be
that naught but care and suffering had been her lot; holding
out wasted hands to the years as they pass—holding them
out always, and always empty. She wore a shabby, faded
calico, and spoke with the peculiar expressionless drawl of
the mountaineer. She was a wonderful contrast to Mrs. Darley, all furbelows and flounces, with her fresh, smooth face
and soft hair, and plump, round arms half-revealed by the
flowing sleeves of her thin, black dress. Mrs. Darley was in
mourning, and therefore did not affect the ballroom. At this
moment, on benevolent thoughts intent, she was engaged in
uncorking sundry small phials, gazing inquiringly at their
labels, and shaking their contents.

In reply to Mr. Kenyon's question, Mrs. Johns, sitting on
the extreme edge of a chair and fanning herself with a pink
calico sun-bonnet, talked about her husband, and a misery
in his side and in his back, and how he felt it "a-comin' on
nigh on ter a week ago." Mr. Kenyon expressed sympathy,
and was surprised by the announcement that Mrs. Johns considered her husband's illness "a blessin', 'kase ef he war able
ter git out'n his bed, he 'lowed ter go down ter Harrison's
Cove ter the dancin' party, 'kase Rick Pearson war a-goin'
ter be thar, an' hed said ez how none o' the Johnses should
come."

"What, Rick Pearson, that terrible outlaw!" exclaimed Mrs.
Darley, with wide open blue eyes. She had read in the newspapers sundry thrilling accounts of a noted horse thief and
outlaw, who with a gang of kindred spirits defied justice and
roamed certain sparsely-populated mountainous counties at
his own wild will, and she was not altogether without a
feeling of fear as she heard of his proximity to the New

Helvetia Springs,—not fear for life or limb, because she was practical-minded enough to reflect that the sojourners and employés of the watering-place would far outnumber the out-law's troop, but fear that a pair of shiny bay ponies, Castor and Pollux, would fall victims to the crafty wiles of the expert horse thief.

"I think I have heard of a difficulty between your people and Rick Pearson," said old Mr. Kenyon. "Has a peace never been patched up between them?"

"No-o," drawled Mrs. Johns; "same as it always war. My old man'll never believe but what Rick Pearson stole that thar bay filly we lost 'bout five year ago. But I don't believe he done it; plenty other folks around is ez mean ez Rick, leastways mos' ez mean; plenty mean enough ter steal a horse, ennyhow. Rick *say* he never tuk the filly; say he war a-goin' ter shoot off the nex' man's head ez say so. Rick say he'd ruther give two bay fillies than hev a man say he tuk a horse ez he never tuk. Rick say ez how he kin stand up ter what he does do, but it's these hyar lies on him what kills him out. But ye know, Mis' Darley, ye know yerself, he never give nobody two bay fillies in this world, an' what's more he's never goin' ter. My old man an' my boy Kossute talks on 'bout that thar bay filly like she was stole yestiddy, an 't war five year ago an' better; an' when they hearn ez how Rick Pearson hed showed that red head o' his'n on this hyar mounting las' week, they war fightin' mad, an' would hev lit out fur the gang sure, 'ceptin' they hed been gone down the mounting fur two days. An' my son Kossute, he sent Rick word that he had better keep out'n gunshot o' these hyar woods; that he did n't want no better mark than that red head o' his'n, an' he could hit it two mile off. An' Rick Pear-son, he sent Kossute word that he would kill him fur his sass the very nex' time he see him, an' ef he don't want a bullet in that pumpkin head o' his'n he hed better keep away from that dancin' party what the Harrisons hev laid off ter give, 'kase Rick say he's a-goin' ter it hisself, an' is a-goin' ter dance too; he ain't been invited, Mis' Darley, but Rick don't keer fur that. He is a-goin' ennyhow, an' he say ez how he ain't a-goin' ter let Kossute come, 'count o' Kossute's sass an' the fuss they've all made 'bout that bay filly that war stole five year ago,—'t war five year an' better. But Rick say ez how he is goin', fur all he ain't got no invite, an' is a-goin' ter dance too, 'kase you know, Mis' Darley, it's a-goin' ter be a dancin' party; the Harrisons hev determinated on that. Them gals of theirn air mos' crazed 'bout a dancin' party. They ain't been a bit of account sence they went ter Cheat-ham's Cross-Roads ter see thar gran'mother, an' picked up all them queer new notions. So the Harrisons hev determinated on a dancin' party; an' Rick say ez how he is goin' ter dance too; but Jule, *she* say ez how she know thar ain't a gal on the mounting ez would dance with him; but I ain't so sure 'bout that, Mis' Darley; gals air cur'ous critters, ye know yer-self; thar's no sort o' countin' on 'em; they'll do one thing one time, an' another thing nex' time; ye can't put no depend-ence in 'em. But Jule say ef he kin git Mandy Tyler ter dance with him, it's the mos' he kin do, an' the gang'll be no whar. Mebbe he kin git Mandy ter dance with him, 'kase the other boys say ez how none o' them is a-goin' ter ax her ter dance, 'count of the trick she played on 'em down ter the Wilkins settlemint—las' month, war it? no, 't war two month ago, an' better; but the boys ain't forgot how scandalous she done 'em, an' none of 'em is a-goin' ter ax her ter dance."

"Why, what did she do?" exclaimed Mrs. Darley, surprised. "She came here to sell peaches one day, and I thought her such a nice, pretty, well-behaved girl."

"Waal, she hev got mighty quiet say-nuthin' sort 'n ways, Mis' Darley, but that thar gal do behave *rediculous.* Down thar ter the Wilkins settlemint,—ye know it's 'bout two mile or two mile 'n a half from hyar,—waal, all the gals walked down thar ter the party an hour by sun, but when the boys went down they tuk thar horses, ter give the gals a ride home behind 'em. Waal, every boy axed his gal ter ride while the party war goin' on, an' when 't war all over they all set out fur ter come home. Waal, this hyar Mandy Tyler is a mighty favo*rite* 'mongst the boys,—they ain't got no sense, ye know, Mis' Darley,—an stiddier one of 'em axin' her ter ride home, thar war five of 'em axed her ter ride, ef ye'll believe me, an' what do ye think she done, Mis' Darley? She tole all five of 'em yes; an' when the party war over, she war the last ter go, an' when she started out 'n the door, thar war all five of them boys a-standin' thar waitin' fur her, an' every one a-holdin' his horse by the bridle, an' none of 'em knowed who the others war a-waitin' fur. An' this hyar Mandy Tyler, when she got ter the door an' seen 'em all a-standin' thar, never said one word, jest walked right through 'mongst 'em, an' set out fur the mounting on foot with all them five boys a-followin' an' a-leadin' thar horses an' a-quarrelin' enough ter take off each others' heads 'bout which one war a-goin' ter ride with her; which none of 'em did, Mis' Darley, fur I hearn ez how the whole lay-out footed it all the way ter New Helveshy. An' thar would hev been a fight 'mongst 'em, 'ceptin' her brother, Jacob Tyler, went along with 'em, an' tried ter keep the peace atwixt 'em. An' Mis' Darley, all them married folks down thar at the party—them folks in the Wilkins settlemint is the biggest fools, sure—when all them married folks come out ter the door, an' see the way Mandy Tyler hed treated them boys, they jest hollered and laffed an' thought it war mighty smart an' funny in Mandy; but she never say a word till she kem up the mounting, an' I never hearn ez how she say ennything then. An' now the boys all say none of 'em is a-goin' ter ax her ter dance, ter pay her back fur them fool airs of hern. But Kossute say he'll dance with her ef none the rest will. Kossute he thought 't war all mighty funny too,—he's sech a fool 'bout gals, Kossute is,— but Jule, she thought ez how 't war scandalous."

Mrs. Darley listened in amused surprise; that these moun-

tain wilds could sustain a first-class coquette was an idea that
had not hitherto entered her mind; however, "that thar
Mandy" seemed, in Mrs. Johns's opinion at least, to merit the
unenviable distinction, and the party at Wilkins settlement
and the prospective gayety of Harrison's Cove awakened the
same sentiments in her heart and mind as do the more ambitious germans and kettledrums of the lowland cities in the
heart and mind of Mrs. Grundy. Human nature is the same
everywhere, and the Wilkins settlement is a microcosm. The
metropolitan centres, stripped of the civilization of wealth,
fashion, and culture, would present only the bare skeleton of
humanity outlined in Mrs. Johns's talk of Harrison's Cove,
the Wilkins settlement, the enmities and scandals and sorrows and misfortunes of the mountain ridge. As the absurd
resemblance developed, Mrs. Darley could not forbear a
smile. Mrs. Johns looked up with a momentary expression of
surprise; the story presented no humorous phase to her per-
ceptions, but she too smiled a little as she repeated, "Scandalous, ain't it?" and proceeded in the same lack-lustre tone
as before.

"Yes,—Kossute say ez how he'll dance with her ef none the
rest will, fur Kossute say ez how he hev laid off ter dance,
Mis' Darley; an' when I ax him what he thinks will become
of his soul ef he dances, he say the devil may crack away at
it, an' ef he kin hit it he's welcome. Fur soul or no soul he's
a-goin' ter dance. Kossute is a-fixin' of hisself this very minit
ter go; but I am verily afeard the boy'll be slaughtered, Mis'
Darley, 'kase thar is goin' ter be a fight, an' ye never in all yer
life hearn sech sass ez Kossute and Rick Pearson done sent
word ter each other."

Mr. Kenyon expressed some surprise that she should fear for
so young a fellow as Kossuth. "Surely," he said, "the man is
not brute enough to injure a mere boy; your son is a mere
boy."

"That's so," Mrs. Johns drawled. "Kossute ain't more 'n
twenty year old, an' Rick Pearson is double that ef he is a

day; but ye see it's the fire-arms ez makes Kossute more 'n a match fur him, 'kase Kossute is the best shot on the mounting, an' Rick knows that in a shootin' fight Kossute's better able ter take keer of hisself an' hurt somebody else nor ennybody. Kossute's more likely ter hurt Rick nor Rick is ter hurt him in a shootin' fight; but ef Rick did n't hurt him, an' he war ter shoot Rick, the gang would tear him ter pieces in a minit; and 'mongst 'em I'm actually afeard they'll slaughter the boy."

Mr. Kenyon looked even graver than was his wont upon receiving this information, but said no more; and after giving Mrs. Johns the febrifuge she wished for her husband, he returned to his seat on the piazza.

Mrs. Darley watched him with some little indignation as he proceeded to light a fresh cigar. "How cold and unsympathetic uncle Ambrose is," she said to herself. And after condoling effusively with Mrs. Johns on her apprehensions for her son's safety, she returned to the gossips in the hotel parlor, and Mrs. Johns, with her pink calico sun-bonnet on her head, went her way in the brilliant summer moon light.

The clear lustre shone white upon all the dark woods and chasms and flashing waters that lay between the New Helvetia Springs and the wide, deep ravine called Harrison's Cove, where from a rude log hut the vibrations of a violin, and the quick throb of dancing feet, already mingled with the impetuous rush of a mountain stream close by and the weird night-sounds of the hills,—the cry of birds among the tall trees, the stir of the wind, the monotonous chanting of frogs at the water-side, the long, drowsy drone of the nocturnal insects, the sudden faint blast of a distant hunter's horn, and the far baying of hounds.

Mr. Harrison had four marriageable daughters, and had arrived at the conclusion that something must be done for the girls; for, strange as it may seem, the prudent father exists even among the "mounting folks." Men there realize the importance of providing suitable homes for their daughters

as men do elsewhere, and the eligible youth is as highly
esteemed in those wilds as is the much scarcer animal at a
fashionable watering-place. Thus it was that Mr. Harrison
had "determinated on a dancin' party." True, he stood in
bodily fear of the judgment day and the circuit-rider; but
the dancing party was a rarity eminently calculated to please
the young hunters of the settlements round about, so he swallowed his qualms, to be indulged at a more convenient season, and threw himself into the vortex of preparation with
an ardor very gratifying to the four young ladies, who had
become imbued with sophistication at Cheatham's Cross-
Roads.

Not so Mrs. Harrison; she almost expected the house to fall
and crush them, as a judgment on the wickedness of a dancing party; for so heinous a sin, in the estimation of the greater
part of the mountain people, had not been committed among
them for many a day. Such trifles as killing a man in a quarrel, or on suspicion of stealing a horse, or wash-tub, or anything that came handy, of course, does not count; but a dancing party! Mrs. Harrison could only hold her idle hands, and
dread the heavy penalty that must surely follow so terrible a
crime.

It certainly had not the gay and lightsome aspect supposed
to be characteristic of such a scene of sin: the awkward
young mountaineers clogged heavily about in their uncouth
clothes and rough shoes, with the stolid-looking, lack-lustre
maids of the hill, to the violin's monotonous iteration of The
Chicken in the Bread-Trough, or The Rabbit in the Pea-
Patch,—all their grave faces as grave as ever. The music now
and then changed suddenly to one of those wild, melancholy
strains sometimes heard in old-fashioned dancing tunes, and
the strange pathetic cadences seemed more attuned to the
rhythmical dash of the waters rushing over their stone barricades out in the moonlight yonder, or to the plaintive sighs
of the winds among the great dark arches of the primeval
forests, than to the movement of the heavy, coarse feet danc-

ing in a solemn measure in the little log cabin in Harrison's Cove. The elders, sitting in rush-bottomed chairs close to the walls, and looking on at the merriment, well-pleased despite their religious doubts, were somewhat more lively; every now and then a guffaw mingled with the violin's resonant strains and the dancers' well-marked pace; the women talked to each other with somewhat more animation than was their wont, under the stress of the unusual excitement of a dancing party, and from out the shed-room adjoining came an anticipative odor of more substantial sin than the fiddle or the grave jiggling up and down the rough floor. A little more cider too, and a very bad article of illegally-distilled whiskey, were ever and anon circulated among the pious abstainers from the dance; but the sinful votaries of Terpsichore could brook no pause nor delay, and jogged up and down quite intoxicated with the mirthfulness of the plaintive old airs and the pleasure of other motion than following the plow or hoeing the corn.

And the moon smiled right royally on her dominion: on the long, dark ranges of mountains and mist-filled valleys between; on the woods and streams, and on all the half-dormant creatures either amongst the shadow-flecked foliage or under the crystal waters; on the long, white, sandy road winding in and out through the forest; on the frowning crags of the wild ravine; on the little bridge at the entrance of the gorge, across which a party of eight men, heavily armed and gallantly mounted, rode swifty and disappeared amid the gloom of the shadows.

The sound of the galloping of horses broke suddenly on the music and the noise of the dancing; a moment's interval, and the door gently opened and the gigantic form of Rick Pearson appeared in the aperture. He was dressed, like the other mountaineers, in a coarse suit of brown jeans somewhat the worse for wear, the trowsers stuffed in the legs of his heavy boots; he wore an old soft felt hat, which he did not remove immediately on entering, and a pair of formidable pistols at his belt conspicuously challenged attention. He had auburn hair, and a long full beard of a lighter tint reaching almost to his waist; his complexion was much tanned by the sun, and roughened by exposure to the inclement mountain weather; his eyes were brown, deep-set, and from under his heavy brows they looked out with quick, sharp glances, and occasionally with a roguish twinkle; the expression of his countenance was rather good-humored,—a sort of imperious good-humor, however,—the expression of a man accustomed to have his own way and not to be trifled with, but able to afford some amiability since his power is undisputed.

He stepped slowly into the apartment, placed his gun against the wall, turned, and solemnly gazed at the dancing, while his followers trooped in and obeyed his example. As the eight guns, one by one, rattled against the wall, there was a startled silence among the pious elders of the assemblage, and a sudden disappearance of the animation that had characterized their intercourse during the evening. Mrs. Harrison, who by reason of flurry and a housewifely pride in the still unrevealed treasures of the shed-room had well-nigh forgotten her fears, felt that the anticipated judgment had even now descended, and in what terrible and unexpected guise! The men turned the quids of tobacco in their cheeks and looked at each other in uncertainty; but the dancers bestowed not a glance upon the newcomers, and the musician in the corner, with his eyes half-closed, his head bent low upon the instrument, his hard, horny hand moving the bow back and forth over the strings of the crazy old fiddle, was utterly rapt by his own melody. At the supreme moment when the great red beard had appeared portentously in the doorway and fear had frozen the heart of Mrs. Harrison within her at the ill-omened apparition, the host was in the shed-room filling a broken-nosed pitcher from the cider-barrel. When he reentered, and caught sight of the grave sun-burned face with its long red beard and sharp brown eyes, he too was dismayed for an instant, and stood silent at the opposite door with the pitcher in his hand. The pleasure and the possible profit of the dancing party, for which he had expended so much of his scanty store of this world's goods and risked the eternal treasures laid up in heaven, were a mere phantasm; for, with Rick Pearson among them, in an ill frame of mind and at odds with half the men in the room, there would certainly be a fight, and in all probability one would be killed, and the dancing party at Harrison's Cove would be a text for the bloody-minded sermons of the circuit-rider for all time to come. However, the father of four marriageable daughters is apt to become crafty and worldly-wise; only for a moment did he stand in indecision; then, catching suddenly the small brown eyes, he held up the pitcher with a grin of invitation. "Rick!" he called out above the scraping of the violin and the clatter of the dancing feet, "slip round hyar ef ye kin, I've got somethin' for ye;" and he shook the pitcher significantly.

Not that Mr. Harrison would for a moment have thought of Rick Pearson in a matrimonial point of view, for even the sophistication of the Cross-Roads had not yet brought him to the state of mind to consider such a half loaf as this better than no bread, but he felt it imperative from every point of view to keep that set of young mountaineers dancing in peace and quiet, and their guns idle and out of mischief against the wall. The great red beard disappeared and reappeared at intervals, as Rick Pearson slipped along the gun-lined wall to join his host and the cider-pitcher, and after he had disposed of the refreshment, in which the gang shared, he relapsed into silently watching the dancing and meditating a participation in that festivity.

Now, it so happened that the only girl unprovided with a partner was "that thar Mandy Tyler," of Wilkins settlement renown; the young men had rigidly adhered to their resolution to ignore her in their invitations to dance, and she had been sitting since the beginning of the festivities, quite neglected, among the married people, looking on at the amusement which she had been debarred sharing by that unpopular bit of coquetry at Wilkins settlement. Nothing of disappointment or mortification was expressed in her countenance; she felt the slight of course,—even a "mounting" woman is susceptible of the sting of wounded pride; all her long-anticipated enjoyment had come to naught by this infliction of penance for her ill-timed jest at the expense of those five young fellows dancing with their triumphant partners and bestowing upon her not even a glance; but she looked the express image of immobility as she sat in her clean pink calico, so carefully gotten up for the occasion, her short black hair curling about her ears, and watched the unending reel with slow, dark eyes. Rick's glance fell upon her, and without further hesitation he strode over to where she was sitting and proffered his hand for the dance. She did not reply immediately, but looked timidly about her at the shocked pious ones on either side, who were ready but for mortal fear to aver that "dancin' ennyhow air bad enough, the Lord knows, but dancin' with a horse thief air jest scandalous!" Then, for there is something of defiance to established law and prejudice in the born flirt everywhere, with a sudden daring spirit shining in her brightening eyes, she responded, "Don't keer ef I do," with a dimpling half-laugh; and the next minute the two outlaws were flying down the middle together.

While Rick was according grave attention to the intricacies of the mazy dance and keeping punctilious time to the scraping of the odd fiddle, finding it all a much more difficult feat than galloping from the Cross-Roads to the "Snake's Mouth" on some other man's horse with the sheriff hard at his heels, the solitary figure of a tall gaunt man had followed the long winding path leading deep into the woods, and now began the steep descent to Harrison's Cove. Of what was old Mr. Kenyon thinking, as he walked on in the mingled shadow and sheen? Of St. Augustin and his Forty Monks, probably, and what they found in Britain. The young men of his acquaintance would gladly have laid you any odds that he could think of nothing but his antique hobby, the ancient church. Mr. Kenyon was the most prominent man in St. Martin's church in the city of B——, not excepting the rector. He was a lay-reader, and officiated upon occasions of "clerical sore-throat," as the profane denominate the ministerial summer exodus from heated cities. This summer, however, Mr. Kenyon's own health had succumbed, and he was having a little "sore-throat" in the mountains on his own account. Very devout was Mr. Kenyon. Many people wondered that he had never taken orders. Many people warmly congratulated themselves that he never had; for drier sermons than those he selected were surely never heard, and a shuddering imagination shrinks appalled from the problematic mental drought of his ideal original discourse. But he was an integrant part of St. Martin's; much of his piety, materialized into contributions, was built up in its walls and shone before men in the costliness of its decorations. Indeed, the ancient name had been conferred upon the building as a sort of tribute to Mr. Kenyon's well-known enthusiasm concerning apostolic succession and kindred doctrine.

Dull and dismal was Mr. Kenyon, and therefore it may be considered a little strange that he should be a notable favorite with men. They were of many different types, but with one invariable bond of union: they had all at one time served as soldiers; for the war, now ten years passed by, its bitterness almost forgotten, had left some traces that time can never obliterate. What a friend was the droning old churchman in those days of battle and bloodshed and suffering and death! Not a man sat within the walls of St. Martin's who had not received some signal benefit from the hand stretched forth to impress the claims of certain ante-Augustin British clergy to consideration and credibility; not a man who did not remember stricken fields where a good Samaritan went about under shot and shell, succoring the wounded and comforting the dying; not a man who did not applaud the indomitable spirit and courage that cut his way from surrender and safety, through solid barriers of enemies, to deliver the orders on which the fate of an army depended; not a man whose memory did not harbor fatiguing recollections of long, dull sermons read for the souls' health of the soldiery. And through it all,—by the camp-fires at night, on the long white country-roads in the sunshiny mornings; in the mountains and the morasses; in hilarious advance and in cheerless retreat; in the heats of summer and by the side of frozen rivers, the ancient British clergy went through it all. And, whether the old churchman's premises and reasoning were false, whether his tracings of the succession were faulty, whether he dropped a link here or took in one there, he had caught the spirit of those staunch old martyrs, if not their falling churchly mantle.

The mountaineers about the New Helvetia Springs supposed that Mr. Kenyon was a regularly ordained preacher, and that the sermons which they had heard him read were, to use the vernacular, out of his own head. For many of them were accustomed on Sunday mornings to occupy humble back benches in the ball-room, where on week-day evenings the butterflies sojourning at New Helvetia danced, and on the Sabbath metaphorically beat their breasts, and literally avowed that they were "miserable sinners," following Mr. Kenyon's lugubrious lead.

The conclusion of the mountaineers was not unnatural, therefore, and when the door of Mr. Harrison's house opened and another uninvited guest entered, the music suddenly ceased. The half-closed eyes of the fiddler had fallen upon Mr. Kenyon at the threshold, and, supposing him a clergyman, he immediately imagined that the man of God had come all the way from New Helvetia Springs to stop the dancing and snatch the revelers from the jaws of hell. The rapturous bow paused shuddering on the string, the dancing feet were palsied, the pious about the walls were racking their slow brains to excuse their apparent conniving at sin and bargaining with Satan, and Mr. Harrison felt that this was indeed an unlucky party and it would undoubtedly be dispersed by the direct interposition of Providence before the shed-room was opened and the supper eaten. As to his soul—poor man! these constantly recurring social anxieties were making him callous to immortality; this life was about to prove too much for him, for the fortitude and tact even of a father of four marriageable young ladies has a limit. Mr. Kenyon, too, seemed dumb as he hesitated in the door-way, but when the host, partially recovering himself, came forward and offered a chair, he said with one of his dismal smiles that he hoped Mr. Harrison had no objection to his coming in and looking at the dancing for a while. "Don't let me interrupt the young people, I beg," he added, as he seated himself. The astounded silence was unbroken for a few moments. To be sure he was not a circuit-rider, but even the sophistication of Cheatham's Cross-Roads had never heard of a preacher who did not object to dancing. Mr. Harrison could not believe his ears, and asked for a more explicit expression of opinion.

"Ye say ye don't keer ef the boys an' gals dance?" he inquired. "Ye don't think it's sinful?"

And after Mr. Kenyon's reply, in which the astonished "mounting folks" caught only the surprising statement that dancing if properly conducted was an innocent, cheerful, and healthful amusement, supplemented by something about dancing in the fear of the Lord, and that in all charity he was disposed to consider objections to such harmless recreations a tithing of mint and anise and cummin, whereby might ensue a neglect of weightier matters of the law; that clean hands and clean hearts—hands clean of blood and ill-begotten goods, and hearts free from falsehood and cruel intention —these were the things well-pleasing to God,—after his somewhat prolix reply, the gayety recommenced. The fiddle quavered tremulously at first, but soon resounded with its former vigorous tones, and the joy of the dance was again exemplified in the grave joggling back and forth.

Meanwhile Mr. Harrison sat beside his strange new guest and asked him questions concerning his church, being instantly, it is needless to say, informed of its great antiquity, of the journeying of St. Augustin and his Forty Monks to Britain, of the church they found already planted there, of its retreat to the hills of Wales under its oppressors' tyranny, of many cognate themes, side issues of the main branch of the subject, into which the talk naturally drifted, the like of which Mr. Harrison had never heard in all his days. And as he watched the figures dancing to the violin's strains, and beheld as in a mental vision the solemn gyrations of those renowned Forty Monks to the monotone of old Mr. Kenyon's voice, he abstractedly hoped that the double dance would continue without interference till a peaceable dawn.

His hopes were vain. It so chanced that Kossuth Johns, who had by no means relinquished all idea of dancing at Harrison's Cove and defying Rick Pearson, had hitherto been detained by his mother's persistent entreaties, some necessary attentions to his father, and the many trials which beset a man dressing for a party who has very few clothes, and those very old and worn. Jule, his sister-in-law, had been most kind and complaisant, putting on a button here, sewing up a slit there, darning a refractory elbow, and lending him the one bright ribbon she possessed as a neck-tie. But all these things take time, and the moon did not light Kossuth down the gorge until she was shining almost vertically from the sky, and the Harrison Cove people and the Forty Monks were dancing together in high feather. The ecclesiastic dance halted suddenly, and a watchful light gleamed in old Mr. Kenyon's eyes as he became silent and the boy stepped into the room. The moonlight and the lamp-light fell mingled on the calm, inexpressive features and tall, slender form of the young mountaineer. "Hy're, Kossute!" A cheerful greeting from many voices met him. The next moment the music ceased once again, and the dancing came to a stand-still, for as the name fell on Pearson's ear he turned, glanced sharply toward the door, and drawing one of his pistols from his belt advanced to the middle of the room. The men fell back; so did the frightened women, without screaming, however, for that indication of feminine sensibility had not yet penetrated to Cheatham's Cross-Roads, to say nothing of the mountains.

"I told ye that ye war n't ter come hyar," said Rick Pearson imperiously, "and ye've got ter go home ter yer mammy right off, or ye'll never git thar no more, youngster."

"I've come hyar ter put *you* out, ye cussed red-headed horse thief!" retorted Kossuth, angrily; "ye hed better tell me whar that thar bay filly is, or light out, one."

It is not the habit in the mountains to parley long on these occasions. Kossuth had raised his gun to his shoulder as Rick, with his pistol cocked, advanced a step nearer. The outlaw's weapon was struck upward by a quick, strong hand, the little log cabin was filled with flash, roar, and smoke, and the stars looked in through a hole in the roof from which Rick's bullet had sent the shingles flying. He turned in mortal terror and caught the hand that had struck his pistol,—in mortal terror, for Kossuth was the crack shot of the mountains and he felt he was a dead man. The room was somewhat obscured by smoke, but as he turned upon the man who had disarmed him, for the force of the blow had thrown the pistol to the floor, he saw that the other hand was over the muzzle of young Johns's gun, and Kossuth was swearing loudly that by the Lord Almighty if he did n't take it off he would shoot it off.

"My young friend," Mr. Kenyon began, with the calmness appropriate to a devout member of the one catholic and apostolic church; but then, the old Adam suddenly getting the upper-hand, he shouted in irate tones, "If you don't stop that noise, I'll break your head! Well, Mr. Pearson," he continued, as he stood between the combatants, one hand still over the muzzle of young Johns's gun, the other, lean and sinewy, holding Pearson's powerful right arm with a vise-like

MARY N. MURFREE 151

grip, "well, Mr. Pearson, you are not so good a soldier as you used to be; you did n't fight boys in the old times."

Rick Pearson's enraged expression suddenly gave way to a surprised recognition. "Ye may drag me through hell an' beat me with a sootbag ef hyar ain't the old fightin' preacher agin!" he cried.

"I have only one thing to say to you," said Mr. Kenyon. "You must go. I will not have you here shooting boys and breaking up a party."

Rick demurred. "See hyar, now," he said, "ye've got no business meddlin'."

"You must go," Mr. Kenyon reiterated.

"Preachin's yer business," Rick continued; " 'pears like ye don't 'tend to it, though."

"You must go."

"S'pose I say I won't," said Rick, good-humoredly; "I s'pose ye'd say ye'd make me."

"You must go," repeated Mr. Kenyon. "I am going to take the boy home with me, but I intend to see you off first."

Mr. Kenyon had prevented the hot-headed Kossuth from firing by keeping his hand persistently over the muzzle of the gun; and young Johns had feared to try to wrench it away lest it should discharge in the effort. Had it done so, Mr. Kenyon would have been in sweet converse with the Forty Monks in about a minute and a quarter. Kossuth had finally let go the gun, and made frantic attempts to borrow a weapon from some of his friends, but the stern authoritative mandate of the belligerent peace-maker had prevented them from gratifying him, and he now stood empty-handed beside Mr. Kenyon, who had shouldered the old rifle in an absent-minded manner, although still retaining his powerful grasp on the arm of the outlaw.

"Waal, parson," said Rick at length, "I'll go, jest ter please you-uns. Ye see, I ain't forgot Shiloh."

"I am not talking about Shiloh now," said the old man.

"You must get off at once,—all of you," indicating the gang, who had been so whelmed in astonishment that they had not lifted a finger to aid their chief.

"Ye say ye'll take that—that"—Rick looked hard at Kossuth while he racked his brains for an injurious epithet—"that sassy child home ter his mammy?"

"Come, I am tired of this talk," said Mr. Kenyon; "you must go."

Rick walked heavily to the door and out into the moonlight. "Them was good old times," he said to Mr. Kenyon, with a regretful cadence in his peculiar drawl; "good old times, them War days. I wish they was back agin,—I wish they was back agin. I ain't forgot Shiloh yit, though, and I ain't a-goin' ter. But I'll tell ye one thing, parson," he added, his mind reverting from ten years ago to the scene just past, as he unhitched his horse and carefully examined the saddle-girth and stirrups, "ye're a mighty queer preacher, ye air, a-sittin' up an' lookin' at sinners dance an' then gittin' in a fight that don't consarn ye,—ye're a mighty queer preacher! Ye ought ter be in my gang, that's whar *ye* ought ter be," he exclaimed with a guffaw, as he put his foot in the stirrup; "ye've got a damned deal too much grit fur a preacher. But I ain't forgot Shiloh yit, an' I don't mean ter, nuther."

A shout of laughter from the gang, an oath or two, the quick tread of horses' hoofs pressing into a gallop, and the outlaw's troop were speeding along the narrow paths that led deep into the vistas of the moonlit summer woods.

As the old churchman, with the boy at his side and the gun still on his shoulder, ascended the rocky, precipitous slope on the opposite side of the ravine above the foaming waters of the wild mountain stream, he said but little of admonition to his companion; with the disappearance of the flame and smoke and the dangerous ruffian his martial spirit had cooled; the last words of the outlaw, the highest praise Rick Pearson could accord to the highest qualities

Rick Pearson could imagine—he had grit enough to belong to the gang—had smitten a tender conscience. He, at this age, using none of the means rightfully at his command, the gentle suasion of religion, must needs rush between armed men, wrench their weapons from their hands, threatening with such violence that an outlaw and desperado, recognizing a parallel of his own belligerent and lawless spirit, should say that he ought to belong to the gang! And the heaviest scourge of this sin-laden conscience was the perception that, so far as the unsubdued old Adam went, he ought indeed.

He was not so tortured, though, that he did not think of others. He paused on reaching the summit of the ascent, and looked back at the little house nestling in the ravine, the lamp-light streaming through its open doors and windows across the path among the laurel bushes, where Rick's gang had hitched their horses.

"I wonder," said the old man, "if they are quiet and peaceable again; can you hear the music and dancing?"

"Not now," said Kossuth. Then, after a moment, "Now I kin," he added, as the wind brought to their ears the oft-told tale of the rabbit's gallopade in the pea-patch. "They're a-dancin' now, and all right agin."

As they walked along, Mr. Kenyon's racked conscience might have been in a slight degree comforted had he known that he was in some sort a revelation to the impressible lad at his side, that Kossuth had begun dimly to comprehend that a Christian may be a man of spirit also, and that bravado does not constitute bravery. Now that the heat of anger was over, the young fellow was glad that the fearless interposition of the warlike peacemaker had prevented any killing, "'kase ef the old man hed n't hung on ter my gun like he done, I'd have been a murderer like he said, an' Rick would hev been dead. An' the bay filly ain't sech a killin' matter nohow; ef it war the roan three-year-old now, 't would be different." (1878, 1884)

JOHN FOX, JR.

John Fox, Jr. was born in 1862 in Paris, Kentucky. After attending Transylvania College for two years, he transferred to Harvard, graduating in 1883. He later worked as a reporter for the *New York Sun*, attended law school at Columbia University, and in 1887 went into the mining business at Big Stone Gap, Virginia. He served briefly with Theodore Roosevelt as a Rough Rider and covered the Russo-Japanese War as a war correspondent for *Scribner's*. He gained national fame with his stories of the Kentucky mountaineers, particularly *The Little Shepherd of Kingdom Come* and *The Trail of the Lonesome Pine*. He died in 1919 of pneumonia contracted on a fishing trip in the mountains.

Students of regional literature have noted Fox's faithfulness to descriptive detail but at the same time his pervading sentimentality which has become a trademark of his fiction. "Christmas Eve on Lonesome," from a collection by the same title, is exemplary.

Christmas Eve on Lonesome

It was Christmas Eve on Lonesome. But nobody on Lonesome knew that it was Christmas Eve, although a child of the outer world could have guessed it, even out in those wilds where Lonesome slipped from one lone log-cabin high up the steeps, down through a stretch of jungled darkness to another lone cabin at the mouth of the stream.

There was the holy hush in the gray twilight that comes only on Christmas Eve. There were the big flakes of snow that fell as they never fall except on Christmas Eve. There was a snowy man on horseback in a big coat, and with saddle-pockets that might have been bursting with toys for children in the little cabin at the head of the stream.

But not even he knew that it was Christmas Eve. He was thinking of Christmas Eve, but it was of Christmas Eve of the year before, when he sat in prison with a hundred other men in stripes, and listened to the chaplain talk of peace and good-will to all men upon earth, when he had forgotten all men upon earth but one, and had only hatred in his heart for him.

"Vengeance is mine!" saith the Lord.

That was what the chaplain had thundered at him. And then, as now, he thought of the enemy who had betrayed him to the law, and had sworn away his liberty, and had robbed him of everything in life except a fierce longing for the day when he could strike back and strike to kill. And then, while he looked back hard into the chaplain's eyes, and now, while he splashed through the yellow mud thinking of that Christmas Eve, Buck shook his head; and then, as now, his sullen heart answered:

"Mine!"

The big flakes drifted to crotch and twig and limb. They gathered on the brim of Buck's slouch hat, filled out the wrinkles in his big coat, whitened his hair and his long mustache, and sifted into the yellow, twisting path that guided his horse's feet.

High above he could see through the whirling of snow now and then the gleam of a red star. He knew it was the light from his enemy's window; but somehow the chaplain's voice kept ringing in his ears, and every time he saw the light he

couldn't help thinking of the story of the Star that the chaplain told that Christmas Eve, and he dropped his eyes by and
by, so as not to see it again, and rode on until the light shone
in his face.

Then he led his horse up a little ravine and hitched it
among the snowy holly and rhododendrons, and slipped
toward the light. There was a dog somewhere, of course; and
like a thief he climbed over the low rail-fence and stole
through the tall snow-wet grass until he leaned against an
apple-tree with the sill of the window two feet above the
level of his eyes.

Reaching above him, he caught a stout limb and dragged
himself up to a crotch of the tree. A mass of snow slipped
softly to the earth. The branch creaked above the light wind;
around the corner of the house a dog growled and he sat still.

He had waited three long years and he had ridden two
hard nights and lain out two cold days in the woods for this.

And presently he reached out very carefully, and noiselessly broke leaf and branch and twig until a passage was
cleared for his eye and for the point of the pistol that was
gripped in his right hand.

A woman was just disappearing through the kitchen door,
and he peered cautiously and saw nothing but darting shadows. From one corner a shadow loomed suddenly out in
human shape. Buck saw the shadowed gesture of an arm,
and he cocked his pistol. The shadow was his man, and in a
moment he would be in a chair in the chimney-corner to
smoke his pipe, maybe—his last pipe.

Buck smiled—pure hatred made him smile—but it was
mean, a mean and sorry thing to shoot this man in the back,
dog though he was; and now that the moment had come a
wave of sickening shame ran through Buck. No one of his
name had ever done that before; but this man and his people
had, and with their own lips they had framed palliation for
him. What was fair for one was fair for the other, they always

said. A poor man couldn't fight money in the courts; and so they had shot from the brush, and that was why they were rich now and Buck was poor—why his enemy was safe at home, and he was out here, homeless, in the apple-tree.

Buck thought of all this, but it was no use. The shadow slouched suddenly and disappeared; and Buck was glad. With a gritting oath between his chattering teeth he pulled his pistol in and thrust one leg down to swing from the tree —he would meet him face to face next day and kill him like a man—and there he hung as rigid as though the cold had suddenly turned him, blood, bones, and marrow, into ice.

The door had opened, and full in the firelight stood the girl who he had heard was dead. He knew now how and why that word was sent him. And now she who had been his sweetheart stood before him—the wife of the man he meant to kill.

Her lips moved—he thought he could tell what she said: "Git up, Jim, git up!" Then she went back.

A flame flared up within him now that must have come straight from the devil's forge. Again the shadows played over the ceiling. His teeth grated as he cocked his pistol, and pointed it down the beam of light that shot into the heart of the apple-tree, and waited.

The shadow of a head shot along the rafters and over the fireplace. It was a madman clutching the butt of the pistol now, and as his eye caught the glinting sight and his heart thumped, there stepped into the square light of the window —a child!

It was a boy with yellow tumbled hair, and he had a puppy in his arms. In front of the fire the little fellow dropped the dog, and they began to play.

"Yap! yap! yap!"

Buck could hear the shrill barking of the fat little dog, and the joyous shrieks of the child as he made his playfellow chase his tail round and round or tumbled him head over heels on the floor. It was the first child Buck had seen for three years; it was *his* child and *hers*; and, in the apple-tree, Buck watched fixedly.

They were down on the floor now, rolling over and over together; and he watched them until the child grew tired and turned his face to the fire and lay still—looking into it. Buck would see his eyes close presently, and then the puppy crept closer, put his head on his playmate's chest, and the two lay thus asleep.

And still Buck looked—his clasp loosening on his pistol and his lips loosening under his stiff mustache—and kept looking until the door opened again and the woman crossed the floor. A flood of light flashed suddenly on the snow, barely touching the snow-hung tips of the apple-tree, and he saw her in the doorway—saw her look anxiously into the darkness—look and listen a long while.

Buck dropped noiselessly to the snow when she closed the door. He wondered what they would think when they saw his tracks in the snow next morning; and then he realized that they would be covered before morning.

As he started up the ravine where his horse was he heard the clink of metal down the road and the splash of a horse's hoofs in the soft mud, and he sank down behind a holly-bush.

Again the light from the cabin flashed out on the snow.

"That you, Jim?"

"Yep!"

And then the child's voice: "Has oo dot thum tandy?"

"Yep!"

The cheery answer rang out almost at Buck's ear, and Jim passed death waiting for him behind the bush which his left foot brushed, shaking the snow from the red berries down on the crouching figure beneath.

Once only, far down the dark jungled way, with the underlying streak of yellow that was leading him whither, God only knew—once only Buck looked back. There was the red light gleaming faintly through the moonlit flakes of snow.

Once more he thought of the Star, and once more the chaplain's voice came back to him.

"Mine!" saith the Lord.

Just how, Buck could not see, with himself in the snow and *him* back there for life with her and the child, but some strange impulse made him bare his head.

"Yourn," said Buck grimly.

But nobody on Lonesome—not even Buck—knew that it was Christmas Eve. (1904)

V. *New Dimensions of Realism: Renaissance in the Hills*

In the first third of the twentieth century reaction was sharp against the local color tradition, and the author most singled out for criticism was John Fox, Jr. Thomas Wolfe in a letter to his mother in 1921, Sherwood Anderson in his moonshining novel *Kit Brandon* in 1936, and minor novelist and business woman Anne W. Armstrong in a critical article all lamented romantic fiction *à la* Fox. Writing in the *Yale Review* in 1935, Mrs. Armstrong expressed a common sentiment among the small group of modern writers who saw the mountaineer in a manner entirely different from that of Fox and Murfree, ". . . if the mountaineers of John Fox, Jr. ever existed in fact, which I seriously doubt—mountaineers whose vices were only the picturesque, never the odious, to say nothing of the unmentionable ones—they do not exist now. I see no reason why we should go on glossing over the defects of the present-day Southern mountaineer. These vital, highly intelligent fellow countrymen are entirely able to stand the fullest light that can be turned upon them. When all their defects are revealed, they still retain characteristics which the rest of us will do well to examine." In her own novel, *This Day and Time* (1930), which according to the late John M. Bradbury added a "new dimension to the realism of mountain fiction," Mrs. Armstrong had revealed the full range of "unmentionables," including incest; but when all is taken into account, the virtues of the mountain people, especially those seen in the heroic Ivy Ingoldsby, do indeed outweigh their many human faults. The same can be said for the mountain characters of Wolfe as well as for those of Anderson. Another story in this section, "Sairy and the Young'uns" by Beulah Childers, reflects not only the new found honesty characteristic of the new writing (for Appalachia) but also the new concern with style and art.

ANNE W. ARMSTRONG

Anne Wetzell Armstrong was born in Grand Rapids, Michigan in 1872. When she was quite young, the Wetzells moved to Knoxville, which provides part of the setting for her first novel, *The Seas of God* (1915). She attended Mount Holyoke College and the University of Chicago and near the end of World War I served as assistant manager of industrial relations for Eastman Kodak and became the first woman to lecture before the Harvard School of Business. In the twenties she retired to the Big Creek Section of Sullivan County, Tennessee where she wrote *This Day and Time* (1930) and where she lived until forced to move by the completion of the South Holston Dam. A friend of Thomas Wolfe, who visited her at Big Creek, she published articles in practically every major American periodical on subjects from cooking to women in business. She died in 1958 at the Barter Inn in Abingdon, Virginia.

This Day and Time is a novel about Ivy Ingoldsby, who has been deserted by her husband and left with her young son in the mountains of East Tennessee to fend for herself. Her struggle to endure is both realistic and heroic. The following chapter depicts some of the difficulties with which Ivy contends in the pre-TVA society. Mr. Pemberton and Shirley are aristocratic summer visitors to the mountains, and

Doak Odom is one of Ivy's neighbors. The title for this incident has been supplied. A discussion of the language in this novel is contained in the essay by Earl Schrock in Part II of the present collection.

The Cow in the Corn

The money Ivy was saving had grown into quite a little horde. Friends of Shirley or her father who stayed at the cottage over Sunday had given her money on their departure, unexpected gifts that filled her with joy and excitement—"tips" Shirley called them. Once she had made fried pies, to surprise Mr. Pemberton, and although, to her distress, he had barely tasted one, he had expressed his pleasure by a five-dollar bill.

Every evening when Ivy returned to her cabin, she looked to see if the money she had hidden was still there.

She began to think of ways to expend this money, ways outside of the bare necessities of life. She thought of a clock. Uncle Jake's clock had stopped running long since, and it was hard to judge time entirely by the light, especially on cloudy mornings. She thought of a rocking-chair. And more and more she thought of having her teeth filled. Maybe she could even afford a gold tooth, such as she had seen in the mouths of mountain folks who had moved to Montana or California and come back on a visit, "rich," from picking oranges or herding sheep. "I reckon them gold teeth is expensive," she thought, a trifle recklessly, "but ef money won't buy what a feller wants, what's money fer?"

The midsummer heat had come. Ivy was working hard. But her step was quick and light. On the whole, she was getting along better than she had ever done before.

Almost her only fret at present was Doke's cow. Sometimes she was late in the mornings now, because she had had to mend her garden-fence again before leaving home, or make her garden-gate more secure. "But a body cain't bar agin a cow like that to do no good," she would explain to Shirley. "She kin lift a gate same as a person. She's nothin' but a aggravation, her a-eatin' all my cabbages, an' she won't be nothin' else long as the breath o' life is in her."

"I tell ye," she would complain angrily to Old Mag or Mrs. Philips, "I tell ye, ef I had me a gun, I 'ud as leave to shoot the sorry old critter as no, me a-workin' hard the endurin' day, an' a sight to do atter I gits home of a night, me a-needin' my sleep, an' then a-havin' to git up from the bed an' run her off! Of course, Doke hain't got no chancet to keep his critters up. He's done burnt all his fence-rails fer firewood. I tell ye, folks, there hain't nothin' a man won't do where burns his fence-rails. But Doke, he's got to do somethin' about that old cow o' hisn. I 'ud put the law on him, I 'ud take a writ, on'y I'm afeared he 'ud witch Enoch or burn me down. I do know Doke Odum is the aggravatin'est man on earth—I won't except none!"

One morning she found that Doke's cow had broken into her corn-field, ravaging the whole small patch. She set out Enoch's breakfast, but she could not eat her own. Bowing her head on the table, she wept bitterly. It was true, she was saving enough money so that she could buy what corn she should need for bread and to feed her chickens through the coming year. But she saw only one thing now—her corn was ruined. Corn meant bread. Corn meant life. Nothing must happen to corn.

Shirley's efforts to console her were of little avail. She asked to go home early. It was hardly later than mid-afternoon when she approached Doke's cabin, still seething with indignation, hot from her long walk in the July sun, and heavily laden with packages, food and other things that Shirley had insisted she take home. She was wearing some new low-cut shoes that she had sent to town for by Uncle Abel, and a dress that had been Shirley's, a cotton print of delicate design, but gay coloring. "I'm afeard you cain't spare hit,"

Ivy had protested, her heart beating high, when Shirley had given her the dress a day or so before.

Doke and Leola were in their yard, bending over a bed-stead they had taken apart and brought outside. Some dirty patchwork quilts hung over the fence, and several badly discolored ticks, with wisps of straw protruding through them. The children were standing around, one of the little girls holding the baby. The hounds, running out from underneath the cabin began to bay, and Doke turned his head.

"Ivy," he greeted her with a good-natured shout, "the chinches has about driv' us out o' the house. Doggone ef they hain't!"

Ivy had stopped outside the gate, resting her packages against it. "Doke," she called back, "you 'ull have to do somethin' about your old cow, an' not be long about hit."

Doke resumed his examination of the greasy wooden bed-stead. After a moment or so he started down towards the gate, unhurryingly, his ragged overalls flopping around his bony legs, the children following at a distance, "Lord, Ivy, you hain't a-stoppin' jest to rare on me, are ye, jest to bless me out? Why, a feller don't see nothin' of ye sence ye heels hit by so fast of a mornin' an' of a evenin', both."

"Doke, I'm plumb wore out! She's et up the last blade o' corn I've got. I had the beautifulest bean-vines in the corn, jest a-startin' nice, an' them all tromped down too"—Ivy was almost crying with vexation. "I've been a-tellin' ye, Doke, an' now she's ruint my patch."

Doke's black eyes were roving over Ivy from head to foot. "Ivy, I hain't never saw ye so fine."

"Doke, you needn't to put me off with sech as that."

"Ivy, what you a-gittin' red as a beet fer?"

"Hesh your mouth, Doke! An' I wisht you'd keep them old bold eyes o' yourn where they belongs, they're bold as a mink's."

Doke ran his hand through his big head of bushy black hair, lazily. "Ivy, you must be a-wantin' a man!"

"Well, hit hain't you!" she blazed out.

"By God, no!" He added something half under his breath, while his eyes continued to travel up and down Ivy's sturdy though not ungraceful figure, from her new shoes and the silk stockings Shirley had given her to her hair, still brushed back smoothly from her low brow and coiled at the nape of her neck, but arranged, in imitation of Shirley's, a little differently from the way she had worn it before.

"Ivy"—a smile curled slowly around Doke's thick lips, vivid as blood under his bushy black mustache—"Ivy, you hain't heern nothin' from Jim, have ye? I 'lowed maybe you was a-lookin' fer Jim in all them fine clothes."

In sudden fury Ivy dropped her packages, shaking her fist in his face. "Doke Odum, I 'ud like to knock out every brain in your head! I 'ull thank ye to mind your own business, you a-throwin' up Jim! I don't never want to lay eyes on Jim Ingoldsby agin long as blood warms my body."

"Oh, ye don't, don't ye?" Doke looked at her searchingly.

"Doke Odum, don't never on earth name sech as that to me agin!"

"I reckon, Ivy," Doke said, after a pause, "them fine clothes must be some of hern—"

"Hern—" Ivy glared.

"—Some of hern she hain't no use fer, that girl you're niggerin' fer."

A choking sound issued from Ivy's throat.

"By Jesus, she don't need much o' none! I seen her in her canoe, hit were day afore yesterday, an' her naked, what you might say."

"You know good an' well, Doke Odum," Ivy shouted, her voice shaking, "them bathin'-suits like hern is all the style. The girls is all a-wearin' 'em this day an' time."

"Oh, I don't reckon Shirley Pemberton is no different, Ivy, from the rest of them town whores."

"Doke," Ivy screamed, stamping her foot now in impotent rage, "Doke," she panted, "ef hit's the last word I say on earth,

I 'ull—" She stopped, in sudden fright at the threat she was about to utter.

"I've fotched a many a gallon o' liquor," Doke went on imperturbably, "to them summer people, to them big rich folks from town. There's cottages I've went to, of a night, an' found 'em a-dancin' to a victroly, an' not a stitch o' clothin' on their naked bodies, bathin'-suits or nothin', on'y their nastiness—men an' women both."

Ivy's eyes started from her head. "Doke—!" The nails of her clenched hands cut into her palms. "Doke—!" she screamed. The children had backed away in fright. Leola came towards them.

"Doke, I've a notion to kill ye!" Ivy cried. "I've a notion to kill ye, you low-down—" A filthy epithet trembled on her lips, but she held it back. "Doke, don't never agin blackguard Shirley Pemberton in my hearin'!" Dry sobs had broken from her, between her panting breaths. "She don't have nothin' to do with them other summer people—an' you knows hit— more 'an to speak."

Leola, in her dark calico wrapper, stiff with soil, had stood by inertly, her white moon-shaped face, her soft dark eyes, alike expressionless. "Ivy," she said now, in a brief lull that had come, "I wouldn't take on so. Doke is on'y a-funnin'. He's on'y a-bein' mean."

Ivy made no answer. She darted another look at Doke, who, with his head turned away, had lifted a chunk of wood, laying it across the chopping-block under an apple-tree near the gate. "Doke, you hain't fitten to take the name o' sech as Shirley Pemberton on them foul lips o' yourn!" She was still half sobbing. "Looks like you delight, Doke Odum, in mouthin' harm words agin folks where's decent."

"I say decent!" Doke gave a guffaw. He picked up his ax and began chopping. "You hain't a-talkin' about Shirley Pemberton's pap, are ye? I reckon," he sneered, between strokes with his ax, "the old man hain't got past scramblin' up to his camp of a day, has he?"

Ivy pretended not to hear. She could feel her fingers, like ice, as they came into contact with each other tremblingly gathering together her packages.

"I reckon old man Pemberton is still a-whorin', hain't he?"

"Doke, don't you start nothin' like that agin! I've tried to live peaceable with you an' yourn. I've took a heap. But I tell ye now, I hain't a-goin' to stand fer you a-blackguardin' the best friends ever I had."

Doke brought his ax up again. "Why, Lord God, Ivy, there hain't a soul in the country where don't know all about old man Pemberton."

Ivy said nothing. She could feel herself shaking from head to foot.

"Nan Buskill, she's up at the camp, jest where she's stayed sence way back yonder in loggin' days. Hit's over Nan that old man Jesse an' his woman, they fallen out. Nan Buskill, she's the cause o' Mis' Pemberton not a-comin' here of a summer no more. Mis' Pemberton, she's jealous-hearted, I reckon."

Leola turned her soft dark eyes towards Ivy. A faint smile crept across her face. "Mis' Pemberton orter married the Scrapin's o' the earth, like I done," she interposed in her list-less manner, nodding towards Doke; "then she wouldn't never 'a been jealous."

Doke threw back his head, laughing uproariously. "Leoly, I wouldn't take nothin' on earth fer you!"

"You hain't good enough, Doke Odum," Ivy muttered, white-faced and still shaking "—you hain't good enough fer me to nasty my hands a-killin' ye!" She started up the path towards the road.

"Ivy," Leola called after her, gently yet detainingly, "you're a-gittin' fat as a bear. Looks like them Pembertons must be a-feedin' ye good!"

"I'm a-gittin' plenty.—Doke, I hain't a-goin' to name hit to ye agin about that cow o' yourn." Ivy stood in the road, pausing before she turned towards home. "I don't want to have no racket with ye, but I hain't a-goin' to be wearied by your old cow no more. She'd done ruint my corn, but ef she breaks in my garden agin, I 'ull have ye indicted, shore as the jedgment day's a-comin'."

"There hain't a-goin' to be no next time," Doke called back, "an', Ivy, I 'ull pay ye fer every God-damned copper o' damage my cow has done ye."

"Keep them promises o' yourn to home," Ivy returned scornfully. "I don't think nothin' of 'em." (1930, 1970)

BEULAH R. CHILDERS

Beulah Childers is a native of Berea, Kentucky, where her family has long been connected with Berea College. She was graduated from the College and received a Master's degree from Columbia University. She taught as a visiting professor at Purdue and the University of Oregon, and has alternated between living in New York City and the mountain area of Kentucky. "Sairy and the Young'uns" is a finely polished story told with insight and humorous affection. It has, to use William Dean Howells' phrase, "the stamp of verity."

Sairy and the Young'uns

Early a-Friday morning, when Bett threw the wash water from the breakfast dishes out the back door, her eyes ran the curving length of the road as far as she could see, from a little to one side of the front gate, which was not visible, into the slatey bed of the creek and out again, hindered here by a clump of willows, there skirting the sloping pasture, to the place about a quarter of a mile away where it ascended a low rise against a mountain and disappeared in the direction of Preacher Jed Pendergrast's. It was the road that led, eventually, to the land beyond the hill-country, which she had once seen; and whatever the Hales got that the hill-country itself did not yield to them, must come this way.

There was no sign of life on the road; for Bett, no sign of any living thing in the valley. A horse cropped grass by the creek, a few cows grazed in the pasture, a gray hawk swooped and circled above the willows in ominous silence, but these were transformed by her mood and partook of the unreality of the hour, so that they seemed to be of a sameness with the clouded mountain top, their movements no more animated than those of the mist that rose and shifted over the trees. They were but parts of a meaningless and insensible landscape on which the road was a crooked, empty vessel with open mouth held up to the horizon, waiting to be filled.

To be filled with what? She did not know; she could not tell, exactly. Her vague, half-fashioned hopes were just for something different, out of the ordinary, contradictory even, whose presence (like salt in butter, fire in the parlor, or an anguished lover in a song) would quicken the valley and lend significance to the hills; would thereby give to her own existence the tang, the spice, the flavor now wholly lacking. The road, she felt, was at once an evidence of incompletion and a promise that all might be fulfilled. She fixed her eyes on the intervening ridges as though they deliberately withheld from her that last indefinite something that was her due, and that they might, by the very intensity of her gaze, be compelled to relinquish.

"Ruth!" she called in a sudden flurry. "Ruth! Come out hyer a minute."

Her sister came and stood in the doorway behind her: "Well, what on earth?"

"I just wish to goodness you'd look an' tell me—who is that a-comin' yonder, over the rise?" Bett asked the question as though she wanted (but hardly expected) to hear another answer than the one she had already shaped for herself.

Moving forms, small with distance, had appeared on the brow of the hill and were now descending in a slow straggling line that expanded and contracted like an accordion played by a lazy man in the heat of the day. There was a fascinating quality in this motion, which was natural and haphazard and yet seemed to have an underlying plan; a suggestion of the inevitable in the patient, unhurried manner of their drawing near that made it akin to the approach of night or the coming of the seasons, which could not be stayed nor made to hasten.

There must have been eight or ten of them at least, and as in a row of wind-sown plants, no two were the same height, the last being taller than any of the others. They were still too far away to be recognized by their features, but Ruth had seen them thus too many times not to know, unmistakably, who they were.

"The Lord ha' mercy!" she groaned. "The Lord ha' mercy if it ain't Sairy Pendergrast as shore as I'm a-livin'. Esther, prepare yoreself; hyer comes Sairy an' the young'uns to spend the day."

Above, on the narrow landing of the outside stairway, Esther was putting quilts to air, hanging them over the railing evenly, so that the dark brilliance of their raw blues and reds and yellows made a neat horizontal pattern against the white clapboards of the house. She studied the road from under the striped shadow of her fingers; getting a bonnet of clean checked percale from a nail on the back porch, she came and stood beside them in the sun.

"Don't she look more like an old Dominecker hen with a brood o' roupy chicks!"

"Why, they're bound to a-slept in their clothes an' a-started before it was purely daybreak."

"Well, don't they always get hyer before the beds are made, an' stay till we're mighty nigh ready to turn 'em down again? Mark my words, they'll have Aunt Cory or somebody bespoken to do their milkin' for 'em, so they can wait long enough that we'll be obliged to offer 'em supper before they go."

"An' us with all them berries to put up," Ruth complained. "You can count on it as sure as summer, an' I never yet knowed it to fail; just let us have an extry big day's work ahead of us that cain't hardly be left over, then Sairy an' the young'uns are bound to come a-meachin' across that hill. Well, it's no earthly use a-startin' in on the cannin' now, for you shorely cain't do nary a thing with that passel o' brats underfoot, a-stompin' in an' out like a herd o' cattle, an' a-gomin' up everything. Not to mention a-havin' 'em to cook fer." She sighed and turned back toward the kitchen. "Bett, you put the berries in the springhouse in middlin' deep water, an' I reckon they ought to keep over another day. I'll have to go pick a couple o' friers if I can wrest 'em from under Naomy's skirts long enough to wring their necks."

"Well," said Esther, "as many times as I've laid the table for 'em I never can keep track of how many young'uns Sairy's got."

"I don't reckon she knows, herself, for certain," said Bett.

"Let's see now, there's one, two, three, four, five—they shift around till I cain't tell which I've counted an' which I haven't."

"Why don't ye get 'em a-comin' out from behind that bunch o' willows? Two, four, six . . . I see ten, an' the older boys not with 'em."

"Well I see twelve myself."

"Try a-callin' 'em by name. Beginnin' at the top, there's Morg an' Went an' Bev at home—"

"Berthy an' Hass—"

"An' Versie an' Flossie an' Pete an' Lige an' Little Jed."

"An' the one that died o' convulsions."

"An' the Baby makes twelve; that's all. No more than Ma's had, when ye come to consider."

"Well, they shorely do seem like a heap more, the way

they can take the place an' turn it upside down. I swan, Bett, I don't see Berthy nowheres; do you reckon she could a-stayed at home?"

"Not likely. Why, there's Lizzie; we forgot her. She makes thirteen."

"An' how about Versie? Whur does she come in?"

"We counted her once a-ready."

"No we didn't."

"I know we did!"

"Well, numberin' 'em won't make 'em no less nor no easier to manage," said Ruth from the window. "An' if I was you girls, I'd quit a-standin' there a-arguin' over nothin' an' run an' put all my good things out o' sight. You moaned for a week last time because they got into yore talcum powders an' spilled 'em. Well, 'pon my honor, Bett Hale, if you don't beat ever'thing! Hyer I been a-huntin' all over creation fer that dishpan to cut up my chickens in, an' you a-standin' right there all the time, a-dawdlin' around with it. I'm plumb put out!"

Naomy, picking beans in the garden, bending over and gathering the long green fingers of the bean vine into her own and heaping them in her lifted apron until it was pregnant, until she looked like a fruitful woman ready to bear, lifted her head at the sound of a joyful cry and saw that Sairy and the young'uns were coming up the lane. To the eager delighted signals of Versie and Flossie and Pete and Lige, she replied without reservation in the same language, her utterance marked by the same convivial accents.

How like Preacher Jed the children were, as though he had stood at the head of a hollow and shouted his own name, to have it echoed back to him from many distances, blurred, and a little twisted, but still more his name than any other. Naomy had never cared much for the Preacher. Her distaste was instinctive, her recoil from his domineering ways something she could not help, which made it seem all the more unaccountable that one of the things that endeared the young'uns to her was their resemblance to him. But Sairy had been a filter in which his characteristics were purified of all the elements that made them repugnant to her; a water-gate past which a clearer stream flowed on in the old familiar curves. And it drew upon the abundant store of her pity that his lineaments—the insistent arch of his nose, the faltering turn of his chin, the vague compassionless blue of his eyes—should be thus imposed upon the innocent and helpless faces of beings powerless to reject them—unaware, even, that there was in them anything that merited rejection.

For Bett, emerging from the dim cool refuge of the spring-house, the young'uns called to mind nothing that was the least bit pleasant; and Sairy, as she calmly marshalled them toward the house, made her think of a picture of General Braddock before his defeat, in one of the old almanacs in the storeroom closet, so purposeful and confident she was, as though about to move upon a place which she knew was unfortified and could offer no resistance whatever.

The girls were dressed in ugly short-waisted garments of brought-on goods or home-woven linsey, unskilfully cut and badly put together; the boys wore anything from new blue overalls to hand-me-down knee pants, each with its own peculiar history; while the Baby, who was a boy and going on five years old, was still in curls and embroidered petti-coats, trailing a little behind the others and nearest to Sairy.

Sairy herself had on her Sunday best, the stiff black silk with the heavy crocheted collar and the bulging placket in the rear. She had taken off her bonnet of black calico and held it in one hand, fanning briskly as she advanced. With the other she had gathered up the folds of her gored and pleated skirt to save it from the dust, an exaggerated delicacy in the curve of her waist and the spread of her fingers by which she expressed her conception of "Elegance," as the children had been taught at school, when speaking a piece, to show "Dis-dain" by a lifted quivering lip, and "Happiness" by a fixed and determined smile. Above her spare form, the heavy pile of her hair, which had been wound neatly on the very top of her head when she left home, had slipped over to one side and hung there at a rakish angle that contrasted oddly with the mournful droop of her mouth.

As she neared the gate, Mrs. Hale came out on the front porch, slender and white-haired, with soft gray eyes in a delicate face. The moment Sairy caught sight of her, her bearing underwent a sudden and violent change. She was no longer the calm general; she was a devout Holy Roller who had managed to hold herself in check all the way to meeting in order to have more power for her emotional outburst when she got there, but who was now in full view of the congregation and need restrain herself no longer. She gave a little preliminary screech, and pushing past the young'uns, rushed up the path, wailing loudly:

"Oh, Lordy Lordy! Oh, Lordy Lordy!"

Right behind her came Hasseltine, with an air of mingled reverence and concern, for all the young Pendergrasts had been nourished in a deep respect for the condition of Sairy's internal organs, which, it was understood, were so weak and ailing as an unavoidable result of the fact that she was a Mother, that the slightest shock might prove too much for them. In which case the young Pendergrasts would be left Motherless, a state which none of them had ever thought through to any definite mental image, but which, as the theme for a ballad, was always accompanied by such a sorrowful tune that they could hardly hold back the tears when they heard it.

"Now Mammy; now Mammy—now Ma!" said Hasseltine. (She meant to say "Ma" all the time, like the Hale girls did, but forgot when she was excited.) "You'll have the high strikes, a-gittin' yoreself all worked up this-a-way."

The high strikes, probably derived from a mispronunciation of hysterics and meaning the same thing, was Sairy's equivalent to a room of her own into which she would retreat if necessary, but never, as now, when her suffering was so well attended.

"The Lord ha' mercy on my soul!" she cried, in her thin tremulous voice. "I thought fer sartin' my time had come; I 'lowed my heart would shorely give way when Morg broke the news to me like he did, right out of a clear sky, without no warnin'. I doan't see how in this mortal world he ever come to do sich a thing, as good as he knows my condition. Well, I reckon they's nary a doubt I would a-dropped in my tracks if I'd a-been a-standin' up, but I was a-settin' down to grind the breakfast coffee. Lucy, I can tell by yore face that yeou ain't yet hyeared the turrible affliction that's come upon me."

Lucy reached for a split-bottomed chair that leaned against the porch wall, slanting downward to shed the rain, and offered it to Sairy, not in the least put out by her carrying on. Sairy carried on a great deal over one thing and another. Her reaction to any event, however remote from her own way of life, was always of an intensely personal nature. Indeed, it seemed as though no external fact could reach her consciousness without being at once translated into bodily discomfort, and her first concern in any tragedy was not with its immediate consequences, which might be cataclysmic, but with how it affected her, physically, at the moment of hearing it told.

When Gabriel blows his trumpet, thought Lucy, I reckon Sairy'll rise up a-sayin' it give her a pain in her ears.

Now, sinking carefully into the proffered chair so as not to mess her pleats, she took up her weeping again like a piece of embroidery that she had been forced to lay down, temporarily, in order to explain the pattern to a neighbor, but which her mind had kept on working busily all the while. Lucy, who had barely glimpsed a few unrelated stitches, despaired of ever getting the whole design from Sairy.

"Hasseltine, maybe you better tell me what's the matter with yore Ma."

"It's Berthy," said Hasseltine breathlessly. "She's done gone an'—"

But a gesture from Sairy was a felled tree at the meeting place of two roads and a creek: it checked Hasseltine, arrested Lucy, and stemmed the flow of her own grief. It cleared a space where she could say all that there was to be said.

"I doan't know," she began with a mournful sigh, "I cain't think what I've ever done that the good Lord should punish me this-a-way. I've allus tried to do right by Berthy, an' teach her to do right—"

"Sairy," Lucy interrupted, "will you stop a-feelin' sorry for yoreself jest a minute, an' tell me what'd happened to Berthy, so's I'll have some inklin' o' what you're a-talkin' about? She ain't dead, is she?"

"Dead!" wailed Sairy. "Dead! Lucy Hale, hit couldn't a-hurt me nary a speck more to a-seen her a-layin' cold an' stiff in her shroud, than hit does to be a-thinkin' she's whur she is today. I want yeou to know, *I want yeou to know*, that after all we've done fer that girl, an' after all the warnin's her Pappy's dinned into her years frum the time she was that high, if she ain't run off with the low-down, stinkin', good-fer-nothin' Mitch Blair!"

"No!"

"Yes! Run right off with 'im, mind ye, without so much as a by-your-leave! Left a note on the dresser, if ye please, a-sayin' he's a-aimin' to marry her when they git to Jackson. Well, he'd best marry her after this, or Jed Pendergrast'll know the reason why. Oh, hit's might' nigh finished me, Lucy, the same as if she'd a-struck me a mortal blow with her own hand. Well, I'll tell ye: I was a-settin' in the kitchen doorway yesterday mornin', a-turnin' the coffee grinder an' a-plannin' how to inside-out Flossie's old white wu'sted fer Versie to be baptized in, when I looked up an' what did I see but the milk pails still a-hangin' by the stove, an' it full five o'clock. Why Morg, I says—Morg was a-standin' by the wash-bench—why Morg, I thought Berthy was out a-milkin', an' thar hangs the pails. Yeou go right upstairs an' tell that young lady to roust herself out o' the bed too quick to talk about.

"Well, I reckon it wasn't no more'n two or three minutes till Morg come a-runnin' back. He stood thar before me—I can see 'im now jest as plain as day, the way he looked, all scared to death, like, an' as pale as if he'd a-seen a ghost. 'Mammy,' he says, 'I swan to goodness Berthy ain't in her room, an' her bed ain't even been slep' in!' "

"Well, I thought to my soul I'd never be able to draw my breath agin. Blurted the whole thing right out, jest like that, Lucy, an' not a-doin' ary thing to prepare me fer what was a-comin'. 'Yes,' he says, 'she ain't in her bed an' the kivers ain't even been mussed!' "

"Why, Sairy!"

"I doan't know; I cain't see a-tall, why things should happen the way they do. Nary a womern on Tejes Creek could a-kep' a closter watch on a girl than I did on Berthy; why, she ain't hardly been out o' my sight since she got to the courtin' age."

"Maybe," said Lucy gently, "you watched her a mite too close."

"No," said Sairy, "Berthy's jest wilful, an' she's been that-a-way since the day she was borned. She et ever'thing on the table afore she was six months old, an' still nothin' ever pacified her. The other young'uns would suck on a sugar-tit fer hours, as peaceable as a body could ask; but Berthy would barely tetch it an' tho'w it away."

She sighed, profoundly; before the inscrutable face of Providence she brooded darkly, trying to read some meaning into this feature or that, longing to trace some permanent readable line between brow and chin, between cheek and cheek. But it was no use. He smiled, and you thought those lines were true, and meant thus and so, and would stay for-ever; he frowned, and they were gone in the twinkling of an eye, so that you couldn't even remember, exactly, how they had looked. Thirteen young'uns Sairy had borne in her womb, and still their doings were to her as mysterious, as unpredictable, as the ways of the rain and wind. More so, for clouds gathered before a thunderstorm, and rain did not turn to sleet in the summertime; a lifted straw showed which direction the breeze was blowing, and a south wind would be warm, as like as not. But there was never any telling how young'uns would turn out. No difference if you raised them the best you know, there wasn't, apparently, any connection between what you did and what they did. Still, you went on doing it just the same, so that at least you could say you had. You kept on struggling against nature, and got what comfort you could from your religion.

"By the by," she said, abruptly cheerful, as though in what she had taken for utter blackness she now perceived a gleam of light. "I knowed thar was somethin' else I'd been a-savin' up to tell ye, an' I better be a-sayin' it naow, afore hit plumb slips my mind. (Hass, yeou run back in the kitchen an' see if thar ain't somethin' yeou can do to help the girls. Me an' Miz Hale wants to talk.)"

With a critical eye, she measured the distance to the corner of the house, where Lige and Pete were seining tadpoles from a rain-barrel, and carefully lowering her voice, leaned forward and placed an impressive hand on Lucy's knee.

"Naow who do you reckon I seed a-comin' out o' Rissie Blair's place last Sunday an' the Sunday 'fore that? Zeb Hammonds, the ornery no-count thing! An' Rissie Blair, of all people! Why, she ain't worth her salt. They do say she lets tomatoes rot on the vine when she ain't got hardly 'ary one put up, an' she doan't dry enough fruit to last till Christmas. Well, it takes a widder to make a fool of a man, pervidin' he ain't a fool to start with. But wouldn't yeou a-thought he'd a had the gumption not to be a-settin' out a-ready, an' pore Cynthy barely three months cold in her grave?"

"Why, Sairy, it must a-been more than three months since

Cynthy was buried; I recollect there was snow on the ground that evenin'.' "

"All the same, I 'low if the truth was known his comb was a-gittin' red afore she was fairly a-dyin'. Come to think of it, Rissie didn't hold back none about goin' to Hammondses when Cynthy took down. Lucy! Do you reckon they could a-been arything . . . ?' "

"Why, no, I don't reckon there was. It 'pears to me like Rissie means well enough, as people go."

Adam Hale, that morning, was grubbing the field that rose to merge with the lower side of Sarvice Mountain, clearing away the saplings and bushes and sprouts that had gotten a hold upon it in fallow years. If he had not observed the arrival of Sairy from its highest point, where he and the men and mules began, or noticed, from middling ground, the young'uns, running over the place, and heard them whooping, he might have been alarmed by the wild and furious clamor of the dinner bell at noon. As it was he made a leisurely end to three small sassafras trees whose roots were interwoven in earth, and took his time on the way home because he never hurried unless he had a reason, and even then he didn't hurry a great deal.

Usually his daughter Ruth rang the bell. She saw to the cooking, mostly, and was the best judge of how much time he would need to get to the house. And as a fruit is latent in the flower, so the clean table, the good plain food, her firmly capable step as she brought more beans or replenished the buttermilk in the pitcher—the order and continuity that characterized their family meals in general—were implicit in the clear steady sound that she produced. But under the hands of Pete and Lige and Lizzie and Little Jed (now one, now another, now two or three or all of them pulling the rope with a different rhythm or else without any rhythm at all), the altered tones of the bell prepared him for the changed atmosphere he would find in the dining-room, suggested to him, without his being fully aware of the cause, how the table would look with two extra leaves, Sairy at the foot, the young'uns wiggling around the edge like suckling pigs at the teats of a sow, and the Bible brought in for the Baby so that his size would be less of a handicap in the struggle that would surely begin (as a feud with a rifle shot), with the word Amen at the end of the blessing.

The vision was by no means disagreeable to him. Oh, not in the least! He enjoyed Sairy and the young'uns. They gave him a complete and satisfying sense of his own power and his own importance as no one else ever did. His tenants, for instance, were meek enough to his face, since his goodwill was their meat and bread, but underneath their apparent servility was something he couldn't quite touch—a wall of reserve that he had never been able to penetrate. He suspected them of laughing at him behind his back. Then, he had every right to expect consideration from Lucy and the girls. And while they took his word for law, they too denied him that deep inner acquiescence that he could not explain, or demand, or put a finger on, yet the want of which kept him forever asserting his will against them in barren success.

But the Pendergrasts—now they were whole-hearted. A warm glow suffused him at the thought of the young'uns' expectant faces awaiting his word of authority over the chicken, and the unconditional admiration that always shone upon him from Sairy's eyes. And he gave it back to her in full measure, not only because she was an old friend and neighbor, a fellow Primitive and a Sister in the Lord, but because he really liked her and knew her for his own kind.

"Well, 'pon my honor!" he exclaimed affably, as he pulled out his big armchair at the head of the table, his hands and face still damp from washing, and drops of cold water falling from his stiff black hair. "I'm proud to see ye out, Sister Sairy. I was a-feared yore trouble would jest about put ye to bed, but ye look to be a-bearin' up mighty well. Jest mighty well."

"If I do look pyeart, Brother Adam, I shorely doan't feel that-a-way. I allus would be to keep a-goin' as long as I could, whether I felt right able or not. Well, I didn't reckon the news had reached ye yet. Naow who on earth could a-told 'im!"

"Yes," said Adam, "I hyeared it from Big Jim Meadors. He rid up the creek not more than a hour ago."

"Up the creek! Well, whur do yeou reckon he could a-been a-startin'?"

"After a cow, he said. But about Mitch an' Berthy—didn't you all have no inklin' o' what was a-goin' on?"

"As true as I live an' breathe this minute, nary a sign did I see!"

"Then hit must a-been a turrible hard blow fer you an' Brother Jed a-comin' so unforeseen. What's he a-doin' today, an' why didn't ye bring him with ye?"

"He's gone to mill."

"Heavenly Father . . . thank . . . blessings . . . showered . . . bless . . . food . . . use . . . nourishment . . . bodies . . . service . . . Christ's sake . . . Amen. Well, hit's quare I never seen 'im pass, nor he didn't stop to say howdy."

"Why, he never come by hyer a-tall, Brother Adam; he went to-wards Sturgeon. We 'lowed we'd try out the miller over thar, fer onct, jest to see how he done. Hit does seem like them Blairs a-bein' sich a ungodly lot, an' a-carryin' on the way they do, hit ain't right Christian to cater to 'em. Besides, they been a-shortin' us a leetle mite."

"Time an' time agin I've said it," Adam declared. "But I jest never had the guts to do nothin' about it. I'm mighty glad to see Brother Jed a-takin' a stand, an' I reckon the rest of us cain't do less than to foller."

"Adam, you better start the chicken around," said Lucy. "The young'uns are helped to everything else, but you've got the chicken whur they cain't hardly get to it."

"Well I declar! I wasn't a-noticin'. All right, Lige, you reach me yore plate; which piece do you favor?"

"The liver."

At this simple declaration, loud howls went up from Little
Jed and the Baby, while the other young'uns stared at Lige,
as outraged, as scornful as if he had said that he meant to
eat the whole chicken himself and leave them nary a bite.

"Hush, hush, hush!" cried Sairy, and Adam raised his
hand.

"Well I swear to goodness," he said, "if this ain't the quarest
chicken I ever laid eyes on! Hit's got two livers!"

"The way we do it at home," said Hasseltine earnestly, "we
begin with the Baby an' go on up."

"I doan't know what in this mortal world makes them
young'uns act so foolish over a liver," said Sairy. "But they
allus have, an' I reckon they allus will. Did I ever tell ye
what Versie said when Flossie was borned?"

"No," said Esther, adding an undertone to Bett: "not over
fifty or sixty times, anyhow!"

"Well," said Sairy, "when they told her we had a new
baby, what did she do but set right daown in the middle o'
the floor an' begin to cry so pitiful like, the tears a-streamin'
as if her pore little heart was plumb broke. An' boo-hoo-hoo,
she says, naow it'll git the liver!"

"Why Mammy," said Flossie, "I thought it was me said
that when Pete was borned."

"Likely yeou did," said Sairy. "Hit doan't make a heap o'
difference whether one said it or t'other. No, Brother Adam,
I jest couldn't eat a bite to save me. Well, maybe a leetle
piece o' that thar breast wouldn' hurt me none; hit does look
mighty good an' tender. Though I doan't feel like I'm able to
swaller. I ain't hardly tetched a morsel o' food since it happened, yesterday morn."

Sairy took her young'uns and went, while a narrow strip of
sky still separated the sun from the trees on the hilltop. She
hated like everything to rush off that-a-way, she said (My
goodness, rush off! thought Ruth), but she'd promised to stop
fer a while with Gran'ma Meadors, though if 'ary more o'

them blackish clouds come up, she wouldn't but set an' rise, fer she recollected she'd aired her parlor the day before an' fergot to close the winders, an' the Lord knew that even if Jed was home, he'd never think o' shuttin' one unless the rain was a-pourin' right in on him, an' even then, like as not, he'd jest shift his chair a few inches.

Lucy saw them off. Her quiet hospitable "come agains" and "good-byes" pursued them down the path and through the gate, until finally, rather than raise her voice to a shout, she left one of Sairy's replies hanging there alone in the growing space between them, sure, unambiguous, prophetic.

"We will, yeou come."

Yeou come; the words fell softly away into silence. But we will, we will, we will, seemed to echo and multiply and spread out on the air like the ripples made by a pebble dropped in water, becoming wider and wider until they encircled the whole of Lucy's future in the assurance that Sairy and the young'uns would come again. And whether she looked at them this way or that, and whether she welcomed them in her heart or bore with them grudgingly, there they would be just the same, to be met, to be dealt with.

She followed them with her eyes as they trudged the length of the lane, in a broken wavering line but presenting to her an almost solid mass composed of spindly legs, dusty bottoms, and thin lumpy backs shrinking smaller and smaller against the same fixed strip of creek and woods and sky. Now they were nearing the main travelled road where it bordered the pasture, and Sairy, who went ahead, turned first and walked for a moment alone, seen in profile, with her hands hanging limp at her sides, her shoulders drooping, the head on her slanting neck pushed forward, inquiring, resentful—the embodiment of a question unhopefully asked and forever unanswered.

As Lucy watched them the past seemed to rise before her, obscuring the present, so that she saw, not Sairy, today, but an earlier and more comely Sairy altering there before her into all the Sairys that she had ever known, and whose seasonal comings and goings had marked off her life into periods. A young and supple Sairy, walking unattended, with lifted head and a quick light step, grew into a Sairy beginning to swell with her first pregnancy, became a Sairy large and shapeless with child, and then, as singly the young'uns turned into the road to join her, appeared as yet other Sairys with one, two, three, four, five of them trailing behind her until the entire line had rounded the corner into the present —Sairy and the young 'uns.

Sairy and the young'uns; what would her life have been if she had never known them? She reached back into the past to blot them out, but withdrew her hand before the thing was accomplished. Let them stay as they were; she didn't mind them; they meant no harm. They even gave to the years a pattern without which her own plain weave might have been a dull, monotonous thing, like the warp of grayish blankets that she had made the winter before out of undyed wool.

It came to her then that if she had not had Sairy's example always before her, with Sairy's faults and blunders continually thrust on her notice, she herself might have been more like Sairy in many ways. And she thought that perhaps she had even done better, accomplished more, with her younger children, who were of an age with Sairy's older ones, because she had had the little Pendergrasts to make them different from.

Now the young'uns were climbing upward, and Sairy was crossing the brow of the hill as she had crossed it that morning. She had reversed her direction, but the sun had moved its place, and she was returning home as she had come, with the light at her back and her shadow before her feet. Nothing gained, apparently; nothing changed except that now she was tired and the young'uns were dirty. And it was as though she had gone so far and stayed so long that she had, in the end, defeated herself by her own tenacity and her determination to get everything that there was to be gotten out of one day.

After the supper dishes were washed and dried and put back on the table (the plates laid upside down, the spoons turned into a tumbler glass, and a wide clean cloth spread over), the girls sat out on the porch in the cooling dusk and talked. Lucy was thumping away at the loom in the lower bedroom, by a lamp whose light streamed through the window upon them, and Adam sat apart, with his stockinged feet on the railing, his shoes beside his chair, and his Bible spread open across his knees although it had been too dark to read for the last half hour.

"I'm plumb worn out," said Ruth. "An' maybe it ain't no trouble to cook fer a dozen young'uns extry! I declare to goodness, the way they eat when they come hyer, it makes it seem as if they'd been a-savin' up their hunger a week beforehand. I do know better, for Sairy fixes a-plenty at home. Not that I grudge 'em the food, but it shore does take a heap o' doin'."

"Not that I grudge 'em the food," said Bett, "but it jest looks so bad to see 'em crammin' it in."

"Now, shucks!" said Esther. "I don't care whether they swaller it by the bushel or smear it all over theirselves. What aggervates me is the way they git into my things. It was all I could do to keep my hands off o' Versie an' Flossie, the nasty brats, when I found 'em into my bureau drawer, a-tyin' knots in my ribbons an' sashes, an' a-puttin' their sticky hands on my clean handkerchiefs an' my best lace collars. Yes, Naomy Hale, an' if you wasn't forever a-given' 'em yore things to play with, they wouldn't be so bad about takin' mine!"

"The Baby pulled a sight o' cornsilks off'n the roastin' ears," said Ruth. "Now he knew better than that. Naomy, it does 'pear to me like if you was bound to have 'im a-follerin' you round in the garden, you might at least a-kept an eye on what he was doin'!"

Naomy turned her face toward the green and purple infinity that crept stealthily down on the hills because there were no moon and stars to hinder. A succession of images drenched her mind like a swift brief pattering of rain: Versie's freckles, rising indeterminately near the edge of her hair and coming to an aimless climax across the bridge of her nose; Flossie's thinly tapering plaits, the color of damp moulded leaves in January; Pete's long baggy pants, and his futile repeated gesture of pulling them up; Hasseltine's dingy petticoat hanging below the attempted finery of her second-best dress; the Baby, brightly expectant, offering her, Naomy, his gift of red and white cornsilks, while behind him stretched the row of listless, despoiled ears; the wide, pale, vaguely wounded, vaguely perplexed gaze that marked them every one—the Pendergrast look. It seemed to sum up their meagre shortcomings, to lay open all their bleak insufficiencies, and leave them completely vulnerable.

"Well, ain't you girls got a spark o' feelin' for the pore little fellers?" she cried.

"Pore little fellers!" Esther exclaimed. "Why they're the sorriest lot that ever was raised on Tejes!"

"An' if Sairy ain't the most worrisome thing in the world," said Ruth, "then I don't know what she is."

"Mercy, yes," said Bett.

"You shet yore mouths," said Adam harshly, rising and closing his Book. "An' don't let me hyear no more sich foolish talk out o' ary one of ye. Sairy Pendergrast is as good a womern as ever drawed breath, an' a mighty fine passel o' young'uns she's got!" (1935)

THOMAS WOLFE

Born in Asheville, North Carolina, in 1900, Thomas Wolfe was bound to the mountains in ways in which the outward incidents of his life do not indicate. He attended the University of North Carolina and entered Harvard Graduate School in 1920. He later lived in New York and taught sporadically at New York University from 1924–1930, while writing *Look Homeward, Angel* (1929). During this time he also journeyed to England and Germany frequently. His award-winning *A Portrait of Bascom Hawke* was published in 1932; *Of Time and the River* and *From Death to Morning* appeared in 1935. Wolfe returned to Asheville in 1937 for the first time since the publication of *Look Homeward, Angel*, and the next year succumbed to pneumonia. Several of his significant works—*You Can't Go Home Again, The Web and the Rock*, and *The Hills Beyond*—were published posthumously.

"The Great Schism" from *The Hills Beyond* illustrates Wolfe's knowledge of the frontier tradition in literature and his skillful use of that tradition for purposes of humor and wisdom. There is much truth to the argument that at least in his later works Thomas Wolfe spiritually did go home again.

The Great Schism

If, as Carlyle says, the history of the world is recorded in the lives of its great men, so, too, the spirit of a people is recorded in the heroes it picks. No better illustration of this fact could be found than in the life of Zachariah Joyner. Historically, his position is secure enough. True, his greatest fame is where he would himself have wished it to be—at home. His name has not attained the national celebrity of a Webster or Calhoun; no doubt most people outside Catawba would have difficulty in placing him. But historians will remember him as a leader in the affairs of his own state for almost fifty years; as an able and resourceful Governor; later, as one of the more forceful and colorful leaders of debate in the affairs of the United States Senate; and all in all, when the whole record of his life is weighed and estimated, as a man of great natural ability and intelligence, considering his place and time and situation.

He directed the affairs of his state through the Civil War, and he directed them courageously and ably. In periods of stress he was unmoved by threat and unswayed by the hysterias of popular feeling. In the closing days of the Confederacy, when the armies were in desperate need, he curtly refused a demand from Jefferson Davis for almost seventy thousand suits of uniforms, shoes, and coats which the state owned and had in its possession. He refused bluntly and without apology, saying that the equipment would be used first of all for the rehabilitation of his own people; and although this act of rebellion brought down upon him bitter denunciation from all quarters, he stuck to his decision and refused to budge.

Later, in the darker days of Reconstruction, military occupation, black legislatures, and night riders, he rendered even greater service to his state. And he concluded a long life, full of honors and accomplishment, as a member of the nation's

Senate, in which capacity he died, during Cleveland's last administration, in 1893.

All these facts are sufficiently well known to make his position in the nation's chronicle secure. But to people in Catawba his name means a great deal more than this. They are well acquainted with the story of his life, and the record of his offices as it has been outlined here. But these honors and accomplishments, splendid as they are, do not in themselves explain the place he holds in Catawba's heart. For he is their hero: in the most local and particular sense, they feel that he belongs to them, is of them, could in no conceivable way belong to anything else, is theirs and theirs alone. Therefore, they love him.

He was not only their own native Lincoln—their backwoods son who marched to glory by the log-rail route—he was their Crockett and Paul Bunyan rolled in one. He was not alone their hero; he was their legend and their myth. He was, and has remained so to this day, a kind of living prophecy of all that they themselves might wish to be; a native divinity, shaped out of their own clay, and breathing their own air; a tongue that spoke the words, a voice that understood and spoke the language, they would have him speak.

They tell a thousand stories about him today. What does it matter if many of the things which they describe never happened? They are true because they are the kind of things he would have said, the kind of things that would have happened to him. Thus, to what degree, and in what complex ways, he was created so in their imaginations, no one can say. How much the man shaped the myth, how much the myth shaped the man, how much Zack Joyner created his own folk, or how much his people created him—no one can know, and it does not matter.

For he was of them, and the rib; and they of him the body and the flesh. He was indigenous to them as their own clay, as much a part of all their lives as the geography of their native earth, the climate of their special weather. No other place on earth but Old Catawba could have produced him. And the people know this: therefore, again, they love him.

In examining the history of that great man, we have collected more than eight hundred stories, anecdotes, and jokes that are told of him, and of this number at least six hundred have the unmistakable ring—or *smack*—of truth. If they did not happen—they *should* have! They belong to him: they fit him like an old shoe.

"But," the pedants cunningly inquire, "*did* they happen? Now, really, *did* they? Ah, yes, they *sound* like him—he *might* have said them—but that's not the point! *Did* he?"

Well, we are not wholly unprepared for these objections. Of the six hundred stories which have the smack of truth, we have actually verified three hundred as authentic beyond the shadow of a doubt, and are ready to cite them by the book—place, time, occasion, evidence—to anyone who may inquire. In these stories there is a strength, a humor, a coarseness, and a native originality that belonged to the man and marked his every utterance. They come straight out of his own earth.

As a result of our researches, we can state unequivocally that there is no foundation in fact for the story that one time, in answer to a lady's wish, he called out to a Negro urchin at a station curb, who had a donkey wagon and a load of peanuts:

"Boy! Back your——over here and show this lady your——!"

But he certainly did make the speech in the United States Senate (in rejoinder to the Honorable Barnaby Bulwinkle) that is generally accredited to him, even though there is no account of it in the *Congressional Record*:

"Mr. President, sir, we are asked by the honorable gentleman to appropriate two hundred thousand dollars of the taxpayer's money for the purpose of building a bridge across Coon Creek in the honorable gentleman's district—a stream,

sir, which I have seen, and which, sir, I assure you, I could
——halfway across."

The Vice-President (pounding with his gavel): "The Senator is out of order."

Senator Joyner: "Mr. President, sir, you are right. If I was *in* order, sir, I could——the whole way across it!"

The last story that is told of Zachariah Joyner is that in his final days of illness (and, like King Charles, in dying, he was "an unconscionable time") he was aroused from coma one afternoon by the sound of rapid hoofs and wheels, and, looking wearily out of the window of his room, he saw the spare figure of his brother Rufus hastening toward the house. Even in his last extremity his humor did not forsake him, for he is said to have smiled wanly and feebly croaked:

"My God! I reckon it's all up with me! For here comes Rufe!"

People told the story later and, despite the grimness of the joke, they laughed at it; for the family trait to which it pointed was well known.

Bear Joyner, in his later years, after he had moved to Libya Hill, when told of the death of one of his sons in Zebulon by his second marriage, is known to have said:

"Well, I reckon some of the children will attend the funeral." Here he considered seriously a moment, then nodded his head with an air of confirmation. "Hit's—hit's no more than right!" And after another pause he added virtuously: "If I was thar, *I'd go myself!*" And with these words, he wagged his head quite solemnly, in such a way as to leave no doubt about the seriousness of his intent.

Zachariah is reported, when asked the number of his kin, to have replied: "Hell, I don't know! You can't throw a rock in Zebulon without hitting one of them!" He reflected on his metaphor a moment, and then said: "However, let him that is without sin among you throw the first stone. I can't!" And with these words he turned virtuously away, scratching himself vigorously in the behind.

Again, when he responded to the greeting of a member of the audience after a political rally at which he had made a speech, he is reported to have said:

"My friend, your face looks familiar to me. Haven't I seen you somewhere before?"

To which the person so addressed replied: "Yes, sir. I think you have. I was yore pappy's ninth child by his second marriage, and you was his fourth 'un by his first. So I reckon you might say that you and me was both half-brothers, distantly removed."

The grimmest story in the whole Joyner catalogue, perhaps, is that old Bear Joyner, when reproached one time for a seeming neglect of his own brood, is reputed to have said to his inquisitor:

"My God Almighty! A man can plant the seed, but he cain't make the weather! I sowed 'em—now, goddamn 'em, let 'em grow!"

There is no reason to believe that either William or his children were as neglectful of each other as these stories indicate, yet they really do denote a trait—or failing—of the clan. The fault—if fault it be—has long been known in Catawba, where it is said that "the only thing that will bring 'em all together is a wedding or a funeral; and it has to be a good one to do that." And yet, this trait has been too easily interpreted. Many people have taken such stories as evidence that the Joyners were lacking in a sense of family feeling; but nothing could be further from the truth.

The truth is that no family ever lived that had a stronger sense of their identity. It is hard to describe the thing in more familiar terms, for the whole tribe violates the standards by which such things are commonly appraised. Of "affection," "love," "devotion," even "clannishness"—as these terms are generally accepted—the family seems to have had little. It is perfectly true that years have gone by when brothers have not seen or spoken to each other, even when they lived in the same town. It is also true that some have grown rich, indifferent to others who have struggled on in obscure poverty; that children have been born, and grown up, and gone away, scarcely familiar with the look of a cousin's face, the identity of a cousin's name.

Many people have observed these things and wondered at them, and then accepted them as further proof that the tribe was "queer." And yet, paradoxically, out of this very indifference came the family unity. From this very separateness came the deep and lasting sense of their identity. In a way, they reversed completely the old adage that if men refuse to hang together, they will all hang separately: of the Joyners it could rather be said that they hang separately because they know they hang together.

To find what produced their sense of "separateness" one must look into the history of the family.

The many children of Bear Joyner by his two marriages— there were more than twenty by the lowest count—grew up in a community where every man had to look out for himself. As for old Bill himself, nothing in his earlier life had prepared him for the exacting duties of parenthood. Whatever his career had been before he came into the hill-bound fastnesses of Zebulon, it had been very hard. He is known to have said: "If a young'un don't learn to root afore fourteen, he never will. A hen'll scrabble for young chicks, but before they're fryin' size they've got to scratch for themselves."

Although he was a man of substance for his time and place, his means were not enough to give two dozen children an easy start in life. Moreover, it must be owned that, like so many men who have been widowed in first marriage, he ventured into a second because it was the best expedient to meet his need. And the fourteen or sixteen children who came later—well, it is a brutal fact, but it was a sowing of blind seed. They came. They just came. And that was all.

Perhaps it is unjust to emphasize the schism of this second marriage. And yet, a separation did exist. It is inevitable

that this should have been. For one thing, the older children
of Bear Joyner's first marriage were fairly well grown when
he married for the second time, and when the children of the
second brood began to come along. Again, the surviving children of the first—Zack, Robert, Hattie, Theodore, and Rufe
—were, if not a different breed, yet of a separate clan. And
they knew it. From the first, instinctively, they seemed to
know it. It was not that, consciously, they felt themselves to
be "superior"—a bitter accusation that was later made—and
yet they seemed to feel they were. And—since the blunt truth
must be spoken—in the light of their accomplishment, and in
the world's esteem, they were.

Another fact—the Joyners, first to last, were a vainglorious
folk. Even old William had his share of this defect, perhaps
even more than the rest of them, for old men thirty years
ago who could remember him, and who would pay due
tribute to his prowess and his extraordinary gifts, would
often add: "Well, he *knowed* that he was good. . . . He was
remarkable, but he *knowed* that he was good. And he was
bigoted. He could be bigoted; and he was overbearing, too. . . .
And as for Zack," old men would smile when they said his
name, "Well, there was Zack, too. He knowed that *he* was
good. Zack was a wonder . . . but no one ever said he was a
blushing violet."

The Joyners of this early flowering not only "knowed that
they was good," but they made little effort to conceal it.
Apparently, none of them—unless it was Robert—hid his
light under a bushel. And the truth is, each of them, in his
own way—even Theodore!—had a light to show.

The reasons? Well, the reasons were complex, but perhaps
the first one was the consciousness they had of special heritage. Bear Joyner's first wife was a "special woman": she was
a Creasman, and the Creasmans were "good people." The
Joyners of the first lot were all proud of their Creasman
ancestry. Of Martha Creasman herself there is little to be
told except that she was a good wife, a quiet and hard-work-

ing mother, and a Presbyterian. This last fact, trifling as it seems, was all important: for it bespeaks a kind of denominational snobbishness which is still more prevalent than the world may know, and which the Joyners of the first lot never lost.

As to Bear Joyner's second wife, she was a Baptist. The first Joyners—Zack, and all the rest of them—were always careful to speak of her respectfully, but with a touch of unconscious patronage that was infuriating to "the country cousins" of the lesser breed:

"Well now, she was a mighty good woman, and all of that. . . . Of course"—with a kind of hesitant and regretful concessiveness—"she was a Baptist. . . . I reckon you might call her a kind of religious fanatic. . . . She had queer religious notions. . . . But she was a good woman. . . . She had some queer ideas, but she was a good mother to those children. . . . Now everyone will have to give her *that!*"

Here then, obviously, were the roots of the great schism. Bear Joyner himself seems to have shared unconsciously in this prejudice of his elder children. He had apparently always been somewhat in awe of his first wife: her family was well known, and there is reason to believe he felt he was making a considerable step forward in the world when he married her. Toward his second wife he had no such feeling: she was one of a hard-shell Baptist tribe, and there is a story that he met her at camp meeting. However that may be, he was "looking for a woman to keep house"; and it was pretty much in this capacity that he married her.

That she worked long and faithfully there can be no doubt; or that she was a patient, strong, enduring woman—"a good mother," as the elder Joyners always willingly admitted, to the numerous family that she now began to bring into the world.

As for Bear Joyner's older children by his previous marriage—Zack, Hattie, Robert, Theodore, and Rufe (Martha and George, the two remaining of the seven, had died in

childhood)—they seem from the beginning to have been outside the sphere of their stepmother's control. Their strongly
marked individualities had already been defined and shaped
by the time their father married again. They had inherited,
in liberal measure, his own strong character, his arrogant
confidence in his own powers, a good measure of his color,
his independence, his intelligence, his coarse and swingeing
humor, his quick wit.

There is no evidence that they were consciously contemptu-
ous of their new mother, but there is no doubt they felt
superior to her. Even in a backwoods community theirs was a
larger, bolder, more tolerant and experienced view of life
than she had ever known; and her narrow prejudice, her
cramped vision, her rigid small moralities (all products of an
inheritance she couldn't help) simply amused them, aroused
their ridicule and mirth.

Zachariah, especially, although in later years he always
spoke feelingly of her excellent qualities, was particularly
active in his humorous analysis of her. Her superstitions and
prejudices amused him; the operations of her mind, and the
narrow cells of her morality seemed grotesque and ludicrous
to him; and he questioned, teased, examined her rather
cruelly in order, as he said, "to see what made her tick."

Hers, indeed, poor woman, was a strange and contradictory
code, and yet, because it was the only one she knew, she
thought it was the only one there was: it seemed natural to
her, and it never occurred to her to question it.

That harsh code to which she adhered was indigenous to
America. It has not only done much to shape our lives and
histories, but it persists to this day, and is at the root of much
of the sickness, the moral complex of America. For example,
she believed it was wrong to take a life "in cold blood," but
it was not nearly so wrong as to take a drink. She was always
warning her children against evil ways and loose living, and
speaking of people who committed "all kinds of immorality
and licentiousness"; but it would have come strangely to her

ears to hear murder referred to as an immoral act. True, it was "an awful crime"—she could understand it in these terms because the Bible told about Cain and Abel, and taught that it was wicked to take life. But, privately, she did not consider it half as bad for a man to take a life as to take a drink, or—what was the most immoral act of all—to sleep with a woman who was not his wife.

Life-taking, the shedding of man's blood, was so much a part of the life of a pioneer community that it occasioned no surprise. To be sure, she would not openly defend the practice of killing, although in a surprising number of individual cases she was willing to defend it, becoming quite aroused, in fact, when Zachariah, with deceptive gravity, would point out that her own brother—whose life in other ways she esteemed as a model of the Christian virtues—had been quite handy with his gun in his hot youth, and was known to have killed three men:

"Now, Zack," she would cry angrily, "don't you go a-diggin' into that. Reese had his faults, like everyone, and I reckon maybe in his young days he may have been hot-tempered. But he's always led a good Christian and God-fearin' sort of life. He never drank or smoked or used bad language or ran around with women—like *some* people I know about." Here she glared accusingly at her erring stepson, who returned her look with an expression of bland innocence. "So don't you start on him: he's always been an upright, moral sort of man."

All of this amused Zachariah no end: he did not mean to be cruel to her, but, as she said, he was "always tormenting" her, rummaging gravely about in the confusing rag-bag of her moral consciousness to see what further mysteries would be revealed.

He is known to have spoken of the physical sharpness of her sense of smell, which really was amazing, and which all of her children inherited (she is said one time to have "smelled burning leaves five miles away upon the mountain, long before anyone else knowed there was a fire"):

"Well, she can smell fire and brimstone farther off than that. And Hell! If I took a drink in Libya Hill, she'd smell it on my breath before I crossed the county line!"

On another occasion, she is said to have called out to him the moment that he came into the house: "Zack Joyner! You've been drinkin' that bad, old, rotten, vile corn licker again. I can smell it on your breath!"

"Now, mother," he answered temperately, "there is no bad, old, rotten, vile corn licker. Some is good—" he went on in a tone of judicious appraisal that she must have found very hard to take—"and some is better. But there is no bad!"

Again, when Bear Joyner returned from Libya Hill one day with this announcement:

"Well, Thad Burton's gone and done it again!"

"Gone and done what?" said Zachariah, looking up.

"Gone and killed a man," Bear Joyner answered.

"Oh!" said Zachariah with a relieved air, casting a sly look toward his stepmother, "I was afraid you were goin' to tell me he'd done something really bad, like gettin' drunk."

Bear Joyner was no less adept than his sons in this sport of teasing his bewildered wife. It is said that having driven in with her one day from Zebulon, to see the boys who at that time were "keeping store" for him in Libya Hill, he went into the store and, finding Zack on duty there, the following conversation then took place between them:

"You boys been leadin' the Christ-life like your mother told you to?"

"Yes, sir," Zachariah said.

"Have you done your chores this mornin'?"

"Yes, sir."

"Watered the milk?"

"Yes, sir."

"Sanded the sugar?"

"Yes, sir."

"*Fixed* the scales?"

"Yes, sir."

"Well," said Bear, "you'd better call in Ted and Bob. Your mother's here, an' we're goin' to have prayers."

Finally, there was the case of Harriet—the "Miss Hattie" of later years, for she never married—to add to the confusion and distress of William Joyner's second wife. Of all Bear Joyner's children, Hattie was the favorite. In her, perhaps, more than in any of the others he saw the qualities—the quick wit, the humor, the independence and intelligence— that in himself he most esteemed. It has been said she was his "love child"—a euphemism maybe for the fact that she was illegitimate—and that this accounted for her father's deeper care. At any rate, although her birth was hidden in an obscurity that was never cleared—for old Bear Joyner never spoke of it, and no one dared to speak of it to him—she was brought up as a member of his elder brood. The story goes that he was gone one time for several weeks upon a journey to the south, and that when he returned he brought the child with him. She was almost eight years old then, and Martha, the first wife, was still alive. The story goes that Joyner brought the child into the house—the family was at dinner, and the faces of the other children wonderingly turned—and sat her down beside them at the table.

"This," he said, "is your new sister. From this time on, she'll be one of the family, and you'll treat her so."

And this is all that was ever spoken. It is said that Martha, Joyner's first wife, took the child as one of her own; and in justice to the second wife, no matter what additional distress and confusion this new proof of Joyner wickedness may have caused that bewildered woman's soul, it was always freely acknowledged, most loyally of all by Harriet herself, as a further tribute to the woman's qualities, that she was a good mother, and brought the girl up as if she were "one of her own."

Historically, time-periods are most curiously defined: the world does not grow up together. The footpads that made Johnson carry his stick at night when he went out alone in London in the Eighteenth Century have been quite actively abroad in recent years in our own land. And as for "human life," a commodity which our editorial writers tell us they most jealously esteem, the security of human life in our own broad land—whether from murder, violence, or sudden death of every kind soever—is perhaps *almost* as great in America at the present time as it was in England at the period of Elizabeth, although our figures are by far the more bloody of the two.

And as for our own Dick Whittingtons—our country boys who went to town—there, too, we ape the European pattern; but we have been late.

The history of human celebrity for the most part is an urban one. In our own land, although children are taught that most of their great men "came from the country," it is not sufficiently emphasized that most of them also "went to town." Certainly, this has been true in America: the national history could almost be written in the lives of men who went to town.

Zachariah Joyner, in his later years, was very fond of using the log-cabin theme for politics, but if he had been more true to fact, he would have admitted that the turning point in his own career had come when he abandoned finally the world-lost fastnesses of Zebulon for the more urban settlement of Libya Hill. There, truly, was *his* starting point, his threshold, the step from which he gained his vantage, took off for the larger community of public life and general notice in which for fifty years he was to play so large a role.

And, in various ways, the same transitional experience was true of his more immediate family—his three brothers, who came with him. In one sense the whole history of the many Joyners, their divided lot and the boundary that separated the lowly from the great, might be stated in one phrase. It was the history of those who stayed at home, and of those who went to town.

As the years passed, the division of each group became more widely marked, the sense of unity more faint and far. Hill-bound, world-lost, locked in the narrow valleys and the mountain walls of Zebulon, the Joyners who remained at home became almost as strange and far away to those who lived in Libya Hill as if their home had been the Mountains of the Moon. True, they lived only fifty miles away, but as Bear Joyner had himself said so many years before, it was "the wrong way." It really was this sense of two directions that divided them. The Libya Hill Joyners were facing ever toward the world, and those in Zebulon away from it; and as years went by, it seemed that this directiveness became more marked than ever—the town Joyners ever more the world's men; those in Zebulon more withdrawn from the world.

By 1900, a whole century since William Joyner crossed the Blue Ridge and came down into the wilderness with his rifle and his grant of land, if some curious historian, gifted with immortality, could have returned there, he would have observed a change as startling as it was profound. He would have found the lives of the town Joyners (for by this time Libya Hill had grown to twelve thousand people) so greatly altered as to be scarcely recognizable; but he would have found the lives of the country Joyners scarcely changed at all.

True, some changes had occurred in Zebulon in those hundred years, but for the most part these were tragic ones. The great mountain slopes and forests of the section had been ruinously detimbered; the farm-soil on hill sides had eroded and washed down; high up, upon the hills, one saw the raw scars of old mica pits, the dump heaps of deserted mines. Some vast destructive "Suck" had been at work here; and a visitor, had he returned after one hundred years, would have been compelled to note the ruin of the change. It was evident that a huge compulsive greed had been at work: the whole region had been sucked and gutted, milked dry, denuded of its rich primeval treasures: something blind and ruthless had been here, grasped, and gone. The blind scars on the hills, the denuded slopes, the empty mica pits were what was left.

And true, the hills were left—with these deteriorations; and all around, far-flung in their great barricades, the immense wild grandeur of the mountain wall, the great Blue Ridge across which they had come long, long ago; and which had held them from the world.

And the old formations of the earth were left: the boiling clamor of the rocky streams, the cool slant darkness of the mountain hollows. Something wild, world-lost, and lyrical, and special to the place called Zebulon was somehow left: the sound of rock-bright waters, birds calls, and something swift and fleeting in a wood; the way light comes and goes; cloud shadows passing on a hill; the wind through the hill grasses, and the quality of light—something world-lost, far, and haunting (special to the place as is the very climate of the soil) in the quality of light; and little shacks and cabins stuck to hill or hollow, sunken, tiny, in the gap; the small, heart-piercing wisps of smoke that coiled into the clear immensity of weather from some mountain shack, with its poignant evidence that men fasten to a ledge, and draw their living from a patch of earth—because they have been here so long and love it and cannot be made to leave; together with lost voices of one's kinsmen long ago—all this was left, but their inheritance was bare. Something had come into the wilderness, and had left the barren land.

And the people—ah, the people!—yes, the people!——
They were left! They were left "singing the same songs" (as college Doctors of Philosophy so gloatingly assure us) "their Elizabethan forebears sang"—which is a falsehood; and no glory—they should have made new and better ones for themselves. "Speaking the same tongue" their Elizabethan forebears spoke—which also is a falsehood; and they should

have made a new one for themselves. "Living the same lives" their forebears lived a hundred years ago—which further is a falsehood. The lives their forebears lived were harsh and new, still seeking and explorative; their own lives often were just squalid, which should have been better.

What remained? It has been said, "The earth remains." But this was wrong. The earth had changed, the earth had eroded, the earth had washed down the gulleys in a billion runnels of red clay; the earth was gone.

But the people—ah, the people!—yes, the people! The people were still there!

Turned backwards now, world-lost, in what was once new land! Unseeking now, in what their forebears with blue vistas in their eyes, alone, in Indian country, sought! Turned in upon themselves, congruent as a tribe, all intermarried (so each man now was cousin to the very blood he took: each Cain among them brother to his very deed!)——

The people!—aye, the people! The people of Zack Joyner, and old Bear, who sought a world, and *found* it, that such as these might lose it; had wandered so that such as these should *stay*; had sought great vistas to the West, so that such as these remain——

The people! To be gloated over by exultant Ph.D's (who find in mountain shacks the accents of Elizabeth); to be gawked at by tourists (now the roads are good) in search of the rare picturesque; to be yearned over by consecrated schoolmarms "from the North"; have their "standards" "improved" by social service workers, who dote upon the squalor, ignorance, and poverty; lasciviously regret the degradations of the people's lot, and who do valiantly their little bit (God bless their little, little souls!) to help the people, teach the people, prop the people, *heal* the people, with their little salves (not too completely, else what are little salves and social service work about?)—and who therefore (in spite of dirt, filth, rickets, murder, lean-tos, children, syphilis, hunger, incest, and pellagra) love the people, adore the people, see

underneath their "drawbacks" and their "lack of opportunities" all "the good" in people—because the people, at the
bottom, "are so fine."

It is a lie! . . . Dear God! . . . Dear Jesus God, protect us, all
men living, and the people, from such stuff as this!

The people are not "fine"—the people are not picturesque—
the people——

Well, after a hundred years of it—denudings, minings, loot-
ings, intermarryings, killings, dyings, bornings, livings, all
the rest of it—the people—in spite of Smike, the lumber thief,
who stole their hills; and Snead, his son, who stole their bal-
ladry; in spite of Gripe, who took their mica and their ore,
and gave them "the lung-sickness" in exchange for it; despite
Grace, Gripe's daughter, who now brings rubber condoms
and tuberculin; and his wife, Gertrude, who schools them in
hand-weaving—despite Gripe, Smike, and Grace, and all
lovers of the picturesque soever—despite rickets, incest,
syphilis, and sham—the people!—ah, the people!—well, the
people——

"Why, goddamn it!" Zachariah Joyner roared— "I'll tell you
what the people are! . . . The people . . . the *people*! . . . Why,
goddamn it, sir, the people are the *people*!"

And so they are!—Smike, Gripe, rickets, Grace, and Snead
—all forces to the contrary notwithstanding.

The people are the people.

And the Joyners—second Joyners; the humble, world-lost
Joyners out in Zebulon—they're the people! (1941)

SHERWOOD ANDERSON

Born in Camden, Ohio, in 1876, Sherwood Anderson spent his boyhood in Ohio towns. For a brief period he attended Wittenberg College in Springfield, and later he served in the Spanish-American War. In 1924 Anderson moved to Marion, in the hills of southwest Virginia, and operated two newspapers (Republican and Democrat). He later built what he called "the most beautiful home in America" on Ripshin Creek near the village of Troutdale. The author of numerous works of fiction and nonfiction, including the celebrated *Winesburg, Ohio* (1919), he died in 1941 on a trip to South America made on behalf of the State Department.

Anderson frequently inveighed against stereotyping people along regional and ethnic lines. While the characters in "A Jury Case" from *Death in the Woods* indulge or participate in those activities usually associated with the Southern mountaineer, particularly moonshining, they are immediately recognizable as authentic human beings.

A Jury Case

They had a still up in the mountains. There were three of them. They were all tough.

What I mean is they were not men to fool with—at least two of them weren't.

First of all, there was Harvey Groves. Old man Groves had come into the mountain country thirty years before, and had bought a lot of mountain land.

He hadn't a cent and had only made a small payment on the land.

Right away he began to make moon whisky. He was one of the kind that can make pretty fair whisky out of anything. They make whisky out of potatoes, buckwheat, rye, corn or whatever they can get—the ones who really know how. One of that kind from here was sent to prison. He made whisky out of the prunes they served the prisoners for breakfast— anyway, he called it whisky. Old man Groves used to sell his whisky down at the lumber mills. There was a big cutting going on over on Briar Top Mountain.

They brought the lumber down the mountain to a town called Lumberville.

Old Groves sold his whisky to the lumberjacks and the manager of the mill got sore. He had old Groves into his office and tried to tell him what was what.

Instead, old Groves told him something. The manager said he would turn old Groves up. What he meant was that he would send the Federal men up the mountains after him, and old Groves told the manager that if a Federal man showed up in his hills he would burn the lumber stacked high about the mills at Lumberville.

He said it and he meant it and the mill manager knew he meant it.

The old man got away with that. He stayed up in his hills and raised a large family. Those at home were all boys. Every

one about here speaks of the Groves girls, but what became
of them I've never heard. They are not here now.

Harvey Groves was a tall, raw-boned young man with one
eye. He lost the other one in a fight. He began drinking and
raising the devil all over the hills when he was little more
than a boy and after the old man died of a cancer, and the
old woman died and the land was divided among the sons
and sold, and he got his share, he blew it in gambling and
drinking.

He went moonshining when he was twenty-five. Cal Long
and George Small went in with him. They all chipped in to
buy the still.

Nowadays you can make moon whisky in a small still—it's
called "over-night stuff"—about fourteen gallons to the run,
and you make a run in one night.

You can sell it fast. There are plenty of men to buy and run
it into the coal mining country over east of here. It's pretty
raw stuff.

Cal Long, who went in with Harvey, is a big man with a
beard. He is as strong as an ox. They don't make them any
meaner. He seems a peaceful enough man, when he isn't
drinking, but when he starts to drink, look out. He usually
carries a long knife and he has cut several men pretty badly.
He has been in jail three times.

The third man in the party was George Small. He used to
come by our house—lived out our way for a time. He is a
small nervous-looking young man who worked, until last
Summer, on the farm of old man Barclay. One day last Fall,
when I was over on the Barclay road and was sitting under
a bridge, fishing, George came along the road.

What was the matter with him that time I've never found
out.

I was sitting in silence under the bridge and he came
along the road making queer movements with his hands. He
was giving them a dry wash. His lips were moving. The road
makes a turn right beyond the bridge and I could see him

coming for almost a half mile before he got to the bridge. I was under the bridge and could see him without his seeing me. When he got close I heard his words. "Oh, my God, don't let me do it," he said. He kept saying it over and over. He had got married the Spring before. He might have had some trouble with his wife. I remember her as a small, red-haired woman. I saw the pair together once. George was carrying their baby in his arms and we stopped to talk. The woman moved a little away. She was shy as most mountain women are. George showed me the baby—not more than two weeks old—and it had a wrinkled little old face. It looked ages older than the father and mother but George was fairly bursting with pride while I stood looking at it.

How he happened to go in with men like Harvey Groves and Cal Long is a wonder to me, and why they wanted him is another wonder.

I had always thought of George as a country neurotic—the kind you so often see in cities. He always seemed to me out of place among the men of these hills.

He might have fallen under the influence of Cal Long. A man like Cal likes to bully people physically. Cal liked to bully them spiritually too.

Luther Ford told me a tale about Cal and George. He said that one night in the Winter Cal went to George Small's house—it is a tumble-down little shack up in the hills—and called George out. The two men went off together to town and got drunk. They came back about two o'clock in the morning and stood in the road before George's house. I have already told you something about the wife. Luther said that at that time she was sick. She was going to have another baby. A neighbor had told Luther Ford. It was a queer per-formance, one of the kind of things that happen in the coun-try and that give you the creeps.

He said the two men stood in the road before the house cursing the sick woman inside.

Little nervous George Small walking up and down the

road in the snow, cursing his wife—Cal Long egging him on. George strutting like a little rooster. It must have been a sight to see and make you a little sick seeing. Luther Ford said just hearing about it gave him a queer feeling in the pit of his stomach.

This Spring early these three men went in together, making whisky.

Between Cal and Harvey Groves it was a case of dog eat dog. They had bought the still together, each putting in a third of its cost, and then, one night after they had made and sold two runs, Harvey stole the still from the other two.

Of course Cal set out to get him for that.

There wasn't any law he and George Small could evoke— or whatever it is you do with a law when you use it to get some man.

It took Cal a week to find out where Harvey had hidden, and was operating, the still, and then he went to find George.

He wanted to get Harvey, but he wanted to get the still too.

He went to George Small's house and tramped in. George was sitting there and when he saw Cal was frightened stiff. His wife, thinner than ever since her second child was born half sick, was lying on a bed. In these little mountain cabins there is often but one room and they cook, eat and sleep in it —often a big family.

When she saw Cal, George's wife began to cry and, very likely, George wanted to cry too.

Cal sat down in a chair and took a bottle out of his pocket. George's wife says he had been drinking. He gave George a drink, staring at him hard when he offered it, and George had to take it.

George took four or five stiff drinks, not looking again at Cal or at his wife, who lay on the bed moaning and crying, and Cal never said a word.

Then suddenly George jumped up—his hands not doing the dry wash now—and began swearing at his wife.

"You keep quiet, God damn you!" he yelled.

Then he did an odd thing. There were only two chairs in the cabin and Cal Long had been sitting on one and George on the other. When Cal got up George took the chairs, one at a time, and going outside smashed them to splinters against a corner of the cabin.

Cal Long laughed at that. Then he told George to get his shotgun.

George did get it. It was hanging on a hook in the house and was loaded, I presume, and the two went away together into the woods.

Harvey Groves had got bold. He must have thought he had Cal Long bluffed. That's the weakness of these tough men. They never think any one else is as tough as they are.

Harvey had set the still up in a tiny, half-broken-down old house, on what had once been his father's land, and was making a daylight run.

He had two guns up there but never got a chance to use either of them.

Cal and George must have just crept up pretty close to the house in the long grass and weeds.

They got up close, George with the gun in his hands, and then Harvey came to the door of the house. He may have heard them. Some of these mountain men, who have been law-breakers since they were small boys, have sharp ears and eyes.

There must have been a terrific moment. I've talked with Luther Ford and several others about it. We are all, of course, sorry for George.

Luther, who is something of a dramatist, likes to describe the scene. His version is, to be sure, all a matter of fancy. When he tells the story he kneels in the grass with a stick in his hand. He begins to tremble and the end of the stick wobbles about. He has taken a distant tree for the figure of Harvey Groves, now dead. When he tells of the scene in that way, all of us standing about and, in spite of the ridiculous figure Luther cuts, a little breathless, he goes on for perhaps five seconds, wobbling the stick about, apparently utterly helpless and frightened and then his figure suddenly seems to stiffen and harden.

Luther could do it better if he wasn't built as he is—long and loose-jointed, whereas George Small, whose part in the tragedy he is playing, is small, and, as I have said, nervous and rather jerky.

But Luther does what he can, saying in a low voice to us others standing and looking, "Now, Cal Long has touched me on the shoulder."

The idea, you understand, is that the two men have crept up to the lonely little mountain house in the late afternoon, George Small creeping ahead with the heavily loaded shotgun in his hands, really being driven forward by Cal Long, creeping at his heels, a man, Luther explains, simply too strong for him, and that, at the fatal moment, when they faced Harvey Groves, and I presume had to shoot or be shot, and George weakened, Cal Long just touched George on the shoulder.

The touch, you see, according to Luther's notion, was a command.

It said, "Shoot!" and George's body stiffened, and he shot.

He shot straight, too.

There was a piece of sheet-iron lying by the door of the house. What it was doing there I don't know. It may have been some part of the stolen still. In the fraction of a second that Harvey Groves had to live he snatched it up and tried to hold it up before his body.

The shot tore right through the metal and through Harvey Groves' head and through a board back of his head. The gun may not have been loaded when George Small brought it from his house. Cal Long may have loaded it.

Anyway Harvey Groves is dead. He died, Luther says, like a rat, in a hole—just pitched forward and flopped around a little and died. How a rat in a hole, when he dies, can do much flopping around I don't know.

After the killing, of course, Cal and George ran, but before they did any running Cal took the gun out of George Small's hand and threw it in the grass.

That, Luther says, was to show just whose gun did the killing.

They ran and, of course, they hid themselves.

There wasn't any special hurry. They had shot Harvey Groves in that lonely place and he might not have been found for days but that George Small's wife, being sick and nervous, just as he is, ran down into town, after Cal and George had left their place, and went around to the stores crying and wringing her hands like a little fool, telling every one that her husband and Cal Long were going to kill some one.

Of course, that stirred every one up.

There must have been people in town who knew that Cal and George and Harvey had been in together and what they had been up to.

They found the body the next morning—the shooting had happened about four in the afternoon—and they got George Small that next afternoon.

Cal Long had stayed with him until he got tired of it and then had left him to shift for himself. They haven't got Cal yet. A lot of people think they never will get him. "He's too smart," Luther Ford says.

They got George sitting beside a road over on the other side of the mountains. He says Cal Long stopped an automobile driving past, a Ford, stopped the driver with a revolver he had in his pocket all the time.

They haven't even found the man who drove the Ford. It may be he was some one who knows Cal and is afraid.

Anyway, they have got George Small in jail over at the county seat and he tells every one he did the killing and sits and moans and rubs his funny little hands together and keeps saying over and over, "God, don't let me do it," just as he did that day when he crossed the bridge, long before he got into this trouble, and I was under the bridge fishing and saw and heard him. I presume they'll hang him, or electrocute him—whichever it is they do in this State—when the time for his trial comes.

And his wife is down with a high fever, and, Luther says, has gone clear off her nut.

But Luther, who acts the whole thing out so dramatically whenever he can get an audience, and who is something of a prophet, says that if they have to get a jury from this county to try George Small, even though the evidence is all against him, he thinks the jury will just go it blind and bring in a verdict of not guilty.

He says, anyway, that is what he would do, and others, who see him acting the thing out and who know Cal Long and Harvey Groves and George Small better than I do, having lived longer in this county and having known them all since they were boys, say the same thing.

It may be true. As for myself—being what I am, hearing and seeing all this . . .

How do I know what I think?

It's a matter, of course, the jury will have to decide. (1933)

VI. *Uses of the Past: The Search for Identity*

Recent Appalachian writing cannot be so handily categorized as that of earlier times, but if there is one characteristic common to most contemporary fiction of the region it is that of the living past. Almost without exception Appalachian writers would belong to what R. W. B. Lewis has called in *The American Adam* the "party of memory," and in story after story there is an attempt on the part of characters to come to terms with the past, which, however, takes many forms. In Jesse Stuart's "Vacation in Hell" it is the pastoral dream of picking peaches, in Mildred Haun's "Melungeon-Colored" the fatalism of folklore handed down since time out of mind, in James Still's "A Master Time" the recollection of the hog-kill and all that went with it, in the passage from Harriette Arnow's *The Dollmaker* the remembered hills of Kentucky, in the chapter from James Agee's *A Death in the Family* an old woman almost unconscious herself but still a living force, and in the selection from Wilma Dykeman's *Return the Innocent Earth*, the past is represented by Cebo's mother. The consciousness of custom and tradition is a theme which mountain literature shares with that of the rest of the South and in all the implied moral is the same: The past may be a burden, but it is also a bond of common humanity.

JESSE STUART

One of the most popular of all American writers, Jesse Stuart
lives with his wife Naomi on the same land in W. Hollow,
Kentucky, where he was born in 1907. Determined to be a
writer for as long as he can remember, he attended a one-
room school and at the age of nine hired out for twenty-five
cents a day working at various jobs. Taking advantage of
every educational opportunity, he eventually entered Lincoln
Memorial University near Cumberland Gap, Tennessee,
where he worked to help pay his way through. Later he
attended Vanderbilt University and came under the influence
of Donald Davidson. Since the publication of *Man with a
Bull-Tongue Plow* in 1934, Stuart has produced fiction,
nonfiction, and poetry at an amazing rate. He has also
farmed, served in the Naval Reserve, taught, and lectured all
over America. Among the many awards he has received are
the Thomas Jefferson Southern Award for *Taps for Private
Tussie* and the Academy of Arts and Sciences Award for
Men of the Mountains, from which the following story is
taken.

Like so much mountain fiction in recent years, "Vacation
in Hell" is replete with symbolic overtones as seen in the use
of the rats, the spider, the snake, and the peaches. Conflicts

in the story are not only between the agrarian and the industrial—farming and mining—but also between original sin and the quest for the Edenic state.

Vacation in Hell

You know how it is here among th' hills. A body's got to make a little money. I've been makin' mine diggin' coal. I make enough durin' th' fall after th' crop's gathered in to buy my youngins some winter clothes and shoes and pay my taxes. I get five cents a bushel fer diggin' th' coal and wheelin' it out where th' jolt-wagons can get to it. I can dig about thirty bushels o' coal a day on an average. That makes a dollar and half a day and honest to God that ain't to be laughed at in times like these. It's better 'n cuttin' timber fer fifty cents a thousand, or hoein' corn fer seventy-five cents a day or doin' gin work fer some farmer fer fifty cents a day.

Lefty Weaver dug coal with me. Lefty and me's been buddies a long time. Atter we'd gather our crops we'd go back to th' coal bank over on Rufus Pratt's place and dig coal together. We allus worked as buddies. I'd hep Lefty gather his crop and he'd hep me. Old Lefty was as good a worker as ever God put breath in. He fit his work. Warn't no standin' back and shirkin' when Lefty took holt o' a thing. When he lifted he didn't stand and holler and grunt like a lot o' fellars. He lifted hard enough to bust a gut. That was Lefty. It took me humpin' all day to do th' work that Lefty done. I shore to God worked to do my half o' work. I jist wouldn't let Lefty out-do me.

Atter we'd worked out in th' fields and farmed all summer, w'y, Lefty called goin' back to th' coal bank a vacation in hell. Th' bank we dug coal from warn't th' best bank Rufus had. He's got four coal banks on his place. But we warn't steady diggers and Rufus give us th' bad bank. It may not be so bad but it got a bad name when th' Right Entry fell in and smashed Sid MacCoy and Lief Porter. It jist got a couple o' fellars is all. That give it sorty a bad name. Th' roof on none o' Rufus Pratt's coal banks ain't any good. It's a brittle rock roof. Got to keep it posted all th' way in. But 'pears like th' roof above our vein o' coal is rottener than any th' roofs.

It was jist two weeks ago. Sall got my breakfast and I drinked a couple o' cups o' good hot black coffee. I was dressed in my bank clothes, and Lord but they's cold in th' December wind when I got out and started down to Lefty's. I hurried down th' path to Lefty's. He'd had his breakfast and was ready. We struck off down th' road to th' mines. It was so cold and our old bank clothes was filled with mud and kindly damp to be wearin'. But we didn't mind that. We jist hurried to th' mines. It's allus warm in th' mines o' a winter time you know. Water a runnin' out and rats livin' back there jist as warm and comfortable.

We put our coal forks and picks and shovels in th' coal buggy. We refilled our lamps with carbite, put in a little water and turned th' little wheel to get th' spark. "Kaflunk" and pop went th' fire and lit our lamps. Then we bent over sorty behind th' buggy and shoved off back to a mile under th' hill. Lefty's big shoulders and mine together nearly spread across some th' nar places in th' coal bank.

"Lefty," I'd say, "you beat anybody diggin' coal I ever saw. Jist lay there on your side and prize around with a crowbar or two a little bit and durned if th' whole vein don't tumble down fer you. In this hard diggin' durned if I don't believe you can dig fifty bushels a day." Lefty'd jist laugh and th' little carbite flame would flicker from his lamp. We could tell when a hot wind was pressin' to th' front o' th' bank. Th' flames on our carbite lamps 'peared to be tryin' to pull away from th' lamps and get back out'n th' mines.

"A lot o' seeps comin' through here," says Lefty, "we must be under that damned sag. We'll need a lot more posts. We'll haf to take a couple o' days off and do a lot o' postin'. If we don't this damned roof goin' to come down shore'n God made th' lumps o' coal. I seen a big rat runnin' out'n here t' other day."

I says: "Lefty, so much o' this bank postin'—havin' to go out and cut tough-butted white oaks fer posts and haulin' em here to th' coal bank—then cartin' back and settin' 'em up—it's that what cuts our average o' coal diggin' down. And look at all th' bone and slate we got to cart out and dump over th' hill."

"I know," says Lefty, "but that ain't it. We got youngins at home. We got a wife ain't we? And wouldn't this be a deep damn grave? All th' tombstones we'd have would be th' saw briars above us, th' green briars, th' tough-butted white oaks and th' rocks! If this entry'd ever fall in I'll be damned if I'd believe anybody could find us where we are now. We've got this hill filled up with enough big holes fer a hundred moonshine stills and a thousand foxes to den in. Th' foxes 'll get it if th' moon-shiners don't beat 'em to it."

It's th' truth that I allus thought o' Sall and my seven youngins when I's back under th' hill. But look at Lefty—he had eleven youngins! Would have another one right soon. Lefty'd have a round dozen! What if th' hill was to get 'im? What if th' hill was to get me? What would his Murt and my Sall and all our youngins do without us? I jist hated to think these thoughts but sometimes I did think 'em. I'd think 'em as I come in behind th' buggy shovin' with all th' strength I had. Sometimes I'd haf to brace my feet on one o' th' little crossties in th' track and above with every ounce o' weight and strength I had.

"See that rat," says Lefty to me, "there he goes! Yander, see 'im! That's th' sign o' a bad roof Hargis. We'd better do some mine postin' tomorrow. We can't go on too fur. I believe we're under that damned sag. It's that big saddle down in th' ridge—dangerous as hell too. We can't tell exactly how we're runnin' with this entry."

I tell you old Lefty's really shovelin' down and prizin' out th' big lumps o' coal. I's loadin' 'em and takin' 'em out'n th' buggy and dumpin' 'em fer th' jolt-wagons and th' teams. By noon I'd shoved out five buggy loads o' coal. Not quite ten bushels to th' buggy. But we'd been doin' good work.

"There goes another rat," says Lefty. "I seen its eyes. Runnin' out'n here."

"Th' moonshiners 'll have a lot o' company when we leave this mine," I says.

"When we leave this mine," says Lefty, "it'll be too dangerous fer th' rats."

"You're about right," I says, "men stay longer in these mines than the rats."

"Th' rats can live a lot easier than men," says Lefty, "they ain't no law to keep them from pilferin'. Jist too bad when they get caught."

"I never liked a rat until I come here," I says. "I didn't know there's one good thing to be said fer a rat. But there is one thing. He warns us when there's danger in th' coal banks. We can see 'im runnin' out. I jist often wonder who warns him!"

"He's more ust to th' ground than we are," says Lefty, "allus lived in a hole in th' hill, under a smoke house, cellar or a hogpen!"

"We jist been in a hole fer ten years," I says.

"We ain't no rats neither," says Lefty, "but if we'd lived back under th' hills all our lives and was born back here, w'y, we'd be changed a lot. You jist think what if a man never saw daylight and worked back here all his life in this night. What would happen to 'im! Jist ast a few o' th' old coal diggers! W'y, he'd get like a varmit. His eyes would get afraid o' th' light. He'd be afraid o' th' light."

"Another rat," I says, "see 'im. Look—watch 'im! There he goes! Where's all th' rats a-comin' from nohow?"

"Don't ast me," says Lefty, "you know as much about 'em as I know. They jist live back in here where it's good and warm is all. They live back here like we do."

Lefty was down on his side diggin' coal. I was jist over on th' other side from Lefty. I was diggin' with a short handled pick. Th' coal it 'peared like was comin' out so easy.

It jist seemed to me like I wasn't diggin' coal. It 'peared to me like I'd been diggin' coal. No, I was not diggin' coal. I was gatherin' peaches. It was July. Th' sun was hot. My how th' sun did come down. It was almost too hot to get my breath. I'd take a big willer basket and walk up th' ladder into th' peach tree. I'd reach up and pick th' peaches. I'd put them in my basket. Th' basket was heavy to hold. Th' leaves on th' peach tree were thick and th' wind was smothery. It was hard fer me to get my breath.

I'd put th' big peaches in th' basket. Once I started to take a bite off'n one and I saw a green snake on a peach tree limb. It was lookin' right into my eye. I jist took aim at 'im with th' peach and drawed back my arm and let th' peach fly. I took th' green snake right above th' eye. He jist bent double like a measurin' worm and tumbled down out'n th' tree. I couldn't see where he hit on th' ground fer I's up in th' peach tree and there's a lot of green wilted leaves below me.

I picked th' basket o' peaches and went down th' ladder with 'em. It was a ladder like we got at home fer th' chickens to walk up in th' oak tree to roost. It bent a little with my weight. Th' peaches was awful heavy. But I helt it against my hip and helt to th' ladder with th' other hand and I got down all right. I dumped th' basket o' peaches in th' barrel that Sall had used to sulphur apples in. I jist didn't like th' smell o' th' durn sulphur. But I poured th' peaches in th' barrel and went back up in th' tree atter more peaches.

I started to take a bite off'n a big ripe peach. I jist looked up in time. It was a durned big stripped-tail spider. He had big hard shiny eyes that looked like agates in th' sun. He's shinin' his two eyes on me right in th' wilted leaves in th' peach tree top. They looked like flashlights after dark. "God," I says to myself, "what's it all about nohow? A body pickin' peaches and can't get to take a bite o' one o' 'em."

I took th' big ripe peach and I cut drive at that spider's eyes. I took one o' 'em casouse. Th' ripe peach jist splattered all over th' spider's face. Th' last I saw o' 'im he's goin' down through th' peach tree limbs a wipin' th' mushy peach from his face with one o' his long hard legs. He was a monstrous spider. About as big as a quart cup I'd say. But I hit 'im in a touchy spot when I plugged his eye. He fell fur below me. I never saw 'im hit th' ground. It was too fur down out'n th' tree.

"Now," I says to myself, "I'll take me a bite o' peach." I pulled me a big peach and started to take a bite. I jist looked in time. It was that durned green snake again. He was right on th' limb in front o' me a-lickin' out his tongue. Fire was dancin' in his eyes too. He was mad. Ripe peach was smeared all over his head where I'd hit 'im before. I didn't know whether to hit his big open mouth with my fist or to hit 'im with another peach. He was at close range. I didn't take a chance with my fist. I jist drawed back and I let 'im have it. Th' peach jist smashed over his face and eyes and he tumbled out'n th' tree like a stuck hog.

"I got 'im this time," I says, "now I can eat a peach in peace."

I reached up and pulled me another peach. Jist as I got ready to take a bite I looked up and seen th' spider. He whetted his front legs across each other and they made a racket like rubbin' two files across each other. He'd cleaned th' peach I'd hit 'im with off'n his face. It was clean as a chip chopped from a tree. His eyes were big and shined like two silver dollars at me. He'd come back to get a bite o' me. Lord, I've allus been more afraid of a spider than I have o' a man. I know how they'll jump twenty feet to bite a body. I intended to get 'im before he got me. I jist drawed back my arm and I cut drive so hard with that peach at his head that

I had to hold to a limb to keep from fallin' out'n th' tree. I busted 'im right between th' eyes and he jist crumpled up like a green leaf scorched by fire—jist wound up like a ball and tumbled out'n th' tree.

"I got you this time," I says, "you damned stripped-tail thing!"

I picked peaches and put 'em in my basket. I jist about had all th' peaches I could carry down out'n th' hot tree. Lord but it was hot up among th' leaves. Jist once in awhile I could get a breath o' wind. I believe it was th' hottest smothery day I ever saw. I'd pick th' peaches fer Sall and then I'd go back to th' coal bank and dig coal. "There's something funny about this," I thought, "I dig coal in th' fall and winter and here I am pickin' peaches fer Sall to can. Maybe it's a dream." Then I thought: "It can't be a dream. Here are th' peaches and here am I up here in th' tree. Right here is a good peach. I'll reach up and get it and take a bite!"

I pulled th' peach down. It had big red spots on it that colored it like a lady's cheeks when th' winter wind stings 'em. I was jist ready to put my mouth over th' peach and bite out a hunk when I looked upon th' limb above me and here was that snake and spider. Both side by side. They'd doubled teamed on me. They'd got together down on th' ground. Now they'd come back up in th' tree to fight me. "I know this tree," I says to 'em both. "It is my peach tree. It is up on th' hill above my pasture field. This peach tree is th' big tree that allus bore so many peaches. It's th' one in th' low swag by th' old rotted white oak stump. It's my tree and by-God I'll defend it. No snake nor spider can run me off'n my own premises."

They jist looked at me. I didn't expect 'em to speak. Who ever heard o' one speakin'. They jist bite a body 's all. "If I hit one o' 'em," I thought, "th' other'n bite me shore as God made th' peaches. I'll jist get down out'n th' empty tree and let 'em have it. I've got th' peaches. They have th' tree." I jist went down the ladder and th' last I saw o' 'em they's settin' upon th' limb like two chickens gone to roost. Eyes a shinin't like silver dollars.

I dumped th' basket o' peaches in th' barrel. I hated to get close to th' barrel fer I smelt th' sulphur. I'd haf to tell Sall about th' snake and th' spider. She wouldn't believe me. She'd say that I'd been dreamin'. I'd ast 'er why she give me th' old sulphurin' barrel to put th' peaches into. I'd have a good'n on 'er! I jist laughed and laughed. But I'd picked th' barrel o' peaches. I's wet with sweat a-doin' it too. Now I'd light my pipe and have a smoke.

I set down on th' ground. I's purty tired-out. I pulled my homemade terbacker crums from my pocket and I put a handful in my pipe. I's tampin' 'em down with my finger. I heard somebody comin' over th' hill talkin'. It was right back o' my peach orchard. You know where that patch comes around th' hill. I never heard as much laughin' in all my life. Sounded like a whole crowd o' men. I felt in my pocket fer a match but I couldn't find one. I says: "It's all damned funny. It's jist like I was when I's a boy. I ust to dream I's tryin' to make water. I'd get about ready and somebody's face would pop up. Then I'd run someplace else and get behind th' sprouts. I'd get ready again and somebody'd slip up on me. I never could find a place. In th' mornin' I'd wake up with a big wet place in my bed—a big yaller circle on th' clean white sheet.

Then Mom would come 'n say: "Why can't you wake up? You big Lummix! Jist lay there and sleep and float th' bed off! Look at my sheet now! It'll be a purty thing to hang out on th' clothes line to dry and all th' neighbor wimmen and th' girls to see! What can I tell them! Hargis floated th' bed away again last night." This must be a dream too. I couldn't eat a peach fer a snake and a spider! A spider big as a quart cup! Huh! I couldn't smoke my pipe fer I couldn't find a match!

"But it's not a dream," I says to myself, "here's my peach orchard. It's in June. It has to be June. I'm gatherin' peaches. Here's th' green leaves wilted in th' sun. Right over there is th' big beech on th' pint. Yander is th' big poplar on th' knoll. Right over yander is my house. I can hear somebody comin'."

When I turned my head around to look th' way I heard th' voices I seen four men comin' down th' hill. They's laughin' and talkin' and havin' a lot o' fun. Jist layin' th' talk off with their hands. They's comin' right down th' path toward me. I didn't know a one o' 'em. They's smokin' cigars and pipes and makin' merry. Big puffs o' smoke were circlin' above their heads.

I says: "Howdy, fellars! One o' you ain't got a match have you?"

"Ain' that funny," says a big freckled-faced fellar with horse-teeth.

Then they all begin to laugh. They'd bend over and pat their knees and laugh.

"He wants a match," says a little sawed-off dumpy fellar with black hair combed straight back over his head.

"What do you know about 'im wantin' a match?" says a tall bean-pole boy with a red face and little mouse teeth. "Jist to think he wants a match."

"Yes," says a big barrel-bellied boy, with red hair and bird-egg blue eyes, "th' poor fellar wants a match. Ain't one of you fellars got a match? Don't you see he's got his pipe filled and wants to smoke? Say, open up your hearts and give th' poor fellar a match. Ain't you wanted to smoke and didn't have a match?"

Then they bent over and laughed again. The fat boy with th' bird-egg eyes jist shook all over when he laughed. "Wants a match," he'd say. Then he'd laugh. "What do you know about that! Ast me fer a match. He don't know who I am?" Then he bent over and laughed again.

"Hep yourself to th' peaches boys," says th' bean pole fellar.

"Don't mind if I do," says th' fat fellar. "Old Hargis don't know who I am. He ust to know me! I know him don't I? Sure, I do. I'd know 'im anyplace."

I says: "How do you know my name? I've never seen you anyplace. I don't know you."

Then all the men laughed. "He don't know you," says th' sawed-off dumpy fellar with th' black hair. "You'd better tell 'im who you are."

"Do you remember th' time your Pap had that little bottom in tame huckleberries below th' old Koonse Saw-Mill?"

"Yes," I says.

"Do you reemember beatin' up Austin Finnie?" he says to me.

"Yes," I says. "And his brother Jim come over and put a shiner under each one o' my eyes!"

"That ain't got a thing to do with it what brother Jim done. I am Austin Finnie!"

"W'y, you've been dead for twenty-six years. You are buried at Three-Mile Hill."

"You jist think I've been dead. I've been alive fer th' first time in my life. Nothin' to bother me now. Nothin' to worry me. I thought I'd come over and bring th' boys to welcome you home. Welcome you to your new life!"

"I'm not dead," I says. "I know damn well I ain't dead. I'm a livin' mortal. This is my peach orchard. These are my peaches. Up in that peach tree is a spider and a snake."

"Yes," says Austin, "they are there. That is right. So am I over at Three-Mile Hill too. Jist a part o' me that don't amount to a damn. You didn't know me because I was a boy when I left here."

"Allright," I says, "I still don't believe you're Austin Finnie. I believe I'm dreamin'. If you're Austin Finnie show me where that tree fell on you and run a limb into your right lung that killed you."

"Allright," says Austin, and he jerked his shirt open and showed me th' big pink scar.

"Good God," I says.

"You don't know th' fellars I got with me either do you?"

"W'y I don't know none o' you fellars. You've jist told me

you's Austin Finnie and showed me th' scar where th' tree fell on you. Th' Austin Finnie I knowed was jist a boy fourteen years old when th' tree fell on 'im."

"Well I've had to grow up damn it," says Austin. "I couldn't stay fourteen forever. Don't you know that!"

"You don't know me neither," says th' tall bean-pole boy. "You ought to."

"No," I says, "I don't know you."

"I'm your brother Wilburn. Jist growed a little is all."

"You don't look like me," I says.

"Of course not," says he, "you take atter Ma's people and I take atter Pa's people."

"My brother Wilburn died when he's eight years old. It was twenty years ago. I can't remember 'im very well."

"I'm Wilburn Dixon. I've jist growed a little 's all. I run around with th' fellars from right around here. You know these two fellars too, Brother Hargis. Buster Broughton, you remember 'im. Died with th' measles in 1914. Pert Rister died with th' fever in 1916."

"Durned if I don't believe I know old Buster," I says, "I thought your coal-black hair and eyes I'd seen sommers before."

I shook his hand. I says: "I'm glad to see you again. Now I'm beginnin' to believe you boys. My new-found Brother Wilburn and my old friend Pert. Let me shake your hands. Boys I'd a-never knowed you!"

"Of course not," says Buster, "we've all growed so. But you've thought a lot about us since we've been gone. That's why we've come to welcome you. Thought we might have a card game or something to show you how glad we are to see you."

"We's jist funnin' with you about th' match," says Pert Rister.

Brother Wilburn, Buster and Pert jist bent over and laughed and laughed.

Austin looked at me with hard eyes. He didn't laugh. He hadn't got over th' beatin I give 'im when we's boys. It allus bore on my mind atter he died. But he ought to forget. We's jist boys then.

"You said you wanted a match," says Pert Rister, "I'll give you one. I ain't got a match but I'll get you some fire."

He just cracked his hands together and a blaze shot up. They all 'peared to vanish in smoke. I never seen which way they went. Nearly all th' peaches had been taken from my barrel. Th' snake spread its thin hard lips up in th' tree and grinned at me. Th' spider's eyes got brighter. They had their heads close together and looked down at me. That was th' last I remember. I was awfully hot.

I wanted to sleep. Th' air got so hot and smothery. I was so wet with sweat. My clothes were wet as water could make 'em.

Then I thought I's in th' bed. Don't remember how I got there. I thought it had all been a dream. Now I was in th' bed with Sall. I thought I had th' kivers wrapped around me and I couldn't get no breath.

Then I got my head out and got a little breath o' fresh air. Then I went to sleep—gradually—a smothery, sweaty, sort of sleep with a heavy quilt upon my back.

Th' next thing I remember was I woke up on t'other side o' th' hill. I was layin' on a quilt on th' ground.

I says: "What's happened?" Sall was beside me cryin'. She says: "Don't you know, Hargis? Honey, don't you know th' mine caved in? They've had to dig you out?"

"Am I hurt," I says, "have I got any bones broke?"

"Ask no questions," says Sall, "but lay right still under th' blankets."

I never saw so many people around th' old mine. But there was a new entry now. It was on t'other side o' th' hill. When th' coal bank caved in it just dropped down.

Where th' earth dropped down all th' other miners

dropped a hole straight down. We's nearly to th' top o' th' ground fer we's runnin' under th' saddle o' th' hill and th' roof was brittle.

"A big piece of rock," says Sall, "was all that saved you. It fell and you fell beside it. Th' roof come down and th' big rock by your side helt it up and made a little room fer you. There was a crack that went down through th' ground to you. Jist looks like th' Lord was with us."

Murt is cryin' as she comes over th' hill and I say to Sall: "What about Lefty?" Murt comes from th' entrance o' th' coal bank on t'other side o' th' hill—she hurries down through th' corn-stalks where th' corn was cut last fall. Th' mud is shoe-mouth deep. Th' sun has come out and melted th' frozen ground.

"He's dead," says Sall. "They took him out at th' main entry. Th' big heap o' dirt fell between you. It got Lefty. Couldn't take 'im out from this side. Lefty is dead."

"Oh he's dead, he's dead," says Murt, wringin' her hands and a cryin'. "Lefty is dead. Lefty is dead."

"Carry me up some, you fellars," I says, "and let me look at that hole where you dug me out." Steve Morton, Shucks Pennix, and Eb Flannery, and John Stableton took a corner apiece o' th' bedsprings I was layin' on and carried me up where I could look over. Lord, I jist couldn't believe I'd been dug out'n that hole. No wonder I's meetin' th' dead and smotherin' pickin' peaches.

I says: "Sall, how long have I been under this hill?"

"Two days, Honey," she says. "Monday night when you didn't come home I knowed something was wrong. So I run down and told Shucks Pennix. He went to th' coal bank and took a crowd o' men. They begin to hunt fer you and found th' coal bank caved in. Th' men know about th' roof. They found th' entry you's in and it was caved in so they come outside and walked over th' hill and found th' slip. One crew o' men dug all night down through th' slip. One crew o' men worked from th' other side o' th' hill. They went back through th' main entrance and dug from th' other side. Then a shift o' men relieved each crew th' next day. Four shifts o' men have been workin' to get you out. About th' time they got you out, they took Lefty out dead from th' other side."

"I'd like to know what's th' matter with me," I says. "Can't move my arms and legs. 'Pears like my breath is short too. I believe my slats are all caved in."

"That's it, Honey," says Sall, "and your spine fractured. Doctor Norris was right here when they hauled you out'n th' hole. You got both arms broke, and one side o' your ribs caved in. But that's all right, Honey. He says you'll live. Look at poor Lefty! Look at poor Murt!"

"I envy Lefty," I says. "Fellars carry me over th' pint on t'other side o' th' hill and let me see old Lefty."

Th' boys took me away from th' deep-deep rabbit hole they dug me from.

They carried me on th' mattress springs over th' muddy ground where I could see thousands o' tracks in th' mud and th' corn-stalks was all mashed down and th' sprouts skint. I tell you it was good to feel th' winter wind against my face and feel th' Kentucky sunshine again. I's jist a old wreck.

My body would never be again what it had been. Th' boys carryin' me'd say: "Be careful now. Don't slip and fall with 'im. Take it easy. Ground is slick from thawin'."

All that stuff atter I'd been under tons o' dirt and rock and got out a livin' mortal to spend th' rest o' my days in bed or in a swing built to th' jyst like old Ephraim Potts did th' time he got his back broke.

There was a big crowd standin' around th' main entrance o' our coal bank. Lefty'd jist been hauled out'n th' mine a little while. He was layin' on th' coal-buggy. Th' buggy was holdin' a different load o' coal.

His face was bloody. His old dirty overalls was a red color

now. They'd been soaked in Lefty's own blood. Murt come back across th' hill with Sall. She's leanin' on Sall's shoulder and cryin'.

I jist laid on my bed and looked at Lefty. It hadn't been very long ago that he was a powerful man. He could dig more coal than any man I'd ever seen go into th' mines. But he wouldn't dig any more coal. He didn't know what it was all about now.

His big body was layin' upon th' buggy like a big lump of red-painted coal. He had th' look o' pain on his lips jist like he'd been shovin' his whole weight against a buggy load o' coal stuck on th' track. His shoulders looked nearly as wide as th' coal-buggy and his powerful big muscled legs fell limp over th' end o' th' buggy. Lefty, my old buddie was dead.

I says to Sall: "I envy Lefty."

"You ought to thank God," says Sall, "that you got out alive. Lefty is dead."

"I got out jist a hull o' a man," I says, "jist like a holler oak. Th' heart o' me is gone, I'm no more. I'll haf to go through life like this. I'll never be th' same. Lefty missed all o' this. He's better off in th' long run."

It took eight men to carry me home. Four carried me until they got tired. They walked along and rested while four more men took me and carried me apiece. I took my last look at th' old hill that had been a killer o' men. Th' roof over th' coal was brittle. That had caused it all. Men feared but they went back and dug th' coal. They had to have money. They had to live.

"It don't matter how many posts a body sets under a roof like that," says Shucks Pennix, "that roof is liable to fall any time. Lefty and Hargis had th' worst coal bank o' th' bunch. But th' other coal banks are jist about as bad!"

I never talked. I jist listened. Sall walked along and looked at me and kept th' blankets tucked around my bed so th' cold winter wind couldn't blow under. I saw th' big heap o' yaller dirt in th' field where they'd gone down and got me. It looked like a big yaller chimney standin' out there in th' cornfield. I looked at th' winter oaks standin' along my patch so silent and contented and waitin' fer th' spring.

I was goin' home now. It jist didn't seem right that I'd been away from home a couple o' days and nights. It seemed like I'd jist waked up in bed atter a night o' sleep.

I jist thought: "Wonder if it ain't that way for Lefty? Jist waked up atter a night o' sleep. But Lefty ain't broke up like I am. Lefty is better off. I hope he is. Old Lefty was a good worker. But we won't dig no more coal together from under this old hill."

I couldn't wipe th' tears from my eyes. Sall would walk along and wipe 'em off. She knowed why I shed 'em. She didn't say anything. I didn't neither. Th' men kept walkin' along with me. I wanted to say but I didn't: "It's my last vacation in Hell. Jist to think about all th' wild dreams I had! That snake and that spider! I can see 'em yet! Gettin' so hot too! Gatherin' peaches!"

I says: "Sall, you got all that sulphur barrel o' peaches I've picked fer you canned yet?"

"What peaches, Honey?" she says.

"I've been pickin' peaches fer you and a stripped-tailed spider and a big green snake tried to run me out'n th' tree. I picked a whole barrel fer you and th' sun was so hot. I thought I's goin' to die. I wanted to smoke and couldn't get a match to light me pipe!"

Atter I told Sall this I laughed. She says: "Oh, yes—I've got 'em canned." She thought I's talkin' out'n my head. Th' men carryin' me begin to look funny at one another and shake their heads and nod.

They thought I's out'n my right mind and all done fer but I warn't. I'd get all right. I'd be like th' big silent oaks they's carryin' me under. I'd jist haf to stand and wait th' long winter through fer th' spring. (1941)

MILDRED HAUN

Born in 1911 in Hamblen County, Tennessee, Mildred Haun grew up in Haun Hollow, Hoot Owl District, Cocke County, where she learned mountain ballads and folklore from her family and neighbors. In 1927 she moved to Franklin in Middle Tennessee to live with an aunt and uncle. She attended Vanderbilt University, where she came under the influence of John Crowe Ransom and Donald Davidson, to whom she gave credit for making her aware of her rich East Tennessee heritage, the essence of which was a mountain folk tradition transmitted orally for generations. Later Miss Haun was Book Review Editor for the *Nashville Tennessean* and an assistant to Allen Tate on the *Sewanee Review*. Her collection of tales, *The Hawk's Done Gone*, was published in 1940 and reissued in 1968 by Vanderbilt University Press, edited by Professor Herschel Gower of the Vanderbilt English Department. "Melungeon-Colored" from this collection illustrates admirably Mildred Haun's artistic use of her mountain antecedents.

Melungeon-Colored
Cordia Owens (born June 1, 1902)

I didn't know what to make of it when I saw Ad come stomping into the house in the middle of the morning. He was white as a lily.

"Cordia runned off and got married last night," he said. "To Mos Arwood."

"Hit's a tale-idle," I said. "It hain't so."

But he said Square Newberry told him. Then he let in to fussing at me because I let her go over there to spend two weeks with Amy. Said after Amy got married and went to Hamblen County to live she had forgot how to take care of anything. Said it looked like I wanted Cordia to run off and get married. I didn't know what to do. Me and Ad had both been tight on Cordia. Tighter than we were on our own young-ons. We never had allowed her to go to any poke suppers or singings or anything like that. Many was the time I had stayed away from things myself just to keep Cordia at home.

Of course, Cordia didn't know but what me and Ad were her real pa and ma. I give Effena a death-bed oath that I never would tell. You know, if you tell something a dying person asks you not to tell you will be haunted by that person the rest of your life. Everybody you tell will be haunted too. It never would have done to have told Cordia—just never would.

I didn't see how I was going to do without Cordia. And having to worry about her. That made it worse. I had missed her them two weeks she had been staying with Amy—missed her worse than a cow misses a baby calf. I told Amy to be careful with her. But I could tell about what had happened. And I was right. Amy let her go to one of them Dunkards' suppers. Of course, a Dunkards' supper is the beatinest place in the world for a boy and girl to start sparking. Cordia couldn't see but what she had as much right to get married as anybody else when she was already seventeen year old. Me and Ad had brought her up with our own youngons and she never did know she was just a grandyoungon.

Effena, she died just two days after she bore Cordia. She had had much to go through on account of her man getting killed and everything. Then taking that long trip to the New Jerusalem church house in the wagon just as it was time for the baby to come. And the baby being a girl instead of the boy she already had named "Little Murf." It was all too much for her. She was always the sickliest one of my youngons anyhow.

So when Effena saw she was going to die she asked me not to ever let Cordia know that her pa had been a Melungeon. Said some folks were getting so they held it against a body for being a Melungeon. I reckon it was because of what that ignorant man from down the country said about them having Negro blood in them. Of course I don't know—I never have seed a Negro. But I've heard tell of them. Ad sees them sometimes when he goes to Newport. But other folks claimed that Melungeons were a Lost Colony or a Lost Tribe or something. I don't know. I just know Effena said for me to raise Cordia up to think she didn't ever have any other pa or ma. And she said for me not to ever let Cordia get married. I could see how Effena thought. I knowed if Cordia ever had any boy youngons they would be Melungeon-colored and her man might not understand. I knew, and I promised Effena just as the breath went out of her.

I set out to keep the promise. Many was the time it was hard to keep from bawling when Cordia would beg like a pup to go somewhere and would think hard of me because I wouldn't let her. But I made up my mind not to worry till I had something to worry about. I told myself there might not be any youngons, or if there were, they might all be girls.

Everything I looked at made me think of Cordia. The blue flowers out in the yard. Cordia had gone out in the woods and dug them up along back in the spring. Cordia liked flowers. I can remember how she liked them even when she wasn't any more than knee-high to a duck—how she would slip off and pluck wild flowers of all sorts and come toting them in. She went all over the side of Reds Run Mountain picking sweet williams in the spring. She would make little round rings out of larkspur blossoms. And press them in the catalogue.

Cordia was handy around the house. She took to cooking like a duck to water. And she was pretty. I wish it had been so I could have let her go to big to-dos and have a good time. If it just hadn't been for that blood in her, I would have let her have a big time. Then when she got married she could have had an infare and everything. But there's no use crying over a burnt-up candle.

Cordia come home that evening and brought Mos with her. I tried not to let her see I was worried. But I did talk to her about all the signs there are that a woman is going to have a baby. I made her promise to come right to me and let me know at the first sign she had. I hate to own up to what I was aiming on doing. All the years that I have been a Granny-woman I never have give anybody a thing to knock a youngon. Heaps of women have begged me to. It is just one of the things I always said no to. But with Cordia it was different. What I aimed on doing was to give her a quart of hot pennyroyal tea. Ma told me about it back when she was teaching me to be a Granny-woman.

I tried to hint around and tell Cordia how to keep from getting big. But Cordia didn't want to keep from it—she said she wanted youngons. So I knew I would have to work easy to keep her from catching on to what it was for. And, on top of it all, right while I was talking to her I heard a dove on top of the house hollering—hollering out its bad luck sound.

Of course I couldn't tell Ad nor the youngons anything about it. And Cordia would know when she had her miscarriage. But I allowed Mos never would know but what Cordia got too hot or jumped down off the fence or something. Then I made up my mind that I wasn't going to worry over a swinging foot-log till I was sure I would have to cross one. I didn't see Cordia e'er a time during that whole winter long. Ad went over there once or twice and he said she was getting on all right. Said she was just broke into harness like an old horse.

It come spring. Spring made me feel so good I didn't stop to worry much over Cordia. I was sure she would let me know. It come a real pretty day. I got up soon that morning because I had a feeling Cordia might take a notion to come home and spend the day. The first thing I seed was Old Puss setting there in front of the door washing her face. I was sure then that somebody was coming. I hurried on and started to milk. I hoped it would be Cordia. I wanted to see her. She hadn't been back any more since her and Mos come the next evening after they were married. Of course, the weather hadn't been fitten for her to come.

I hung the milk bucket across my arm and started out the door. It seemed like I couldn't get my work turned off very well. I just poked around like the dead lice were dropping off me. It seemed like the chickens and turkeys and everything else were hungry. They all started to yelping and running after me. They got on my nerves. I stopped to feed them. Everything I saw made me think of a baby being born, of a ma trying to save a youngon. I could see the egg hanging in the old gray goose's belly. One of the old turkey hens acted sneaking, like she was going to slip off and hunt herself a nest. I seed a little robin skipping about up there in the cow field. Singing because it was fixing to build itself a nest. Happy even before its babies were hatched out. I had to go plumb to the furderest corner of the field. Old Heif always used around the oak trees over there soon of a morning.

I felt all shook up inside. I kept turning around and looking back. I could see somebody coming down the side of Sals King Mountain. I knowed they couldn't be going anywhere else save here. I couldn't think of it being anybody save

Cordia. I went on to milk. I couldn't tell for sure who it was. But I knew in reason it was Cordia. Nobody else would be coming this way. I kept on looking back. It looked to me like everwho it was had on a green hat, a yellow waist, and a blue skirt, and big red shoes. She was leading a cow that had a green head and a yellow neck, a blue body and red legs. Then I caught myself.

I thought if it was Cordia she would go on in the house and make up the beds. I thought nothing had got wrong with her. She never had sent word by Ad that she wanted to see me about anything.

Old Heif was away over in the edge of the pine thicket. I thought I would milk her over there where she stood. It would take less time than driving her up. I seed a snake skin right in front of me. Another bad luck sign. But I had already made up my mind not to let things bother me.

Old Heif had been dry in one tit for over a week. I never had thought much about it before. But I thought about it then. That was the worst of bad luck. Then the sun hid behind a cloud and things looked dark and gloomy. I felt tired and dilitary for some reason. I felt like I was just about ready to fall to staves. The old wet filth in the gullies stunk worse than carrion. I nigh stepped on a tumblebug. It let loose of its ball quick as a frog could jump into the water. That set me to thinking again. Tumblebugs knew how to take care of their youngons. Spiders made a ball to tote their youngons around in too. And dirt dobbers.

And birds—if they thought somebody was going to pester their nests—would grab up the little birds in their mouths and hide them in the bushes somewhere. Then they would perch themselves on a limb and holler. They wanted a body to kill them instead of the little birds. Snakes—even snakes took care of the little snakes. They would swallow them. Then I told myself to stop thinking about such. And then I told myself again that any ma that loved her youngon wouldn't let harm come to it. Cordia was more than my youngon.

I moseyed on back to the house. Seemed like I couldn't hurry no matter how hard I tried. I heard somebody making a racket in the house. I couldn't help but notice that old hen standing in the door. Just as I hollered shoo at her she stuck out her head and crowed. I went over that old saying:

> "A whistling girl and a crowing hen
> Is sure to come to some bad end."

I took note of which one it was so I could ring her old neck for her.

Cordia heard me holler and she come to the door with the broom in her hand.

"Well, howdy doo," I said. "What crooked wind blowed you here?"

"I don't know. How are you all getting along?"

"We are perusing about. How are you and Mos?"

"As well as common, I reckon," she said. She went to talking about needing to be at home. "By rights I ought to be at home working now. But this is the first day it has been fitten to come."

I looked at her. She looked like an old woman—tired and without color. "How many chickens have you'ns got?" I asked her.

"We've not had very good luck. We had about thirty-seven hatched off. We don't have but nineteen now."

"I'll get this milk strained so we can set down and talk," I told her.

She said for me to go on with my work. Then she said, "I guess I might as well tell you now. I'm that way, Ma."

I jumped. "You don't know for sure yet? You might not be."

"Yeah, it couldn't be anything else. I've been that way for three months now."

"Three months?" I knew I mustn't let on. I didn't know what to do. Pennyroyal tea won't do any good after a woman is that far gone. I tried to think it would be a girl baby. I begun saying to myself that I wished Cordia would die before it was born. Of course I didn't wish anything of the sort. I tried to make out like I was proud. "Who are you going to have with you, Cordia?"

"You and Mos's ma," she said.

For the next six months that was all I could think of. I tried to tell myself it was good enough for Cordia because she didn't come and tell me sooner. I tried to think it would be sure to be a girl baby, and not be black. But soon I got to the place where I couldn't believe anything save that it would be a boy. Then when I recollected that Ad had told me Mos had a Melungeon boy from Newman's Ridge in Hancock County staying over there with him during the winter to help saw wood, I seed that would make things worse.

I had a feeling it would have to happen that night, that night it did happen. It was an awful night. A stormy night in the fall of the year. It was the worst storm I ever saw. I didn't see how Ad could lay there and sleep like a knot on a log. I had to stay up and look out the window. I couldn't have slept if I had all the jimpson weed seeds in the world in my shoes.

The water was slushing against the house. There wasn't any air—not enough for a body to breathe. I thought I was going to smother. I opened the window door and kept it open, even if the lightning did scare me. The hard splashes of water. I had to shut it once or twice—for a short while. It was a regular cloudbust.

I felt certain something terrible was bound to happen that very night. I had been feeling it all day. I dreamed of snakes the night before—green snakes. I hadn't slept any the rest of the night. The wind. I buttoned the door and the window too. And propped the door good. But every puff that come I thought it was going to blow open. I feared to breathe. If the door should blow open the wind would suck through and blow the top off the house. I felt like the wind coming through the window was about to blow me away.

"Ad," I yelled.

"Shet your mouth," he said. Then real quick, "What the hell?"

"The door. Quick," I told him.

I bit my tongue as I watched him fight against the wind. He got it pushed to. I knew he couldn't hold it there. "Hand me the hammer and nails here," I heard him yell. I went to turning around and around. To save my life I couldn't think where the hammer was. A big flash of lightning come. It run all over the house. I thought the world was coming to an end. It looked like the whole world was on fire. "God damn it, hurry up," I heard Ad yelling. "On the fireboard."

I handed him the hammer. I couldn't hold the door to. I tried to drive the nails while he held it. Mashed my finger. More bad luck. And I stopped to think of that right there. I wondered how Cordia was taking the storm. I hoped she wouldn't have the baby that night. It come a keen crash. I hollered out that lightning struck the house. Ad said for me to come on to bed and stop that damned foolishness.

I couldn't go to bed. For the last nine days I had been feeling all turned upside down. The feeling I always had when something was going to happen. Something was bound to take place that night. I recollected about hearing death bells in my ears before midday that day. That meant somebody was going to die before midnight. I thought it meant the whole world. It looked to me like everybody was going to burn up.

I caught myself hoping the world would come to an end. So Cordia wouldn't have any trouble. I tried not to think on Cordia. I went to telling Ad the world was coming to an end and singing, "Will you be ready for that day to come?" I kept thinking about that Melungeon boy that had helped Mos all winter. Ad said he was mighty talky around Cordia. That made it worse. It all hopped around through my mind. I got in the bed behind Ad. I didn't even fool to turn my shoes upside down. Corns didn't matter any more. Not then.

I pulled the quilt up over my head. I had rather not see the lightning. I thought there wasn't any use in trying to stop God's plans. I had almost been warned but I hadn't done anything about it. I thought the Lord would understand.

I heard a noise that wasn't just thunder. It was a tree falling. Sounded like the whole earth was being tore up by the roots. I made up my mind to go. I never had done any harm to anybody that I could think of.

I thought I heard somebody calling, "Granny." I was scared so bad I thought it was the Lord. I heard it again. I was making up my mind to do what Preacher Jarven said and answer, "Yes, Lord," when I heard knocking at the window. I called Ad again.

"Aw, God damn it," he said. Then I heard him hollering louder. "Yeah—yeah, all right, Mos." I felt Ad getting out of bed. It was Mos instead of the Lord. I listened. "Cordia wants Granny to come over there," I heard Mos say. All I could think of then was getting over there and helping Cordia. I remembered that the door was nailed. I was afeared to open the window on account of the wind. The only thing I could think of was to lift up a plank and crawl out under the house.

I heard Ad scolding me. "What are you doing?" he yelled. "Go on out the window like somebody with some sense." I minded him. It looked like the whole ground was a branch. I thought I would be drowned. I heard a screech owl hollering. "A screech owl hollering in the rain, Mos," I told him. Then I said to myself that it needn't be telling me. I already knew death was nigh.

Mos said, "Slop Creek is rising like smoke from a brush pile. I guess the foot-log is gone by now."

That meant we would have to go way up the creek and cross that swinging foot-log. I didn't think I could ever get across it. It was kind of rickety anyhow. I made up my mind I didn't care if I did fall in. The wind was something awful. Things kept roaring in my head till I thought it was going to bust. "Mos, what was that?" I asked.

"A tree. It just blowed up by the roots," he said.

I kept talking to Mos. "Mos, we'll be kilt dead before we get there. I know we will. I dreampt about snakes last night. That lightning."

He answered me real calm-like, "The ground is soggy. These here sod soakers make pine trees and cedars easy to blow up by the roots."

I heard a loud noise—sounded like a gun going off in my ear. The woods were roaring in my ears. I felt like the whole woods were blowing up. It looked like there was a tree falling right on me. I wanted to yell. But I didn't have enough breath to yell. "That was just a limb broke off in front of us," Mos said. He said we had better go straight up the edge of the creek from then on. Then he said, "You will be the only one there. The Shin-Bone branch is up so big I can't go after Ma."

I was almost glad he couldn't. The water was roaring so I was afraid to go near the bank. I was afraid it might come down in a big gush and wash us away before we got to Cordia. Then I pert nigh wished it would. I never would have known how it all ended up. I heard something squealing—some kind of animal squealing. "Look," Mos said. "There goes Dona Fawyer's hogs down the creek. And good God, cow too."

I was so tore up I didn't care what washed away. I made up my mind to pull myself together. I never had been into such a shape before. Then was the time I needed to keep my head. We got to the foot-log. When it lightened I could see the foot-log swing in the wind. I wished it wouldn't lighten so keen. I didn't want to see it swinging in the wind. I felt like if I set my foot on the foot-log I would fall right off. Then I would go down the creek with Dona's hogs and cow. Hogs and cows and me, I thought. There were worse things to be with.

Mos took hold of my hand. Both of us would go together, I thought. I wondered why the wind had to blow like that, why the branch had to roar. I got to thinking maybe the world had already come to an end. I thought maybe that was hell. Preacher Jarven said it would be raining lightning bolts all the time in hell. Every drop would be an arrow of blazing lightning and it would go through your body.

I went to thinking about that song:

"Will the waters be chilly,
Will the waters be chilly
When I am called to die?"

The water would roar and the sinner would fall into it. It would freeze around his neck. His head would be left up on top for the burning arrows to stick into. And the thunder. But I had enough sense left to know that wasn't hell. I told myself I had better keep my head. Something picked me up. I thought it was the water. I could feel myself floating against a cow.

"I'll carry you across," Mos said.

"Don't drop me," I kept on telling him.

He set me down. I couldn't bear to look back. The foot-log would be gone in another second. Mos walked so fast it was hard for me to keep up with him. We got in sight. It looked like the house was on fire. The tree in the yard was blowed up by the roots. I seed that the next thing. I wondered if Cordia had heard all that racket. We had to surround the tree to get up on the porch. Cordia didn't open the door. The first thing I thought about was that she was dead. "Push it open—I can't come," I heard her say from inside. Mos pushed the button off with one big lunge. I followed him in.

"It is done over. Hurry up," Cordia said.

I threw back the quilt. "Heat me some water. Bring me the scissors, Mos," I said.

Mos come running with the scissors. "Its skin!" I said. "A Melungeon! I knowed it." I don't know what made me say it. Mos give the baby one look. "That's why that devil wanted to stay here," he yelled.

I seed him pick up a stick of stove wood. I didn't know what had made me blurt it out. I just didn't know anything. I reckon Cordia was too weak to pay any attention to what we were saying. She was shaking. I seed she was having convulsions. That was what it was. And I took note of the stuff by the side of her bed. She had took too much gunpowder.

"Mos!" I yelled. "Don't!"

But it was too late to yell. I stood there like a post, trying to think. I felt Mos take a hold of me. I thought he was going to kill me too.

"Listen to reason," he said to me. "Are you in your right senses?"

I jumped. I don't think I knowed for sure whether I was or not. I saw I would have to quiet myself down. The baby was alive. With Cordia dead. Mos's eyes—they were as green as a glow worm.

"Me and you can bury her up yander on the hill in the morning," he said.

I stood there. But I recollected the hill. Mos's grandpa and grandma were buried up there. It would be for Cordia's good. It would save her name. All that went through my head. Nobody would blame Mos. Nobody would know about the burying. Nobody would come to the burying anyhow. Both creeks were up too high. I seed it was best. We could tell that we had to bury her. I thought of the baby.

I've thought about the things that happened that night. All night me and Mos hammered on the coffin. Old rough planks that he tore out of the house loft. Right there in the room where Cordia was. And her more than my girl. And the little funny-colored baby that I prayed the Lord would let die before we got the coffin made. But it didn't. It kept on whimpering and gasping. I never could have stood it if I had been in my right mind. I was scared out of my right senses. Scared Mos would hit me in the head with that hammer. Somehow, I wasn't willing to die, even if I did think I wanted to.

When we got the coffin done we didn't even stuff it and put a lining in it. We piled some quilts down in it and laid Cordia on them. I did wash Cordia and wrap her up in a new quilt. But we had to break her knees to get her legs to go down into the coffin.

And the baby, it kept on living. Mos, he just picked it up and put it on in. I stood and watched him. Stood stone-still and watched him. We nailed the lid down. It was about chicken crow then. I had to stay there in the room while Mos went to dig a grave. And the baby alive.

It poured down rain while Mos was gone. It was dark as pitch outside. And that cat. That cat kept on clawing at the window. It meowed and screamed and went on. Then I heard that panther scream right out there in the yard. It sounded like a woman's screaming.

A big puff of wind come and blew the door open. And that cat kept on. I was afraid the panther would get in the house if I didn't go shut the door. But I couldn't move toward the door. I couldn't move any which way.

The grave, it was full of water by the time me and Mos got Cordia carried up there. About halfway there we had to set the coffin down in the mud so we could rest a spell. And that cat. When we set the coffin down, it jumped upon it. Mos couldn't knock it off. It fit him right back. It followed us every jump of the way. I could hear the baby smothering and that cat meowing.

I'm not even sure we buried Cordia with her head to the west. We might not have. Cordia may have her back turned to the Lord when she raises up to meet him.

It was seven months after we buried her that the funeral was. I had a good notion not to go to the funeral. But I wanted to hear what was said about Cordia. Mos tried all winter to get a preacher man. The roads were gouted out so bad he had to wait till spring. Then Preacher Jarven come. It was a pretty day. A spring day when the bees and birds and spiders and hens and everything thought about their babies.

It would have been a pretty day for Cordia to get married.

It was a big funeral. Everybody in Hoot Owl District was there. I wished there hadn't so many folks come. They all said they pitied me and Mos because the branches were up so big we had to do the burying by ourselves.

There were already several folks at the church house when me and Ad got there. I thought we would be the first ones. We started soon. Looked as if the folks were all staring at me like a cat trying to charm a bird. I thought I saw Cordia setting up there on the front seat by Mos. I told myself to keep my senses. But there was a woman setting by the side of Mos.

"Me and you are supposed to set up hyear with Mos and his woman, ain't we?" I heard Ad asking. Then it come to me who that woman was. It was Mos's new woman. He hadn't waited till the dirt settled on Cordia's grave. That woman looked like Cordia. Cordia pale as a sheet. Mos was pale too. I wanted to tell Mos how it was. But I knowed that would disturb Effena's peace, because I had promised her. Effena would come back and haunt Mos. Mos would be haunted and I would be haunted.

I tried to listen to what the preacher man was saying. Something about Cordia. Something about he wished everybody was as ready to go as Cordia was when the Lord saw fit to call her home. Something about them that weren't ready would cook in biling molasses the rest of their lives, and smell burning sulphur. Something about Cordia making a bee-line for Heaven.

It begun to get dark. I thought a cloud must be coming up. It was time of year for such. "April showers make May flowers," I went to saying, and thinking about how everything was planned out. Then I heard the leaves. Sounded like there was a whirlwind outside. I thought I could smell something burning. I thought about sulphur, about the church being on fire, about the woods—but the woods were green.

I took note that everybody was standing. Ad pulled me up.

It seemed like everybody was hollering about something. Then I seed. They were just singing loud. I went to singing too:

> "In vain to Heaven she lifts her eyes
>   But guilt, a heavy chain,
> Still drags her downward from the skies
>   To darkness, fire and pain."

Darkness, fire and pain. They were what I had been through. But God said he understood.

Me and Ad went on out behind Mos. We stopped down there in the hollow and I picked my dress tail full of poke sallet for supper. The sun was going down and the air felt good and cool-like. A honey bee flew around my head, and some pretty pied butterflies. I felt peaceful as a kitten. (1940, 1968)

JAMES STILL

Born in 1906 at Double Creek in the red hills of Alabama, James Still is the descendant of English and Scotch-Irish stock who fought in the American Revolution, the War of 1812, and in the Civil War on the side of the Confederacy. After attending Lincoln Memorial University, he received an M. A. from Vanderbilt University and a degree in library science from the University of Illinois. For several years he was associated with the Hindman Settlement School at the forks of Troublesome Creek in the Kentucky mountains. The recipient of numerous awards, he is perhaps best known for his remarkable novel, *River of Earth*. A writer of high aesthetic standards, he has been called by Appalachian novelist Wilma Dykeman the "Flaubert of Southern literature." He makes his home at Wolfpen Creek near Mallie, Kentucky. Americans today can purchase pre-packaged food and products, but James Still in "A Master Time" reminds us vividly of the community effort that was often involved in obtaining basic provisions in the Southern mountains.

A Master Time

Wick Jarrett brought the invitation of his eldest son, Ulysses. "He's wanting you to come enjoy a hog-kill at his place next Thursday," Wick said. "Hit's to be a quiet affair, a picked crowd, mostly young married folks. No old heads like me—none except Aunt Besh Lipscomb, but she won't hinder. 'Lysses and Eldora will treat you clever. You'll have a master time."

Thursday fell on January 4, a day of bitter wind. I set off in early afternoon for Ulysses's home-seat on Upper Mule Creek, walking the ridge to shun the mud of the valley road. By the time I reached the knob overtowering the Jarrett farm my hands and ears were numb, my feet dead weights. A shep dog barked as I picked my way down and Ulysses opened the door and called, "Haste to the fire." I knocked my shoes at the doorstep. "Come on in," Ulysses welcomed. "Dirt won't punish our floors."

A chair awaited me. Before the living-room hearth sat Ulysses's cousins, Pless and Leander Jarrett, his brothers-in-law, Dow Owen and John Kingry, a neighbor, Will Harrod, and the aged midwife, Aunt Besh Lipscomb, who had lived with Ulysses and Eldora since the birth of their child. From the stoveroom came sounds of women's voices.

"Crowd to the fire and thaw," Ulysses said, "and pull off your jacket."

"Be you a stranger?" Aunt Besh asked.

"Now, no," Ulysses answered in my stead. "He lives over and across the mountain."

"He's got a tongue," Aunt Besh reproved. And she questioned, "Was I the granny-doctor who fotched you?"

Ulysses jested, "Why, don't you remember?"

Aunt Besh said, "I can't recollect the whole push."

The fellows chuckled under their breaths, laughing quietly so as not to disturb the baby sleeping on a bed in the corner.

The heat watered my eyes. My hands and feet began to ache.

"You're frozen totally," Aunt Besh declared. "Rid your boots and socks and warm your feet. Don't be ashamed afront of an old granny."

"Granny-doctors have seen the world," Ulysses said.

"Hush," Aunt Besh cried, and as I unlaced my boots she said, " 'Lysses, he needs a dram to warm his blood."

Ulysses shrugged. "Where'd I get it?"

"A medicine dram. Want him to catch a death cold?"

"I ought to got a jug for the occasion," Ulysses said. "We're all subject to take colds. I forgot it plumb."

"I'd vow there's a drap somewhere."

"This is apt to be the driest hog-kill ever was," Ulysses said.

"Humph," Aunt Besh scoffed.

I had my boots on again when the wives gathered at the fire. Eldora took up the baby, scolding Ulysses, "You'd let it freeze. Its nose is ice." And Ulysses said, "Men, we might's well allow the petticoats to hug the coals a spell. Let's get air." We followed him through the front door, and on around to the back yard. The wind tugged at us. We pulled our hats down until the brims bent ears.

Ulysses led us into the cellar-house. "Look sharp," he invited, "and see how I fare." We noted the baskets of Irish and sweet potatoes, cushaws and winter squash, the shelves loaded with conserved vegetables and fruits. "Anybody give out o' victuals," he went on, "come here and get a turn." Will Harrod glanced about impatiently, and Dow Owen uncovered a barrel. Ulysses said, "Dow, if you want to crack walnuts, the barrel's full." Pless and Leander Jarrett took seat on a meat box and grinned.

"Ah, 'Lysses," Will Harrod groaned, "quit stalling."

"Well, s'r," Ulysses said, "I've got a little stuff, but it's bad, my opinion. I'd hate to poison folks." The bunch livened.

Pless and Leander, knowing where to search, jumped off the salt box and raised the lid; they lifted a churn by the ears. Will said, "Say we drink and die." Ulysses cocked his head uncertainly at me. I said, "Go ahead, you fellows."

A gourd dipper was passed hand to hand, and Will, on taking a swallow, yelled joyously. Ulysses cautioned, "Don't rouse Aunt Besh. We'd never hear the last." The gourd was eased from Dow Owen's grasp. Ulysses reminding, "A job o' work's to do. We'll taste lightly right now." A jar of pears was opened to straighten breaths.

We returned to the fire and the wives laughed accusingly, "Uh-huh" and "Ah-hah." Leander's wife clapped a hand on his shoulder, drew him near, and sniffed. She said, "The sorry stuff and don't deny it."

"Pear juice," Leander swore. "Upon my honor."

"You've butchered the swine quick," Aunt Besh said scornfully. No attention was paid to her and she jerked Ulysses's coattail. "Are ye killing the hogs or not?"

"Can't move a peg till the women are fixed," Ulysses answered.

"It's you men piddling," one of the women reported. "We've had the pots boiling an hour."

Eldora spoke, "Who'll mind the baby? I won't leave it untended."

Aunt Besh said, "Don't leave me watchdogging a chap."

Pless's wife volunteered to stay with the baby. She was the youngest of the wives, sixteen at the most.

"Aunt Besh," Ulysses petted, "you just set and poke the fire."

"Go kill the hogs," Aunt Besh shrilled.

"She's the queen," Ulysses told us.

"Go, go."

Ulysses got his rifle. "John," he said, "come help." They made off.

There being two hogs for slaughter we waited until the

second shot before rushing toward the barn, men through the front door, women the rear. The hogs lay on straw, weighing between 350 and 400 pounds. The wind raced, flagging blazes beneath three iron pots. An occasional flake of snow fell.

We men scalded the carcasses in a barrel; we scraped the bristles free with knives while the women dabbled hot water to keep the hair from "setting." The scraping done, gambrels were caught underneath tendons of the hind legs and the beasts hefted to pole tripods; they were singed, shaved, and washed, and the toes and dewclaws removed. Ulysses and John served as butchers, and as they labored John questioned:—

"Want the lights saved?"

"Yes, s'r," Ulysses replied.

"Heart-lump?"

"Yip."

"Sweetbreads?"

"Fling them away and Aunt Besh will rack us. The single part she'll eat."

Will Harrod laid a claim: "The bladders are mine. I'll raise balloons."

The shep dog and a gang of cats dined well on refuse.

The wind checked and snow fell thicker. The women hurried indoors, carrying fresh meat to add to the supper they had been preparing nearly the day long. Ulysses and John hustle their jobs, the rest of us transporting hams, loins, shoulders, and bacon strips to the cellar-house. No hog-kill tricks were pulled. Nobody had a bloody hand wiped across his face; none dropped a wad of hog's hair inside another's breeches.

John complained to Ulysses, "The fellars are heading toward the cellar-house faster'n they're coming back."

"We'll join 'em in a minute," Ulysses said.

2

When I entered the living room Aunt Besh asked, "Got the slaughtering done finally?" And seeing I was alone she inquired, "Where's the crowd?"

"They'll come pretty soon," I said, removing my hat and jacket and brushing the snow onto the hearth. "We put by the sweetbreads," I added.

Aunt Besh gazed at me. Pless's wife clasped the baby and lowered her face. Aunt Besh said, "Son, speak while 'Lysses hain't here to drown you. Was I the granny-doctor who fotched you into life?"

"Aunty," Pless's wife entreated, "don't embarrass company."

"Daresn't I ope my mouth?" Aunt Besh blurted.

I said, "Who the granny was, I never learned."

"Unless you were born amongst the furren I'm liable to 'a' fotched you. I acted granny to everybody in this house, nigh everybody on Mule Creek."

Pless's wife blushed. She stirred on her chair, ready to flee.

"There's a way o' telling," Aunt Besh went on. "I can tell whether I tied you or not."

Up sprang Pless's wife, clutching the infant. She ran into the stoveroom.

"I wasn't born on Mule Creek," I explained.

"Upon my word and honor!" Aunt Besh cried. "Are ye a heathen?"

Eldora brought the child back to the fire, and she came laughing. The husbands tramped in, Dow walking unsteadily, for he had made bold with the churn dipper. Will dandled two balloons. Hearing mirth in the stoveroom John asked, "What's put the women in such good humor?"

Aunt Besh watched as a chair was shoved under Dow, and she began to wheeze and gasp. Presently Ulysses queried, "What's the trouble, Aunt Besh?"

"My asthma's bothering," she said. "The cold's the fault."

"Why, it's tempering," Ulysses remarked. "It's boiling snow, but the wind's stilling."

"My blood's icy, no matter."

"I'll wrap you in a quilt."

"No."

"I'll punch the fire."

"Devil," Aunt Besh blurted, "can't you understand the simplest fact?"

Eldora scolded, " 'Lysses, stop plaguing and go mix a cup of ginger stew to ease her."

Ulysses obeyed, and Aunt Besh raised her sleeves and poked forth her arms. "See my old bones," she whimpered. "There's hardly flesh to kiver 'em. I'll need good treatment, else I'm to bury." Tears wet her eyes.

"Aunty," Will comforted, "want to hold a balloon?"

"Keep the nasty thing out o' my view," Aunt Besh said.

Ulysses fetched the stew—dram in hot water, dusted with ginger and black pepper. Aunt Besh nursed the cup between quivering hands and tasted. " 'Lysses," she snuffed, "your hand was powerful on the water."

Supper was announced and Ulysses told us, "Rise up, you fellers," and Eldora said, "You'll find common victuals, but try to make out." We tarried, showing manners. Ulysses insisted, "Don't force us to beg. Go, the bread's smoking." After further prompting we trooped into a narrow gallery lighted by bracket lamps, which was the dining room. John hooked a wrist under Dow's arm, leading him. Aunt Besh used the fire-poker for walking stick.

"Why don't you eat with us women at the second table?" Eldora asked Aunt Besh.

"I don't aim to wait," Aunt Besh said. "I'm starving."

We sat to a feast of potatoes, hominy, cushaw, beans, fried and boiled pork, baked chicken, buttered dumplings, gravy, stacks of hand-pies, and jam cake. Ulysses invited, "Rake your plates full. If you can't reach, holler."

As we ate, laughter rippled in the stoveroom. Leander's

wife came with hot biscuits and her face was so merry Leander inquired, "What's tickled you feymales?" She made no reply.

John said, "They've been giggling steady."

"We ought to force them to tell," Leander said. "Choke it out."

"If you'll choke your woman," John proposed, "I'll choke mine."

"Say we do," Leander agreed. "And everybody help, everybody strangle his woman, if he's got one. But let's eat first."

A voice raised in the stoveroom: "You'll never learn, misters." The laughter quieted.

"We'll make them pray for air," Leander bragged loudly. He batted an eye at us. "We'll not be outsharped."

"Cross the women," Ulysses said, "and you'll have war on your hands."

"Suits me," Leander said, and Pless and John vowed they didn't care. Will, his mouth full, gulped, and nudged Dow. Dow, half asleep, said nothing.

Of a sudden the women filed through the gallery, their necks thrown, marching toward the fire. Only Eldora smiled.

Ulysses said, "You big talkers have got your women mad. But I didn't anger mine."

"Ah," Pless said, "they know we're putting-on."

"Eat," Aunt Besh commanded, "eat and hush."

Dow nodded in his chair and Ulysses arose and guided him to a bed.

3

While we were at table the wives hid the churn, and when they joined us in the living room later in the evening the four estranged couples sat apart, gibing each other. Ulysses tried making peace between them. The wives wouldn't budge, though the husbands appeared willing.

John sighed, "Gee-o, I'm thirsty," and his wife asked

sourly, "What's agin pure water?" "Hit's weaky," was the reply.

Finally Ulysses threw open the door. The wind had calmed, the snowing ceased. Moonlight behind clouds lighted the fields of snow. Ulysses said, "Maybe the way to end the ruckus is to battle. Who's in a notion to snowball-fight?"

"Anything to win the churn," Leander said.

"The churn's what counts," Pless baited, "the women don't matter."

"A fight would break the deadlock," Ulysses declared.

The four wives arose.

Will groaned, "I'm too full to move," and John testified, "I can't wiggle." Pless and Leander were as lief as not, yet Pless reminded, "Me and Leander are old-time rabbit rockers."

Ulysses urged, "Tussle and reach a settlement."

The wives pushed John and Will onto the porch and shoved them into the yard. "Get twenty-five steps apart," Ulysses directed, "and don't start till I say commence." He allowed the sides to prepare mounds of snowballs.

I had followed to witness the skirmish, as had Eldora and Dow's wife. Behind us Aunt Besh spoke, "Clear the door. Allow a body to see."

Ulysses halloed, "Let 'em fly," and the wives hurled a volley. A ball struck Will's throat and he appealed to Ulysses, "Rocks, unfair." Aunt Besh hobbled to the porch, the better to watch; she shouted and we discovered the sides she pulled for. Will and John fought halfheartedly, mostly chucking crazy; Leander and Pless, deadeye throwers, practiced near-hits, tipping their wives' heads, grazing shoulders, shattering balls poised in hands. The women dodged and twisted and let fly.

Will sat in the snow when the hoard of balls was exhausted, and John quit—quit and yanked up his collar.

Leander and Pless stopped tossing and batted the oncoming missiles.

The women crept nearer, chucking point-blank. They rushed upon Will and before he could rise to escape had him pinned. They stuffed snow in his mouth and plastered his face. Then they seized John, a docile prisoner, rolling him log-fashion across the yard. And they got hands on Pless. Pless wouldn't have been easily caught had not Leander grabbed his shoulders and shielded himself. Leander stood grinning as snow was thrust down Pless's neck.

Leander's feet wouldn't hold at his turn. It was run, fox, run around the house, the women in pursuit. He zigzagged the yard, circled the barn, took a sweep through the bottom. They couldn't overhaul him. His wife threatened, "Come take your punishment, or you'll get double-dosed." He came meekly, and they buried him in snow. They heaped snow upon him and packed and shaped it like a grave. He let them satisfy themselves until he had to rise for air.

The feud ended and all tramped indoors good-humoredly, the wives to comb rimy hair, the husbands to dry wet clothes and accuse Aunt Besh of partiality. Hadn't Aunt Besh bawled "Kill 'em" to the women? An argument ensued, Aunt Besh admitting, "Shore, I backed the girls."

The husbands fire-dried, chattering their teeth exaggeratedly, and their wives had the mercy to bring the churn from hiding and place it in the gallery. The dipper tapped bottom as its visitors heartened themselves. Aunt Besh eyed the gallery-goers. "I got chilled a-watching," she wheezed.

Ulysses said, "I don't hear your gums popping."

"Are ye wanting me to perish?" she rasped.

Eldora chided Ulysses into brewing a ginger stew, and Aunt Besh instructed, "This time don't water hit to death."

It was Leander who remembered to inquire, "Now, what tickled you feymales back yonder?"

The women turned their heads and smiled.

The night latened, and Aunt Besh dozed. Husbands and wives, reconciled, sat side by side. The balloons were kept spinning aloft. Apples were roasted on the hearth, potatoes baked in ashes; and popcorn was capped and pull-candy cooked.

Past one o'clock Eldora made known the retiring arrangements. Aunt Besh would sleep in her chair, on account of asthma. Two beds in the upper room would hold five women, two in a lower provide for six men. Ulysses and Eldora, occupying the living-room bed, could keep the child near the fire and attend Aunt Besh's wants in the night.

My roommates sauntered off. When I followed they were snoring. John, Will, and Dow lay as steers strawed to weather a blizzard; Pless and Leander, my assigned bedfellows, were sprawled, leaving little of the mattress unoccupied. I decided to go sleep in front of the hearth, though I waited until the house quieted, until smothered laughter in the upper room hushed.

I found the coals banked, the lamp wick turned low. Aunt Besh sat wrapped in a tower of quilts and I thought her asleep. But she uncovered her face and spoke, "See if there's a drap left in the churn." I investigated, and reported the churn empty. She eyed me coldly, as she might any creature who had not the grace to be born on Mule Creek. "I'll endure," she said. (1949)

HARRIETTE ARNOW

Harriette Louisa Simpson Arnow was born in Wayne County, Kentucky, and spent most of her childhood in the town of Burnside, in Pulaski County. She attended Berea College and received her Bachelor's degree from the University of Louisville. In addition to *The Dollmaker* her works include *Mountain Path* (1936), *Hunter's Horn* (1949), *The Weed Killer's Daughter* (1970), and two volumes on the social history of the old Southwest: *Seed Time on the Cumberland* (1960), and *Flowering of the Cumberland* (1963). She is married to former newspaperman Harold B. Arnow, is the mother of two children, and presently lives in Ann Arbor, Michigan.

One of the major social problems of Southern Appalachia and America has been the relatively recent out-migration of the mountain people to the great cities of the North; and if one had to identify a definitive novel dealing with this social upheaval, *The Dollmaker* would be the obvious choice.

Gertie Nevels, the protagonist, finds herself in an almost completely alien environment in wartime Detroit; and her memories of the Kentucky hills play a major role in her own quest for identity and raise huge questions about the quality of urban life, especially as it relates to the rural heritage of America. The following chapter from *The Dollmaker* examines in both direct and subtle ways the conflict of two dissimilar worlds. The title has been supplied.

Adjusting

After supper, when the radio was still at last and Clovis and the children had gone to bed, Gertie sat a while whittling in the kitchen. She finished one of Homer's dolls and began the rough work on another. She soon got so sleepy that for some minutes she did little but nod and yawn and try to blink her eyes into wakefulness. Since Clovis had been put on this shift, she dreaded to go to bed even worse than formerly, for as soon as she got into bed she always came wide awake.

Tonight was no better than other nights. She lay rigidly still, inviting sleep, but it would not come. Half her mind wondered how soon the alarm would go off. The other half listened to the wind, or in the spells of silence between the sob and shriek of it, the night sounds of the city, lonelier seeming than by day, as if she lived in a world where nothing else lived. If in the silence she could hear the creek over rocks, the wind in living trees, the bark of a fox, the cry of a screech owl—anything alive, not dead like the clock and the Icy Heart.

She thought of their debts on the car, Icy Heart, washing machine, radio, dishes, curtains. Her mind kept wanting to add the total, reckon up the interest, that must be more, way more than John's 5½ per cent. She turned restlessly from side to side, but her mind wouldn't turn from the debts. What if Clovis got sick? She wouldn't think. She'd put herself back home. Pretty soon the war would be over and they'd be going back. She still had the more than three hundred dollars she'd saved in fifteen years. And she musn't go back without a face for the block of wood. It must be a happy, laughing face even though she'd lost the Christ with the red leaves in his hands.

She was, instead of the laughing Christ, seeing Reuben's hurt and angry eyes when the alarm sounded. Clovis, whose hands always awakened first, reached and turned it off. Sleep pulled him back on the pillow, but Cassie awakened whimpering, and Clytie cried sleepily, "Is it school time?"

Clovis protested as always that there was no need for her to get up. But as always she did, though his lunch was fixed, and there was nothing to do but make coffee. She'd rather be up in the kitchen than in bed unable to sleep for reading the sounds of Clovis—the opening of the icebox, hiss of the gas, slide of the lunch box across the table. Sound for sound that Whit made in the Meanwell kitchen behind the other wall. If she drowsed, the sounds might mix, and Clovis, her man, would cease to be a man and become instead a numbered sound, known only by the number.

She thought of numbers still when Clovis was gone, and she was back in bed. Numbers instead of people. But she wanted people. People to call her, "Gertie." If she could have an animal to nose her hand, a red bird to watch, even a potted plant. Something alive, she had to have something alive. Remembering roused her to lift on one elbow, smiling a little. She had forgotten the ice flowers on the kitchen window. This morning, before the wind rose to scatter the loose snow and make a body think there was another blizzard, the ice flowers on the glass had shone red as if alive when through them she had watched the sun rise between Mrs. Daly's chimney and the telephone pole.

She was glad when two or three days later the children brought from school word that at the term end there was to be a thing called an "open house" to which the mothers were invited so that they could see how it was in school and talk to the teachers about their children. It would be nice to see

Mr. Skyros, the art teacher, again, and she wanted to talk with some of the other teachers, especially Mrs. Whittle, who taught Reuben.

He had come slamming through the door that same afternoon, his eyes blazing, not speaking, and it had taken three questions to find out what ailed him. He was to have "that ole Miz Whittle" another term. Cassie, who would be six in February, had come home shivering. Next term she'd have to learn to read for true. She had to go into "Ole Miz Huffacre's room," the meanest teacher, Clytie had warned her, in the whole school.

"You'll learn to read same as th others," Gertie had comforted Cassie, and to Reuben, "You've jist got off on th wrong foot with her—keep a tryen."

However, doubts tore at her as three days later she walked to the school after having accepted Max's offer to watch Amos and Cassie until it was time for her to go to work at four-thirty.

She would, she decided, go first to Miss Vashinski. Cassie liked her so, and maybe she would warn this Miss Huffacre that Cassie might have a lot of trouble in learning to read. Then it came to her that Cassie had only the one Miss Vashinski, but Miss Vashinski had a lot of Cassies' most of whom had been with her for months instead of only a few weeks. The woman wouldn't recollect her.

She was hardly prepared when Miss Vashinski right off gave her a great big smile and said: "How do you do, Mrs. Nevels. I hate to lose Cassie. She was so sweet."

Gertie smiled, "She hates to leave you, but how can you recollect all th"—Clytie didn't want her to say "youngens," but she couldn't think of the other word—"youngens," she said at last, remembering too late the word Clytie liked was "kids." But she went on, flushing, flustered, "Let alone recollect their mamas."

Miss Vashinski laughed until her dangling earrings trembled. "I don't always remember, but I remember you," she said, savoring a victory. "On Cassie's first day Garcia spoke, remember? I was almost ready to give up."

"He must be talken right along now," Gertie said. "Cassie says somethen about him ever once in a while."

"He's fine, just fine," Miss Vashinski said. "You should hear him and Cassie together. The other day we'd had a story about a little girl in Holland—I'd told the children Holland was a country across the ocean, and of course they started talking about countries—you know we have many countries here. Garcia said to Cassie, 'My country is Mexico,' and Cassie said to Garcia, 'My country is Kentucky.' Wasn't that sweet?" and she turned to the next mother, but after smiling, turned back to Gertie, who was saying, worried:

"Cassie's so afeared that she won't learn to read."

"She'll learn," Miss Vashinski said. "She has a high intelligence rating; if she should have trouble, have her eyes checked right away."

"Her eyes is good," Gertie insisted. "She can see th stars an she don't git up close; she backs off . . ." She had just remembered her father before he got his double-vision glasses.

Miss Vashinski had stopped in the middle of a great big smile after getting only as far as, "How do you do, Mrs.—" She couldn't remember the other mother's name, and was glad to look at Gertie again. "She could have a kind of far-sightedness. I'll make a note." She turned back to the other mother, a dark dumpling of a woman in a red and yellow scarf with blue roses, perspiring as she said slowly and timidly, "I—Michael Ospechuk's mother."

Gertie turned away. The woman looked too scared to talk. Maybe she had older ones like Clytie who didn't like the words she used and told her what to say. She followed a group to the basement, where in a little crowded, sweat-smelling room a great gang of children played with balls and jumping ropes. She realized she was looking at the "gymnasium" of which Reuben had dreamed. Its ceiling wasn't high enough for even a basketball goal, and it was smaller than a classroom.

The teacher, a tired, middle-aged woman, smiled as the mothers introduced themselves, pretending like, Gertie thought, she remembered their children. She couldn't, because she taught all the children in the school above the third grade, and there were, she had heard, 642 children in a building put up forty years before for three hundred. This tired teacher looked as if in her time she had taught them all. But when Gertie introduced herself she smiled and said: "Your son is so cute. At first he was so bashful, and he still won't do couple dancing with anyone but me. He's just getting to that age, you know; but in the folk games he's already one of the best—such a good sense of rhythm."

"Seems like Enoch's smart in everything," Gertie said.

"Enoch," the woman said, looking disappointed, trying to remember an Enoch, "I thought you were Reuben Nevels's mother."

Gertie laughed. "I'm Reuben's too. I just didn't figger Reuben 'ud be good at dancen."

"Why? I'll bet you are," she said, smiling, already turning to another mother who was wanting to know why her Eva Marie had got a *U* in self-control.

Gertie looked over her shoulder as she left the room. If she'd been a little girl here, her black sin would have been no sin at all. Clytie had been troubled the first time the gym class danced. Folk games the teacher had called it, she told her mother, but still it was dancing. She had been relieved when Gertie assured her that it was no sin, not the sinful dancing of which her Grandmother Kendrick had warned so many times.

Gertie tramped on up and down the building, a big perspiring woman in the crowd of mothers. The warm lights in her eyes grew warmer when she heard Clytie, the blue band of a traffic director on her arm, talking to the telephone in the principal's office easy as if she'd been born in a house with a ringing telephone. She was smiling widely by the time she had seen Enoch's home-room teacher and heard what a good boy he was, how well he had adjusted, and how quickly he learned his lessons. She felt proud and happy, remembering that until their coming to Detroit she, with help from Clytie, had given him most of the schooling he had had. She saw him sitting up near the front of the room with a book and some papers on his desk. She looked at him, smiling, until he lifted his head. He turned red, looked quickly away, then down, and began a furious scribbling. She stood an instant watching, her smile dying slowly.

Mr. Skyros, with his questions about the head in the wood he had heard she was making, and his praise of Reuben's carving—for in art class he taught, along with lots of other things, carving in wood and soap, even potatoes—brought back a lot of the lost warmth. She lingered a while in the art room, studying the exhibits, and wishing her father could have seen such a room. A hound dog, a clumsy, ugly thing with too little chest and too much belly, made by Reuben, was there for everybody to see. She was ashamed of it and half thought to put it out of sight until two mothers admired it, and then she lingered, reaping the nice remarks for a harvest for Reuben.

It was getting late, the children marching homeward through the halls, before she reached the one room she dreaded—Mrs. Whittle's. It was empty save for one other mother just coming out, and a woman who Gertie knew was Mrs. Whittle, for she was taking her purse from an open desk drawer. She hesitated in the doorway. She wished the woman, a tall, thinnish, middle-aged person with a pink and white face above a yellow stringy neck, would invite her in. Mrs. Whittle did glance up briefly, but only turned sharp around to a cupboard in the corner behind her desk. Gertie studied her hair, so neatly and so smoothly fixed in rows and rows of little yellow curls that it made her think of the hard and shiny scallops on some piece of her mother's starched embroidery.

She waited a moment longer, then cleared her throat and said, "Miz Whittle."

The woman opened the cupboard door and gave a slight backward nod as if to indicate that she had heard. Gertie watched as she lifted carefully off a paper-wrapped hanger a long dark green coat. She held the coat for an instant at arm's length, turning it slowly, inspecting it. She found something on a sleeve which she lifted off with the fingertips of one pale bright-nailed hand. She then put one arm into the coat, crooked the arm, and studied the coat over it for possible specks. The hand of the coated arm took the purse while she went through the same careful procedure with the other sleeve, then tied and buttoned the coat.

Gertie moved a step nearer and stood by the desk. The woman was now taking a dark green felt hat from a shelf and did not look around when Gertie said, "I come to talk to you about my youngen—boy."

Mrs. Whittle, with a crinkling hiss of paper, was removing the hat from a green paper sack. "You'll have to hurry," she said, her voice somehow matching the paper. "It's late and I've been teaching and talking to mothers all afternoon."

"Th slip my youngens brung home said th teachers ud talk to us after school," Gertie said, speaking with difficulty, choked up at being forced to speak to the woman's back.

Mrs. Whittle put the hat an instant on her head while she folded the bag and laid it upon the shelf. She then took the hat carefully between the tips of her fingers, and bending so as to get her face exactly in the center of a mirror affixed to the door, eased the hat gently onto the bright hair so that no one of the close-coiled ringlets was disturbed. The business required her utmost concentration, and she could not speak again until the hat was on and she was opening her purse, looking into it. "The child's name?" she asked, bringing out her lipstick, turning again to the mirror.

"Reuben—Reuben Nevels."

Mrs. Whittle gave no sign that she had heard. The lipstick

needed even more time and concentration than the hat. Gertie came round to the end of the desk, tried to see the woman's eyes in the mirror, but saw only their lids drooping over the eyes fastened onto the mirrored slowly shaping mouth. The precise red bow was finished at last. Mrs. Whittle turned, looked briefly at Gertie, then spoke as she opened the desk drawer, and took out gloves, "Well, what is the matter? Did your child fail to pass? A percentage do, you know."

"No, he passed," Gertie said, fighting to keep her voice smooth. "But—but you're his . . ." She had forgotten the name, the kind of teacher. "You've got him more'n th other teachers, an you'll keep on a haven him an . . ."

"Are you trying to say that I'm his home-room teacher?" Mrs. Whittle asked, drawing on a glove.

Gertie nodded.

"Well, what is the matter?" She was smoothing the drawn-on gloves finger by finger now.

"He—he don't seem to be a doen so good—not in his home room. He ain't happy; he don't like school, an I thought mebbe . . ."

Her words, though halting and stumbling as they were, caused Mrs. Whittle to glance up from the second glove, and for the first time the two women looked at each other. Mrs. Whittle smiled, the red mouth widening below the old woman's angry glaring eyes. "And of course it's his teacher's fault your child is unhappy. Now just what do you expect me to do to make him happy?"

"That's what I come to ask you," Gertie said. "He kinda likes his other classes, an back home he was . . ."

"Back home," Mrs. Whittle said, as if she hated the words, her voice low, hissing, like a thin whip coming hard through the air, but not making much noise. "You hill—southerners who come here, don't you realize before you come that it will be a great change for your children? For the better, of course, but still a change. You bring them up here in time of war to an overcrowded part of the city and it makes for an over-crowded school. Don't you realize," she went on, looking again at Gertie, looking at her as if she alone were responsible for it all, "that until they built this wartime housing—I presume you live there—I never had more than thirty-two children in my section—and only one section." She opened her purse. "Now I have two sections—two home rooms, one in the morning with forty-three children, one in the after-noon with forty-two—many badly adjusted like your own—yet you expect me to make your child happy in spite of . . ." Words seemed inadequate, and she was silent while she reached into her purse.

"But I've got three more in school, an they git along an—"

"What did you say your name was?"

"Nevels. My boy's name is Reuben. Maybe you don't recol-lect him, but—"

"I don't what?" And she frowned as she might have at a child giving the wrong answer.

" 'Recollect,' I said," Gertie answered.

"Does that mean 'remember'?"

When Gertie continued to stand in choked silence staring down at her, she went on, after taking a bunch of keys from her purse and closing it. "I do remember now—too well. Your children came up for discussion in faculty meeting the other day." She stopped to select a key, a small steel-colored one. "The others have, I understand, adjusted quite well, especially the younger boy and the older girl, but Reuben—I remember him," and she looked up from locking a desk drawer, toward a back seat in the row farthest from her desk and the windows. She looked down, choosing another key, then bent to the other drawer. "He has not adjusted. His writing is terrible—he's messy; quite good in math but his spelling is terrible. I'm giving him a *U* in conduct because he just won't get along with other children."

"He warn't bad to fight," Gertie said to the woman's back, for she had turned now to lock the cupboard doors.

"I have had one mother complain most bitterly. Her son had a toy gun. He was talking to Reuben, teasing him a little perhaps. You know how children tease—learning to take is a part of their adjustment to life." She took out a ring holding car keys. "Reuben lost his temper—he's forever sullen with a chip on his shoulder—and bragged to the other boy that he wouldn't have a toy gun." She shook one drawer to make certain it was locked, shook the other, but looked at Gertie the better to emphasize her revelations. "He bragged he had a real gun all his own, and that he'd taken it off in the woods and hunted alone and that once he'd seen a bear. He never tried to kill it, just shot at it and it ran away, the boy said Reuben said. The boy, of course, called him a liar, and Reuben—are you certain he is only twelve years old?— slapped him down. The mother came to me. I told her to go to the principal." She turned toward the door, jingling the car keys impatiently.

Gertie's face was pale. Her wide mouth was a straight line above her square, outthrust chin, her big hands gripped into fists until the knuckle bones showed white, her voice husky, gasping with the effort to keep down all that rose within her. "Reuben warn't lyen. He's had a rifle since he was ten years old. They's bear an deer clost to our place back home. We're right nigh th edge of a gover'ment game preserve. One year the deer eat up my late corn."

She drew a long shivering breath. "I don't want any a my youngens ever a playen with a toy gun, a pointen it at one another, an a usen em fer walken canes er anything. Some day when they've got a real gun they'll fergit—and use it like a toy."

Mrs. Whittle smiled. "Your psychology, and your story, too, are—well—interesting and revealing, but . . ." She stepped into the hall. "I see no point in carrying this discussion further. He will have to adjust."

"Adjust?" Gertie strode ahead, turned and looked at the woman.

"Yes," Mrs. Whittle said, walking past her. "That is the most important thing, to learn to live with others, to get along, to adapt one's self to one's surroundings."

"You teach them that here?" Gertie asked in a low voice, looking about the dark, ugly hall.

"Of course. It is for children—especially children like yours —the most important thing—to learn to adjust."

"You mean," Gertie asked—she was pulling her knuckle joints now—"that you're a teachen my youngens so's that, no matter what comes, they—they can live with it."

Mrs. Whittle nodded. "Of course."

Gertie cracked a knuckle joint. "You mean that when they're through here, they could—if they went to Germany— start gitten along with Hitler, er if they went to—Russia they'd git along there, they'd act like th Russians an be"— Mr. Daly's word was slow in coming—"communists—an if they went to Rome they'd start worshippen th pope?"

"How dare you?" Mrs. Whittle was shrill. "How dare you twist my words so, and refer to a religion on the same plane as communism? How dare you?"

"I was jist asken about adjustments," Gertie said, the words coming more easily, "an what it means."

"You know perfectly well I mean no such thing." Mrs. Whittle bit her freshly lipsticked lips. "The trouble is," she went on, "you don't want to adjust—and Reuben doesn't either."

"That's part way right," Gertie said, moving past her to the stairs. "But he cain't hep th way he's made. It's a lot more trouble to roll out steel—an make it like you want it—than it is biscuit dough." (1954)

JAMES AGEE

James Agee was born in 1909 in Knoxville, Tennessee. He attended St. Andrews school, Exeter Academy, and Harvard, where he was graduated in 1932. Since the posthumous publication of *A Death in the Family* in 1957, he has increasingly been recognized as one of the most extraordinary literary talents of his time. His other works include *Morning Watch* (1951), *Let Us Now Praise Famous Men* (1941) with Walker Evans, a book of poems, *Permit Me Voyage* (1934), and the film script for the *African Queen*.

Any student of Appalachian life perceives immediately the tremendous role played by the family and the importance of family traditions. Nowhere has this subject been given more sensitive and artistic treatment than in James Agee's masterful *A Death in the Family*. The Sunday trip into the hills of East Tennessee is in effect a journey into the past, where Rufus is awakened to the significance of ancestral ties. Though Agee leaves the reader to his own conclusions, there seems to be no doubt that in the coming together of generations Rufus as well as other members of the family acquires a wisdom of the heart. The title for this selection has been supplied.

Family Ties

After dinner the babies and all the children except Rufus were laid out on the beds to take their naps, and his mother thought he ought to lie down too, but his father said no, why did he need to, so he was allowed to stay up. He stayed out on the porch with the men. They were so full up and sleepy they hardly even tried to talk, and he was so full up and sleepy that he could hardly see or hear, but half dozing between his father's knees in the thin shade, trying to keep his eyes open, he could just hear the mild, lazy rumbling of their voices, and the more talkative voices of the women back in the kitchen, talking more easily, but keeping their voices low, not to wake the children, and the rattling of the dishes they were doing, and now and then their walking here or there along the floor; and mused with half-closed eyes which went in and out of focus with sleepiness, upon the slow twinkling of the millions of heavy leaves on the trees and the slow flashing of the blades of the corn, and nearer at hand, the hens dabbing in the pocked dirt yard and the ragged edge of the porch floor, and everything hung dreaming in a shining silver haze, and a long, low hill of blue silver shut off everything against a blue-white sky, and he leaned back against his father's chest and he could hear his heart pumping and his stomach growling and he could feel the hard knees against his sides, and the next thing he knew his eyes opened and he was looking up into his mother's face and he was lying on a bed and she was saying it was time to wake up because they were going on a call and see his great-great-grandmother and she would most specially want to see him because he was her oldest great-great-grandchild. And he and his father and mother and Catherine got in the front seat and his Granpa Follet and Aunt Jessie and her baby and Jim-Wilson and Ettie Lou and Aunt Sadie and her baby got in the back seat and Uncle Ralph stood on the running board because he was sure he could remember the way, and that was all there was room for, and they started off very carefully down the lane, so nobody would be jolted, and even before they got out to the road his mother asked his father to stop a minute, and she insisted on taking Ettie Lou with them in front, to make a little more room in back, and after she insisted for a while, they gave in, and then they all got started again, and his father guided the auto so very carefully across the deep ruts into the road, the other way from LaFollette as Ralph told him to ("Yeah, I know," his father said, "I remember *that* much anyhow."), that they were hardly joggled at all, and his mother commented on how *very* nicely and carefully his father always drove when he didn't just forget and go too fast, and his father blushed, and after a few minutes his mother began to look uneasy, as if she had to go to the bathroom but didn't want to say anything about it, and after a few minutes more she said, "Jay, I'm awfully sorry but now I really think you *are* forgetting."

"Forgetting what?" he said.

"I mean a little too fast, dear," she said.

"Good road along here," he said. "Got to make time while the road's good." He slowed down a little. "Way I remember it," he said, "there's some stretches you can't hardly ever get a mule through, we're coming to, ain't they Ralph?"

"Oh mercy," his mother said.

"We are just raggin you," he said. "They're not all *that* bad. But all the same we better make time while we can." And he sped up a little.

After another two or three miles Uncle Ralph said, "Now around this bend you run through a branch and you turn up sharp to the right," and they ran through the branch and turned into a sandy woods road and his father went a little slower and a cool breeze flowed through them and his mother said how lovely this shade was after that terrible hot sun, wasn't it, and all the older people murmured that it sure was, and almost immediately they broke out of the woods and ran through two miles of burned country with stumps and sometimes whole tree trunks sticking up out of it sharp and cruel, and blackberry and honeysuckle all over the place, and a hill and its shadow ahead. And when they came within the shadow of the hill, Uncle Ralph said in a low voice, "Now you get to the hill, start along the base of it to your left till you see your second right and then you take that," but when they got there, there was only the road to the left and none to the right and his father took it and nobody said anything, and after a minute Uncle Ralph said, "Reckon they wasn't much to choose from there, was they?" and laughed unhappily.

"That's right," his father said, and smiled.

"Reckon my memory ain't so sharp as I bragged," Ralph said.

"You're doin fine," his father said, and his mother said so too.

"I could a swore they was a road both ways there," Ralph said, "but it was nigh on twenty years since I was out here." Why for goodness sake, his mother said, then she *certainly* thought he had a wonderful memory.

"How long since *you* were here, Jay?" He did not say anything. "Jay?"

"I'm a-studyin it," he said.

"There's your turn," Ralph said suddenly, and they had to back the auto to turn into it.

They began a long, slow, winding climb, and Rufus half heard and scarcely understood their disjointed talking. His father had not been there in nearly thirteen years; the last time was just before he came to Knoxville. He was always her favorite, Ralph said. Yes, his grandfather said, he reckoned that was a fact, she always seemed to take a shine to Jay. His father said quietly that he always did take a shine to her. It turned out he was the last of those in the auto who had seen her. They asked how she was, as if it had been within a month or two. He said she was failing lots of ways, specially getting around, her rheumatism was pretty bad, but in the mind she was bright as a dollar, course that wasn't saying how they might find her by now, poor old soul; no *use* saying. Nope, Uncle Ralph said, *that* was a fact; time sure did fly, didn't it; seemed like before you knew it, this year was last year. She had never yet seen Jay's children, or Ralph's, or Jessie's or Sadie's, it was sure going to be a treat for her. A treat *and* a surprise. Yes it sure would be that, his father said, always supposing she could still recognize them. Mightn't she even have died? his mother wanted to know. *Oh* no, all the Follets said, they'd have heard for sure if she'd died. Matter of fact they *had* heard she had failed a good bit. Sometimes her memory slipped up and she got confused, poor old soul. His mother said well she should *think* so, poor old lady. She asked, carefully, if she was taken good care of. Oh, yes, they said. That she was. Sadie's practically giving her life to her. That was Grandpa Follet's oldest sister and young Sadie was named for her. Lived right with her tending to her wants, day and night. Well, isn't that just wonderful, his mother said. Wasn't anybody else could do it, they agreed with each other. All married and gone, and she wouldn't come live with any of them, they all offered, over and over, but she wouldn't leave her home. I raised my family here, she said, I lived here all my life from fourteen years on and I aim to die here, that must be a good thirty-five, most, a good near forty year ago, Grampaw died. Goodness sake, his mother said, and she was an old *old* woman *then!* His father said soberly, "She's a hundred and three years old. Hundred and three or hundred and four. She never could remember for sure which. But she knows she wasn't born later than eighteen-twelve. And she always reckoned it might of been eighteen-eleven."

"*Great heavens,* Jay! Do you *mean* that?" He just nodded, and kept his eyes on the road. "Just *imagine that,* Rufus," she said. "Just *think* of *that!*"

"She's an old, old lady," his father said gravely; and Ralph gravely and proudly concurred.

"The things she must have seen!" Mary said, quietly. "Indians. Wild animals." Jay laughed. "I mean *man*-eaters, Jay. Bears, and wildcats—terrible things."

"There were cats back in these mountains, Mary—we called em painters, that's the same as a panther—they were around here still when *I* was a boy. And there is still bear, they claim."

"Gracious Jay, did you ever *see* one? A panther?"

"Saw one'd been shot."

"Goodness," Mary said.

"A mean-lookin varmint."

"I know," she said. "I mean, I *bet* he was. I just can't get over—why she's almost as old as the country, Jay."

"*Oh*, no," he laughed. "Ain't nobody *that* old. Why I read somewhere, that just these mountains here are the oldest . . ."

"Dear, I meant the nation," she said. "The United States, I mean. Why let me see, why it was hardly as old as I am when she was born." They all calculated for a moment. "*Not* even as old," she said triumphantly.

"By golly," his father said. "I never thought of it like that." He shook his head. "By golly," he said, "that's a fact."

"Abraham Lincoln was just two years old," she murmured. "Maybe three," she said grudgingly. "Just try to *imagine* that, Rufus," she said after a moment. "Over a hundred years." But she could see that he couldn't comprehend it. "You know what she is?" she said, "she's Granpa Follet's *grand-mother!*"

"That's a fact, Rufus," his grandfather said from the back seat, and Rufus looked around, able to believe it but not to imagine it, and the old man smiled and winked. "Woulda never believed you'd hear *me* call nobody 'Granmaw,' now would you?"

"No sir," Rufus said.

"Well, yer goana," his grandfather said, "quick's I see her."

Ralph was beginning to mutter and to look worried and finally his brother said, "What's eaten ye, Ralph? Lost the way?" And Ralph said he didn't know for sure as he had lost it exactly, no, he wouldn't swear to that yet, but by golly he was damned if he was sure this was *hit* anymore, all the same.

"Oh *dear,* Ralph how *too bad,*" Mary said, "but don't you mind. Maybe we'll find it. I mean maybe soon you'll recognize landmarks and set us all straight again."

But his father, looking dark and painfully patient, just slowed the auto down and then came to a stop in a shady place. "Maybe we better figure it out right now," he said.

"Nothin round hyer I know," Ralph said, miserably. "What I mean, maybe we ought to start back while we still know the *way* back. Try it another Sunday."

"Oh, Jay."

"I hate to but we got to get back in town tonight, don't forget. We could try it another Sunday. Make an early start." But the upshot of it was that they decided to keep on ahead awhile, anyway. They descended into a long, narrow valley through the woods of which they could only occasionally see the dark ridges and the road kept bearing in a direction Ralph was almost sure was wrong, and they found a cabin, barely even cut out of the woods, they commented later, hardly even a corn patch, big as an ordinary barnyard; but the people there, very glum and watchful, said they had never even heard of her; and after a long while the valley opened out a little and Ralph began to think that perhaps he recognized it, only it sure didn't look like itself if it *was* it, and all of a sudden a curve opened into half-forested meadow and there were glimpses of a gray house through swinging vistas of saplings and Ralph said, "By golly," and again, "By golly, that is *hit.* That's hit all right. Only we come on it from behind!" And his father began to be sure too, and the house grew larger, and they swung around where they could see the front of it, and his father and his Uncle Ralph and his Grandfather all said, "Why sure enough," and sure enough it was: and, "There she is," and there she was: it was a great, square-logged gray cabin closed by a breezeway, with a frame second floor, and an enormous oak plunging from the packed dirt in front of it, and a great iron ring, the rim of a wagon wheel, hung by a chain from a branch of the oak which had drunk the chains into itself, and in the shade of the oak, which was as big as the whole corn patch they had seen, an old woman was standing up from a kitchen chair as they swung slowly in onto the dirt and under the edge of the shade, and another old woman continued to sit very still in her chair.

The younger of the two old women was Great Aunt Sadie, and she knew them the minute she laid eyes on them and came right on up to the side of the auto before they could even get out. "Lord God," she said in a low, hard voice, and she put her hands on the edge of the auto and just looked from one to the other of them. Her hands were long and narrow and as big as a man's and every knuckle was swollen and split. She had hard black eyes, and there was a dim purple splash all over the left side of her face. She looked at them so sharply and silently from one to another that Rufus thought she must be mad at them, and then she began to shake her head back and forth. "Lord God," she said again. "Howdy, John Henry," she said.

"Howdy, Sadie," his grandfather said.

"Howdy, Aunt Sadie," his father and his Aunt Sadie said.

"Howdy, Jay," she said, looking sternly at his father, "howdy, Ralph," and she looked sternly at Ralph. "Reckon you must be Jess, and yore Sadie. Howdy, Sadie."

"This is Mary, Aunt Sadie," his father said. "Mary, this is Aunt Sadie."

"I'm proud to know you," the old woman said, looking very hard at his mother. "I figured it must be you," she said, just as his mother said, "I'm awfully glad to know you too." "And this is Rufus and Catherine and Ralph's Jim-Wilson and Ettie Lou and Jessie's Charlie after his daddy and Sadie's Jessie after her Granma and her Aunt Jessie," his father said.

"Well, Lord God," the old woman said. "Well, file on out."

"How's Granmaw?" his father asked, in a low voice, without moving yet to get out.

"Good as we got any right to expect," she said, "but don't feel put out if she don't know none-a-yews. She mought and she mought not. Half the time she don't even know me."

Ralph shook his head and clucked his tongue. "Pore old soul," he said, looking at the ground. His father let out a slow breath, puffing his cheeks.

"So if I was you-all I'd come up on her kind of easy," the old woman said. "Bin a coon's age since she seen so many folks at onct. Me either. Mought skeer her if ye all come a whoopin up at her in a flock."

"Sure," his father said.

"*Ayy*," his mother whispered.

His father turned and looked back. "Whyn't you go see her the first, Paw?" he said very low. "Yore the eldest."

"Tain't me she wants to see," Grandfather Follet said. "Hit's the younguns ud tickle her most."

"Reckon that's the truth, if she can take notice," the old woman said. "She shore like to cracked her heels when she heared *yore* boy was born," she said to Jay, "Mary or no Mary. Proud as Lucifer. Cause that was the first," she told Mary.

"Yes, I know," Mary said. "Fifth generation, that made."

"Did you get her postcard, Jay?"

"What postcard?"

"Why no," Mary said.

"She tole me what to write on one a them postcards and put hit in the mail to both a yews so I done it. Didn't ye never get it?"

Jay shook his head. "First I ever heard tell of it," he said.

"Well I shore done give hit to the mail. Ought to remember. Cause I went all the way into Polly to buy it and all the way in again to put it in the mail."

"We never did get it," Jay said.

"What street did you send it, Aunt Sadie?" Mary asked. "Because we moved not long be . . ."

"Never sent it to no street," the old woman said. "Never knowed I needed to, Jay working for the post office."

"Why, I quit working for the post office a long time back, Aunt Sadie. Even before that."

"Well I reckon that's how come then. Cause I just sent hit to 'Post Office, Cristobal, Canal Zone, Panama,' and I spelt hit right, too. C-r-i . . ."

"Oh," Mary said.

"Aw," Jay said. "Why, Aunt Sadie, I thought you'd a known. We been living in Knoxvul since pert near two years before Rufus was born."

She looked at him keenly and angrily, raising her hands slowly from the edge of the auto, and brought them down so hard that Rufus jumped. Then she nodded, several times, and still she did not say anything. At last she spoke, coldly, "Well, they might as well just put me out to grass," she said. "Lay me down and give me both barls threw the head."

"Why, Aunt Sadie," Mary said gently, but nobody paid any attention.

After a moment the old woman went on solemnly, staring hard into Jay's eyes: "I knowed that like I know my own name and it plumb slipped my mind."

"Oh what a shame," Mary said sympathetically.

"Hit ain't shame I feel," the old woman said, "hit's sick in the stummick."

"Oh I didn't m . . ."

"Right hyer!" and she slapped her hand hard against her stomach and laid her hand back on the edge of the auto. "If I git like that too," she said to Jay, "*then* who's agonna look out fer her?"

"Aw, tain't so bad, Aunt Sadie," Jay said. "Everybody

slips up nown then. Do it myself an I ain't half yer age. And you just ought see Mary."

"Gracious, yes," Mary said. "I'm just a perfect scatter-brain."

The old woman looked briefly at Mary and then looked back at Jay. "Hit ain't the only time," she said, "not by a long chalk. Twarn't three days ago I . . ." she stopped. "Takin on about yer troubles ain't never holp nobody," she said. "You just set hyer a minute."

She turned and walked over to the older woman and leaned deep over against her ear and said, quite loudly, but not quite shouting, "Granmaw, ye got company." And they watched the old woman's pale eyes, which had been on them all this time in the light shadow of the sunbonnet, not changing, rarely ever blinking, to see whether they would change now, and they did not change at all, she didn't even move her head or her mouth. "Ye hear me, Granmaw?" The old woman opened and shut her sunken mouth, but not as if she were saying anything. "Hit's Jay and his wife and young-uns, come up from Knoxvul to see you," she called, and they saw the hands crawl in her lap and the face turned towards the younger woman and they could hear a thin, dry crack-ling, no words.

"She can't talk any more," Jay said, almost in a whisper. "Oh *no*," Mary said.

But Sadie turned to them and her hard eyes were bright. "She knows ye," she said quietly. "Come on over." And they climbed slowly and shyly out onto the swept ground. "I'll tell her about the rest a yuns in a minute," Sadie said.

"Don't want to mix her up," Ralph explained, and they all nodded.

It seemed to Rufus like a long walk over to the old woman because they were all moving so carefully and shyly; it was almost like church. "Don't holler," Aunt Sadie was advising his parents, "hit only skeers her. Just talk loud and plain right up next her ear."

"I know," his mother said. "My mother is very deaf, too."

"Yeah," his father said. And he bent down close against her ear. "Granmaw?" he called, and he drew a little away, where she could see him, while his wife and his children looked on, each holding one of the mother's hands. She looked straight into his eyes and her eyes and her face never changed, a look as if she were gazing at some small point at a great distance, with complete but idle intensity, as if what she was watching was no concern of hers. His father leaned forward again and gently kissed her on the mouth, and drew back again where she could see him well, and smiled a little, anxiously. Her face restored itself from his kiss like grass that has been lightly stepped on; her eyes did not alter. Her skin looked like brown-marbled stone over which water has worked for so long that it is as smooth and blind as soap. He leaned to her ear again. "I'm Jay," he said. "John Henry's boy." Her hands crawled in her skirt: every white bone and black vein showed through the brown-splotched skin; the wrinkled knuckles were like pouches; she wore a red rubber guard ahead of her wedding ring. Her mouth opened and shut and they heard her low, dry croaking, but her eyes did not change. They were bright in their thin shadow, but they were as impersonally bright as two perfectly shaped eyes of glass.

"I figure she knows you," Sadie said quietly.

"She can't talk, can she?" Jay said, and now that he was not looking at her, it was as if they were talking over a stump.

"Times she can," Sadie said. "Times she can't. Ain't only so seldom call for talk, reckon she loses the hang of it. But I figger she knows ye and I am tickled she does."

His father looked all around him in the shade and he looked sad, and unsure, and then he looked at him. "Come here, Rufus," he said.

"Go to him," his mother whispered for some reason, and she pushed his hand gently as she let it go.

"Just call her Granmaw," his father said quietly. "Get right up by her ear like you do to Granmaw Lynch and say, 'Granmaw, I'm Rufus.'"

He walked over to her as quietly as if she were asleep, feeling strange to be by himself, and stood on tiptoe beside her and looked down into her sunbonnet towards her ear. Her temple was deeply sunken as if a hammer had struck it and frail as a fledgling's belly. Her skin was crosshatched with the razor-fine slashes of innumerable square wrinkles and yet every slash was like smooth stone; her ear was just a fallen intricate flap with a small gold ring in it; her smell was faint yet very powerful, and she smelled like new mushrooms and old spices and sweat, like his fingernail when it was coming off. "Granmaw, I'm Rufus," he said carefully, and yellow-white hair stirred beside her ear. He could feel coldness breathing from her cheek.

"Come out where she can see you," his father said, and he drew back and stood still further on tiptoe and leaned across her, where she could see. "I'm Rufus," he said, smiling, and suddenly her eyes darted a little and looked straight into his, but they did not in any way change their expression. They were just color: seen close as this, there was color through a dot at the middle, dim as blue-black oil, and then a circle of blue so pale it was almost white, that looked like glass, smashed into a thousand dimly sparkling pieces, smashed and infinitely old and patient, and then a ring of dark blue, so fine and sharp no needle could have drawn it, and then a clotted yellow full of tiny squiggles of blood, and then a wrong-side furl of red-bronze, and little black lashes. Vague light sparkled in the crackled blue of the eye like some kind of remote ancestor's anger, and the sadness of time dwelt in the blue-breathing, oily center, lost and alone and far away, deeper than the deepest well. His father was saying something, but he did not hear and now he spoke again, careful to be patient, and Rufus heard, "Tell her 'I'm Jay's boy.' Say, 'I'm Jay's boy Rufus.'"

And again he leaned into the cold fragrant cavern next her ear and said, "I'm Jay's boy Rufus," and he could feel her face turn towards him.

"Now kiss her," his father said, and he drew out of the shadow of her bonnet and leaned far over and again entered the shadow and kissed her paper mouth, and the mouth opened, and the cold sweet breath of rotting and of spice broke from her with the dry croaking, and he felt the hands take him by the shoulders like knives and forks of ice through his clothes. She drew him closer and looked at him almost glaring, she was so filled with grave intensity. She seemed to be sucking on her lower lip and her eyes filled with light, and then, as abruptly as if the two different faces had been joined without transition in a strip of moving-picture film, she was not serious any more but smiling so hard that her chin and her nose almost touched and her deep little eyes giggled for joy. And again the croaking gurgle came, making shapes which were surely words but incomprehensible words, and she held him even more tightly by the shoulders, and looked at him even more keenly and incredulously with her giggling, all but hidden eyes, and smiled and smiled, and cocked her head to one side, and with sudden love he kissed her again. And he could hear his mother's voice say, "Jay," almost whispering, and his father say, "Let her be," in a quick, soft, angry voice, and when at length they gently disengaged her hands, and he was at a little distance, he could see that there was water crawling along the dust from under her chair, and his father and his Aunt Sadie looked gentle and sad and dignified, and his mother was trying not to show that she was crying, and the old lady sat there aware only that something had been taken from her, but growing quickly calm, and nobody said anything about it. (1957)

WILMA DYKEMAN

Born and raised in Asheville, North Carolina, and a graduate of Northwestern University, Wilma Dykeman is a columnist for the Knoxville *News-Sentinel*. She is the author of three novels—*The Tall Woman, The Far Family* and *Return the Innocent Earth*—and six works of nonfiction, three of which she co-authored with her husband, James Stokely. She is also the author of several articles and reviews and the recipient of numerous awards, including the Thomas Wolfe Memorial Award and a Guggenheim Fellowship. A popular and dynamic speaker, she averages about seventy lectures a year across the country before college groups and civic, religious, and service organizations. Presently she resides at Newport, Tennessee.

The novel *Return the Innocent Earth* deals with the quest for a usable and acceptable past on the part of Jon Clayburn, an executive in a nationwide canning industry established by his ancestors in East Tennessee. He has returned home to investigate an accidental poisoning of one of the workers by a new pesticide. His investigation, however, encompasses much more than the causes of the poisoning, since he obviously sees much in his past with which he hopes to become reconciled. The symbol for this past becomes in part his old uncle Cebo, to whose mother injustice has been done. The legacy of that injustice haunts the narrator as much as some modern commercial methods. The title has been supplied.

Sins of the Fathers

That was the way it came to me: larger than life, less than life. Legend and anecdote, fact and imagination, pieced together like a stained-glass window that is not a window at all—opening neither out nor in—but an illumination of legend, of belief, myth, or transcendent passion carefully created, frozen in rich and brilliant permanence.

Stained glass, of course, is obsolete today. As our memory is considered obsolete by many. It has been replaced by ingenuity. Information systems they are called. They store facts, statistics, formulas, names, data. And when someone in Clayburn-Durant needs an answer he can go to George Hodges' computer and feed in the question—and after a momentary rumble of digestion the Word will come forth.

But that elaborate tool cannot supply the answers for me. It cannot even direct the search, the search more important than answers. These come from my own information systems: labyrinths of brain, organs, senses, spasms of fear, loneliness, intuition, and hungers. There is more here than any computer can contain. There is layer beneath layer of myself and others.

The past is dead! Long live the past! If I think Stull Clayburn or Nat Lusk or Deborah Einemann are more real than my father, Jonathan Clayburn, or my grandmother Mary Ransom Clayburn or even Laura Rathbone, I am a fool.

For how is it that we come to knowledge of ourselves and those strangers around us masquerading as lovers, parents, children, friends, adversaries? A dozen names and roles which are assigned in pompous singleness but which in fact are always fluid, overlapping, and several.

By so-called facts: dates and places, figures, events, a neat record of births and deaths and marriages and mergers, reports in newspapers and journals, which the mothers, aunts, cousins accumulate in fat, neat scrapbooks where the paste crumbles and yellows, the paper clippings turn brittle and brown as dead leaves, and gray mildew finally whiskers the untouched crevices and spine of the bindings.

By unwitting fragments: a word, a glance, a breath, telling nothing but revealing all, buried only in some convolution of the brain until it surfaces at an unexpected moment to slice through accepted myth like a laser beam of reality.

By legend: gradual, constant, unconscious flow of family stories, anecdotes, reverences, judgments, communicating more by the single turn of a phrase, the lift of an eyebrow, the tone of a voice, than pages of words can suggest. All these sucked into us with milk and water, fed to us as surely as bread. Finally we "know"—not what happened so much as what someone, or several, believe happened. And at last not so much what someone believes happened but what it meant to those who were there. That is the legend we receive and transmit: of something that happened somewhere and sometime and how someone was there—one person at the beginning, a different person at the conclusion.

What happened on that remote, fog-wrapped mountain during the incredible morning when my young father (is it ever possible to see one's father young, smooth-cheeked, naive, frightened?) found that paltry pair who had blasted the orderly Clayburn life: Were they real, those horses stamping on the green turf before the old brick home, the trapped black man sweating the oil and juice of flesh because he smelled the unjust presence of death, those bearded neighbors hot for blood until traded out of it by my father?

Violence was a part of the air and place and time our fathers knew. Public hangings with the stretched neck and the gorged eyes of a man like a pulled gander, impromptu burnings with kerosene sloshed on at the excruciating moment or pine splinters stuck in the flesh ablaze, chain gang labor: these were justice.

Heavyweight, lightweight fights until a mortal brain was sufficiently damaged to permit only blackout, knockout: these were entertainment. The lash, the cudgel, the bullet: these were strength. Oddest, most difficult for me to realize, is the fact that this recognizable one-to-one physical violence, which my father Jonathan knew, was infinitely easier to encounter than the subtly masked total violence surrounding my son Lee.

When I was young I sometimes fell asleep at night longing to have been with him, with my father and Janus Rathbone, during that dreadful moment of discovery when they knew beyond dispute that Elisha Clayburn had been killed for money, money only, money all. I would lie under the eiderdown comforter listening to my mother pace the carpeted hallway beyond the door and I would think of the protection and strength I should have given my father. But I cannot seem to give them to my son who is here, now.

Whenever I return to Churchill for more than an afternoon's inspection, they seem to return, too: those who first shaped this company which now shapes me. There are men in the Clayburn-Durant Company, able, hard-hitting managers and salesmen and directors, who can barely remember the maiden names their aging wives once bore; they would consider me a madman if I should lay aside our gin rummy cards on the plane one day and mention the name of my grandmother.

What would I say of Mary Clayburn? What do I even know of her? Only my suspicion that the dogma which was her faith and strength became the doom and weakness of some who came afterward?

Her seven children revered her. I heard their voices, even in elderly years, grow meek and respectful when they mentioned her name. Yet I never "knew" her. What was behind the plain solemn face with its high forehead, slightly flaring nostrils, brown wavy hair? What unspent force within her called forth that religion which totally controlled her and reached into all our lives? What was her strength which left its legacy of weakness?

Not only the blood-kin, the obviously influential, are part of my information systems, however. There are those who were taken for granted as the scenery, and as essential. The forgotten ones. Old Cebo. Lonas Rankin. Delia. Serena, later on. How else except through them and through a childhood of white innuendoes, nods, grins, frowns, approvals, rejections, could I have gained the love/fear, need/hate, identity/indifference sunk deep beneath my tanned and tended flesh? Lonas and Delia I never saw, but a dozen not unlike them moved through my boyhood—the proud strangers destined to stir unease and guilt and destruction, and the unassuming hands and feet, carrying and fetching, lifting and building, doing for—always for.

Cebo was no faceless name to me, however. Cebo was a pair of enormous eyes whose dark pupils were surrounded by purple-veined orbs the yellowish color of aged mutton suet. With those eyes which seemed as ancient as the pyramids and his rasping voice as raw and harsh as rock, that small, inescapable man held me motionless, intent, for hours of childhood.

There is no need now for me to be ashamed or unashamed of the small square room of our big brick garage where my father brought him from old Major Lawes' Riverbend Farm, where he hunched before a round, coal-choked stove in winter and steeped himself in the sunlight which slanted through the open door in summer. There I would find him.

"Hello, Uncle Cebo."

No spoken greeting from him. The lid of one round old yellow eye would descend in the long slow ritual of a wink. That one small gesture enclosed us in a private world. I hunkered down on my haunches until he, on his low-slung, tattered cane-bottom chair, and I were face to face.

"How's your spirits today, Uncle Cebo?"

"Spirits low today, dragging low, boy." His head, small and shriveled as a sun-baked prune, shook slowly from side to side. In my mind I could see clouds of demons, magicians, and protectors hovering in this dusky little room, armed with knowledge given only to Cherokee shaman, African priest, Highland chieftain. For he would tell me then, or later perhaps, some bizarre tale of his encounters with a world that seemed to lie all about us but that I could never enter.

A fierce dog met on the road one midnight was not a dog at all but a man disguised for evil reasons.

The distorted leaf of a certain shrub was a token for making medicine.

The deep-throated gurgle of a mourning dove before rain bespoke warning.

And anyone who would shoot such a dove would call down on himself the curse of heaven, for his name was written in the Bible.

I reveled in the tingle and chill his words aroused in me but I was ashamed to share it with anyone else, even my brother Monty. Now I feel differently. I know there is mystery. Even in the coils of company finances and crises, clubs and committees, and cars and planes, I have been reminded. Teena's death and Deborah's presence and numerous stifled intimations are my link back to that smoky cubbyhole and a touch with old Cebo.

Yet he has come forward with me, too, into my city, my now, my business. The Community Human Relations Council on which I sit is there because of Cebo. Memory of his gnarled hands with their bleached pale palms affects me more than all the volumes of statistics our council has compiled. Wasn't it delayed recall of Cebo's repeated nightmare of a strange fettered wolf—crippled, stifled, dying—that finally made me undertake a new labor-hiring program for our company? But if it was Cebo's memory, then why didn't I move sooner? How our actions and beliefs are barnacled with self-deceptions and comfortable justifications that help us survive, only to drown more deeply!

Only once did I ever visit with Cebo outside his little room. My mother planned a day's journey "down into the country," as she called it, which meant that we would go from our house in Churchill down to the Old Home-Place, the River-bend Farm, our father's home and not hers, as she always reminded my brother and me. And since our father could not leave business that day but had duties to attend, Cebo came along. There was no danger that Cebo could overcome by his frail knotted hands or legs, there was no mechanical repair that he knew how to make on our cumbersome new automobile, but my mother insisted on taking him as symbol of protection and assistance. Symbolism was reality to her.

Aunt Nora and Uncle Joshua Clayburn lived at the River-bend Farm then. Of their children only Stull aroused my curiosity. I did not see him often but he seemed aloof and perplexing, different and therefore interesting, and on this day he was to teach me the gulf between our years, between ourselves.

When we arrived my mother and aunt met in a flurry of all those niceties that are the distillation of a perpetual hostility. Before they could turn their attention and kisses to me I fled around the house. Uncle Cebo was standing in the back yard. His eyes were fixed on a stump beyond us, near the barn. It was a new stump, clean and wide as a table-top, only at its heart there was dark decay.

"Next to last," Cebo was muttering. "I remember you, hard-hearted old man. But now you cut down, gone, and your heart rotted. Nowhere no more. Next to last."

I looked again at the new stump and saw beside it a great, wide-branched tree still standing. "What kind is that, Uncle Cebo?"

He looked at me scornfully. "Oak, boy."

"Was it there when you were a boy?"

His scorn doubled. "That old oak sprouting there long ago

as your great-great-great-grandpa, or maybe long ago as old Nebuchadnezzar himself. Just growing quiet and steady." Then he turned his gaze on me, weighing, making judgment on the ripeness of a moment. "Come along, boy."

We walked across the brown grass of late summer and into the deep shade of the tiers of oak leaves layered above us. We walked up to the tough round trunk of the tree so large I could not embrace even half of it between my outspread arms. Cebo reached out to touch the shaggy bark and so did I. Then I saw that where he touched, higher than his shoulder, there was a difference in the bark and the wood underneath. The scar was old, very old.

"Major Lawes was his name, boy. Major Lawes. He owned this land and all on it, above and underneath. He put the ring in this oak, the iron ring." Cebo's hoarse old voice paused a moment as he stroked the scab of bark beneath his bony fingers.

"They making the brick for this big fine house, toting the brick for the mansion, all the black slaves working for Pharaoh in the latter days. And when the firing didn't go right, when the fetching and laying wasn't fast enough, somebody got fastened to the iron ring."

Suddenly I was listening more attentively than I had ever listened to Cebo before. I knew that this was something I had not even heard whispered before, something as vicious and compelling as a lurking copperhead. I did not move. I scarcely breathed.

"My mammy, she one of the fast toters. Lots of days she set the pace and I toddled behind her, a nubbin of a boy with two bricks in my hands, proud to hear her named the fastest, looked up to. A high-built brainy Ibo tribeswoman, they always said she was, although born this side the ocean. But one day toward the end of the building, they was topping off that last chimney on the northeast corner there—"

We turned and looked at it in the full hot sun, as strong

and steady as if it had always stood and would remain so in centuries to come.

"Things was going hard and whatever anybody tried to do just seemed like they were trading the witch for the devil. Old Major Lawes had lost time—and his temper to boot. And just after noontime thunderheads began to roll up out of the west, I guess my mammy was nervous and all. . . ."

When he paused there wasn't any sound but the rustle of a bluejay high up in the oak leaves.

"What did she do, Cebo?" I asked at last.

He leaned against his hand flattened against the tree. "She dropped two of them satchels of bricks, one first, then right on the next trip up the hill another. And the bricks, striking against one another and the ground, chipped and broke. I was running along close behind and when they fell I saw all those scattered pieces and the look in my mammy's eyes and I fell on my bare knees and started trying to put them bricks back together again. But they wasn't no going back. . . ."

I waited.

"They tied her up to the iron ring. Laid her back open with a special little whip Major Lawes had traded once from an Indian packman."

I tried to visualize a back "laid open" and the "little whip" but even with my vivid child's mind I could not see it plainly. Its blur of blood and pulpy flesh made my stomach churn. "What happened then?" I had to know.

"She passed." He looked at me patiently, then acknowledged my ignorance again. "My mammy died."

I looked back at the scar on the tree in horror.

"Not right there. Not then. Soon after. While Major Lawes' foreman was whipping her, that storm broke loose. Everybody run to shelter, didn't have time to unloose her. During that hard lightning and thunder and then the downpour of rain that come after, she was out here chained to this old tree. I remember one of the workmen held onto me, finally fastened me up in the corncrib when he got tired holding, so I wouldn't run out to my mammy and get in trouble, too."

"But Cebo," I cried, "why didn't your daddy look after you?" My throat was tight. I didn't want his story to end this way. To me it was still a story he could make up as he chose. "Why didn't your daddy come and protect your mother and you?"

"Lord God, boy," Cebo shook his head, "it was Major Lawes doing the punishing."

I still didn't understand. Even when he added, "Major Lawes would have to protect us from hisself," and I knew enough to hush. I didn't actually understand what Cebo said until years later when I became familiar with the arrangements by which a man divides himself.

"I'm sorry, Cebo," I said. But even then I knew my easy regrets were useless. They cost me nothing, made no restitution.

We waited. I could feel the tree all around me. "Then what happened?"

"That evening, after the storm moved on, they moved her back to the cabin, her teeth chattering, her eyes wild as a doe's caught in the light on a fire-hunt. Lung fever carried her off."

There was a pause. The bluejay had long since abandoned his perch in the oak tree, and all was quiet.

"Major Lawes mighty regretful of his loss. Even after the war and jubilee had been laid on him, he still sickest at losing mammy. That and freedom drove him to the old black pit." And for one of the few times in my life, I heard Cebo chuckle. It was not a good sound. And the lines of his face did not seem to fit into a smile. "When your grandpappy buy this place, old Major Lawes a lunatic roaming its rooms calling on the devil to snatch all niggers into hell and brimstone."

I had no knowledge to fit his words or the glee of his high mirthless cackle. Lung fever. Death. Madness. But I mourned his proud, industrious mother. God, I mourned her.

Even then, however, a cool, self-centered corner of my mind was thankful that the cruelty and sadness had not actually driven my stomach to rebellion and betrayed me into sickness. I was glad I had not vomited in childish upset, because I had seen my cousin Stull, fifteen years older than I, during the final minutes of my conversation with Cebo, watching from the porch in the distance. Now he came toward us.

He was medium-tall and plump. His hair lay flat against his head. It was never possible to guess what he was thinking. Or feeling.

"What are you two doing down here?" he asked. No greeting, no pleasantry, no acknowledgment of us as visitors.

"Hello, Stull," I tried to be older. But he did not respond. He waited. "Oh, Cebo and I were talking about this old tree."

I looked to Cebo to find some signal about whether or not I should tell any more. But he was gazing off toward the mountains. "This old tree has a lot of stories," I went on desperately. Somehow my words seemed to be separating me from Cebo, pushing me toward my indifferent cousin.

"Stories?" Stull said. His tone, his face, discounted the word and all it described.

"But Cebo's are true," I rushed on. "They really happened. Didn't they, Cebo?"

He did not answer.

Then Stull demolished me. "Well, it must be fun to be a child, able to spend the day telling tales." He turned, in ballooning knickers and self-esteem, and walked back toward the house. "As for me, I have to go in to Churchill," he was saying as he left, "and help Uncle Jonathan with the sauerkraut pack."

There was no sound after Stull's words. Presently the screen at the back door slammed behind him.

Cebo only looked at me. I was brimming with disappointment and chagrin and jealousy. Then Cebo shuffled away, moving toward the barn. I looked at the scar on the oak again. Actually it wasn't a very large wound. Considering the size of the whole tree it was almost nothing.

At dinner I asked Aunt Nora if Stull had really gone in to work with my father at the plant.

"Goodness yes." She smiled, pleased, and gave me an extra helping of banana fritters. Then she said to my mother, "Jonathan is one person who seems to appreciate Stull's abilities. You know—"

My mother nodded. "Jonathan has put himself out to train and teach the boy—"

It seemed to me that when my mother and aunt talked, none of their sentences was ever quite completed. They trailed off into labyrinths of meaning I could not follow.

But I did know that being part of the emotion-rich backyard world of an old black man was nothing compared to being Stull and part of the practical upper world of making and selling, of trade and profit. The food I ate, even Aunt Nora's banana fritters, had lost all flavor.

On the way home I had nothing to say. I thought about Cebo's story. My attention, my caring, seemed weak and insignificant before Stull's detachment. I thought about Stull working with my father. And I was miserable with jealousy.

After all the years, the jealousy is weaker, easier understood and dismissed. But Cebo's iron ring and mother are fastened in my mind. Not consciously—I haven't thought of them in ten, maybe twenty years. But now I have discovered they are still with me.

Cebo was only one of the first and now forgotten. Time carries them away and they all—even the central ones—diminish in the family and public vision just as a figure standing at the wrong end of a telescope recedes to a speck of dust with a few twists of the lens adjustor. Yet they all made Clayburn-Durant, wrought it from nothingness, sweated it into stability until now it grows larger each day and magnifies at the other end of the telescope.

In our information systems somewhere we must have filed at least a memo of the awkwardness and intuition, the vision and error, the lonely decision and grinding labor which accrued, accumulated, became this company and us. Yet we do not reach for it. Deborah says we are terrified to look back and so we keep running. But that is because she has seen the wolf pit, the snake den, the bare fang—not over her shoulder or far away but gaping at her feet, tearing at her flesh. I am determined to cancel out her memories with mine —or discover the point within us where they merge. (1973)

VII. *Muse of the Mountains: Appalachian Poetry*

Folk music and Appalachia have become almost synonymous, but long before the white man brought his ballads from the old world to the Southern mountains, the songs of the Cherokee echoed among the hills and valleys. Like the songs of the Indians, the ballads of the white conquerors were anonymous, expressing as they do, not the thoughts of one man but the life view of a people. The ballad has remained a favorite in Appalachia as can be seen in the works of such modern poets as Louise McNeill and Billy Edd Wheeler. Another old form, the sonnet, has also lived on, especially as seen in the poems of Jesse Stuart.

Just as the forms and techniques of Appalachian poetry tend to be traditional, so do the themes: the beauty of nature, independence, and the exploitation of man and the earth. Verse of the mountains has much in common with that of other parts of the nation, but it differs generally in one important respect: its success does not in circuit lie, to paraphrase Emily Dickinson. Rather it says what it has to say as directly and simply as possible, like most of the inhabitants whom it concerns. It is indeed rich in metaphor but metaphor which rarely obfuscates. A symbol hunter or subtlety-lover would more than likely opt for the lines of T. S. Eliot or Wallace Stevens. In any event, the thoughtful reader will find in these uncomplicated lines succinct expressions of old verities.

SIDNEY LANIER

This poem reflects Sidney Lanier's basic concern with independence and self-reliance. For biographical information on Lanier, see p. 121

Thar's More in the Man Than Thar Is in the Land

I knowed a man, which he lived in Jones,
Which Jones is a county of red hills and stones,
And he lived pretty much by gittin' of loans,
And his mules was nuthin' but skin and bones,
And his hogs was flat as his corn-bread pones,
And he had 'bout a thousand acres o' land.

This man—which his name it was also Jones—
He swore that he'd leave them old red hills and stones,
Fur he couldn't make nuthin' but yallerish cotton,
And little o' *that*, and his fences was rotten,
And what little corn he had, *hit* was boughten
And dinged ef a livin' was in the land.

And the longer he swore the madder he got,
And he riz and he walked to the stable lot,

And he hollered to Tom to come thar and hitch
Fur to emigrate somewhar whar land was rich,
And to quit raisin' cock-burrs, thistles and sich,
And a wastin' ther time on the cussed land.

So him and Tom they hitched up the mules,
Pertestin' that folks was mighty big fools
That 'ud stay in Georgy ther lifetime out,
Jest scratchin' a livin' when all of 'em mought
Git places in Texas whar cotton would sprout
By the time you could plant it in the land.

And he driv by a house whar a man named Brown
Was a livin', not fur from the edge o' town,
And he bantered Brown fur to buy his place,
And said that bein' as money was skace,
And bein' as sheriffs was hard to face,
Two dollars an acre would git the land.

They closed at a dollar and fifty cents,
And Jones he bought him a waggin and tents,
And loaded his corn, and his wimmin, and truck,
And moved to Texas, which it tuck
His entire pile, with the best of luck,
To get thar and git him a little land.

But Brown moved out on the old Jones' farm,
And he rolled up his breeches and bared his arm,
And he picked all the rocks from off'n the groun',
And he rooted it up and he plowed it down,
Then he sowed his corn and his wheat in the land.

Five years glid by, and Brown, one day
(Which he'd got so fat that he wouldn't weigh),
Was a settin' down, sorter lazily,
To the bulliest dinner you ever see,
When one o' the children jumped on his knee
And says, "Yan's Jones, which you bought his land."

And thar was Jones, standin' out at the fence,
And he hadn't no waggin, nor mules, nor tents,
Fur he had left Texas afoot and cum
To Georgy to see if he couldn't git sum
Employment, and he was a lookin' as hum-
Ble as ef he had never owned any land.

But Brown he axed him in, and he sot
Him down to his vittles smokin' hot,
And when he had filled hisself and the floor
Brown looked at him sharp and riz and swore
That, "whether men's land was rich or poor
Thar was more in the *man* than thar was in the *land*."
(1869, 1882)

DONALD DAVIDSON

Educator and writer Donald Davidson was born in Camp-
bellsville, Tennessee, in 1893. He received his A.B. and M.A.
degrees from Vanderbilt University after teaching high school
and completing military service. In 1920 he joined the faculty
of Vanderbilt and at the time of his death in 1968, he was a
professor *emeritus*. The author of many critical essays and
books on English composition, he was co-founder and editor
of the *Fugitive*, the magazine which influenced the Southern
literary renaissance and all of American literary criticism
from 1922–25, and was literary editor of the *Nashville Tennessean* from 1924–1930. Among Davidson's most notable
achievements, however, is his own poetry which evinces the
artist's concern for form and the scholar's knowledge of subject. "Sanctuary" from *Donald Davidson: Poems 1922–1961*
reveals his thorough knowledge of Tennessee history as well
as his belief that man's basic security lies in a rapport with
the wilderness.

Sanctuary

You must remember this when I am gone,
And tell your sons—for you will have tall sons,
And times will come when answers will not wait.
Remember this: if ever defeat is black
Upon your eyelids, go to the wilderness
In the dread last of trouble, for your foe
Tangles there, more than you, and paths are strange
To him, that are your paths, in the wilderness,
And were your fathers' paths, and once were mine.

You must remember this, and mark it well
As I have told it—what my eyes have seen
And where my feet have walked beyond forgetting.
But tell it not often, tell it only at last
When your sons know what blood runs in their veins.
And when the danger comes, as come it will,
Go as your fathers went with woodsman's eyes
Uncursed, unflinching, studying only the path.
First, what you cannot carry, burn or hide.
Leave nothing here for *him* to take or eat.
Bury, perhaps, what you can surely find
If good chance ever bring you back again.
Level the crops. Take only what you need:
A little corn for an ash-cake, a little
Side-meat for your three days' wilderness ride.
Horses for your women and your children,
And one to lead, if you should have that many.
Then go. At once. Do not wait until
You see *his* great dust rising in the valley.
Then it will be too late.
Go when you hear that he has crossed Will's Ford.
Others will know and pass the word to you—
A tap on the blinds, a hoot-owl's cry at dusk.

Do not look back. You can see your roof afire
When you reach high ground. Yet do not look.
Do not turn. Do not look back.
Go further on. Go high. Go deep.

The line of this rail-fence east across the old-fields
Leads to the cane-bottoms. Back of that,
A white-oak tree beside a spring, the one
Chopped with three blazes on the hillward side.
There pick up the trail. I think it was
A buffalo path once or an Indian road.
You follow it three days along the ridge
Until you reach the spruce woods. Then a cliff
Breaks, where the trees are thickest, and you look
Into a cove, and right across, Chilhowee
Is suddenly there, and you are home at last.
Sweet springs of mountain water in that cove
Run always. Deer and wild turkey range.
Your kin, knowing the way, long there before you
Will have good fires and kettles on to boil,
Bough-shelters reared and thick beds of balsam.
There in tall timber you will be as free
As were your fathers once when Tryon raged
In Carolina hunting Regulators,
Or Tarleton rode to hang the old-time Whigs.
Some tell how in that valley young Sam Houston
Lived long ago with his brother, Oo-loo-te-ka,
Reading Homer among the Cherokee;
And others say a Spaniard may have found it
Far from De Soto's wandering turned aside,
And left his legend on a boulder there.
And some that this was a sacred place to all
Old Indian tribes before the Cherokee
Came to our eastern mountains. Men have found
Images carved in bird-shapes there and faces
Moulded into the great kind look of gods.

These old tales are like prayers. I only know
This is the secret refuge of our race
Told only from a father to his son,
A trust laid on your lips, as though a vow
To generations past and yet to come.
There, from the bluffs above, you may at last
Look back to all you left, and trace
His dust and flame, and plan your harrying
If you would gnaw his ravaging flank, or smite
Him in his glut among the smouldering ricks.
Or else, forgetting ruin, you may lie
On sweet grass by a mountain stream, to watch
The last wild eagle soar or the last raven
Cherish his brood within their rocky nest,
Or see, when mountain shadows first grow long,
The last enchanted white deer come to drink.

(1938, 1966)

JESSE STUART

To millions of Americans, Jesse Stuart is perhaps best known as a writer of prose fiction and nonfiction, but his most lasting achievement may be verse; in fact, Stuart's poetry has never been widely assessed or given the attention it truly deserves. In any event, a perceptive reader can detect immediately in his lines a lyrical voice of power and beauty. The first two sonnets are from *Man With a Bull-Tongue Plow* and their titles have been supplied. "Robert Diesel," "Anannis Tabor," "Issiac Splinters," and "Lonnie Biggers" are from *Album of Destiny*. The remaining poems are from *Kentucky Is My Land*.

Spring in Kentucky Hills

Spring in Kentucky hills will soon awaken;
The sap will run every vein of tree.
Green will come to the land bleak and forsaken;
Warm silver wind will catch the honey bee.
Blood-root will whiten on the barren hill;
Wind-flowers will grow beneath the oaks and nod
To silver April wind against their will.

Bitterns will break the silence of the hills
And meadow's grass sup dew under the moons,
Pastures will green and bring back whippoorwills
And butterflies that break from stout cocoons.
Spring in Kentucky hills and I shall be
A free-soil man to talk beneath the trees
And listen to the wind among the leaves
And count the stars and do as I damn please.

Autumn is Coming

Autumn is coming now; plowing is over.
Pastures are sprouted clean and gardens tended;
The cane is thinned and all the fences mended;
It's cool for bees to gather from late clover.
And we must gather now the rakes and plows,
And mattocks, spades, pitchforks, and garden hoes,
Stack them away just as the summer goes;
And we must watch the water for the cows
And keep the holes cleaned out, for land is dry
And pasture grass is short this time of year.
The martins gather and the autumn's near—
And August clouds go floating slow and high.
When it's too cool for bees to work in clover,
It's time to gather tools, for summer's over.

(1934)

Robert Diesel

You ask me if there is a living God.
I say it does not matter when I see
God in the fresh turned slopes of loamy sod,

God in the white blooms on the apple tree.
I feel God in the lilac lips of night
And see Him in the sky and sun and star;
To be with Him is laughter and delight,
To feel and touch these parts of Him that are.
I know spring-scented wind that bites my cheeks
Is God caressing me in showers of spring;
I know in April winds it's God who speaks;
His language is such quiet and simple thing.
God walks with me around the slopes I plow
And soothes me with the fern and wild jonquils;
He often sees the sweat run from my brow. . . .
God is eternal here among these hills.

Anannis Tabor

The words of earth turn over from my plow.
I notice every shining mellow word
As it rolls over from the white mould-board.
You'd laugh to see the chattering blackbirds
Follow the furrows, picking at my words.
They understand the mellow words somehow.
Dirt words are words no printer sets to print
For they will never lie on the clean page.
Dirt words will never be the people's rage.
Dirt words will lie on pages of the world
And speak through tender blossoms first unfurled
About the last of March or first of April . . .
When men go forth to plow the greening tendril
Green words of earth are speaking to the world.

Issiac Splinters

These dark hills stood before me and I wept
To step upon their rugged slopes again;
Life started over as if I had slept
Under a quilt of snow and sleet and rain . . .
And peace was here, I never knew we had,
Time for to work, to talk, to sing and play;
My heart beat fast with joy, I was so glad
To smell the wilted corn and fork the hay.
Each oak was friendly and we soon renewed
Old friendship with a sigh and nod of leaf;
My blood ran warm, my body felt so good,
I dreamed it was a dream that would be brief.
But it was real for hills are here to see,
And I am here, my guns, my bed, my shack;
And I'm content to be here and be free,
To walk these paths and shout that I am back!

Lonnie Biggers

You telling me when I am making dough!
I make the silver, nickel, copper, gold!
But it's the big green-backs I'm after though.
Look at the land and timber I have sold!
I've sold a million trees beneath these skies.
I sold the timber, sold the treeless land,
Even to fence-posts and the small cross-ties;
And I have made some dough, you understand.
I never went a day to any school.
I cannot read nor write nor cipher figures.
I think an educated man's a fool
For all I know still come to Lonnie Biggers
To borrow cash and ask me for advice!

It's easier than it is for wind to blow
If you will scratch your head and just think twice
To timber lands and make cart-loads of dough!

(1941)

Builders of Destiny

They lie, our pioneers, where highways run.
They lie where railroads go and cities stand.
Their brittle bones have been exposed to sun
And wind. Their bones are restless in this land.
What does it matter if their bones do lie
Beneath the turning wheels where millions pass,
Builders and dreamers born to live and die
Like white plum petals on the April grass?
What does it matter if their bones turn stone,
Their flesh be richer dust our plowshares turn,
Builders who made America our own,
Whose blood has fed the roots of grass and fern?
Dreamers and builders of our destiny,
They left their epitaph for all to read:
A land of dream and wealth and energy,
A land where freedom is the greatest greed.

Modernity

Before the hard roads came my legs were strong.
I walked on paths through bracken and the fern,
And five to thirty miles were not too long
On paths I knew by tree and rock and turn.
I knew in March where trailing arbutus
Bloomed under hanging cliffs and dogwood groves

And thin-leafed willows were wind-tremulous.
I knew where April percoon bloomed in coves.
But since I drive, my legs are losing power,
For clutch and brake are not leg exercise.
I cannot drive contented by the hour,
For driving is not soothing to the eyes.
The road's grown old that I am forced to see
Above the stream where water churns to foam,
Where great green hills slant up in mystery . . .
I sometimes see a bird or bee fly home.

These Hills I Love

This night a million stars pin back the sky
To make a jeweled roof above this earth
And I must go to hear the night winds cry
Over these ancient hills that gave me birth.
I will hear messages from whispering leaves
That grow from trees in forests such as mine
Where beech and birch and ash are friendly trees,
Where sycamore is neighbor to the pine.
For months I've been away from life my own,
I've heard the song of wheels against cold steel;
I've climbed skyward, trusting the motors' moan
Across the continent. And, now, I feel
The sweet true surge of life in every vein,
Herein this night with brighter stars above
With beauty, song and peace to soothe my brain
Among these rugged hills of home I love.

(1950)

LOUISE McNEILL

Louise McNeill was born in 1911 at Buckeye, West Virginia, on a mountain farm her ancestors "took out" in 1768. She received her A.B. degree from Concord College, an A.M. from Miami of Ohio, and a Ph.D. from West Virginia University. She has taught at all levels from one-room mountain schools to the university. In addition to *Gauley Mountain* and *Paradox Hill*, she is the author of *Mountain White* and *Time is Our House*, a Breadloaf Prize book. She is also the winner of *The Atlantic Monthly* Poetry Award for 1938 and other honors. In 1973 she retired from Fairmont State College and is currently working on *Appalachia Heart*, a prose manuscript. The poetry of Louise McNeill is characterized by versatility and simplicity. It exhibits a thorough understanding and appreciation of the Appalachian culture, as seen in the following selections from *Gauley Mountain*. "Scotch Irish," "Appalachian Mountaineer," and "Overheard on a Bus" are from a collection entitled *Paradox Hill*.

Jacob Marlin and Stephen Sewell
(Hunters who lived in adjoining tree trunks and disagreed on theology.)

Their hollow trees stood bark to bark,
They built two fires to melt one dark
And to disperse one copper fear.
They notched two sticks to count one year.

The English Rubric was the bone
To chew together, gnaw alone.
Since Jake confirmed and Steve denied,
And both beliefs seemed justified
In scripture which they knew by rote
And did not hesitate to quote,

Each mountain dawn the hill-domed air
Carried two versions of one prayer:
"Guide poor blind Steve for Jesus' sake"—
"Send Wisdom, Lord, to lame-brained Jake."

Katchie Verner's Harvest

It pleasures her to gather
A hoard when autumn comes:
Of grapes in scroll-worked silver,
Red-streaked-with-amber plums,
Winesaps and seek-no-farthers,
Green peppers, russet pears,
White roastin'-ears for drying
On frames above the stairs,
Queer handled gourds for dishes
And dippers at the spring,
Long butternuts, fat pumpkins,
Cream-colored beans to string,

Wild meats to jerk and pickle,
Brown chestnuts tipped with cold,
Cranberries from the marshes,
Tree honey dripping gold.

In barrels and crocks and suggins,
In pokes upon the floor
And hanging from the rafters
Is Katchie Verner's store
Against the mountain winter
When sleet-hard drifts will freeze
The deep loam of her garden
And gird her orchard trees.

Mountain Corn Song

Oak leaves are big as a gray squirrel's ear
And the dogwood bloom is white,
While down in the crick the bull frogs boom
For a "Jug O' Rum" all night.
Out in the fields while the dawn is still
Four bright grains to each sandy hill
With, *"One for the beetle and one for the bee*
One for the devil and one for me."

A drouth wind gasps and the clouds move on
So the red clay fields bake dry,
But pea vines throttle the green young blades,
And the grass stands boot top high.
This is the time for scraping the hoe
Around each plant in the hard-packed row,
"One stalk for the smut and one for the weed,
One for the borer and one for need."

A drizzle sinks in the stubble field
And the wigwam shocks are brown,

While under the thorny, brush-pile fence
The leaves are bedded down,

So this is the season to kneel in muck
And strip each ear from its withered shuck,
With, *"One for dodger and one to feed,*
One for likker and one for seed."

Faldang

Cider in the rain barrel, corn in the popper,
Shoats in the mast woods, mash in the hopper,
Taffy on the window sill, rosin on the bow,
Grab your partners, Boys, dance the "Do Si Do"!

Logs in the fireplace, pone in the baker,
Taters in their jacket coats, salt in the shaker,
Kick the rhythm with your heel, catch it on your toe,
Grab your partners, Boys, dance the "Hoe Down Hoe"!

Pick and shovel in the loft, boss man under kivver,
Dish pan in the chicken yard, boat gone down the river,
Rags stuffed in the broken pane, wind a-howlin' low,
Grab your partners, Boys, "How you oughta know"!

"Old Dan Tucker," "Old Zip Coon,"
"Old Ninety Seven," any old tune!
Pat-a-foot, Granny! Break down, Ma!
Hug-em-tight, Annie! Step high, Pa!

Cider in the rain barrel, corn in the popper,
Shoats in the mast woods, mash in the hopper,
Taffy on the window sill, rosin on the bow,
Grab your partners, dance the "Do Si Do"!

Jeemes MacElmain

This scar is where he slashed me in the throat
But he thought better, took me south alive.
In Libby Prison . . . eighteen months, it was,
Until the first of April '65.
Camp itch and dysentery, the scurvy too,
And hunger pains until we hunted meat,
You won't believe,—but prison rats are tame
And fat as porkers. Well, a man must eat.
One evening when the guard was laid out drunk
I stole some gutta percha and a knife,
Began to carve a chain for Mary Reed. . . .
You never knew her. . . . Ann's my second wife.
I whittled at the stuff to pass the time. . . .
I carved the circles true and fit them well.
Nigh seven hundred links, I had, when Grant
Rode into Richmond and unlocked our cell.

It will be forty years when April comes
But still I hope Old Scratch's fireman lay
Great cords of wood around the red-barred pit
Where old Jeff Davis and his rebels stay.
We licked his gang but now that I am old
And need my rest, the habit sets so deep
I often curse because I have to fit
Black links into my chain of broken sleep.

(1939)

Scotch Irish

In Appalachia—our family graveyards—
Where all the headstones standing face the east—
Of Keltic blood, when Stonehenge was the portal,
Our fathers' fathers watched the Druid priest . . .

Bring me at morning to our weedy hilltop;
With all my pagan kindred lay me there—
The wine is crimson in the spiles of sunlight;
The priest intones the prayer . . .

Liter by liter down my life stream running—
The blood and fog and flame—
Remembering when Stonehenge was the portal
Before the Roman came.

Appalachian Mountaineer

Ohio . . . Indiana . . . Illinois . . .
While in our mountain cabins still we kept—
Our kinfolk led the way across the prairie,
And up the dark Sierra climbed and crept.

Our women took their slips of rose and lilac;
Our menfolk took the plowshare and the gun—
Nebraska . . . Utah . . . Idaho . . . Nevada . . .
Montana . . . Colorado . . . Oregon.

The wind blew east: we smelled our purple lilacs,
And campfire smoke and bison meat and pine,
Resin and oil and tar and sand and ocean,
The very scent of salt and stinging brine.

Deserts of heat blew into our cool dooryards;
Sequoia forests mingled with our rain;
And so we kept our own forever after—
The ties of bloodship grafted down the vein.

—Mixture of lilac, rose, and wild persimmon,
Of sage brush, green savannahs, dusky laurel,
Of Texas . . . California and Wyoming—
Of ponderosa pine and pennyroyal.

The pasque flower of Dakota, wheat, and clover
Blowing across our rooftrees—wind and smoke
Of sassafras and bison grass and river,
America and oak.

Overheard on a Bus
(Miner's Wife)

"He must go down in the mine—
It's all he knows;
Certain as morning shine
Then off he goes—
Me standing there in the door
A-seeing black
And wondering evermore
If he'll come back. . . .

Asked him, I have, to quit.
I can beg and whine,
But there's nothing to do for it,
It's the mine, the mine—
And him cast under its spell,
So off he goes—
Black as the mouth of hell,
And when it blows—
But I reckon they pay him well,
And it's all he knows. . . ."

(1972)

BILLY EDD WHEELER

Born in the coal town of Whitesville, West Virginia in 1932, Billy Edd Wheeler attended Warren Wilson College in Swannanoa, North Carolina, and Berea College where he received his B.A. in English. He later studied playwrighting at Yale School of Drama and has had seven plays produced in colleges and summer stock. He is best known as a folk and country singer, and as a highly successful song writer for Glen Campbell, Johnny Cash and June Carter, Judy Collins, Bobby Goldsboro, Nancy Sinatra, the Kingston Trio, and many others. The winner of several awards from the American Society of Composers, Authors, and Publishers, he has given hundreds of concerts throughout America. He is married to the former Mary Mitchell Bannerman, and he makes his home in Swannanoa. The poems in *Song of a Woods Colt* are marked by their musical quality and social commentary on subjects ranging from sterile tourism to strip mining.

Mountain Fertility Rite

There was a farmer so superstition bound
That every time spring planting came around
He'd take his wife and put her on the ground

Under full moon and fertilize his plowin'
While his family of kids danced up and down
At edges of field, naked and making sounds
Like singing—rituals quaint and past profound.
They made quare signs and led a snow white hound.
Everyone laughed and called him *Almanac Clown*.
But he always had the best corn crop in town!

Christmas in Coaltown

Tonight the men lift pokes instead of coal.
Their backs are puzzled by the lack of weight
And wish it were as easy lifting slate.
This work is play and good for a miner's soul.

They ride in the company truck by every door
Opening as they approach from the house below.
The fire spreads across the bluish snow
Tinting bearers of gifts from the company store.

And not a man but wishes these light sacks
Of nuts and candy and sweet tangerines
Were costlier gifts to suit the children's dreams,
Toys, and clothes to wear upon their backs.

But the men laugh. They laugh and they spread cheer
To the kid who takes a bag and darts back in
Behind the window, sending out his grin.
They may not laugh again the rest of the year.

The Craft Shop

"If you like somebody treatin' ye quaint,
You wait on 'em. I tell ye I ain't
About to be exhibit A

For snobby tourists hunting a way
To color their trip along the edge
Of our mountains. Let's see you wedge
A dollar out of their deep pockets.
They gawk till their eyes pop the sockets,
But buy? No, they're eyeing you
Mostly, glancing to see if one shoe
Matches the other. You love Mankind,
Or so you talk. See if you find
One thing to love about city folks
That figure us for dumb slowpokes.
Ah, Lordy!"
   It was my brother's defense
Which bowed daily to his business sense
And put him through the curtained door
With: "Howdy, and what can I do-ye-for?"

I never saw more genuine ardor
Or humor in a mountain martyr.

Coal Tattoo

Traveling down that coal town road
Listen to my rubber tires whine!
Goodbye to buckeye and white sycamore,
I'm leaving you behind.
I been a coal man all my life,
Layin' down track in the hole
Got a back like an ironwood
Bent by the wind,
Blood veins blue as the coal.
Blood veins blue as the coal.

Somebody said "That's a strange tattoo
You have on the side of your head."

I said that's the blueprint left by the coal,
Just a little more and I'd be dead.
But I love the rumble and I love the dark,
I love the cool of the slate,
But it's on down the new road
Looking for a job.
This traveling and looking I hate.

I've stood for the Union, I've walked in the line,
I've fought against the company.
Stood for the U.M.W. of A.
Now who's gonna stand for me?
I got no house and I got no pay,
Just got a worried soul
And this blue tattoo on the side of my head
Left by the number nine coal.

Some day when I die and go
To heaven the land of my dreams,
I won't have to worry on losing my job
To bad times and big machines.
I ain't gonna pay my money away
On dues and hospital plans,
I'm gonna pick coal while the blue heavens roll
And sing with the angel bands.
And sing with the angel bands!

An Old Man

"Before missionaries came
And Federal planners
And men who organized
Under selfish banners
Their own gravy trains
And took us a ride,

I saw in mountain men
A little pride.

"I'd rather be poor and dumb
Than see a line
Of neighbors taking free food
And licking the behind
Of politicians. God,
It can't be right
If it makes me have to lock
My barns at night."

Goliath
(They Can't Put It Back)

Down in the valley 'bout a mile from me
Where the crows no longer cry
There's a great big earth-moving monster machine
Stands ten stories high
The ground he can eat is a sight
Takes a hundred tons at a bite
He can dig up the grass
It's a fact
But he can't put it back

They come and tell me I got to move
Make way for that big machine
But I ain't movin' unless they kill me
Like they killed the fish in my stream
But look at that big machine go
Took that shady grove a long time to grow
He can rip it out with
One whack
But he can't put it back

I never was one to carry signs
Picket with placards
Walk in lines
Maybe I'm behind the times!

You can bet your sweet life they're gonna hear from me
I ain't gonna take it layin' down
Cause I'm gettin' tired seein' rocks that bleed
On the bare guts of the ground
I ain't goin' to sell my soul
So they can strip out another little tiny vein of coal
I ain't a-movin' out of my tracks
Cause they can't put it back
THEY CAN'T PUT IT BACK!

(1969)

LEE PENNINGTON

The ninth of eleven children, Lee Pennington was born in White Oak in the western end of Greenup County, Kentucky. He attended the same one-room school which his mother and father had attended, and taught his first class when he was in the fourth grade. "You see," he has said, "the teacher spent most of her time making hook-rugs and she had the older students teach the lower ones. I taught first grade, three students. I passed two students to the second grade and double promoted the other one to the third grade." While at McKell High School in Southshore, Kentucky, he came under the influence of Jesse Stuart, the principal, and Lena Nevisin, his English teacher, both of whom encouraged him to write. He received a B.A. in English in 1962 from Berea College and an M.A. in English from the University of Iowa. He has published over 700 poems in more than 100 magazines and anthologies, has written numerous stories and articles, and has given folk-song concerts all over America. Both he and his wife teach at Jefferson Community College in Louisville, Kentucky. Like Jesse Stuart, to whom he addresses one of his poems in *Scenes from a Southern Road*, Pennington has a deep sense of the soil and an appreciation of all that is entailed in that relationship.

Poet of the Soil

You stood there against the Kentucky sky
And watched the wind settle the dust
Following your plow like birds, and I
Under your shadow, proud, with a gooseneck hoe
Leaned to watch the soil where you'd been.
It must have been your hand, loose from plowlines,
Around my shoulder and then your mountain voice
Pointing like echoes across the ridges,
For I remember coming back from where romping
Thoughts had played in the growing corn
And standing there by your side and hearing
You say it takes a million tumbling stones
To make soil worthy of the earth.

The Singer of W-Hollow

Now where did I first hear you sing?
Down along the creekbed by the hornet's nest?
Upon the hill bringing water from the spring?
Or coming out with autumn brightly dressed

In fabric woven by a poet's brain?
I guess I heard you sing in December
When snows covered fence-posts by the lane
And left their grey heads looking. I remember

Your wading through drift to your waist,
Carrying a crippled bird you had found.
You held it to the warmth of under-vest,
And sang to it recuperating sound.

Man With A Dream

Once there was a man
With a pack of dreams,
A fisher on the banks
Of frothy mountain streams.

He knew that he was dreaming
And thought he'd pinch his skin.
Now he dreams of dreaming
Back into dreams again.

Robert Williams Sings His Song

I cannot tell the time by lifting fog.
I cannot hear the song you claim of wind.
Nor can I smell the wild blooming rose,
Nor tell when the fox hunt nears its end.

I cannot name the birds by their song.
I cannot smell that rain is in the air.
I cannot hear and count the honking geese.
These are things of which I'm unaware.

I got my education from great books.
I got my learning from the greatest schools.
Now I wonder if I've been taken by crooks
Who sold to me the song that's sung by fools?

Poet of the Flowers
(For Naomi Deane)

Kentucky woman, tall against the sun,
I've seen you gather from the hills
Earth flowers and bring them one by one

To grow in places they say no flowers can;
I've seen your gentle hands in love
With growing things—A love which falls
Like rain when April's gone. I've seen
Them bloom as though a magic moon
Touched each tender petal when the dew
Was down. They bloom in sound; they bloom
In song: Poet of the Flowers
Writing for the wind in evening hours.

In The Field

Given equal opportunity
And equal needs,
Victory always comes
To the fighting weeds.
                   (1969)

JANE STUART

Jane Stuart, daughter of Jesse Stuart, was born in 1942 in Ashland, Kentucky. She pursued a rigorous academic and teaching career from the receipt of a B.A. from Case-Western Reserve University in 1964, to two masters' degrees and the Ph.D. in Greek, Latin, and Italian literature from Indiana University in 1971. Her three volumes of published poetry include *A Year's Harvest* (1957); *Eyes of the Mole* (1967); and *White Barn* (1973). *Yellowhawk*, the first of three novels, appeared in 1973; *Passerman's Hollow* and *Land of the Fox* are scheduled for early publication. Presently writing, translating, and lecturing, she lives with her husband and two children in Gainesville, Florida. The following poems from *Eyes of the Mole* reflect those themes dear to any native of the Kentucky hills.

Where Stuarts Lie

If ever fields were flecked with sun-gold green
and hollows high, between tall tree-clumped hills
that, circled with mauve mists, shoulder sky,
it is here, in Shelbyanna, where Stuarts lie.

If pine-cone chimes can sound the evensong,
white wind-fingers pluck the willow harp,
as night-things purr a silver slumber song,
it is here where sleeping earthlings dream of dawn:

of violets and melons wet with dew—
cornfields ripening in lush river beds—
a hummingbird sucking pink hollyhocks—
on hills where they shall no more walk.

Here they are buried with their mighty dreams,
weary giants sleeping in the soil—
in mottled fields of green and sun-flecked gold
and misty hills that echo tales yet told

about the Stuarts.

Corn Shuck Dolls

Red hills laced with honey suckle,
kneaded by the sun's silk knuckle,
sprinkled now and then with rain—
shall sweet corn grow here again,

straight and sprouting ruffled hair?
Will the farmer's children dare
to pluck the silk and roughened blade
for the blind girl in the shade

who weaves their dolls and hears their laughter,
lemon light and lingering after
night has swept the sounds away
of little children lost in play

with corn shuck dolls in green-leaf dresses;
the blind girl smiles and softly blesses
these barren hills for feeble birth
of dusty corn from red-rust earth.

Song of Blackbirds

I know a song
the blackbirds sing
when perched upon
a blue-tipped wing.
They peck at grains
of Indian corn
early on
an autumn morn
beneath a sleezy
sleepy sun
before cross scarecrows
have begun
to wave their
tattered, blue-stuffed sleeves
at shattered cornstalks,
falling leaves.
They sing of
their prosperity,
their fortune,
their longevity,
and of the good grain
they have found
thriving in
my river ground.

Roots

Roots dug in this hungry craw of land
are badly tangled. No resolute hand
can jerk them up from the mesh of grass
that entwines them to languishing eons that pass
in a cloud of grey mildew, clogged with the sperm
of man's endless renewal, from dust unto worm.

Eyes of the Mole

An astute wizard who lives in the woods
in a vacated woodpecker's hole
swears that the world would be simple and gay
if man had the Eyes of the Mole.
The wizard is shriveled from living on nuts
and the roots of the weeping willow.
His head has grown soft because he has slept
with it propped on a dank moss pillow.
But he says that man would return to the course
of the gods from whose image he strays
if he would close his eyes to the wrongs
of civilization's ways.

(1967)

DAVID McCLELLAN

Newspaperman turned poet-professor, David M. McClellan is a native of Bristol, Tennessee-Virginia, where he worked for several years as a reporter, feature writer, and book reviewer for the *Bristol Herald-Courier*. He has published poetry and fiction widely, had two critical articles appear in the *Fitzgerald-Hemingway Annual*, and wrote the introduction to the reprinting of Anne W. Armstrong's *This Day and Time*. He attended Emory and Henry College, East Tennessee State University and the University of South Carolina, where he studied under the poet James Dickey. McClellan is a charter member of the Thomas Wolfe Memorial Association. Associate Professor of English at East Tennessee State University, he is at work on a novel and a critical work on *Hemingway and the American West*.

Luther Lamp is a picaresque character in a collection of verse and the novel-in-progress. The author sees Lamp as the combination in one fictional personality of a swashbuckling, roughneck vagabond and a self-taught seer and sage. His adventures in *Leaves from the Legend of Luther Lamp* occur in various parts of the world in the World War II and post-war period.

The Ballad of the Captain's Scars

When Pvt. Lamp met Capt. Klein
they didn't sing Lili Marlene
they fought with knives as dark came on
in the dull Bavarian rain

Lamp swung a Barlow knife
lugged from Fox Green Beach to the Rhine
he got it from a drunk in Nashville town
in a swap for a quart of wine

Capt. Klein of the SS Guard
used a dirty skull-handled dirk
it had killed before for Hitler
this time it wouldn't work

Lamp had been wandering the wet German woods
since his outfit had smashed the Kraut
he had marched and fought thru long long days
now he wanted a quick way out

Wandering alone in those haunted woods
where Wolfe once fought in the fall
he stumbled at dusk on Capt. Klein
and that Kraut was having a ball

In a black uniform that was dirty and torn
he was finding salve for defeat
by bragging to Wotan his nasty war god
about killing some Jewish meat

He bragged about women stripped and hung
in Dachau prison camps
he laughed about babies thrown in the fire
and this maddened old Luther Lamp

So Lamp walked up on the Captain
as the setting sun burned like a bruise

bleeding under that dirty wet sky
and Klein didn't have time to choose

Lamp reached up quick with his right knife hand
a movement soft as a girl's caress
and when he drew that knife hand back
Klein's cheek was a bloody mess

Lamp cut him again on the other cheek
before the fall of the dark
and he cut some more with an artist's eye
he was leaving a certain mark

and Capt. Klein as the blood dripped down
could make only one feeble jab
he couldn't fight with a Tennessee man
when that man was fighting mad

Lamp left him reeling on his knees
like a rummy begging for wine
and on Klein's cheeks till the end of his life
was carved the swastika sign

Lamp hurried away to wander the world
dodging the Yankee patrol
he'd already been a lot in the clink
and didn't want back in that hole

But they caught him again as they had before
for a year he looked through the bars
but then and later when he felt low
he remembered the captain's scars

(1972)

East Side Manhattan-Brooklyn Resurrection Vision

Sad one summer Saturday in lower Manhattan

I found a tall bulky man who took me walking

He wore a baggy brown suit and his brown eyes flashed
      beneath his black unruly hair

His nose had been busted in a beer hall brawl
      in the cultured city of Munich

A cigarette butt hung from his mouth and he held
      a tattered map

One of his fingers had a huge, ugly wart from writing
      with a pencil for many years

Harsh dusty light on the lower East Side

Delancy Street swarmed with Jews eating stale
      pushcart sandwiches

A bum with urine on his pants shouted screw
      the government

In an old Greek Orthodox Church candles burned
      before the icons

Below the rusty bridge under the pukey yellow sky
      the East River ran greasy green

In Brooklyn a Williamsburg bus driver in undershirt
      and filthy pants

Shouted he didn't know where in the hell
      Red Hook was

On a cracked doorstep an aged rabbi from Prague
      chanted over a crumbling scroll

We found a dingy cafe with beer in iced glasses
      and a TV ballgame

The jukebox played I Wonder Who's Kissing Her Now

The tall man felt the flank of a waitress
        and whooped for a homerun

Outside the moon rose and mirror-blazed bright
        in the clear blue river

Horns howled in the harbor

I forgot my losses

(1972)

MARION HODGE

A native of Elizabethton, Tennessee, and a graduate of East Tennessee State University, Marion Hodge received his Ph.D. degree from the University of Tennessee and is an instructor in English at Demorest College, Piedmont, Georgia. His first published work appeared in 1973 in the *Green River Review*. "Cole's First Song" is the first poem of a planned epic, with Cole being the central figure. This poem, in contrast to much of the poetry of the Appalachian past, is an indictment of traditional heroes and their aims.

Cole's First Song

There is no glory on the Watauga,
where fierce, pale, gaunt fugitives slew justice
for greed and solitary unrestraint
two hundred years ago; and where they formed
no haven of the green heaven they stole,
but pressed from oppression to oppression,
from sane law to the mindless lunge of beasts.

From terror to trackless terror they ran,
delivering unto their sun-dark sons

the worm writhing about their brains,
the knotting agony that jarred their hearts
even from the shelter of long valleys
cleaved by Doe and Holston and Watauga.

They could not settle down, nor go at dawn
into curving fields fertile and lighted
with gentleness; nor sweat and let their lives
grow with the corn, slowly and peacefully
to grow homes amid the clean wilderness;
nor be still and love; for the writhing grief
always aroused a restlessness,
a detestation of development,
a hatred for the very walls they raised,
those remote fortresses barricading
their delight from the verdant blush of earth
and their flesh from the frontier's flint revenge.

So those sycamore walls became prisons
isolating destroyers and death men,
damning the grim, ungovernable flood,
and sealing Eden from its ravagers,
bastards grown heroes in white eyes,
Richardson, Bean, Boone, Robertson, Sevier,
violent saints, old men, power-mad priests,
disciples of sure destruction, swift death,
weeds which choked the flowers, the Cherokee,
and sucked nutrition from the mountain soil
until, torn whole and helpless by their roots,
they were swept westward with a venal wind
and cultivated by twisted decades.

Wataugans, you bequeathed your sons one skill—
you have taught us usurpation.

Watauga! America's genesis!

Though your fame is dim, your spirit remains
in our impulse to pour desolation
upon fecundity, sterility
upon natural profusion and vigor.

(1973)

JIM WAYNE MILLER

Jim Wayne Miller is a native of the mountain country of western North Carolina. He graduated from Berea College and in 1965 received his Ph.D. in German language and literature from Vanderbilt University where he studied under Donald Davidson and Randall Stewart (see pages 308 and 419). He has taught courses on the secondary school and college levels, and is the author of over 20 short stories, 200 poems, and numerous articles. Presently a professor of German at Western Kentucky University, Miller, like a number of young, native, Appalachian poets, is especially sensitive to the decline of folk ways in an industrialized society. His concern has been made evident in lectures and essays, but perhaps most powerfully in his collection *Dialogue with a Dead Man* from which all of the following poems are taken with the exception of "Small Farms Disappearing in Tennessee."

For S. F. S.

Graveward to this green tent I too came burdened,
though other hands than mine, yet none more willing,
waited to man the metal grips, to bear

you briefly through this rain up Newfound Hill.
Walking beside the water-beaded coffin,
I saw how feet, schooled in these hills at yours,
climbed on the rutted clay; where others slipped,
they did not even soil their Sunday shoes.

In Dogget's Gap, by Double Springs where we
made camp, we knew another tent, another
time, squirrel-time in the Bearwallow,
and rain rolled from our blue-barreled rifles.
Climbing the hill head-down behind you, I marked
how wisely your feet held, fast on the slippery rocks.

Family Reunion

Sunlight glints off the chrome of many cars.
Cousins chatter like a flock of guineas.

In the shade of oaks and maples
six tables stand
filled with good things to eat.
Only the jars of iced tea sweat.

Here the living and dead mingle
like sun and shadow under old trees.

For the dead have come too,
those dark, stern departed who pose
all year in oval picture frames.

They are looking out of the eyes of children,
young sprouts
whose laughter blooms
fresh as the new flowers in the graveyard.

The Bee Woman

She carried the eggs in her straw hat and never
reached into a nest with her bare hand.
A woman who could conjure warts, who knew
charms for drawing fire, spells to make
butter come, and mysteries of bees
and hummingbirds, besides, knew to roll
eggs from a guinea's nest with a gooseneck hoe.

There is a mountain cove and light is leaving.
Speckled guineas fly to roost in trees,
their potterick and screech drift far away,
becomes the faintest peeping in my dream
of stifling afternoons when we would stand,
the old woman and I, by fencerows and cowtrails
listening for half-wild guineas screeching
as they came off nests they'd stolen away
in thickets, briers, scrub pines and chinquapins.

And no matter where I wake—horn's beep,
ship's bells, clatter of garbage cans,
strange tongues spoken on the street below,
in a rising falling bunk out at sea,—
everywhere I stand on native ground.
The bee woman may pass through my dream:
running under a cloud of swarming bees,
she beats an empty pie pan with a spoon
till the swarm settles, black on a drooping pine bough
and guineas re-group pottericking—all
moving toward waking's waterfall.

(1974)

Small Farms Disappearing in Tennessee
—Headline

Sometimes a whole farm family comes awake
in a close dark place over a motor's hum
to find their farm's been rolled up like a rug
with them inside it. They will be shaken onto
the streets of Cincinnati, Dayton or Detroit.

It's a ring, a syndicate dismantling farms
on dark nights, filing their serial numbers
smooth, smuggling them north like stolen cars,
disposing of them part by stolen part.

Parts of farms turn up in unlikely places:
weathered gray boards from a Tennessee burley tobacco
barn are up against the wall of an Ohio
office building, lending a rustic effect.
A Tennessee country church suddenly appeared
disguised as a storefront in Uptown Chicago.
Traces of Tennessee farms are found on the slopes
of songs written in Bakersfield, California.
One missing farm was found intact at the head
of a falling creek in a recently published short story.
One farm that disappeared without a clue
has turned up in the colorful folk expressions
of a state university buildings and grounds custodian.
A whole farm was found in the face of Miss Hattie Johnson,
lodged in a Michigan convalescent home.

Soil samples taken from the fingernails
of Ford plant workers in a subdivision
near Nashville match those of several farms
which recently disappeared in the eastern end of the state.
A seventy-acre farm that came to light
in the dream of a graduate student taking part

in a Chicago-based dream research project
has been put on micro-card for safe keeping.

Divers searching for a stolen car
on the floor of an Army Corps of Engineers
impoundment, discovered a roadbed, a silo, a watering
trough and the foundations of a dairy barn.
Efforts to raise the farm proved unsuccessful.
A number of small Tennessee farms were traced
to a land-developer's safe-deposit box
in a mid-state bank after a bank official
entered the vault to investigate roosters
crowing and cows bawling inside the box.

The Agriculture Agency of the state
recently procured a helicopter to aid
in the disappearing farm phenomenon.
"People come in here every week," the Agency head,
Claude Bullock reports, "whole families on tractors,
claiming their small farm has disappeared."

Running the Small Farms arm of the agency
is not just a job for Bullock, born and brought up
on a small Tennessee farm himself. "We're doing
the best we can," says Bullock, a soft-spoken man
with a brow that furrows like a well-plowed field
over blue eyes looking at you like farm ponds.
"But nowadays," he adds, "you can punch a farm,
especially these small ones, onto computer cards.
You can store them away on magnetic tapes.
So they're hard to locate with a helicopter."

Bullock's own small farm, a thirty-acre
remnant of "the old home place," disappeared
fourteen months ago, shortly before
he joined the Small Farms arm of the agency.

(1974)

PART II

Echoes and Reverberations: Essays in Criticism and Culture

As Harry Caudill observes in the essay with which this book concludes, "The Appalachian Mountain range is the least understood and the most maligned part of America." While the literature of the Appalachians has often counteracted the maligning of the region, it has also contributed to it. The purpose of the essays which follow is to help put the problems of myths and realities of Appalachia in some sort of perspective. Toward that end the editors have chosen essays and articles by critics and scholars on a wide variety of aspects of Appalachian life. These authors deal with the problems of regionalism in general (Warren), history of the region (Theodore Roosevelt, Houston, and Toynbee), myth and stereotyping (Blair, Wilson, and Stewart), religion (Mencken), education (Weller and Miller), language (Schrock and Reese), and cultural identity (Williams, Jones, and Caudill). Their views can easily be related to the fiction and poetry of Southern Appalachia. In the research for this book it became apparent that practically every critic of note of American culture has had something to say either directly or indirectly about the Appalachian experience. Their frequently conflicting views are not apt to lead to a unanimity of opinion among readers but will, hopefully, lead to a deeper interest.

ROBERT PENN WARREN

Born in 1905 in Todd County, Kentucky, Robert Penn Warren attended public schools in Kentucky before entering Vanderbilt where he graduated in 1925. Later he did graduate work at University of California, Yale, and Oxford where he was a Rhodes Scholar. He has taught in various parts of the nation, served as editor for the *Southern Review*, and consistently produced works of high quality, winning the Pulitzer Prize for both fiction and poetry. Perhaps best known for his magnificent *All the King's Men*, he has long been regarded as one of America's most able critics. "Some Don'ts for Literary Regionalists" is an essential caveat for any study of regionalism whatsoever.

Some Don'ts for Literary Regionalists

Americans are sometimes accused of having a get-rich-quick psychology; and accused with some justice. It has not been confined to the purely economic sphere of our activities, where it no doubt contributes substantially to our booms and depressions. It has been carried over into matters such as religion, and year after year we have had new sects and cults, each claiming to have a brand-new technique for getting results from God. It has been carried over into politics, where it makes possible the cure-all, the panacea, the short cut—prohibition, for instance, or the Townsend Plan. And in intellectual and artistic matters it produces "Culture" with a capital C, the five-foot shelf, which might be called a sort of educational Townsend Plan, or William Lyon Phelps, who might be called the Father Coughlin of literature. And this attitude, this get-rich-quick psychology, has contributed heavily to the current vogue of regionalism.

This regionalism is not merely a literary invention. It is a present manifestation of a force that has expressed itself in many ways in the past. In relation to our national concept it may be termed a centrifugal force. It was a force with which the founding fathers of the Republic had some difficulty in dealing, and it has emerged again and again in practical affairs, in the Hartford Convention, for instance, or more dramatically at Gettysburg. A fundamental element in the force was the deeply ingrained instinct of the human creature to resent the attempt on the part of someone who lived a good many miles away and whose name, even, was unknown to take the gold out of his teeth. This force used to be called sectionalism. It expressed itself in the doctrine of states' rights, and, presumably, was embodied in the Constitution of the United States, where it died gradually of asphyxiation. But the decline of the force of the centrifugal principle did not bring perpetual prosperity, and with the collapse of 1929 the sentiment became almost general that, economically at least, the victory over the centrifugal principle had been somewhat Pyrrhic; and so the new regionalism, in that aspect, is apparently a polite attempt on the part of benevolent social philosophers to put back in the teeth of people who didn't happen to live where high tariff was an unmixed blessing some of the gold that was once complacently extracted. Regionalism is a more polite expression than sectionalism of the centrifugal principle, for it doesn't carry the threat of direct political, or other, action. Regionalism is a somewhat disinfected version of the centrifugal principle, which, when it manifested itself as unvarnished sectionalism, tended to be deficient in the Christian virtue of humility. Regionalism, then, we may take in its more practical aspects as an attempt to balance our economy—perhaps, metaphorically speaking, as a belated recognition of the fairly obvious fact that a circle cannot have a center without having a circumference.

But the decline of the centrifugal principle economically and politically was not an isolated thing. It was accompanied by an increasing pressure to stereotype American life, to throttle whatever diverged from the standard in favor of some local or regional sentiment. Official manifestations of regional or local pride, booster clubs and Chambers of Commerce, in fulfilling their function of advertising local benefits, merely advertised a belief that their special community was more like the ideal stereotype than the next stop down the line. That was, also, the period of hick-baiting. The hick was the appropriate butt, for he was apparently at that time the only surviving opponent of the stereotype, an inadequate opponent, with his blundering native conservatism and his inarticulate attachment to what he already knew.

But into what did the hick-baiters want to turn the hick? They never said. Into a drug-store cowboy, a bar-fly, a citizen whose view of human destiny was conditioned by the literature snuggling coyly and superfluously among the pants ads in *Esquire*, whose contact with real L-I-F-E was gained from the columns of O. O. McIntyre, and whose politics were defined by Arthur Brisbane? Probably not, but that was what the hick-baiter got in most cases, when he got any results whatsoever. Frequently the hick-baiter—Mencken, for instance—was impelled by the highest motives and hated the standard stereotype; but the irony of his labor was that he usually did nothing more than make the hick ready to accept the stereotype, because he was not offering the hick a substitute. He accomplished that instead of trying to define and encourage a spirit that might develop a broader cultural integrity in local terms.

But the hick-baiters are now middle-aged and tired. They are also finished. They are sufferers from technological unemployment, for their special talents are no longer required in our rapidly advancing civilization. The hick is not to be baited but pampered now, a process that may have its own dangers and may accomplish with a genial smile what ridicule and high-pressure salesmanship left undone. But, in any case, the hick-baiters are superseded. The issue is drawn along different lines.

The literature of the pre-depression period furnishes a considerable amount of documentation to the effect that writers found it impossible to write unless they could "get away." That was the period when first novels were frequently about the struggle of a young man or woman of genius—genius, for nothing less would do in most cases—to escape from the sordid surroundings of youth. Escape to what? That question was always unanswered. Or rather, it was answered only in a geographical sense. Escape to New York or Paris. But the question was never really answered, for the novel always stopped at that point. The trouble was not in New York or Paris; it was in the attitude of the writer who was escaping. He wanted to escape in search of a subject, a theme. Once in New York, let us say, he felt that he would discover not *how* to write but *what* to write; he went to learn *what* to think and not to say what he thought. Edgar Lee Masters once complained of this failure to observe the meaning of the local scene in a poem on Petit, the poet in *Spoon River Anthology*:

> Seeds in a dry pod, tick, tick, tick,
> Tick, tick, tick like mites in a quarrel—
> Faint iambics that the full breeze wakens—
> But the pine tree makes a symphony thereof.
> Triolets, villanelles, rondels, rondeaus,

Ballades by the score with the same old thought:
The snows and the roses of yesterday are vanished;
And what is love but a rose that fades?

Life all around me here in the village:
Tragedy, comedy, valor, and truth,
Courage, constancy, heroism, failure—
All in the loom, and oh, what patterns
Woodlands, meadows, streams, and rivers,
Blind to all of it all my life long.
Triolets, villanelles, rondels, rondeaus,
Seeds in a dry pod, tick, tick, tick,
Tick, tick, tick, what little iambics,
While Homer and Whitman roared in the pines?

But most poets now know better than Petit did; and so do the novelists and the rest. For the country is now full of stanch regionalists.

The propagandizers for regionalism who talk about literature like to dwell on the "regionalism" of great writers of the past, and analyze complacently, with the terminology of "regional" criticism, the work of Hawthorne or Shakespeare. As a matter of fact, it scarcely requires a fanatical regionalist to approach Milton in the same terms, or even the paradoxical Henry James. We exclaim at what now seems to be the beautiful organic relation of the work of such writers to the social matrix of their time and place, and remark: "Ah, if we can only achieve a true regional spirit, then we'll have literature!" Perhaps we shall have a great literature. And the regional impulse, as I believe, may contribute something to a healthy literary development. But, on the other hand, it is not an inescapable conclusion; perhaps our age is incurably eclectic in temper, diffuse, sceptical, faithless, and tentative.

Perhaps our current interest in regionalism is but one aspect, after all, of our incurable eclecticism, is but the nostalgia of the Alexandrian epoch. Perhaps we should ask ourselves: "Did Hawthorne have to reason or to will himself into his regionalism, into appropriate relation to his place and its past and present? Did he have to argue the point with himself and with other people, and did he attend conventions to discuss the matter?" Probably not; it was as natural as breathing, or at least that is the picture we now see. But in any case, can we be Hawthorne, or Melville? Even then forces were afoot that would destroy the vitality of the spirit from which Hawthorne wrote. There was, in fact, Emerson, who was a disintegrating influence—an eclectic, a philosopher who stood to the past of his little place and culture somewhat as the Neo-Platonists stood to a sterner and earlier Greece—Emerson with noble, vague, and intoxicating periods, laying the foundation that has served, how unwittingly, as the partial basis of our stereotype.

We may say that history does not repeat itself except in deceptive details, and that we can argue from it nothing of our future. We can say that we are not able to use our will and our reason to bring about a healthy and functional relation of the writer to his region and its society. But if we are to assume anything, we assume that we can use, however incompletely and defectively, our will and reason for realizing ends that seem desirable to us.

But it will not do to expect too much. We have the get-rich-quick psychology about regionalism, as we have had it about certain matters in the past. There have been other booms. A dozen get-rich-quick formulae for literature have appeared—humanism, communism, imagism, objectivism, regionalism—all holding out the promise of the gold brick to the writer and the reader.

If regionalism is to mean anything at all, it must not be approached in this spirit. It must not be another fad, another facet of our eclecticism. And there are other things a literary regionalism must not be.

(1) Regionalism is not quaintness and local color and folklore, for those things when separated from a functional idea are merely a titillation of the reader's sentimentality or snob-

bishness. A novel loaded with folklore or local color, no matter how accurate, is not necessarily any better than a novel about adulterers who quote the poetry of Emily Dickinson in penthouses. The study of such material as folklore is valuable in precisely the same way as the study of various other things—and may be in certain hands, most hands, in fact, as irrelevant for the meaning of literature as the making of a card index of five-syllable words in the poetry of John Milton. The value of the study of folklore, etc., depends entirely on the context and the critical implications of the subject. Literary regionalism does not ascribe a privileged place to such investigation. It might be better for a literary regionalist who wanted to write a novel about Mississippi to read the stock-market reports and cotton quotations. Folklore and dialectal accuracy do not guarantee literary merit.

(2) Regionalism based on the literary exploitation of a race or society that has no cultural continuity with our own tends to be false and precious. It is a touristic regionalism. The cult of Indian worship, as we often find it, is an example.

(3) Regionalism does not necessarily imply an emphasis on the primitive or underprivileged character. A novel about a brave cowpuncher or an honest sharecropper is not necessarily more honest, more regional, more convincing, more important, or more anything else, except faked, than a novel about J. P. Morgan or the late Fatty Arbuckle. There is a literature of false primitivism as well as the literature of superficial sophistication; and most of this literature has claimed the label of regionalism.

(4) Regionalism does not mean that a writer should relinquish any resource of speculation or expression that he has managed to achieve. Even simplicity does not mean simple-mindedness. There is no compulsion in regionalism that a modern poet should write fake folk ballads or that a novelist should cultivate illiteracy as a virtue. The poet might learn something from folk ballads, but he could never write them, in any case. A writer's worst dishonesty would be to deny,

on the ground of theory, part of his own temper and own resource; to limit, arbitrarily, the sensibility he would bring to his material. Regionalism does not mean literature by exclusion rather than by inclusion.

(5) Regionalism does not mean that literature is tied to its region for appreciation. When it is so tied, it is so much the less literature. Literature that is only good on the local market probably depends for its interest on purely adventitious factors. Literature, as has often been said, is exportable, and does not, like the wines of the old simile on this subject, lose its flavor in transit. Regionalism does not imply in any way a relaxing of critical standards.

(6) Even literary regionalism is more than a literary matter, and is not even primarily a literary matter. If it is treated as a purely literary matter it will promptly lose any meaning, for only in so far as literature springs from some reality in experience is it valuable to us. The regimen for the regionalist who wanted to be a writer would have its public as well as its private aspect.

The danger in regionalism lies in its last syllable, in the *ism*. As a fad it is meaningless. And those who profess a sympathy for the ideal might do well to realize that it scarcely promises quick returns, is not a cure-all, and provides for the writer no substitute for talent or intelligence. (1936)

THEODORE ROOSEVELT

Theodore Roosevelt, twenty-sixth President of the United States, was born in New York, New York in 1858. Writer, naturalist, explorer, and soldier, he is one of the most extraordinary individuals in American history, surpassing in his spare time what most people can accomplish in a specialized field of interest in an entire lifetime. His highly readable *The Winning of the West* helped to open up the hitherto relatively neglected areas of research in American history. Included in this encyclopedic work is Roosevelt's interpretation of the Watauga Settlement.

Sevier, Robertson, and the Watauga Commonwealth, 1769–1774

Soon after the successful ending of the last colonial struggle with France, and the conquest of Canada, the British king issued a proclamation forbidding the English colonists from trespassing on Indian grounds, or moving west of the mountains. But in 1768, at the treaty of Fort Stanwix, the Six Nations agreed to surrender to the English all the lands lying between the Ohio and the Tennessee;[1] and this treaty was at

[1] Then called the Cherokee

once seized upon by the backwoodsmen as offering an excuse for settling beyond the mountains. However, the Iroquois had ceded lands to which they had no more right than a score or more other Indian tribes; and these latter, not having been consulted, felt at perfect liberty to make war on the intruders. In point of fact, no one tribe or set of tribes could cede Kentucky or Tennessee, because no one tribe or set of tribes owned either. The great hunting-grounds between the Ohio and the Tennessee formed a debatable land, claimed by every tribe that could hold its own against its rivals.

The eastern part of what is now Tennessee consists of a great hill-strewn, forest-clad valley, running from northeast to southwest, bounded on one side by the Cumberland, and on the other by the Great Smoky and Unaka Mountains; the latter separating it from North Carolina. In this valley arise and end the Clinch, the Holston, the Watauga, the Nolichucky, the French Broad, and the other streams, whose combined volume makes the Tennessee River. The upper end of the valley lies in southwestern Virginia, the headwaters of some of the rivers being well within that State; and though the province was really part of North Carolina, it was separated therefrom by high mountain chains, while from Virginia it was easy to follow the watercourses down the valley. Thus, as elsewhere among the mountains forming the western frontier, the first movements of population went parallel with, rather than across, the ranges. As in western Virginia the first settlers came, for the most part, from Pennsylvania, so, in turn, in what was then western North Carolina, and is now eastern Tennessee, the first settlers came mainly from Virginia, and, indeed, in great part, from this same Pennsylvanian stock. Of course, in each case there was also a very considerable movement directly westward. They were a sturdy race, enterprising and intelligent, fond of the strong excitement inherent in the adventurous frontier life. Their untamed and turbulent passions, and the lawless freedom of their lives made them a population very productive of wild, headstrong characters; yet, as a whole, they were a God-fearing race, as was but natural in those who sprang from the loins of the Irish Calvinists. Their preachers, all Presbyterians, followed close behind the first settlers, and shared their toil and dangers; they tilled their fields rifle in hand, and fought the Indians valorously. They felt that they were dispossessing the Canaanites, and were thus working the Lord's will in preparing the land for a race which they believed was more truly His chosen people than was that nation which Joshua led across the Jordan. They exhorted no less earnestly in the bare meeting-houses on Sunday, because their hands were roughened with guiding the plow and wielding the axe on week-days; for they did not believe that being called to preach the word of God absolved them from earning their living by the sweat of their brows. The women, the wives of the settlers, were of the same iron temper. They fearlessly fronted every danger the men did, and they worked quite as hard. They prized the knowledge and learning they themselves had been forced to do without; and many a backwoods woman by thrift and industry, by the sale of her butter and cheese, and the calves from her cows, enabled her husband to give his sons good schooling, and perhaps to provide for some favored member of the family the opportunity to secure a really first-class education.

The valley in which these splendid pioneers of our people settled, lay directly in the track of the Indian marauding parties, for the great war trail used by the Cherokees and by their northern foes ran along its whole length. This war trail, or war trace as it was then called, was in places very distinct, although apparently never as well marked as were some of the buffalo trails. It sent off a branch to Cumberland Gap, whence it ran directly north through Kentucky to the Ohio, being there known as the warriors' path. Along these trails the Northern and Southern Indians passed and repassed when they went to war against each other; and of course they were ready and eager to attack any white man who might settle down along their course.

In 1769, the year that Boone first went to Kentucky, the first permanent settlers came to the banks of the Watauga, the settlement being merely an enlargement of the Virginia settlement, which had for a short time existed on the head-waters of the Holston, especially near Wolf Hills. At first the settlers thought they were still in the domain of Virginia, for at that time the line marking her southern boundary had not been run so far west. Indeed, had they not considered the land as belonging to Virginia, they would probably not at the moment have dared to intrude farther on territory claimed by the Indians. But while the treaty between the crown and the Iroquois at Fort Stanwix had resulted in the cession of whatever right the Six Nations had to the south-western territory, another treaty was concluded about the same time with the Cherokees, by which the latter agreed to surrender their claims to a small portion of this country, though as a matter of fact before the treaty was signed white settlers had crowded beyond the limits allowed them. These two treaties, in the first of which one set of tribes surrendered a small portion of land, while in the second an entirely differ-ent confederacy surrendered a larger tract, which, however, included part of the first cession, are sufficient to show the absolute confusion of the Indian land titles.

But in 1771, one of the new-comers, who was a practical surveyor, ran out the Virginia boundary line some distance to the westward, and discovered that the Watauga settlement came within the limits of North Carolina. Hitherto the set-tlers had supposed that they themselves were governed by the Virginian law, and that their rights as against the Indians were guaranteed by the Virginian government; but this dis-covery threw them back upon their own resources. They suddenly found themselves obliged to organize a civil gov-ernment, under which they themselves should live, and at the same time to enter into a treaty on their own account with the neighboring Indians, to whom the land they were on apparently belonged.

The first need was even more pressing than the second. North Carolina was always a turbulent and disorderly colony, unable to enforce law and justice even in the long-settled districts; so that it was wholly out of the question to appeal to her for aid in governing a remote and outlying community. Moreover, about the time that the Watauga commonwealth was founded, the troubles in North Carolina came to a head. Open war ensued between the adherents of the royal governor, Tryon, on the one hand, and the Regulators, as the insurgents styled themselves, on the other, the struggle ending with the overthrow of the Regulators at the battle of the Alamance.

As a consequence of these troubles, many people from the back counties of North Carolina crossed the mountains, and took up their abode among the pioneers on the Watauga and upper Holston; the beautiful valley of the Nolichucky soon receiving its share of this stream of immigration. Among the first comers were many members of the class of desperate adventurers always to be found hanging round the outskirts of frontier civilization. Horse-thieves, murderers, escaped bond-servants, runaway debtors—all, in fleeing from the law, sought to find a secure asylum in the wilderness. The brutal and lawless wickedness of these men, whose uncouth and raw savagery was almost more repulsive than that of city criminals, made it imperative upon the decent members of the community to unite for self-protection. The desperadoes were often mere human beasts of prey; they plundered whites and Indians impartially. They not only by their thefts and murders exasperated the Indians into retaliating on innocent whites, but, on the other hand, they also often deserted their own color and went to live among the redskins, becoming their leaders in the worst outrages.

But the bulk of the settlers were men of sterling worth; fit to be the pioneer fathers of a mighty and beautiful state. They possessed the courage that enabled them to defy outside foes, together with the rough, practical common-sense that allowed them to establish a simple but effective form of government, so as to preserve order among themselves. To succeed in the wilderness, it was necessary to possess not only daring, but also patience and the capacity to endure grinding toil. The pioneers were hunters and husbandmen. Each, by the aid of axe and brand, cleared his patch of corn land in the forest, close to some clear, swift-flowing stream, and by his skill with the rifle won from canebrake and woodland the game on which his family lived until the first crop was grown.

A few of the more reckless and foolhardy, and more especially of those who were either merely hunters and not farmers, or else who were of doubtful character, lived entirely by themselves; but, as a rule, each knot of settlers was gathered together into a little stockaded hamlet, called a fort or station. This system of defensive villages was very distinctive of pioneer backwoods life, and was unique of its kind; without it the settlement of the West and Southwest would have been indefinitely postponed. In no other way could the settlers have combined for defence, while yet retaining their individual ownership of the land. The Watauga forts or palisaded villages were of the usual kind, the cabins and blockhouses connected by a heavy loop-holed picket. They were admirably adapted for defence with the rifle. As there was no moat, there was a certain danger from an attack with fire unless water was stored within; and it was of course necessary to guard carefully against surprise. But to open assault they were practically impregnable, and they therefore offered a sure haven of refuge to the settlers in case of an Indian inroad. In time of peace, the inhabitants moved out, to live in their isolated log-cabins and till the stump-dotted clearings. Trails led through the dark forests from one station to another, as well as to the settled districts beyond the mountains; and at long intervals men drove along them bands of pack-horses, laden with the few indispensable necessaries the settlers could not procure by their own labor. The pack-horse was the first, and for a long time the only, method of carrying on trade in the backwoods; and the business of the packer was one of the leading frontier industries.

The settlers worked hard and hunted hard, and lived both plainly and roughly. Their cabins were roofed with the clap-boards, or huge shingles, split from the log with maul and wedge, and held in place by heavy stones, or by poles; the floors were made of rived puncheons, hewn smooth on one surface; the chimney was outside the hut, made of rock when possible, otherwise of logs thickly plastered with clay that was strengthened with hogs' bristles or deer hair; in the great fireplace was a tongue on which to hang pot-hooks and kettle; the unglazed window had a wooden shutter, and the door was made of great clapboards. The men made their own harness, farming implements, and domestic utensils; and, as in every other community, still living in the heroic age, the smith was a person of the utmost importance. There was but one thing that all could have in any quantity, and that was land; each had all of this he wanted for the taking, —or if it was known to belong to the Indians, he got its use for a few trinkets or a flask of whiskey. A few of the settlers still kept some of the Presbyterian austerity of character, as regards amusements; but, as a rule, they were fond of horse-racing, drinking, dancing, and fiddling. The corn-shuckings, flax-pullings, log-rollings (when the felled timber was rolled off the clearings), house-raisings, maple-sugar-boilings, and the like were scenes of boisterous and light-hearted merri-ment, to which the whole neighborhood came, for it was accounted an insult if a man was not asked in to help on such occasions, and none but a base churl would refuse his assist-ance. The backwoods people had to front peril and hardship without stint, and they loved for the moment to leap out of the bounds of their narrow lives and taste the coarse pleasures that are always dear to a strong, simple, and primitive race. Yet underneath their moodiness and their fitful light-heartedness lay a spirit that when roused was terrible in its ruthless and stern intensity of purpose. . . .

Thus the Watauga folk were the first Americans who, as a separate body, moved into the wilderness to hew out dwellings for themselves and their children, trusting only to their own shrewd heads, stout hearts, and strong arms, unhelped and unhampered by the power nominally their sovereign. They built up a commonwealth which had many successors; they showed that the frontiersmen could do their work unassisted; for they not only proved that they were made of stuff stern enough to hold its own against outside pressure of any sort, but they also made it evident that having won the land they were competent to govern both it and themselves. They were the first to do what the whole nation has since done. It has often been said that we owe all our success to our surroundings; that any race with our opportunities could have done as well as we have done. Undoubtedly our opportunities have been great; undoubtedly we have often and lamentably failed in taking advantage of them. But what nation ever has done all that was possible with the chances offered it? The Spaniards, the Portuguese, and the French, not to speak of the Russians in Siberia, have all enjoyed, and yet have failed to make good use of, the same advantages which we have turned to good account. The truth is, that in starting a new nation in a new country, as we have done, while there are exceptional chances to be taken advantage of, there are also exceptional dangers and difficulties to be overcome. None but heroes can succeed wholly in the work. It is a good thing for us at times to compare what we have done with what we could have done, had we been better and wiser; it may make us try in the future to raise our abilities to the level of our opportunities. Looked at absolutely, we must frankly acknowledge that we have fallen very far short indeed of the high ideal we should have reached. Looked at relatively, it must also be said that we have done better than any other nation or race working under our conditions.

The Watauga settlers outlined in advance the nation's work. They tamed the rugged and shaggy wilderness, they bid defiance to outside foes, and they successfully solved the difficult problem of self-government. (1912)

SAM HOUSTON

Sam Houston was born in Rockbridge County, Virginia, in 1793. Following the death of his father, he in 1807 with his mother and eight other children moved to Tennessee. Largely self-educated, he lived for three years with the Cherokee who called him "the Raven," and whom he defended throughout a long and remarkable career. He fought with Jackson against the Creeks at Horseshoe Bend and later served two terms in Congress. In 1827 he was elected governor of Tennessee but resigned in 1829 following separation from his wife, Eliza Allen. Leaving Tennessee for Arkansas, he was united in the custom of the Cherokee to Tiana Rogers, collateral ancestor of Will Rogers, but left her in 1832 to go to Texas. Distinguishing himself in the battle of San Jacinto, Houston was overwhelmingly elected first President of the Republic of Texas. He died in 1863 at Huntsville, Texas, still opposed to secession from the Union. Houston's defense of the Cherokee Indians remains one of the most eloquent of any major American historical figure. The selection below is taken from the *Writings of Sam Houston*.

Opposing the Kansas-Nebraska Bill

. . . I am aware, Mr. President, that in presenting myself as the advocate of the Indians and their rights, I shall claim but little sympathy from the community at large, and that I shall stand very much alone, pursuing the course which I feel it my imperative duty to adhere to. It is not novel for me to seek to advocate the rights of the Indians upon this floor and elsewhere. A familiar knowledge of them, their manners, their habits, and their intercourse with this Government for the last half century, from my early boyhood through life, have placed within my possession facts, and, I trust, implanted in me a principle enduring as life itself. That principle is to protect the Indian against wrong and oppression, and to vindicate him in the enjoyment of rights which have been solemnly guaranteed to him by this Government; and *that* is the principle, Mr. President, which I shall insist grows out of the course of policy avowed by this Government as far back as 1785. The Hopewell treaty was then negotiated with the Cherokee Indians of Tennessee. The country in which they lived was solemnly guaranteed to them. It was promised that they should be regarded as a people in alliance with the United States, and that they should have a delegate in Congress. How far that has been complied with, the history of more than fifty years can testify.

Successive promises were made from 1785 to 1802, during the administration of General Washington; and the pledges of amity and regard that were made to the Indians by him, inured to Mr. Jefferson, for he, in 1809, made solemn promises to them, provided they would migrate west of the Mississippi. Long anterior to that they had been seduced by the promises of this Government. They went west of the Mississippi, and were recognized by the United States so soon as that territory was acquired from France. They continued there up to 1814, 1816 and 1817, under the promises of the

Government, battling against the hostile, wild Indians, and relying upon the pledges of the different Presidents of the United States, their great father, that they should not be molested in their settlement there. The treaty of 1817 was negotiated after the war of 1812, in which it will be recollected that the Cherokees, as allies of the United States, enlisted under the banner of this Government, and marched to battle, under the immediate command of General Jackson. They were engaged in all the scenes of the Creek war of 1813 and 1814. Here was an earnest of their fidelity to the pledges which *they* had given to the Government of the United States. In consequence of these services, they were considered in the treaties of 1814, made with the Creeks. After that, the policy of the Government became more stringent upon them; and a disposition arising, owing to pressure from surrounding States, to remove them to Arkansas, it was proposed that the whole nation of Cherokees east of the Mississippi should migrate, and exchange their lands on the east for lands lying to the far west. The white people had surrounded them. It was suggested that it was necessary for them to remove; that when the white man and the Indian were in contact, and particularly when the Indians were surrounded by white men, they could no longer prosper; that they were now surrounded, and had no outlet; that they were not prepared precisely to go into the abodes of civilized men; and, therefore, it was necessary to withdraw them from that vicinity, and to give them a boundless latitude in the west.

These were the suggestions, and the most solemn pledges were made by this Government—that if they would remove to the west of the Mississippi they should never again be surrounded by white men, and that they should have a boundless and interminable outlet, as far as the jurisdiction of the United States extended. This was most solemnly guaranteed to those Indians; and in obedience to that, and to the desire of the Government, most emphatically expressed, almost amounting to a command, the nation divided, and a portion of them went to Arkansas. They had been driven from their first settlement; they had gone up beyond the white settlements in Arkansas Territory, and had located themselves at Point Remove; so-called from the fact of their removal to it. They remained there until Lovely's purchase was made north of the Arkansas from the Osage Indians. White people immediately flocked in beyond them, cutting off again their outlet, and circumscribing them within limits. A treaty was negotiated in 1828, I think, in which it was declared to them that in exchange for the territory they *then* occupied several hundred miles below Lovely's purchase, and by the settlers on Lovely's purchase, the Neosho and Grand rivers and Verdigris, they should be removed below Fort Smith, and that they should have eternal possession of that land. The exchange took place; the settlers on Lovely's purchase were removed down; head rights or preëmptions were granted to them as a recompense for the sacrifice which they had made, by surrendering the cabins which they had occupied, and each man received three hundred and twenty acres of land. The Cherokees received for their compensation a nominal sum, and removed to the country in which they now abide. This country was given to them under every solemn obligation of perpetuity. Every right that the United States possessed was invested in them, and it was declared that it should inure to them and their posterity perpetually. The most solemn pledge had been made that a boundless outlet should be given; that the white man should never again be settled beyond them in the jurisdiction of the United States. In conformity with that the Cherokees made the treaty. Up to 1833, I think it was, the nation was divided, one portion of it remaining east of the Mississippi, the other west, where they had migrated. The Government gave that portion of land that they were settled upon to the Western Cherokees, and they were treated as an independent and separate tribe from that east of the Mississippi. . . .

In 1817 a delegation of two, I think, came from Arkansas to the Cherokee agency, where I then was, a subaltern detailed from the army in the capacity of assistant agent to Colonel Meigs. These Indians came in his absence, and Governor McMinn, ex-officio superintendent of Indian affairs, held a council. The Cherokee authorities east of the Mississippi refused positively to send any delegation to this Government, relying on the pledges given to them of their rightful possession of the country lying east of the Mississippi; and contending that the Government had no right to the territory on which they resided. They claimed that the treaty of Hopewell had guaranteed to them the perpetual possession of it, not as aboriginal inhabitants, but as having acquired it by grant and treaty. A delegation was sent on, formed of Indians east of the Mississippi associated with those west, constituting a delegation from the west, for the purpose of making a treaty with this Government. Though the Indians in the east had never been to the west of the Mississippi, they were detailed from the Cherokee nation, in opposition to the counsel and the action of their chiefs. A chief was appointed for the time being that had never been recognized by their people, thus constraining those east of the Mississippi to yield to the dictation of the superintendent, acting in obedience to the will, as he supposed, if not the express direction, of the Government of the United States. The delegates came to Washington City. Its leader, a man who had been a distinguished warrior of the eastern Cherokees under General Jackson, became indisposed, and in Rogersville, Tennessee, deceased. There was then no other leader but the senior chief from the western Cherokee nation. They presented themselves in Washington City under the auspices of the superintendent; and I was directed by the President of the United States, or by the Secretary of War, to attend at the Executive mansion upon a certain day—in 1818—I think, in March.

Upon the Indians presenting themselves to the President

of the United States, he made a few remarks to them; told them he was desirous to hear what they had to say to him; that they had come a great distance to see their Great Father; that he had understood from the agent they had important communications to make and favors to ask, and that he was prepared to hear them with the greatest consideration. They represented in detail pretty much what I have given as the history of their tribes, and the circumstances under which they had become located in the far West. The President, after hearing all they had to say upon the subject, gave a reply, in which he assured them of the constancy, friendship, and protection of the Government of the United States; the consideration to which they were entitled from the fact of their having emigrated west of Arkansas at the suggestion of the President, and assured them that it entitled them to the most favorable consideration of this Government. He told them, you are now in a country where you can be happy; no white man shall ever again disturb you; the Arkansas will protect your southern boundary when you get there. You will be protected on either side; the white man shall never again encroach upon you, and you will have a great outlet to the West. As long as water flows, or grass grows upon the earth, or the sun rises to show your pathway, or you kindle your camp fires, so long shall you be protected by this Government, and never again removed from your present habitation.

Reposing full confidence in these pledges, the Indians have acted; though the United States, in carrying out their portion of the contract in relation to a part of the tribe west of the Mississippi, without adding to their territory, or without making it distinct, located the Indians east of the Mississippi river—after giving them millions of dollars for their lands—upon the territory of the Western Cherokees. The men who had organized themselves into a government, and lived upon the territory guaranteed to them as a separate and distinct people, found these others thrown upon and intermingling with them; and although there was an additional and distinct territory to the north of them, designated and laid off for the Eastern Cherokees, they did not settle there, but located in the midst of the Old Settlers, dispossessed them of their homes, their improvements, their salt-works, and everything valuable, and formed a new government superseding the former one, and usurping the rights vested in the former tribe.

I need not rehearse to gentlemen who are familiar with the past, the tragedies that followed, the sanguinary murders and massacres, the mid-night conflagrations—these attest the inharmonious action which arose from this faithless conduct on the part of the Government or its agents. I know this may appear a very harsh assertion to make here, that our Government acts in bad faith with the Indians. I could ask one question that would excite reflection and reminiscences among gentlemen. When have they performed an honest act, or redeemed in good faith a pledge made to the Indians? Let but a single instance be shown, and I will be prepared to retract. I am not making a charge against the Government of the United States which is not applicable to all civilized Governments in relation to their aboriginal inhabitants. It is not with the intention to derogate from the purity of our national character or from the integrity of our institutions that I make the accusation; but it is because it is verified by history.

It may be said that my remarks apply only to the Cherokees. I selected them as an example; not as the only nation affording examples; but, as I was more familiar with the circumstances in connection with that nation than any other; and having been more immediately identified with them, I selected them as an illustration of our policy. Look at the Creeks, at the Choctaws, the Chickasaws; look at every tribe that has ever been within our jurisdiction, and in every instance our intercourse has resulted in their detriment or destruction.

Well, sir, what is now proposed to be done? Is it to redress any wrongs that the Indians have sustained? Is it to establish a new course of policy in relation to them? Is it to redeem any pledges given, or is it to violate our most solemn treaty stipulations, that they should not be further molested? Have we not land enough for the occupancy of our citizens? I believe we have one billion three hundred and sixty odd million of acres of vacant or public lands in the United States. What necessity, then, is there on the part of our citizens, that they require to have a spot, peculiarly consecrated by the pledge of national faith, and guaranteed to the Indians, in order to give them room and latitude? Are their necessities so great that it is unpatriotic to restrain them, and can our true policy be carried out only by their molestation, and the exercise of greater injustice towards them? It seems to me that it is an object worthy of the highest consideration of an enlightened, I might say, Christian people and that they should adopt at this late period some system calculated not only to ameliorate the condition of the Indians, but to civilize and christianize them. If that object is not worthy of the gravest contemplation of Senators and legislators, as well as the high functionaries of the Government, I shall realize the most melancholy apprehensions which I have entertained in relation to the fate of this devoted people. It seems to be a foregone conclusion that the Indians must yield to the progress of the white man—that they must surrender their country—that they must go from place to place, and that there is to be no rest for them. Is not the earth wide enough for all the creatures the Almighty has placed upon it? But they seem not to be regarded in the light of human beings, and are driven like wild beasts; and when their habitation is made in one place, they are only considered as temporary residents, to be transferred at will to some more distant station. If they commence the arts of civilization; if they remain in homes; if the domestic circle is formed, and little neighborhoods begin to rise; if schools are established, and scholars sent, it is but a little while before the *necessities* of the white man demand the territory, and they are pushed forward, to some new home, to some wilderness scene, and told that it will be of great advantage to them, and a great deal more pleasant. Dissuade them from their passion for hunting; give them a place for agriculture, and the means to pursue it, and then you civilize them; for no man can become civilized unless he cultivates agricultural and social arts. Do this, and you save this people; neglect it, and you only carry out the process of annihilation. If you are prepared, it is in your power, gentle-men, to do it. Be *just*, and posterity, at least, will appreciate it. The country will be filled up some day, and our actions will be estimated by some moral standard, and not by the passions of men for accumulation of soil, or a disposition to transgress upon the public domain. . . . (1854)

ARNOLD J. TOYNBEE

One of the most noted historians of all time, Arnold J. Toynbee was born in 1889 in London and was educated at Winchester and Balliol College, Oxford. The following selection comes from his magnum opus, *A Study of History*, which is often compared to and contrasted with Oswald Spengler's *The Decline of the West*. Since its publication in 1935, Toynbee's view of the Appalachian as white barbarian has frequently been criticized by defenders of all Southern mountain culture, especially by natives.

Scotland, Ulster, and Appalachia

At the present day, there is a notorious contrast between Ulster and the rest of Ireland. While Southern Ireland is a rather old-fashioned agricultural country, Ulster is one of the busiest workshops in the modern Western World. The city of Belfast ranks in the same company as Glasgow or Newcastle or Hamburg or Detroit; and the modern Ulsterman has as great a reputation for being efficient as he has for being unaccommodating.

In response to what challenge has the Ulsterman made

himself what he now is? He has responded to the dual challenge of migrating to Ulster across the sea from Scotland and contending, after his arrival in Ulster, with the native Irish inhabitants whom he found in possession and proceeded to dispossess. This twofold ordeal has had a stimulating effect which may be measured by comparing the power and wealth of Ulster at the present day with the relatively modest circumstances of those districts on the Scottish side of the border between Scotland and England and along the Lowland fringe of "the Highland Line" from which the original Scottish settlers in Ulster were recruited some three centuries ago by King James I/VI. The comparison reveals that, in the course of the intervening centuries, the dual challenge presented by Ulster has administered a noteworthy stimulus to those descendants of the original Scottish settlers who have remained on the Irish soil on which King James once planted their ancestors.

The modern Ulstermen, however, are not the only living representatives of this stock; for the migratory habit, once acquired, is apt to persist; and the Scottish pioneers who migrated to Ulster in the seventeenth century begot "Scotch-Irish" children and grandchildren who re-emigrated in the eighteenth century from Ulster to North America. At the present day, the twice-transplanted offspring of these "Scotch-Irish" emigrants to the New World survive, far away from their kinsmen in Ireland and their kinsmen in Scotland, in the fastnesses of the Appalachian Mountains: a highland zone which runs through half a dozen states of the North American Union from Pennsylvania to Georgia.

What has been the effect of this second transplantation upon the Scotch-Irish stock? In the seventeenth century King James's colonists crossed the sea from Scotland to Ulster and took to fighting "the Wild Irish" instead of "the Wild Highlanders." In the eighteenth century, their grandchildren crossed the sea again to become "Indian fighters" in the North American backwoods. Obviously this American challenge has been more formidable than the Irish challenge, and this in both its aspects. In the human sphere, the "Red Indian" heathen was of course a more savage adversary than the "Wild Irish" Catholic (however wilfully the difference may have been ignored by the Scotch-Irish frontiersman in his Protestant fanaticism). In the physical sphere, the Appalachian Mountains are wilder in scenery and vaster in scale than any landscape in Scotland or in Ulster, with the consequence that the Scotch-Irish immigrants who have forced their way into these natural fastnesses have come to be isolated and segregated here from the rest of the World to a much greater extent than their ancestors ever were, or than their cousins ever have been, in their Irish and Scottish habitats. In terms of the total environment, the severity of the challenge has been enhanced in the transition from Ulster to Appalachia to such a degree that "the law of diminishing returns" has come into operation with unmistakable force.

If the modern citizen of industrial Belfast has in some respects outstripped his Scottish cousin who has never migrated from the rural neighbourhoods of "the Highland Line" and the English Border, he has certainly not been outstripped in his turn by his American cousin who has migrated for the second time from Ulster to the Appalachian fastnesses. On the contrary, the stimulus which was once administered by the migration from Scotland to Ireland, so far from being reinforced by the subsequent migration from Ireland to America, has been more than counteracted—as we shall find if we now compare the Ulsterman and the Appalachian as they each are to-day, some two centuries since the date when they parted company.

Let us compare them, for example, on the point of their respective proneness to bloodshed: a point on which Ulster has by no means a good record. The old war to the knife between intrusive Protestants and indigenous Catholics is still carried on by gunmen from the windows of Belfast; and at this day the toll of political murders is heavier in the capi-

tal of Ulster than in any other great city of Western Europe.*
Yet even in Ulster, where this political bloodshed still persists, there is no longer any survival of the family blood-feud
which has remained one of the regular social institutions of
"the Mountain People" of Appalachia. The Ulsterman, again,
is unlikely to forget the sea, considering that one of his principal industries is shipbuilding, whereas the Appalachian,
whose ancestors actually crossed the Atlantic five or six generations ago, has lost touch with the sea so completely that
he no longer attaches any clear meaning to the word itself—
which is preserved in his vocabulary solely through its occurrence in his folk-songs. In the third place, the Ulsterman has
retained the traditional Protestant standard of education,
whereas the Appalachian has relapsed into illiteracy and into
all the superstitions for which illiteracy opens the door. His
agricultural calendar is governed by the phases of the Moon;
his personal life is darkened by the fear, and by the practice,
of witchcraft. He lives in poverty and squalor and ill-health.
In particular, he is a victim of Hook-Worm: a scourge which
lowers the general level of vitality in Appalachia just as it
does in India and for just the same reason. (The children
persist in going about barefoot, and their parents either cannot afford to give them shoes, or will not take the trouble to
insist upon their wearing them, or are too ignorant to be
aware that Hook-Worm gains entry into human bodies
through sores in naked soles.)

In fact, the Appalachian "Mountain People" at this day
are no better than barbarians. They are the American counterparts of the latter-day White barbarians of the Old World:
the Rifis and Kabyles and Tuareg, the Albanians and Cau-
casians, the Kurds and the Pathans and the Hairy Ainu.
These White barbarians of America, however, differ in one
respect from those of Europe and Asia. The latter are simply
the rare and belated survivals of an ancient barbarism which

---

* These lines were written before the National-Socialist Revolution in
Germany at the beginning of the year 1933. [Toynbee's note]

has now passed away all around them; and it is evident that their days, too, are numbered. Through one or other of several alternative processes—extermination or subjection or assimilation—these last lingering survivals will assuredly disappear within the next few generations, as other survivals of White barbarism have disappeared in other parts of the Old World at earlier dates: in the Scottish Highlands in the eighteenth century and in Lithuania in the fourteenth. It is possible, of course, that barbarism will disappear in Appalachia likewise. Indeed, the process of assimilation is already at work among a considerable number of Appalachians who have descended from their mountains and changed their way of life in order to earn wages in the North Carolinian cottonmills. In this case, however, there is no corresponding assurance; for the White barbarism of the New World differs from that of the Old World in being not a survival but a reversion.

The "Mountain People" of Appalachia are *ci-devant* heirs of the Western Civilization who have relapsed into barbarism under the depressing effect of a challenge which has been inordinately severe; and their neo-barbarism is derived from two sources. In part, they have taken the impress of the local Red Indians whom they have exterminated.* Indeed, this impress of Red Indian savagery upon the White victors in this grim frontier-warfare is the only social trace that has been left behind by these vanquished and vanished Redskins. For the rest, the neo-barbarism of Appalachia may be traced back to a ruthless tradition of frontier-warfare along the border between Western Christendom and "the Celtic Fringe"

* "The wilderness masters the colonist. It finds him a European in dress, industries, tools, modes of travel, and thought. It takes him from the railroad car and puts him in the birch canoe. It strips off the garments of civilization and arrays him in the hunting shirt and the moccasin. It puts him in the log cabin of the Cherokee and Iroquois and runs an Indian palisade around him. Before long he has gone to planting Indian corn and plowing with a sharp stick; he shouts the war-cry and takes the scalp in orthodox Indian fashion. In short, at the frontier the environment is at first too strong for the man." (Turner, F. J.: *The Frontier in American History* (New York, 1921, Holt), p. 4.) [Toynbee's note]

which had never died out among their ancestors in the British Isles and which has been revived, among these Scotch-Irish settlers in North America, by the barbarizing severity of their Appalachian environment. On the whole, the nearest social analogues of the Appalachian "Mountain People" of the present day are certain "fossils" of extinct civilizations which have survived in fastnesses and have likewise relapsed into barbarism there: such "fossils" as the Jewish "wild highlanders" of Abyssinia and the Caucasus or the Nestorian "wild highlanders" of Hakkiari.

It will be seen that industrial Ulster is a social "optimum" between rural Scotland on the one hand and barbarian Appalachia on the other; and that this "optimum" is the product of a response to a challenge which, in point of severity, presents itself as a "mean" between two extremes. The challenge to which King James's colonists were exposed in Ulster was distinctly more severe than the challenge that had been faced by their ancestors along the English Border or "the Highland Line." On the other hand, it was very much less severe than the challenge which afterwards presented itself to their Scotch-Irish descendants when these migrated from Ulster to North America in order to become "Indian-fighters" in the Appalachian hills. The contrast between rural Scotland and industrial Ulster bears out, as far as it goes, the law of "the greater the challenge the greater the response"; but in the sharper contrast between industrial Ulster and barbarian Appalachia we see this particular law overridden by the general "law of diminishing returns": a law which, in any situation, infallibly comes into operation at some point or other when things are pushed to extremes.

In this sequence "Scotland—Ulster—Appalachia," the challenge is on the borderline between the physical sphere and the human; but the operation of "the law of diminishing returns" appears quite as clearly in other instances in which the challenge is presented in the human sphere exclusively. (1934, 1935)

WALTER BLAIR

Walter Blair was born in Spokane, Washington, in 1900. He was educated at Yale and the University of Chicago, where he later returned to teach and to serve as department chairman. Long recognized as one of the most able students of American culture, he is known for his works, *Native American Humor*, *Horse Sense in American Humor*, and *Mark Twain and Huck Finn*. He presently lives in Chicago. "Six Davy Crocketts" illustrates a major problem in historicity, that of separating myth from reality. Where does a legend end and a man begin? In the case of Davy Crockett the problem is especially compounded, as Blair's article shows.

Six Davy Crocketts

One who studies what historians say about David Crockett (1786 to 1836), hunter in the Tennessee canebrakes, Congressman, and hero of the Alamo, will find many contradictions in their interpretations. Some call him a rascal, some call him a hero, and some claim that—in alternate periods—he was each. Outside the history books, a great deal has been written about a mythical Davy Crockett, a legendary giant who still lives and accomplishes superhuman feats. It has seemed worth while to examine the documents about this man to find out the reason for these contradictory versions.

The basic fact that emerges from such a study is that one source of information about a man active in politics in the 1830's—the newspapers—in this instance may easily confuse the scholar. The reason, probably, is that in journals of the day Crockett was unmercifully exploited for political purposes. Journalists used him thus, I think, because he happened to offer very good material for a type of political argument which was being discovered in his heyday—the argument based on the great respect in America for mother wit. Most of what was written about the man, in other words, was definitely shaped to appeal to the national love for gumption.

The image the name of Crockett conjures up today is, it appears, anything but that of a person tied up with a virtue so unimaginative as horse sense. The Tennessean, as he is now recalled, is a backwoods demigod, a fabulous hunter and fighter wafted to immortality in the rifle smoke of the Alamo. And the frontier yarnspinners created an even more fantastic figure than people now recall. In the 1830's and 1840's, a series of almanac stories, some of them written by Crockett's one-time neighbors, set forth details of a biography which claimed that even when he was born, Davy was the biggest infant that ever was and a little the smartest that ever will be; that, watered with buffalo milk and weaned on whiskey, he grew so fast that soon his Aunt Keziah was saying it was as good as a meal's vittles to look at him. The biography went on to tell about his boyhood. The family used his infant teeth to build the parlor fireplace. At eight, he weighed two hundred pounds and fourteen ounces, with his shoes off, his feet clean and his stomach empty. At twelve, he escaped from an Indian by riding on the back of a wolf which went like a streak of lightning towed by steamboats.

That was just the start of his amazing life story. According

to the almanacs, by the time he was full grown Crockett
had got such a name, among the animals themselves, that
some would die when he just grinned at them, and others,
looking down from a tree and seeing him reach for his gun,
would holler, "Is that you, Davy?" Then when he'd say,
"Yes," they'd sing out, "All right, don't shoot! I'm a-comin'
down." In the almanacs of a century ago, there were many
details just as amazing as these. According to the almanacs,
for instance, instead of getting killed at the Alamo Davy
actually gave Santa Anna an awful licking. Then, riding his
tame bear, Death Hug, from place to place in Mexico, he
wrought havoc among the enemy armies. At last accounts he
was still alive and kicking.

Such a preposterous biography would seem to be very
remote from common sense. It seems, one would say, to be a
creation of the West which passed hours by campfires
genially manhandling facts until those facts vanished in
woodsmoke from the workaday world and, greatly changed,
turned up in fantastic fairylands inhabited by the Big Bear
of Arkansaw and other creatures as imaginary. If the tall
tales of wilderness yarnspinners gave the only clue to the
character of Crockett, one might decide that he had nothing
to do with homespun philosophy.

But there was a quirk of Crockett's character, in real life,
which made frontier folk elect him and re-elect him to the
state legislature and to the United States House of Representatives. That he was poor, that he was uneducated, made no
difference to them: they thought he could get along because
they guessed he had good horse sense. This fact suggests the
paradox of Crockett's renown. He won fame and office
because he had horse sense; he remained famous because of
the nonsense associated with his memory. How this came
about is an interesting story.

The pre-eminent rôle of horse sense in Crockett's rise to
fame is made clear in the account of his first activity in government, which appeared in the book purporting to be his

autobiography. This book shows that he reached manhood in a sparsely settled part of Tennessee after suffering only four days of schooling; then, as a man, he went to school perhaps a hundred days. "In that time," he says, "I learned to read a little in my primer, to write my own name, and to cypher some in the three first rules in figures. And this is all the schooling I ever had in my life. . . ."

This untaught man was living with his second wife and their children in a clearing on Shoal Creek when, about 1818, the people of the district decided they had to have a temporary government. So, he says,

. . . we met and made what we called a corporation; and I reckon we called *it* wrong . . . . we lived in the backwoods, and didn't profess to know much, and no doubt used many wrong words. But we met, and appointed magistrates and constables to keep order. We didn't fix any laws for them, tho'; for we supposed they would know law enough, whoever they might be; and so we left it to themselves to fix the laws.

Appointed one of the magistrates, Colonel Crockett carried on his work in a way which would have made any lawyer shiver with horror, but which seemed to him sensible enough. When he wanted to judge a man, he would say to his constable, "Catch that fellow, and bring him up for trial." This seemed a proper way to do things, he says, "for we considered this a good warrant, even if it was only in verbal writings."

In time, the legislature gave the district a more formal government, and Crockett, now a squire, had the task of writing out warrants and recording proceedings, a chore which was, he said, "at least a huckleberry over my persimmon." Helped by his constable, though, the squire eventually learned to put everything in writing. His procedure was still a bit irregular, but this irregularity troubled the officer not a whit. The account of his squireship ends with a smug summary:

My judgments were never appealed from, and if they had been they would have stuck like wax, as I gave my decisions on the principles of common justice and honesty between man and man, and relied on natural born sense, and not on law learning to guide me; for I had never read a page in a law book in all my life.

From that time the Colonel moved onward and upward, running for elective offices and winning campaigns which would have ended in dismal beatings anywhere except in a section where book learning was thought less of than mother wit. When, for instance, in 1821, he offered for the legislature, he had read no newspapers, had never seen a public document, could not make a speech about governmental affairs. But this tall hunter in buckskin could knock down plenty of squirrels at a neighborhood hunt and, between horns of chain-lightning whiskey, he could tell good stories; so he more than doubled the vote of his rival. After another session in the state legislature, in 1827 he offered for the United States Congress, told more jokes, passed around horns of the creature to possible supporters, "not to get elected of course," he said righteously, "for that would be against the law; but just . . . to make themselves and their friends feel their keeping a little."

Not long after, Alexis de Tocqueville, over here to study the ways of a democracy, was on the steamboat *Louisville* on the Mississippi. After talking to some Tennesseans, he thus recorded his newest discovery:

When the right of suffrage is *universal*, and when the deputies are paid by the state, it's singular how low and how far wrong the people can go.

Two years ago the inhabitants of the district of which Memphis is the capital sent to the House of Representatives . . . an individual named David Crockett, who has no education, can read with difficulty, has no property, no fixed residence, but passes his life hunting, selling his game to live, and dwelling continuously in the woods.

His competitor, a man of wealth and talent, failed.

Again today, they (my fellow passengers) assured me that in the western states the people generally made very poor selections. Full of pride and ignorance, the electors want to be represented by people of their own kind. Moreover, to win their votes one has to descend to manoeuvres that disgust distinguished men. You have to haunt the taverns and dispute with the populace; that's what they call *electioneering* in America.

The Frenchman de Tocqueville made one or two misstatements in this passage about the Congressman from Tennessee. This is hardly surprising, since he got his information from readers of the press; already many readers were beginning to be misled by stories appearing in scores of newspapers. In time, the real Davy was to disappear into a thicket of such stories, and modern scholars who tried to follow him into the tangled growth were to emerge with strange tales of what they had found.

Writing about the Tennessean, some of these historians were to say that along the trail they had found traces of more than one Davy Crockett—of two Davies, or three, or even four. Claude G. Bowers, for example, says: "The present generation scarcely realizes that there were two Davy Crocketts —the man of the woods and the fight, and the less admirable creature who made a rather sorry figure in the Congress." And V. L. Parrington listed four distinct species of the genus Crockett and described each of them. The bewildering multiplication of Crocketts proves less strange, after study, than one would suppose. A correction is suggested by the documents, however, for it appears that even Parrington was too conservative. There were, it seems, six Davy Crocketts. All of them had affiliations with the great gospel of horse sense so important to the people who lifted Davy to fame.

It is hardly necessary to say that the first Crockett, the flesh and blood being who was born in Tennessee, who married, had children, and went to Congress, was no figment of the imagination. People who saw him—a man more than six feet tall, broad-shouldered, red-cheeked, black-haired, dressed in buckskin—had no feeling that he was an impalpable spirit. An old gaffer who had heard him speak in the Big Hatchie district in the late 'twenties had no doubts, two score years later, about having heard a speech which was "plain and sensible . . . with now and then a dry, witty allusion to his educated opponents, which would bring thunders of applause."

But though Crockett the First offered no difficulty to people who saw and heard the man, keen Americans of the time who learned of Davy only through the newspapers may have had trouble believing that the backwoodsman was any more real, say, than a character in a joke book story. The reason was that, shortly after the Tennessean started to Congress, newspaper wags began to print tales about him which were more fictional than factual. It was a fiction of the time, for instance, that, just as all Scotchmen were frugal, all frontiersmen were both great drinkers and prodigious boasters. Jokes pictured Westerners spending most of their waking hours bending their elbows. When they arose each day, said the stories, all had eye-openers; then they had phlegm-cutters; and then they nursed mint juleps until bedtime. And partly because they drank so much, partly because they were so cocky, frontiersmen by habit introduced themselves to strangers (in stories) with a rambunctious boast, perhaps like scores of such flapdoodle challenges printed here and there, perhaps like those in Nimrod Wildfire's story, thus reported in a joke book published in Kentucky:

"I was ridin' along the Mississippi in my wagon, when I came acrost a feller floating down stream . . . in the starn of his boat. . . . Mister, says he, I can whip my weight in wild cats, and ride straight thro' a crab apple orchard on a flash of lightning . . . . Says I, ain't I the yellow flower of the forest? And I'm all brimstone but the head, and that's aquafortis! . . . My name is Nimrod Wildfire—half horse, half alligator, and a touch of the airthquake —that's got the prettiest sister, fastest horse, and ugliest dog in the district, and can out run, out jump, throw down, drag out and whip any man in all Kentuck!"

Such an exchange, in the lore of the day, conventionally preceded a fight.

Soon after his election, several newspaper yarns showed Congressman Crockett behaving exactly like a jest-book frontiersman. In one about a stump speech, after saying he was a candidate, Davy went on:

"Friends, fellow-citizens, brothers and sisters: Carroll is a statesman, Jackson is a hero, and Crockett is a *horse*!!

"Friends, fellow-citizens, brothers and sisters: They accuse me of adultery, it's a lie—I never ran away with any man's wife, that was not willing, in my life. They accuse me of gambling, it's a lie —for I always plank down the cash.

"Friends, fellow-citizens, brothers and sisters: They accuse me of being a drunkard, it's a d—d eternal lie—for whiskey can't make me drunk."

This story, of course, might easily have been cooked up by any wit who knew only two things—that Crockett was a frontiersman, and that the frontiersman had a name for boasting and drinking. Another tale, supposedly in Davy's own words, told how, when he stopped at a Raleigh tavern on his trip to Washington, he found a crowd of guests blocking his way to the hearth:

". . . . I was *rooting* my way 'long to the fire, not in a good humor, when some fellow staggered up towards me, and cried out, 'Hurrah for Adams.' Said I, 'Stranger, you had better hurrah for hell, damn you, and praise your own country.'

"Said he, 'And who are you?'

"I'm the same David Crockett, fresh from the backwoods, half horse, half alligator, a little touched with the snapping turtle— can wade the Mississippi, leap the Ohio, ride upon a streak of lightning, and slip without a scratch down a honey locust—can whip my weight in wildcats . . . and whip any man opposed to Jackson.'

"While I was telling what I could do, the fellow's eyes kept getting larger and larger. . . . I never saw fellows look as they all did. They cleared the fire for me, and when I got warm, I looked about, but my Adams man was gone."

The very wording shows that this is after the same model as the almanac story; and another version of the yarn is still closer to the original.

These stretchers suggest that, in the papers, caricatures showed a person very different from the real Crockett. At first, probably, these yarns were tossed off without any motive. But in time, journalists found that anecdotes like these could be used for political purposes. That was the start of the multiplication of Crocketts.

The Westerner went to Washington in 1827, when followers of Andrew Jackson were still growling because Congress had made Adams President instead of Jackson in 1824. The Jacksonites were going strong in a drive which was to carry Old Hickory into the White House in the next election.

When the canebrake politician arrived at the Capitol, as Constance Rourke, his best biographer, says, "He attracted attention at once. He . . . became quickly known in Washington as the 'coonskin Congressman.' No one at all like him had appeared in office; he aroused great curiosity. His tall figure was striking. His casual speech was often repeated because of its pithy center. Tall talk was easily attributed to him. . . . Such stories [as the one about Davy in the tavern] were printed in many eastern newspapers of the time, and they all stressed Crockett's loyalty to Jackson."

Naturally enough, in their stories—if facts were not to be taken too seriously—the anti-Jackson papers would picture Crockett as an unworthy person and the pro-Jackson papers would show him as a fine fellow. Pieces in all the papers agreed he was uneducated, that he talked tall, that he was funny. But in unfriendly papers, because he had these traits, the man was pictured as a rambunctious clown of the cane-brakes—and it was implied that Old Hickory, in the White House, would be just as inept. Papers favoring Old Andy, by contrast, showed the Congressman as a backwoodsman who used boastful talk and humor to put enemies in their places.

Examples are two tales of how Davy, new in Washington, dined at the White House. An anti-Crockett reporter printed this story (allegedly by the Congressman) of the affair:

"I stepped into the President's house—thinks I, who's afraid? . . . Says I, 'Mr. Adams, I'm Mr. Crockett, from Tennessee.' 'So,' says he . . . and he shook me by the hand . . . I went to dinner, and walked around the long table, looking for something that I liked. At last I took my seat, just beside a fat goose, and I helped myself to as much of it as I wanted. But I hadn't took three bites, when I looked way up the table at a man they called *Tash* (attaché). He was talking French to a woman on t'other side of the table. He dodged his head and she dodged hers and then they got to drinking wine across the table. If they didn't I wish I may be shot. But when I looked back again, my plate was gone, goose and all. So I just cast my eyes down to t'other end of the table, and sure enough I seed a white man walking off with my plate. I says, 'Hello, mister, bring back my plate.' He fetched it back in a hurry . . . ; and . . . how do you think it was? Licked as clean as my hand. If it wasn't I wish I may be shot. Says he, 'What will you have, sir?' And says I, 'You may well say that, after stealing my goose.' And he began to laugh. . . . Then says I, 'Mister, laugh if you please; but I don't half like such tricks upon travellers. If I do I wish I may be shot.' I then filled my plate with bacons and greens; and whenever I looked up or down the table, I held to my plate. . . . When we were all done eating . . . I saw a man coming 'long carrying a great glass thing . . . stuck full of little glass cups. . . . Thinks I, let's taste them first. They were mighty sweet and good—so I took six of 'em. If I didn't I wish I may be shot."

Crockett was so riled by this caricature of him that he wrote two friends who had been at the dinner, asking their testimony that it was "a slander" by "enemies, who would take much pleasure in magnifying the plain rusticity of my manners into the most unparalleled grossness and indelicacy." Congressmen Clark of Kentucky and Verplanck of New York prepared for the press statements that, as one of them said, his behavior at the dinner was "perfectly becoming and proper."

The pro-Jackson papers had a different story of the same function. Probably just as untrue as the "slander," it purported to be the Colonel's story of his talk after dinner, in the White House drawing-room, with the President's son. When this young aristocrat had tried to lead him on with questions about backwoods pastimes, "I know'd he wanted to have some fun at my expense," said uneducated but canny Crockett. So he told about the four classes of people on the frontier. Yarning about the first class, "the quality," he got in a little dig at the President's son, who had been much criticized by the anti-administration press for bringing a billiard table into the President's mansion. This stratum of society, he said, "have a table with some green truck on it, and it's got pockets, and they knock a ball about on it to get it into the pockets." Then, telling about the other classes, he stretched the truth until, he said, "the whole house was convulsed with laughter"—presumably at the expense of the dude who had tried to trick the pawky backwoodsman. The tale had touches as indelicate as the one which so angered Crockett, but there is no evidence that he refuted it.

By contrast with Crockett the First, presumably created by God, Crockett the Second and Crockett the Third were created, then, by anti-Jackson papers and pro-Jackson papers, respectively. Crockett the Second was a Westernized version of a fool character like the one Benjamin Franklin had used to advocate, in such a futile fashion, the hateful policies of the British; Crockett the Third was a Westernized version of Poor Richard, uneducated but rich in common sense gained by experience. These propagandistic versions of the frontiersman were just getting established when the real Davy did something which caused the two sets of political journalists to bring out clean canvases and start new pictures of him.

He changed sides—joined the anti-Jackson forces. And that, eventually, meant the creation of a Crockett the Fourth and a Crockett the Fifth.

The pro-Jackson papers, in this second period (from January, 1829, when the Colonel switched allegiance, until his death in 1836), turned the picture of Crockett the Third—of a bumptious but canny frontiersman—to the wall. In its place they hung a picture of Crockett the Fourth. The new portrait drew some details from the earlier anti-Jackson portraits: it showed "the coon killer, the Jim Crow of Congressmen, the buffoon of the House of Representatives . . . the authorized Whig jester." These were the titles bestowed on Crockett by the New York *Times*, in one vituperative editorial. The Washington *Globe* emphasized the man's alleged grossness by ironically calling him "Dainty Davy."

But the Jacksonians added new touches which made the backwoodsman not only stupid and clownish but also vicious. James K. Polk, for example, prepared for Tennessee newspapers five articles, signed "Several Voters" and so written that they seemed to come from Davy's constituents. They claimed that Crockett had often missed House meetings, that he had done "literally nothing" for the poor in his district. And they stressed a detail constantly emphasized in the new portrait in various papers—that the Congressman had been bought out and used as a tool. Similarly, the Washington *Globe*, the official Jackson organ, made much of the enlistment by the opposition of "mercenaries," with Crockett as the "first recruit." Frequent mention of "David Crockett & Co." suggested organization on a commercial basis. Jackson, now President, stormed at his enemies and "crockett their tool," and often spoke of "Crockett & Co."

The anti-Jacksonites in turn set up their picture of Crockett the Fifth, akin to Crockett the Third, but greatly added to the earlier suggestion of their subject's shrewdness. He now became a homespun oracle, outraged by the horrible carry-ings-on of the party in power and capable of attacking them with telling digs because he was so abundantly blessed with unerring horse sense. Aphorisms headed "Crockett's Latest" —shrewd witticisms hurled at the Jackson crowd—came out in the newspapers.

With the campaign to show that Davy was wise went a drive to show that, contrary to reports (some of which the anti-Jacksonites themselves had been perpetrating) that he was an uncouth Westerner, he was a normal gentleman. A "respectable gentleman of Tennessee" wrote to the Jackson-ville *Banner* as follows:

"I apprehend very many have entertained erroneous opinions of the character of Col. Crockett. He is indeed a specimen of the frontier character, but a very favorable specimen. He is an honest, independent, intelligent man, with strong and highly marked traits of originality, which renders him very interesting and agree-able. . . ."

The Philadelphia *Courier*, in its description of the Colonel when he stopped in Philadelphia on his Eastern tour, wanted readers to know that he was dressed like other men—"in dark clothes," Byronic collar and white hat. The Columbia *Spy* and an Elizabethtown, Kentucky, newspaper, in their reports of visits by "the Hon. David Crockett" to Columbia and Elizabethtown, also pointed out that he was not a wild man but a person, to quote one of the papers, "with a com-manding, lofty aspect, and a dignified, manly countenance."

Late in 1833, the Congressman from Tennessee sent to the newspapers an announcement that he was very angry about the way he had been misrepresented, particularly in a book which retold many newspaper stories about him. He was therefore going to write an autobiography, to "strive to represent myself, as I really am, *a plain, blunt, Western man,* relying on honesty and the woods, and not on learning and the law, for a living." In February, 1834, he had his preface ready, and it too was sent to the papers. It repeated the charge that people had been so misled by portrayals of him that they had "expressed the most profound astonishment at finding me in human shape, and with the *countenance, appearance,* and *common feelings* of a human being. It is to correct all these false notions . . . that I have written." When the book, titled *A Narrative of the Life of David Crockett,* appeared, the Boston *Transcript* said of it that it was the "Simon Pure edition," published to correct lies about Crockett cooked up by "the roguish wags of the Capitol."

The newspaper notice makes it clear that the *Narrative* was part of the campaign of the anti-Jackson forces to show Davy as a normal being, worthy of much respect. This "plain, homespun account," as its author called it, was, in other words, a full length portrait of the Crockett the Fifth sketched in friendly newspapers. The same politically useful character appeared also in *An Account of Col. Crockett's Tour to the North and Down East* (1835). Here is a blunt, honest man, pathetically misrepresented—a man so chockful of mother wit and humor, however, that he can laughably state the obvious case against his rivals.

Many times the author of the *Narrative* makes a supposedly autobiographical account a springboard for political arguments. In Chapter VI, for example, the Colonel interrupts his story of how, when he was fighting under Jackson against the Indians before Jackson became nationally famous, he rebelled against orders, to draw forced parallels between the past situation and the contemporary rebellion against Jackson's unreasonable bank policy. Numerous similar passages occur. The very end of the book stresses Crockett's political independence: "Look at my arms, you will find no party hand-cuff on them! Look at my neck, you will not find there any collar, with the engraving

MY DOG
ANDREW JACKSON."

The *Tour* describes a trip Davy took during the spring of
1834 through cities of the Northeast, speaking at each stop,
under the auspices of the anti-Jacksonites, to crowds who
shared his political notions. The book contains many speeches
in which certain notes are struck again and again: "I am a
plain, uneducated backwoodsman, and find some embarrass-
ment in making an appropriate speech to such an intelligent
audience as that in— . . . I am from the far West, and have
made but little pretensions of understanding the government,
but one thing I know. . . ." This beginning, synthesized from
two speeches, is a typical one.

Crockett's partisans urged readers to believe that the
Crockett the Fifth of these two books was the real article—
Crockett the First. "Veracity," said one newspaper firmly, "is
stamped on every page." But the matter is open to doubt.
The public figure of the man is so well fitted to political
appeals that one suspects the character is at least partly
assumed. In fact, anyone looking for a beginner of the tradition of the "just folks" politician in America will do well to
study the case of the coonskin Congressman.

And all the credit, in the end, will not go to Davy, since
both books clearly were touched up by collaborators (both
of whom have been identified) eager to give the writings
partisan usefulness. A result is that almost anywhere you look
for Crockett the First you are baffled. In the Congressional
records you will find speeches which obviously were doctored
up before they were printed. Authentic letters in the Colonel's
own hand show, first, that they support the guess that his
other writings have been thoroughly edited, and second, that
they do not offer a sure basis for guessing at his character.

Hence, as has been suggested, historians have trouble dealing with the details about this man's life; they study the
documents and announce findings which vary a great deal.

"Restless, assertive, unsocial . . . obsessed with the faith that better land lay farther west, cultivating a bumptious wit . . ." says one, "he was only an improvident child who fled instinctively from civilization." He was "the incipient poor white," says another, with "the elements of decay in him." Another finds that he was a valiant hunter, an efficient farmer, a far-seeing legislator, and a heroic warrior. Still another cannot explain him except as a split personality. The one thing that is sure is that a clean-cut image of him was fogged up by the factional portraits all labeled with his name.

The creators of the imaginary portraits so far considered clearly appealed to common sense readers, expecting them to censure Davy when he was shown as a clown, to back him when he was pictured as a log cabin prophet. But none of these caricatures, any more than a picture of the authentic Crockett, was to survive. An Englishman, Captain R. G. A. Levinge, traveling through Kentucky about a decade after the Tennessean's heroic death at the Alamo, learned there about the Crockett who was to be immortal.

> Everything here [he said] is Davy Crockett. . . . His voice was so loud that it could not be described—it was obliged to be drawn as a picture. He took hailstones for "Life Pills" when he was unwell—he . . . fanned himself with a hurricane. . . . He had a farm, which was so rocky, that, when they planted corn, they were obliged to shoot the grains into the crevices with muskets. . . . He could . . . drink the Mississippi dry—shoot six cords of bear in one day. . . .

This was Crockett the Sixth, the mythical demigod whose fantastic life history was unfolded in the almanacs.

This Crockett had little or no political value, and the happenings in his comic career leaped from the green earth into a backwoods fairyland. Is it possible to think of this rider of thunderbolts as a natural product of a section worshipful of gumption? I believe that this hero of frontier fantasy is such a product, in two ways:

First, these yarns originated by fireside tale-tellers, or written down to be enjoyed by fireside readers, are escape literature of a kind likely to be peculiarly charming to farmers and woodsmen. Their demigod hero, in one aspect, is less notable for his tremendous abilities than he is for his limitations. Another demigod might have used his superhuman powers to create a great symphony, a great work of art, or a great epic; he might have set up a perfect system of government under which all men were free and happy; he might have conquered new realms of knowledge—but not Davy. The nonsense about Davy showed him conquering with ridiculous ease the stubborn physical world which frontier folk had to battle with the aid of common sense. Sickness, rocky farm land, cold, Indians and varmints—the pests of the common sense world—were the effortless conquests of this campfire creation. Even the fantasies of frontier folk, in other words, were given practical chores to perform.

In the second place, this picture of Crockett the Sixth was a sort of horse sense "rationalization." The one interesting aspect of characterization which persisted in all the newspaper Crocketts—the one element of consistency—was the mythical element. The boasts of Davy the Second and Third, "whiskey can't make me drunk; I can wade the Mississippi, leap the Ohio, ride upon a streak of lightning," and so forth, were talk fitting for a superhuman being. Crockett the Fourth displayed his clownishness partly by making similar boasts. Even the *Narrative*, official autobiography of Crockett the Fifth, used expressions which were appropriate to a fantastic creature rather than a common man—a man (to quote what were supposedly his own words) whose "love was so hot it nigh to burst my bilers;" who—if his sweetheart accepted him, "would . . . fight a whole regiment of wild cats;" who got "so mad that I was burning inside like a tarkiln, and I wondered that the smoke hadn't been pouring out of me at all points." Other phrases in the book pictured strange figures the coon-hunter encountered—figures more at home in fan-

tasy than in actuality. The Westerner told, for instance, how
he met a woman "as ugly as a stone fence . . . so homely
that it almost gave me a pain in the eyes to look at her;" how
he spied "a little woman streaking along through the woods
like all wrath" or a bear so big that "he looked like a large
black bull."

What myth-makers did, then, was make Davy's boasts come
true—put him in an imaginary world consistent with the
kind of beasts and people his tall talk described. Temporary
things such as changing political alignments vanished, but
the one abiding element—strangeness—remained. As early
as 1832, the legend-makers had begun to develop this abiding version of their hero: the apotheosis was suggested in a
news story, widely reprinted, which read:

APPOINTMENT BY THE PRESIDENT. David Crockett, of Tennessee,
to stand on the Allegheny Mountains and catch the Comet, on its
approach to the earth, and wring off its tail, to keep it from
burning up the world!

The *Narrative* was written not only as a protest against political misrepresentation but also as an antidote to the legendary
picture already being sketched. Ironically, it stimulated
legends: the women, for example, whom Davy had sketched
in a few phrases in the book, were given complete life histories in the almanac tales. There, they were fit companions
of Demigod David: they wore hornets' nests garnished with
eagle feathers for Sunday bonnets; they could wade the Mississippi without wetting their shifts; they could outscream a
catamount or jump over their own shadows.

The folk mind, in short, refusing to be misled by the political propaganda associated with Crockett the First, the Second, the Third, the Fourth and the Fifth, in time made known
the People's Choice for immortality—the only consistent character it could find in a mess of contradictory portraits,
Crockett the Sixth. And today, if you get far enough away

from paved roads and roadside pop stands in Tennessee and
Kentucky and sit by the fire with backwoods yarnspinners,
you will learn that this Crockett, somewhere or other, is still
carrying out his boasts in superhuman ways. (1940)

EDMUND WILSON

One of the most versatile of American men of letters, Edmund Wilson distinguished himself in fiction, criticism, and reporting. Born in Red Bank, New Jersey, in 1895, he graduated from Princeton University where he was a friend of F. Scott Fitzgerald. His 1955 article on George Washington Harris in the *New Yorker* brought quick responses from the defenders of Sut Lovingood.

"Poisoned!"

"We have no literature—we don't need any yet," said Senator Louis T. Wigfall of Texas to Mr. W. H. Russell of the London *Times*, at the beginning of the Civil War. "We have no press—we are glad of it." Among the few not particularly distinguished exceptions to the literary impoverishment of the South was a Tennessean journalist named George Washington Harris, who invented a comic character called Sut Lovingood and exploited him for fifteen years as a narrator of fantastic stories and as a mouthpiece for political satire. These sketches, of which the first appeared in 1854, were printed not only in the local press but also in a New York sporting paper called the *Spirit of the Times*, and they were collected in 1867 in a volume called "Sut Lovingood: Yarns Spun by a Nat'rl Born Durn'd Fool." Mark Twain reviewed this book in a San Francisco paper and perhaps owed something to it, but Harris, after his death in 1869, seems to have been soon forgotten, and it was only in the thirties of the present century that—in the course of the current rediscovery and revaluing of American literature—such writers as Bernard DeVoto, Constance Rourke, and F. O. Matthiessen began to take an interest in him. A selection from "Sut Lovingood," Harris's sole volume, has now been brought out (Grove) by Mr. Brom Weber, who has drastically edited the text and contributed an introduction.

This reprint is not a success. In attempting to clean up Sut Lovingood and make him attractive to the ordinary reader—an ambition probably hopeless—Mr. Weber has produced something that is all but valueless to the serious student of literature. He is correct in pointing out that the author, in trying to render Sut's illiterate speech, has inconsistently mixed written misspelling, intended to look funny on the printed page—though Sut has never learned to write —with a phonetic transcription of the way he talks, but the writing does have a coarse texture as well as a rank flavor, and to turn it, as the editor does, into something that is closer to conventional English, and to dilute it with paragraphs and strings of dots, is to deprive it of a good deal of this. By the time Mr. Weber gets done with him, Sut Lovingood hardly even sounds like a Southerner; it is fatal to the poor-white dialect to turn "naik" and "hit" into "neck" and "it." What is worst, from the scholarly point of view, is to comb out "words [that] are obsolete and others [that] are probably meaningless to all but a handful of contemporary readers." If the book was to be reprinted, the text should have been given intact, and the unfamiliar words as well as the topical allusions explained. Mr. Weber makes no effort to do this, nor—though Harris, at the time of his death, was preparing a second vol-

ume—does he add any new material except for three little
lampoons of Lincoln. Sut himself is depicted on the jacket as
a stalwart and bearded mountaineer, a portrayal that has
nothing in common with the dreadful, half-bestial "cracker"
of the original illustrations.

One is also rather surprised at the editor's idea of deleting
"three lines of an extremely offensive nature." One of the
most striking things about "Sut Lovingood" is that it is all as
offensive as possible. It takes a pretty strong stomach to get
through it in any version. I should say that, as far as my
experience goes, it is by far the most repellent book of any
real literary merit in American literature. The sort of crude
and brutal humor it contains was an American institution all
through the nineteenth century. The tradition of the crip-
pling practical joke was carried on almost to the end of the
century with "Peck's Bad Boy," and that of the nasty school-
boy by "The Tribune Primer" of Eugene Field, a professional
sentimentalist. But the deadpan homicides and corpses of the
early Mark Twain are given a certain dignity by the stoicism
of the pioneer, and the nihilistic butcheries of Ambrose
Bierce a certain tragic force by his background of the Civil
War. The coarse or macabre joke, on the part of the early
Western writers, had often a purgative function in making as
ridiculous as possible grim hardships and calamitous adventures. But Sut Lovingood is something special. He is not a
pioneer contending against the wilderness; he is a peasant
squatting in his own filth. He is not making a joke of his
hardships; he is avenging his inferiority by tormenting other
people. His impulse is avowedly sadistic. The keynote is
struck in the following passage (I give it in the original Tennessean):

"I hates ole Onsightly Peter [so called because he was
selling encyclopedias], jis' caze he didn't seem tu like tu hear
me narrate las' night; that's human nater the yeath over, an'
yer's more universal onregenerit human nater: ef ever yu dus
enything tu enybody wifout cause, yu hates em alleers arter-

wards, an' sorter wants tu hurt em agin. An' yere's anuther
human nater: ef enything happens sum feller, I don't keer
ef he's yure bes' frien, an' I don't keer how sorry yu is fur
him, thar's a streak ove satisfackshun 'bout like a sowin thread
a-runnin all thru yer sorrer. Yu may be shamed ove hit, but
durn me ef hit ain't thar. Hit will show like the white cottin
chain in mean cassinett; brushin hit onder only hides hit. An'
yere'sa littil more; no odds how good yu is tu yung things,
ur how kine yu is in treatin em, when you sees a littil long
laiged lamb a-shakin hits tail, an' a dancin staggerinly onder
hits mam a-huntin fur the tit, ontu hits knees, yer fingers will
itch tu seize that ar tail, an' fling the littil ankshus son ove a
mutton over the fence amung the blackberry briars, not tu
hurt hit, but jis' tu disapint hit. Ur say, a littil calf, a-buttin
fus' under the cow's fore-laigs, an' then the hine, wif the pint
ove hits tung stuck out, makin suckin moshuns, not yet old
enuf tu know the bag aind ove hits mam frum the hookin
aind, don't yu want tu kick hit on the snout, hard enough tu
send hit backwards, say fifteen foot, jis' tu show hit that but-
tin won't allers fetch milk? Ur a baby even rubbin hits heels
apas' each uther, a-rootin an' a-snifflin arter the breas', an'
the mam duin her bes' tu git hit out, over the hem ove her
clothes, don't yu feel hungry tu gin hit jis' one 'cussion cap
slap, rite ontu the place what sum day'll fit a saddil, ur a
sowin cheer, tu show hit what's atwixt hit an' the grave; that
hit stans a pow'ful chance not tu be fed every time hits
hungry, ur in a hurry?"

In view of all this, the comments of academic critics on the
humor of Sut Lovingood are among the curiosities of recent
American scholarship. We find Mr. J. Franklin Meine, in
"Tall Tales of the Southwest," speaking of this hero's "keen
delight for Hallowee'n [sic] *fun* [italics the author's]—there
is no ulterior motive (except occasionally Sut's desire to 'get
even'), no rascality, no gambling, no sharping. . . . Sut is
simply the genuine naïve roughneck mountaineer, riotously
bent on raising hell," and again, "For vivid imagination,

comic plot, Rabelaisian touch and sheer *fun*, the 'Sut Lovingood Yarns' surpass anything else in American humor."
"Ultimately," asserts Mr. Weber, "the mythic universalities
such as heroism, fertility, masculinity, and femininity emerge
over a bedrock of elemental human values which Sut has
carved out in the course of his adventures, values such as
love, joy, truth, justice, etc. These are only some of the positive concepts which Sut has admired and championed, and it
is no small feat that they emerge from behind a protagonist
who has ironically been deprecated by his creator. This is
humor on a grand scale."

Now, Sut Lovingood can be called "Rabelaisian" only in
the sense that he is often indecent by nineteenth-century
standards and that he runs to extravagant language and
monstrously distorted descriptions. Unlike Rabelais, he is
always malevolent and always extremely sordid. Here is an
example of his caricature at its best:

"I seed a well appearin man onst, ax one ove em [the
proprietors of taverns, evidently carpetbaggers] what lived
ahine a las' year's crap ove red hot brass wire whiskers run tu
seed, an' shingled wif har like ontu mildew'd flax, wet wif saf-
fron warter, an' laid smoof wif a hot flat-iron, ef he cud spaɪ
him a scrimpshun ove soap? The 'perpryiter' anser'd in soun's
es sof an' sweet es a poplar dulcimore, tchuned by a good
nater'd she angel in butterfly wings an' cobweb shiff, that he
never wer jis' so sorry in all his born'd days tu say no, but
the fac' wer the soljers hed stole hit;' 'a towil then,' 'the soljers
hed stole hit;' 'a tumbler,' 'the soljers hed stole hit;' 'a lookin-
glass,' 'the soljers hed stole hit;' 'a pitcher ove warter,' 'the
soljers hed stole hit;' 'then please give me a cleaner room.'
Quick es light com the same dam lie, 'the soljers hed stole
hit too.' They buys scalded butter, caze hit crumbles an' yu
can't tote much et a load on yer knife; they keeps hit four
months so yu won't want to go arter a second load. They
stops up the figgers an' flowers in the woffil irons fur hit takes
butter tu fill the holes in the woffils. They makes soup outen

dirty towils, an' jimson burrs; coffee outen niggers' ole wool socks, roasted; tea frum dorg fennil, and toas' frum ole brogan insoles. They keeps bugs in yer bed tu make yu rise in time fur them tu get the sheet fur a tablecloth. They gins yu a inch ove candil tu go tu bed by, an' a littil nigger tu fetch back the stump tu make gravy in the mornin, fur the hunk ove bull naik yu will swaller fur brekfus, an' they puts the top sheaf ontu thar orful merlignerty when they menshuns the size ove yer bill, an' lasly, while yu're gwine thru yer close wif a sarch warrun arter fodder enuf tu pay hit, they refreshes yer memory ove other places, an' other times, by tellin yu ove the orful high price ove turkys, aigs, an' milk. When the devil takes a likin to a feller, an' wants tu make a sure thing ove gittin him he jis' puts hit intu his hed to open a cat-fish tavern, with a gran' rat attachmint, gong 'cumpanimint, bull's neck variashun, cockroach corus an' bed-bug refrain, an' dam ef he don't git him es sure es he rattils the fust gong. An' durn thar onary souls, they looks like they expected yu tu b'leve that they am pius, decent, an' fit tu be 'sociated wif, by lookin down on yu like yu belonged tu the onregenerit, an' keepin' a cussed ole spindel-shank, rattlin crazy, peaner, wif mud daubers nests onder the soundin board, a-bummin out 'Days ove Absins' ur 'the Devil's Dream,' bein druv thar too, by thar long-waisted, greasey har'd darter, an' listen'd to by jis' sich durn'd fools es I is."

As for the "fun" of Sut Lovingood, it is true that Harris explained his aim as merely to revive for the reader, "sich a laugh as is remembered wif his keerless boyhood," and that he liked to express his nostalgia for the dances and quiltings of his youth, but even in a pre-Lovingood sketch of one of these, the fun seems mainly to consist of everybody getting beaten to a pulp, and in the Lovingood stories themselves, the fun entirely consists of Sut's spoiling everybody else's fun. He loves to break up such affairs. One of his milder devices is setting bees and hornets on people. In this way, he ruins the wedding of a girl who has refused his advances and dismissed him with an unpleasant practical joke, and puts to rout a Negro revivalist rally—for he runs true to poor-white tradition in despising and persecuting the Negroes. He rejoices when his father, naked, is set upon by "a ball ho'nets nes' ni ontu es big es a hoss's hed" and driven to jump into water. Sut gloats over "dad's bald hed fur all the yeath like a peeled inyin, a bobbin up an' down an' aroun, an' the ho'nets sailin roun tuckey buzzard fashun, an' every onst in a while one, an' sum times ten, wud take a dip at dad's bald hed." This leaves the old man "a pow'ful curious, vishus, skeery lookin cuss. . . . His head am as big es a wash pot, an' he hasent the fust durned sign ove an eye—jist two black slits." Sut, who supposed himself to be his mother's only legitimate child, has nothing but contempt for his father as an even greater fool than himself, who has bequeathed to him only misery, ignorance, and degradation. Most of all, however, his hatred is directed against anybody who shows any signs of gentility, idealism, or education. On such people, under the influence of bad whiskey, to which he refers as "kill-devil" or "bald face," he revenges himself by methods that range from humiliation to mayhem. His habit of denouncing his victims as hypocrites, adulterers, or pedants is evidently what has convinced Mr. Weber that Sut Lovingood cherishes "values such as love, joy, truth, justice, etc." But he is equally vicious with anyone who happens for any other reason to irritate him. In the case of an old lady who loves to make quilts, he rides into her quilting party with a horse he has driven frantic, ripping up all the quilts and trampling the hostess to death. This is his only human killing, but animals he has more at his mercy, and he loves to kill dogs, cats, and frogs and to watch their agonized reactions. It is not in the least true, as another of Sut's encomiasts says, that pain does not exist in Sut Lovingood's world. On the contrary, the sufferings of his victims are described with considerable realism, and the furtively snickering Sut enjoys every moment of them. It is good to be reminded by Mr.

Meine that his hero is never shown as guilty of gambling or sharping.

Nor is it possible to imagine that Harris is aiming at a Swiftian satire. It is plain that he identifies himself with Sut, and his contemporaries referred to him as Sut, just as Anatole France in his day was referred to as M. Bergeret. "Sometimes, George, I wishes," says Sut, addressing his creator, "I could read and write just a little." George Harris himself had had—apparently at intervals—only eighteen months of schooling, and it is obvious that he is able to express himself a good deal better as Sut than he can in his own character. He had been steamboat captain, farmer, metalworker, glassworker, surveyor, sawmill manager, postmaster, and railroad man—none of them for very long and none with any great success. It is not known how Harris got along during the years of the Civil War. He seems to have dragged his family from pillar to post in Tennessee, Alabama, and Georgia. His wife died in 1867, leaving him with three small children. He is evidently speaking of himself, in his preface to "Sut Lovingood," when he makes Sut Lovingood say that he will "feel he has got his pay in full" if he can rouse to a laugh "jis' one, eny poor misfortinit devil hu's heart is onder a mill-stone, hu's raggid children are hungry, an' no bread in the dresser, hu is down in the mud, an' the lucky ones a-trippin him every time he struggils tu his all fours, hu has fed the famishin an' is now hungry hisself, hu misfortins foller fas' an' foller faster, hu is so foot-sore an' weak that he wishes he wer at the ferry." Harris had a little education and some training as a jeweller's apprentice, but his origins seem to have been humble—we do not know what his father did nor what became of his parents—and he shared with the "poor white trash" something of their consciousness of limitation and of their rancor against those better off than they.

In Unionist eastern Tennessee, Harris never wavered from his allegiance to the Democratic Party, which represented the artisans and farmers, as against the industrializing

Whigs. But he failed in his attempt at farming as well as at his industrial projects, and it is plain that a sense of frustration—"flustratin'" is one of Sut's favorite words—is at the root of the ferocious fantasies in which he indulges himself in the character of Sut Lovingood. Yet he also uses Sut as a spokesman for his own sometimes shrewd observations, and this somewhat throws the character out as a credible and coherent creation, since he is made to see the world from a level above his intellectual range. The effect of this is more disconcerting than if Sut were simply a comic monster, for one feels that his monstrous doings are a part of the author's mentality, like the comments on local life. It is embarrassing to find Caliban, at moments, thinking like a human being.

Yet the book has a certain power, the language is often imaginative, and Sut Lovingood is a type that it is perhaps well to have recorded. Mr. Weber says truly that Harris has something in common with Caldwell and Faulkner. He is thinking of the tradition of "folk humor," but what is more fundamental is that these writers are all trying to portray various species of the Southern poor white. Sut Lovingood is unmistakably an ancestor of Faulkner's Snopeses, that frightening low-class family (some of them stuck at Sut's level, others on their way up), who, whether in success or crime or both, are all the more formidable to deal with because they have their own kind of pride—who are prepared, as Mr. Weber points out in connection with their predecessor, to "take on the whole world." All that was worst in the worst of the South found expression in Harris's book, and the book is needed, perhaps, to balance the idylls of the old regime, the chivalrous idealism of such a writer as Sidney Lanier, in whose romantic novel "Tiger Lilies," a work of the same period, you have a kind of Sut Lovingood villain, an envious and mutinous boor, who does not want to fight for the Confederacy and who burns down the fine mansion of his masters. The dreamy nobility of a man like Lanier and the murderous clowning of Harris are products of the same society.

George Harris, however, was an advocate of secession, and from the moment Lincoln was nominated turned Sut Lovingood loose on the Unionists. Here is a passage from one of his libels on Lincoln—to call them satires would be to give them too much dignity—of which still another infatuated editor, Mr. Edd Winfield Parks, has said that "though good-humored, they reveal his [Harris's] feelings," and of which Mr. Weber, who includes them in his volume, has said that Lincoln "might not have enjoyed [them] as much as a secessionist would" but that "he would have laughed at the exaggeration of ugliness so customary in frontier humor." Sut Lovingood is supposed to be accompanying Lincoln on the latter's incognito journey through Baltimore on his way to his inauguration, and Lincoln is supposed to be terrified at the threats of the Maryland secessionists:

"I kotch a ole bull frog once an druv a nail thru his lips inter a post, tied two rocks ta his hine toes an stuck a durnin needil inter his tail tu let out the misture, an lef him there tu dry. I seed him two weeks afterwurds, and when I seed ole Abe I thot hit were an orful retribution cum outa me; an that hit were the same frog, only strutched a little longer, an had tuck tu warin ove close ta keep me from knowin him, an ketchin him an nailin him up agin; an natural born durn'd fool es I is, I swar I seed the same watry skery look in the eyes, an the same sorter knots on the backbone. I'm feared, George, sumthin's tu cum ove my nailin up that ar frog. I swar I am ever since I seed old Abe, same shape same color same feel (cold as ice) an I'm d— ef hit ain't the same smell."

Sut's tirades after the war are vituperative on a level that makes the above seem almost the work of an artist. A new rancor, a new crushing handicap have been added to his previous ones. He can only spew abuse at the Yankees. The election of Grant seems a death-blow. One of his last stories, "Well!, Dad's Dead," was inspired, it seems, by this event. One wishes that Mr. Weber had included it. The principal authority on Harris, Professor Donald Day, says that Sut's moronic father has here come to represent the Old South. He passes without lament: "Nara durn'd one ove 'em [the neighbors] come a nigh the old cuss, to fool 'em into believin' that he wanted him to stay a minit longer than he were obleeged to. . . . That night [after they had buried him], when we were hunker'd round the hearth, sayin' nothin' an' waitin for the taters to roast, mam, she spoke up—'oughtent we to a scratch'd in a little dirt, say?' 'No need, mam,' sed Sal, 'hits loose yearth, an' will soon cave in enuff.'" Sut has always claimed that his father sired him as "a nat'ral born durn'd fool," and his habitual falling back on this as an excuse for both his loutish inadequacies and his sly, calculated crimes strikes the deepest note in these farces. He has come to despise the Old South itself, along with so many other things.

The creator of Sut himself did not long survive Sut's father. Returning from a trip to Lynchburg, where he had gone on railroad business and to try to arrange for the publication of his second Sut Lovingood book, he became very ill on the train—so helpless that the conductor at first thought him drunk. He was carried off at Knoxville, and died there. His manuscript disappeared. The cause of his death is unknown, but just before he died, he whispered the word "Poisoned!" (1955)

RANDALL STEWART

Randall Stewart was born in Fayetteville, Tennessee, in 1896. Following his graduation from Vanderbilt University, he received the A.M. degree from Harvard and the Ph.D. from Yale. After holding a number of teaching positions in various parts of the country, he returned to the faculty at Vanderbilt, where he also served as department chairman. Noted for his editorial work on Nathaniel Hawthorne and his book, *American Literature and the Christian Tradition*, in "Tidewater and Frontier" he replied to Edmund Wilson, defending Sut Lovingood and the belief in original sin. The article is actually a lecture given while he was Walker-Ames Professor at the University of Washington, Seattle.

Tidewater and Frontier

Southern literature from the beginning has been more diverse, more varied, than the literature of New England, or of the Middle West. There have been greater extremes in Southern literature, and the basic difference is that which separates two traditions, which one may call the Tidewater tradition and the Frontier tradition. There is no such division in New England literature, for the frontier in New England was never very pronounced or articulate; nor in the literature of the Middle West, because that region has been more homogeneously democratic. But in the South, the contrast has been marked, indeed. It would be difficult to find writers more different than William Byrd of Westover and George Washington Harris, the author of the *Sut Lovingood Yarns*; or, to take more recent examples, Ellen Glasgow of Richmond and Jesse Stuart of W-Hollow, in the Kentucky mountains. It is a remarkable fact about Southern literature that both traditions have had a great deal of vitality, and have flourished side by side.

In modern times, the Tidewater tradition is represented by (among others) the Virginians, Ellen Glasgow and James Branch Cabell; by John Crowe Ransom and Allen Tate of the Nashville School; by Mississippians like Stark Young and Eudora Welty. These writers stem spiritually and culturally from William Byrd's Tidewater: they are courtly, sophisticated, intellectual; they cultivate "wit" in the older sense, and a fine irony; they address an inner circle; they possess restraint, dignity, a sense of form; they are classicists.

The Frontier first found expression in the early Nineteenth Century. This was a full one hundred years after Byrd's *History of the Dividing Line*, but it is remarkable that the Frontier should have been represented in literature at all, let alone so early. The Frontiersman—whether in the mountains of East Tennessee or the canebrakes of Arkansas—was a pretty lively fellow, and he had his niche—and a secure one it is turning out to be—in such writings as Longstreet's *Georgia Scenes*, *The Autobiography of David Crockett*, Harris' *Sut Lovingood Yarns*, Hooper's *Adventures of Captain Simon Suggs*, Baldwin's *Flush Times in Alabama and Mississipi*, Thorpe's *Big Bear of Arkansas*. In modern times, the tradition is represented by such literary descendants as Erskine Caldwell and Jesse Stuart. Thomas Wolfe, who came from the same mountain region as George Washington Harris, belongs with the members of this Frontier school in some respects, though he lacked their sense of humor and their mastery of the vernacular.

The two traditions—Tidewater and Frontier—have maintained a good deal of separateness from each other down to our time, though Faulkner and Warren, as I shall suggest presently, have combined elements from both. You will find, as a general thing, little truck between writers of the two schools. I shouldn't expect Ransom to have a high opinion of Wolfe, and I shouldn't expect Jesse Stuart to think very well of James Branch Cabell. (I mean, of course, of their writings.) I doubt if Tate admires Caldwell, and I should be surprised if Caldwell reads Tate. Tidewater and Frontier are still Tidewater and Frontier.

William Byrd, of course, is the grand prototype in literature of the Tidewater, and he is best seen in his delightful *Progress to the Mines* (1732). The journey was undertaken to investigate the state of the mining industry in Virginia, and the account shows that Byrd was a most painstaking investigator, but the more lively parts of the narrative concern the social entertainment along the way. The *Progress to the Mines* was indeed a royal progress, for Byrd was most hospitably received by the neighboring gentry. The account of his visit with the Spotswoods is revealing:

Here I arrived about three o'clock, and found only Mrs. Spotswood at home, who received her old acquaintance with many a gracious smile. I was carried into a room elegantly set off with pier glasses, the largest of which came soon after to an odd misfortune. . . . A brace of tame deer ran familiarly about the house, and one of them came to stare at me as a stranger. But unluckily spying his own figure in the glass, he made a spring over the tea table that stood under it, and shattered the glass to pieces, and falling back upon the tea table, made a terrible fracas among the china. This exploit was so sudden, and accompanied with such a noise, that it surprised me, and perfectly frightened Mrs. Spotswood. But it was worth all the damage, to show the moderation and good humor with which she bore this disaster.

The moderation and good humor with which Mrs. Spotswood bore the disaster is clearly the point to underscore. She was, as Alexander Pope put it in that most elegant of all compliments to a gentlewoman, "mistress of herself though china fall."

Col. Spotswood, whom Byrd called the "Tubal Cain of Virginia," and who modestly substituted for "Virginia" in the appellation, "North America," was generous with his knowledge of the mining and smelting of iron ore; like many a Southerner after him, he was a great talker. After business, which was not scanted, came the social hour with the ladies, Mrs. Spotswood and her spinster sister, Miss Theky. The conversation with the ladies (Byrd recorded in this private narrative; the *Progress* was not published until after his death) was "like whip sillabub—very pretty, but nothing in it." Southern gallantry, it would seem, was not incompatible with a certain amount of masculine condescension toward the ladies.

At the home of the Chiswells, Byrd was shocked to discover that the twenty-four years which had passed since he last saw Mrs. Chiswell

had made great havoc with her pretty face, and plowed very deep furrows in her fair skin. It was impossible to know her again, so much the flower was faded. However, though she was grown an old woman, yet she was one of those absolute rarities, a very good old woman.

Of Col. Jones's plantations, situated nearby, Byrd recorded:

The poor negroes are a kind of Adamites, very scantily supplied with clothes and other necessaries; nevertheless (which is a little incomprehensible), they continue in perfect health, and none of them die, except it be of old age. However, they are even with their master, and make him but indifferent crops, so that he gets nothing by his injustice, but the scandal of it.

During his visit at the Flemings, the company were confined indoors all day by rainy weather, and Byrd, always the agreeable guest, "began to talk of plays," and, he goes on to say,

finding Mrs. Fleming's taste lay most towards comedy, I offered my service to read one to her, which she kindly accepted. She produced the second part of the Beggar's Opera [*Polly*, 1729], which had diverted the town [London Town] for forty nights successively, and gained four thousand pounds to the author. . . . After having acquainted my company with the history of the play, I read three acts of it, and left Mrs. Fleming and Mr. Randolph to finish it, who read as well as most actors do at a rehearsal. Thus we killed the time, and triumphed over the bad weather.

I resist with difficulty the temptation to quote further from this classic of the colonial South. The *Progress to the Mines* contains most of the essential elements which will recur, with modifications of course, as we attempt to trace the history of the Tidewater tradition: the good manners, the decorum, the sense of community, the sense of justice, the interest in polite literature, the gallantry, the wit. Byrd has never had justice done him as a writer. His taste and style were formed under Restoration and early Augustan auspices, and his writing as writing compares favorably with some of the best in contemporary London. Particularly noteworthy is the wit, which illustrates well enough Addison's definition in *Spectator* No. 62. Wit, Addison says, involves a turn of surprise, as in the statement, "My mistress' bosom is as white as snow, *and as cold.*" Byrd has similar turns of surprise: "Though she was grown an old woman, yet she was one of those absolute rarities, *a very good old woman*"; "So that he gets nothing by his injustice *but the scandal of it.*"

If we divide the Nineteenth Century South into two periods—the ante-bellum and the post-bellum—we find that the best book in each period to illustrate the Tidewater tradition is still, appropriately enough, a product of Virginia: I refer to John Pendleton Kennedy's *Swallow Barn* (1832), and Thomas Nelson Page's *In Ole Virginia* (1884).

Kennedy was a Baltimorean, but his mother's family were Virginians, and Kennedy, like his narrator Mark Littleton, was a welcome guest in the Old Dominion. In writing *Swallow Barn*, the author, therefore, enjoyed the double advantage of detachment and sympathy. His picture is faithfully drawn. Kennedy is less witty than Byrd; his closest literary affinity seems to have been with Irving. But (like Irving) he is a good observer, he has a sense of humor, and he can be, and often is, amusing.

"Swallow Barn," he says, "is an aristocratic old edifice which sits, like a brooding hen, on the Southern bank of the James River." "It gives," he says, "the idea of comfort." Frank Meriwether, "the master of this lordly domain," is "a very model of landed gentlemen." He is most hospitable: "a guest is one of his daily wants." He is a good citizen and attends to business, but, contrary to the expectation and desire of his friends, "he has never set up for Congress." "He is not much of a traveller. He has never been in New England, and very seldom beyond the confines of Virginia. He makes now and then a winter excursion to Richmond, which he considers the center of civilization" (matching Dr. Holmes' view of Boston as the hub of the solar system). He is a Jeffersonian Agrarian, thinking "lightly of the mercantile interest," and believing that those who live in large cities are "hollow-hearted and insincere." He opposed the re-election of John Quincy Adams to the Presidency in 1829, and voted for Andrew Jackson, without, I imagine, being an ardent Jacksonian. "He piques himself upon being a high churchman, but is not the most diligent frequenter of places of worship, and very seldom permits himself to get into a dispute upon points of faith." "He is somewhat distinguished as a breeder of blooded horses." These are some of the main points in Kennedy's "character" of the Virginia planter of the 1830s. . . .

We must look now at the other tradition—the tradition of the Frontier.

The Frontier referred to is, first of all, that of the Old Southwest, which comprised the states now known as the South, if we exclude Virginia and the Carolinas. The literature which flourished in this region between 1830 and the Civil War is the opposite, in most respects, of the literature which we have been considering. Instead of courtliness, sophistication, restraint, there is uninhibited nature. Instead of chivalry, gallantry, polite learning, there is rough-and-tumble. Instead of wit, there is slapstick. The region in this period specialized in the tall tale. The liveliest and most amusing of the frontier humorists is George Washington Harris, author of *Sut Lovingood Yarns*, published in 1867.

The 1867 edition is long since out of print, and now difficult to come by. A new edition has been recently published, but the editor committed the unpardonable error of revising the language and orthography. The intention was to make the tales more intelligible to the general reader. The original work *is* difficult for many educated Northerners, but the difficulty is not insuperable (not greater, for example, than in Chaucer), and to revise a Sut Lovingood tale is to destroy it.

On the occasion of the appearance of the "revised" edition, Mr. Edmund Wilson wrote a long article in the *New Yorker* on the Sut Lovingood yarns in which he deals so harshly with his subject that one suspects he does not rightly understand what is going on. The work is, he says, "by far the most repellant book of any real merit in American literature." He objects to the "crude and brutal humor." Sut, he says, "avenges his inferiority by tormenting other people; his impulse is avowedly sadistic." He quotes as an example of the sadism the following statement by Sut about "universal onregenerit human nater":

Ef enything happens to some feller, I don't keer ef he's yure bes frien, an I don't keer how sorry you is for him, thar's a streak ove

satisfacshun 'bout like a sowin thread a-runnin all thru yer sorrer.
Yu may be shamed ov hit, but durn me ef hit aint thar.

Can it be that Mr. Wilson is so unaware of "universal
onregenerit human nater"—possesses indeed so little of it
himself—that this is a shockingly new thought to him? If so,
he needs a course in Original Sin, and I suggest that he read,
as a starter, Robert Penn Warren's poem entitled *Original
Sin,* where he will find the accusing line: "You hear of the
deaths of friends with sly pleasure."

The truth is that the Lovingood yarns are rowdy slapstick
fun, the most hilarious, uninhibited compositions in American literature, and the broadest humor written in Nineteenth
Century America; and if time permitted I would prove it to
you by reading one—I should like nothing better. They were
not printed in the *Atlantic Monthly*, but in a subliterary journal, the *Spirit of the Times* (published in New York), whose
importance has only recently been discovered by the historians. The fun is often rough, but we read these yarns, if we
read them correctly, with the willing suspension of the senti-
mental-humanitarian attitude, which is as inappropriate here
as a Puritan-moralistic attitude toward a comedy by Con-
greve or Noel Coward. As for sadism, and taking pleasure
in spoiling other people's fun, Sut is himself as often as not
the butt. Many of the funniest things, moreover, do not
involve physical pain at all. "Rare Ripe Garden Seed" might
easily be mistaken for a Chaucerian fabliau, and the discourse on the "points" of young widows is hardly surpassed
anywhere for its appreciation of sexual pleasures.

Mr. Wilson's crowning error is the statement that Sut is a
direct ancestor of Flem Snopes. Faulkner, as I shall suggest
presently, does owe a good deal to Harris, but Sut and Flem
are as unlike as two human temperaments can very well be.
Did Flem Snopes ever go to a party, get drunk, spark the
girls? Flem never had any good healthy fun in his life—he
was mercenary, calculating, and impotent. Sut, on the other

hand—indiscreet, fun-loving, practical joker extraordinary —wasn't exactly the kind to get himself elected president of a bank.

Bernard DeVoto pointed out twenty-five years ago, in his *Mark Twain's America*, Mark Twain's debt to the Old Southwest humorists. Sut belonged in the East Tennessee mountains, in the neighborhood where Mark Twain's parents lived before they moved to Missouri. Mark Twain was almost certainly *conceived* in Sut's neighborhood, and if he had been born there, and had not gone East and come under the dispiriting influence of Livy, Howells, and the Reverend Mr. Twitchell, he might have become the great Rabelaisian author whom Van Wyck Brooks, with a good deal of insight, thought him capable of being.

One must recognize the bearing of Southern topography on these matters, and the age-old distinction between the highlands and the lowlands: between the Shenandoah and the Tidewater, the up-country and the low-country in South Carolina, the Kentucky mountains and the Blue Grass, East Tennessee and Middle Tennessee. The Southern Appalachians —comprising Eastern Kentucky, East Tennessee, and Western North Carolina—are a homogeneous region, and a kind of modern Frontier. This region was Union in sympathies during the Civil War, and is still Republican. There were no plantations in these mountains and few slaves. The Clemenses had one Negro slave, a girl, who accompanied the family to Missouri, and today there are in this region comparatively few Negroes. The mountain people are, or have been, less restrained than their neighbors in the lowlands. They are, or have been, characterized by a special kind of wildness, and it is worth noting in this connection that Tom Wolfe's Altamont is just over the range from the Sut Lovingood country. Wolfe, of course, attended Chapel Hill, studied drama in Professor George Pierce Baker's 47 Workshop at Harvard, taught English in N.Y.U., Washington Square, lived in Brooklyn, read Shelley and Walt Whitman, and came under other "corrupting" influences, but he was a Southern mountaineer, and the mountain wildness is the most autochthonous fact about him. There is a particularly interesting passage in *Of Time and the River*, where Eugene and his cronies go for an automobile ride, drinking as they ride, careering from the hills to the plains, and landing in jail after a wildly drunken time of it. The passage, except for the somewhat Shelleyan treatment of landscape, recalls Lovingood.

It must have been, in part at least, Faulkner's admiration for the mountain wildness which led him to rank Wolfe first among the American novelists of the Twentieth Century (placing himself second). For this wildness—whether of the mountains or the plains—is an important part of Faulkner's inheritance, and it comes out in some of his best writing. Perhaps the best example is the story *Spotted Horses* (later incorporated in *The Hamlet*). Complete pandemonium can be carried no further than in Faulkner's account of what happens after the Texas ponies (the liveliest ever created by God or man) break out of the corral, and run pellmell down the country roads, upsetting many a cart, wagon, and surrey, and trampling their occupants under foot. For a sheer all-hell-broke-loose narrative, it has no equal unless in one of Sut Lovingood's farm-yard escapades. Faulkner's yarn, like many of Sut's, is hilariously funny, despite the fact that several people get hurt, and I don't quite see how Mr. Wilson can escape his old difficulty here. But the difficulty, in fact, is quite common. Non-Southerners often react to the Southern wildness in the wrong way.

If I may be permitted the pedantry of a footnote (without actually relegating the matter to the bottom of the page) on Southern folklore in general, and in particular the special kinship of Faulkner and Wolfe, I should like to quote from each author (from *Of Time and the River*, and from *Sartoris*) a description of the proper way to drink moonshine out of a jug. It is an important subject, and the correct technique is a matter of importance. Each author is obviously proud of this bit of connoisseurship. Wolfe says: "They hooked their thumbs into the handle of the jug, and brought the stuff across their shoulders with a free-hand motion, and let the wide neck pour into their tilted throats with a fat thick gurgle. . . ." Faulkner says: "Bayard was already drinking, with the jug tilted across his horizontal forearm, and the mouth held to his lips by the same hand, as it should be done." The methods are not quite identical, but basically similar. An allowance can be made for a small variation between North Carolina and Mississippi. (Young Sartoris, at the time, is hob-nobbing with the neighboring farm boys, and one of them is saying to another, "I knowed he was all right.") In each case, it is a ritual, not to be familiar with which marks one as lacking the proper initiation into good Frontier society.

We have been considering two traditions in the literature of the South—the Tidewater and the Frontier—and we have seen that they have flourished side by side, and somewhat separate from each other. There is just one more point which I wish to suggest: it is that the two traditions are united in the works of the writer who, all agree, is the greatest in the South today, and possibly this is one important reason why he *is* the greatest. For like Shakespeare, Faulkner embraces the high and the low, the aristocratic and the plebeian, the courtly and the uncouth, the educated and the illiterate, the literary and the vernacular, the traditional and the modern. I have already glanced at his affinity with the Frontier tradition. His sympathetic interest, on the other hand, in the Sartorises, the Compsons, and other aristocrats (Faulkner's treatment of these people can rise to the high-tragic mode) allies him with the Tidewater. It is this comprehensiveness, among other things, which sets Faulkner apart from his contemporaries in the South, though I should add that Robert Penn Warren has some of this same comprehensiveness.

I hope these remarks have at least suggested a genetic relationship (I believe not much appreciated) between the new literature of the South, and the old. However important various influences from outside the South may have been in the present century (and it has not been my intention to deal with these), modern Southern literature—both Tidewater and Frontier—has had a long background in Southern writing. (1959)

H. L. MENCKEN

Born in 1880 in Baltimore, H. L. Mencken is one of the most famous and influential journalists of the century. Reporter, critic, and student of language, he took the whole American culture as his province of study. His coverage of the world famous Scopes "monkey trial" in Dayton, Tennessee, in 1925 as a reporter for the Baltimore *Evening Sun* helped to bring to the attention of the nation and the world the image of the South as the "Bible Belt," a term popularized by Mencken himself. John T. Scopes was accused of breaking the state law by teaching evolution in a public school. He was defended by the brilliant agnostic lawyer Clarence Darrow. The prosecution was in the hands of William Jennings Bryan, a fundamentalist who was nationally known as "the silver-tongued orator." Bryan obtained a token conviction, but was covered with ridicule in the process; he died shortly after.

The following selection appears in his *Prejudices: Fifth Series*. Mencken explains in an introductory note: "In its first form this was a dispatch to the Baltimore *Evening Sun*, in July 1925. I wrote it on a roaring hot Sunday afternoon in a Chattanooga hotel room, naked above the waist and with only a pair of BVD's below."

The Hills of Zion

It was hot weather when they tried the infidel Scopes at Dayton, Tenn., but I went down there very willingly, for I was eager to see something of evangelical Christianity as a going concern. In the big cities of the Republic, despite the endless efforts of consecrated men, it is laid up with a wasting disease. The very Sunday-school superintendents, taking jazz from the stealthy radio, shake their fire-proof legs; their pupils, moving into adolescence, no longer respond to the proliferating hormones by enlisting for missionary service in Africa, but resort to necking instead. Even in Dayton, I found, though the mob was up to do execution upon Scopes, there was a strong smell of antinomianism. The nine churches of the village were all half empty on Sunday, and weeds choked their yards. Only two or three of the resident pastors managed to sustain themselves by their ghostly science; the rest had to take orders for mail-order pantaloons or work in the adjacent strawberry fields; one, I heard, was a barber. On the courthouse green a score of sweating theologians debated the darker passages of Holy Writ day and night, but I soon found that they were all volunteers, and that the local faithful, while interested in their exegesis as an intellectual exercise, did not permit it to impede the indigenous debaucheries. Exactly twelve minutes after I reached the village I was taken in tow by a Christian man and introduced to the favorite tipple of the Cumberland Range: half corn liquor and half Coca-Cola. It seemed a dreadful dose to me, but I found that the Dayton illuminati got it down with gusto, rubbing their tummies and rolling their eyes. I include among them the chief local proponents of the Mosaic cosmogony. They were all hot for Genesis, but their faces were far too florid to belong to teetotalers, and when a pretty girl came tripping down the main street, which was very often, they reached for the places where their neckties should have been with all the amorous enterprise of movie actors. It seemed somehow strange.

An amiable newspaper woman of Chattanooga, familiar with those uplands, presently enlightened me. Dayton, she explained, was simply a great capital like any other. That is to say, it was to Rhea county what Atlanta was to Georgia or Paris to France. That is to say, it was predominantly epicurean and sinful. A country girl from some remote valley of the county, coming into town for her semi-annual bottle of Lydia Pinkham's Vegetable Compound, shivered on approaching Robinson's drug-store quite as a country girl from up-State New York might shiver on approaching the Metropolitan Opera House. In every village lout she saw a potential white-slaver. The hard sidewalks hurt her feet. Temptations of the flesh bristled to all sides of her, luring her to Hell. This newspaper woman told me of a session with just such a visitor, holden a few days before. The latter waited outside one of the town hot-dog and Coca-Cola shops while her husband negotiated with a hardware merchant across the street. The newspaper woman, idling along and observing that the stranger was badly used by the heat, invited her to step into the shop for a glass of Coca-Cola. The invitation brought forth only a gurgle of terror. Coca-Cola, it quickly appeared, was prohibited by the country lady's pastor, as a levantine and Hell-sent narcotic. He also prohibited coffee and tea—and pies! He had his doubts about white bread and boughten meat. The newspaper woman, interested, inquired about ice-cream. It was, she found, not specifically prohibited, but going into a Coca-Cola shop to get it would be clearly sinful. So she offered to get a saucer of it, and bring it out to the sidewalk. The visitor vacillated —and came near being lost. But God saved her in the nick of time. When the newspaper woman emerged from the place she was in full flight up the street. Later on her husband, mounted on a mule, overtook her four miles out the mountain pike.

This newspaper woman, whose kindness covered city infidels as well as Alpine Christians, offered to take me back in the hills to a place where the old-time religion was genuinely on tap. The Scopes jury, she explained, was composed mainly of its customers, with a few Dayton sophisticates added to leaven the mass. It would thus be instructive to climb the heights and observe the former at their ceremonies. The trip, fortunately, might be made by automobile. There was a road running out of Dayton to Morgantown, in the mountains to the westward, and thence beyond. But foreigners, it appeared, would have to approach the sacred grove cautiously, for the upland worshipers were very shy, and at the first sight of a strange face they would adjourn their orgy and slink into the forest. They were not to be feared, for God had long since forbidden them to practise assassination, or even assault, but if they were alarmed a rough trip would go for naught. So, after dreadful bumpings up a long and narrow road, we parked our car in a little woodpath a mile or two beyond the tiny village of Morgantown, and made the rest of the approach on foot, deployed like skirmishers. Far off in a dark, romantic glade a flickering light was visible, and out of the silence came the rumble of exhortation. We could distinguish the figure of the preacher only as a moving mote in the light: it was like looking down the tube of a dark-field microscope. Slowly and cautiously we crossed what seemed to be a pasture, and then we stealthily edged further and further. The light now grew larger and we could begin to make out what was going on. We went ahead on all fours, like snakes in the grass.

From the great limb of a mighty oak hung a couple of crude torches of the sort that car inspectors thrust under Pullman cars when a train pulls in at night. In the guttering glare was the preacher, and for a while we could see no one else. He was an immensely tall and thin mountaineer in blue jeans, his collarless shirt open at the neck and his hair a tousled mop. As he preached he paced up and down under the smoking flambeaux, and at each turn he thrust his arms into the air and yelled "Glory to God!" We crept nearer in the shadow of the cornfield, and began to hear more of his discourse. He was preaching on the Day of Judgment. The high kings of the earth, he roared, would all fall down and die; only the sanctified would stand up to receive the Lord God of Hosts. One of these kings he mentioned by name, the king of what he called Greece-y.[1] The king of Greece-y, he said, was doomed to Hell. We crawled forward a few more yards and began to see the audience. It was seated on benches ranged round the preacher in a circle. Behind him sat a row of elders, men and women. In front were the younger folk. We crept on cautiously, and individuals rose out of the ghostly gloom. A young mother sat suckling her baby, rocking as the preacher paced up and down. Two scared little girls hugged each other, their pigtails down their backs. An immensely huge mountain woman, in a gingham dress, cut in one piece, rolled on her heels at every "Glory to God!" To one side, and but half visible, was what appeared to be a bed. We found afterward that half a dozen babies were asleep upon it.

The preacher stopped at last, and there arose out of the darkness a woman with her hair pulled back into a little tight knot. She began so quietly that we couldn't hear what she said, but soon her voice rose resonantly and we could follow her. She was denouncing the reading of books. Some wandering book agent, it appeared, had come to her cabin and tried to sell her a specimen of his wares. She refused to touch it. Why, indeed, read a book? If what was in it was true, then everything in it was already in the Bible. If it was false, then reading it would imperil the soul. This syllogism from the Caliph Omar complete, she sat down. There followed a hymn, led by a somewhat fat brother wearing silver-rimmed country spectacles. It droned on for half a dozen stanzas, and

[1] Grecia? Cf. Daniel viii, 21. [Mencken's note.]

then the first speaker resumed the floor. He argued that the gift of tongues was real and that education was a snare. Once his children could read the Bible, he said, they had enough. Beyond lay only infidelity and damnation. Sin stalked the cities. Dayton itself was a Sodom. Even Morgantown had begun to forget God. He sat down, and a female aurochs in gingham got up. She began quietly, but was soon leaping and roaring, and it was hard to follow her. Under cover of the turmoil we sneaked a bit closer.

A couple of other discourses followed, and there were two or three hymns. Suddenly a change of mood began to make itself felt. The last hymn ran longer than the others, and dropped gradually into a monotonous, unintelligible chant. The leader beat time with his book. The faithful broke out with exultations. When the singing ended there was a brief palaver that we could not hear, and two of the men moved a bench into the circle of light directly under the flambeaux. Then a half-grown girl emerged from the darkness and threw herself upon it. We noticed with astonishment that she had bobbed hair. "This sister," said the leader, "has asked for prayers." We moved a bit closer. We could now see faces plainly, and hear every word. At a signal all the faithful crowded up to the bench and began to pray—not in unison, but each for himself. At another they all fell on their knees, their arms over the penitent. The leader kneeled facing us, his head alternately thrown back dramatically or buried in his hands. Words spouted from his lips like bullets from a machine-gun—appeals to God to pull the penitent back out of Hell, defiances of the demons of the air, a vast impassioned jargon of apocalyptic texts. Suddenly he rose to his feet, threw back his head and began to speak in the tongues[2]— blub-blub-blub, gurgle-gurgle-gurgle. His voice rose to a higher register. The climax was a shrill, inarticulate squawk, like that of a man throttled. He fell headlong across the pyramid of supplicants.

[2] Mark xvi, 17. [Mencken's note.]

From the squirming and jabbering mass a young woman gradually detached herself—a woman not uncomely, with a pathetic homemade cap on her head. Her head jerked back, the veins of her neck swelled, and her fists went to her throat as if she were fighting for breath. She bent backward until she was like half a hoop. Then she suddenly snapped forward. We caught a flash of the whites of her eyes. Presently her whole body began to be convulsed—great throes that began at the shoulders and ended at the hips. She would leap to her feet, thrust her arms in air, and then hurl herself upon the heap. Her praying flattened out into a mere delirious caterwauling. I describe the thing discreetly, and as a strict behaviorist. The lady's subjective sensations I leave to infidel pathologists, privy to the works of Ellis, Freud and Moll. Whatever they were, they were obviously not painful, for they were accompanied by vast heavings and gurglings of a joyful and even ecstatic nature. And they seemed to be contagious, too, for soon a second penitent, also female, joined the first, and then came a third, and a fourth, and a fifth. The last one had an extraordinary violent attack. She began with mild enough jerks of the head, but in a moment she was bounding all over the place, like a chicken with its head cut off. Every time her head came up a stream of hosannas would issue out of it. Once she collided with a dark, undersized brother, hitherto silent and stolid. Contact with her set him off as if he had been kicked by a mule. He leaped into the air, threw back his head, and began to gargle as if with a mouthful of BB shot. Then he loosed one tremendous, stentorian sentence in the tongues, and collapsed.

By this time the performers were quite oblivious to the profane universe and so it was safe to go still closer. We left our hiding and came up to the little circle of light. We slipped into the vacant seats on one of the rickety benches. The heap of mourners was directly before us. They bounced into us as they cavorted. The smell that they radiated, sweating there in that obscene heap, half suffocated us. Not all of them, of course, did the thing in the grand manner. Some merely moaned and rolled their eyes. The female ox in gingham flung her great bulk on the ground and jabbered an unintelligible prayer. One of the men, in the intervals between fits, put on his spectacles and read his Bible. Beside me on the bench sat the young mother and her baby. She suckled it through the whole orgy, obviously fascinated by what was going on, but never venturing to take any hand in it. On the bed just outside the light the half a dozen other babies slept peacefully. In the shadows, suddenly appearing and as suddenly going away, were vague figures, whether of believers or of scoffers I do not know. They seemed to come and go in couples. Now and then a couple at the ringside would step out and vanish into the black night. After a while some came back, the males looking somewhat sheepish. There was whispering outside the circle of vision. A couple of Model T Fords lurched up the road, cutting holes in the darkness with their lights. Once someone out of sight loosed a bray of laughter.

All this went on for an hour or so. The original penitent, by this time, was buried three deep beneath the heap. One caught a glimpse, now and then, of her yellow bobbed hair, but then she would vanish again. How she breathed down there I don't know; it was hard enough six feet away, with a strong five-cent cigar to help. When the praying brothers would rise up for a bout with the tongues their faces were streaming with perspiration. The fat harridan in gingham sweated like a longshoreman. Her hair got loose and fell down over her face. She fanned herself with her skirt. A powerful old gal she was, plainly equal in her day to a bout with obstetrics and a week's washing on the same morning, but this was worse than a week's washing. Finally, she fell into a heap, breathing in great, convulsive gasps.

Finally, we got tired of the show and returned to Dayton. It was nearly eleven o'clock—an immensely late hour for those latitudes—but the whole town was still gathered in the courthouse yard, listening to the disputes of theologians. The

Scopes trial had brought them in from all directions. There was a friar wearing a sandwich sign announcing that he was the Bible champion of the world. There was a Seventh Day Adventist arguing that Clarence Darrow was the beast with seven heads and ten horns described in Revelation xiii, and that the end of the world was at hand. There was an evangelist made up like Andy Gump, with the news that atheists in Cincinnati were preparing to descend upon Dayton, hang the eminent Judge Raulston, and burn the town. There was an ancient who maintained that no Catholic could be a Christian. There was the eloquent Dr. T. T. Martin, of Blue Mountain, Miss., come to town with a truck-load of torches and hymn-books to put Darwin in his place. There was a singing brother bellowing apocalyptic hymns. There was William Jennings Bryan, followed everywhere by a gaping crowd. Dayton was having a roaring time. It was better than the circus. But the note of devotion was simply not there; the Daytonians, after listening a while, would slip away to Robinson's drug-store to regale themselves with Coca-Cola, or to the lobby of the Aqua Hotel, where the learned Raulston sat in state, judicially picking his teeth. The real religion was not present. It began at the bridge over the town creek, where the road makes off for the hills. (1925)

JACK WELLER

A native of New York, Jack E. Weller graduated from the University of Rochester and received the Bachelor of Divinity degree from Union Theological Seminary, New York City. In 1964 he was named "minister of the year" by the West Virginia Council of Churches for his contributions to the state, and in 1965 he became minister-at-large for the United Presbyterian Church in Eastern Kentucky. His book *Yesterday's People*—from which the following selection is taken—has been one of the most widely discussed books ever written on Southern Appalachia. Weller's assessment of education in the mountains deals with basic problems which still plague many hill communities.

Education

Almost every mountain child has the opportunity (at least, as we see it) to attend public school. Only in relatively few cases is attendance not possible—where families live on top of the mountains or far up the twisting valleys, remote from schools or school-bus routes. Schools vary from the one-room variety up to modern, centralized systems with hundreds of students. Often long bus rides are necessary, over rough and dangerous roads, but few children do not have the possibility, at least, of having twelve years of public schooling. But they do not always get it. Since the forms of education were imposed from the outside and did not grow up as an expression of the culture, teaching what the mountaineer wanted his children to learn, there has traditionally been a resistance to "book learning." A person was thought well enough educated if he could read and write and count, and "too much" schooling was thought to be unnecessary and even dangerous—and so was unwanted.

In the past, children were sent to school as early as allowed, but whenever they were old enough to be helpful at home or on the farm or in the mine, they were taken out of school either for a time or for good. Sometimes the girls were needed at home to help their mothers with the smaller ones or to serve as mother substitutes in cases of sickness or disability. School was always secondary to something else. One day, for instance, I picked up a boy thumbing a ride in front of the school. It was several hours before school was to be dismissed, and I asked him whether he had to go to the doctor, or perhaps had been called home because of some emergency. No, he replied, he had gotten an excuse from his father to come home early to help dig potatoes. Since it was Friday, I asked whether he weren't going to do that the next day. "Why no," he said, in a tone which seemed to indicate that I must not be very discerning. "Tomorrow's the start of hunting season."

Parents now want their children to have an education, because they have become increasingly aware that it is necessary; yet they fear that it will separate children from their families or destroy the common level of the reference group. To be educated means to be "uppity" or snobbish, or to feel that one is better than the rest. A young person who has gone off to college may return at vacation time to find his family and reference group asking, in so many words, "Do you think you're better than we are now?" There is almost a fear of an education that goes very far above the community level. A man who could not find a job because of his limited education expressed to me a great deal of hostility against companies which advised him to go back to school and get some basic courses, such as English. "Why do I need more English to get a job?" he stormed. "I can talk all right. What's the difference if I tell him that I ain't got no job and I need the money in plain talk or some fancy way. He knows what I mean—or he should." Education must have immediate and specific application before the mountain man counts it important or necessary. Yet most mountain schools have taught standard college preparatory courses, with little emphasis on crafts or skills. Most of the education has been object oriented, presenting the kind of information that the mountaineer simply does not understand and ideals that he does not share.

In these adult-centered mountain families, separation between adults and children begins about the time the child enters school and increases rapidly. Because the realm of ideas is not his world, the parent lacks interest in the school. Probably there are no books at all in the home, the child has never been read to, and when he begins having trouble with homework he finds little help or encouragement from parents who may actually have had less education than he has. In some cases, adults may revel in the fact that through "just common sense" they can solve arithmetic problems, for example, faster than their children, who use school-taught methods.

Quite common in the mountains is the unspoken attitude that education is mainly for girls. Most of the teachers are women, and for the boys and men this fact alone smacks of education's being "sissy." As a natural consequence, the best students are girls, the scholastic striving is among them, and they are most likely to go to college. This is unfortunate, for many a mountain boy finds himself at the same disadvantage in life as his father. The women generally have reached a considerably higher education level than the men. It is not uncommon to find a college-trained teacher married to a man who has not even finished high school. Another factor is the action-seeking trait among the boys; coupled with the dullness of daily mountain life, it certainly does not enhance for them the idea of sitting still to listen and learn. Caudill notes that during the early years of school building in the mountains: "[S]uch new schools as the bond issues provided fell prey to athletics to an extent that is difficult to overstate. The miner (and mountaineer) learned quickly to escape from the dreary routines of camp life and coal digging into the exhilaration of a basketball gymnasium or a football stadium, and was far more interested in the hoopla of school sports than in the riddles of grammar and mathematics. His enthusiasm went to the sterile playing fields and his children, imbued with his infectious zeal, sought to emulate his heroes on grid and court."[1]

Motivation for learning is often lacking among both boys and girls. For one thing, educational achievement requires the ability to handle concepts and ideas, to concentrate on the study at hand to the exclusion of other concerns. The mountain child's training in home and reference group has not schooled him to do this well. The reference-group society trains its members to be sensitive to people rather than to ideas. Words are used not to express ideas but to impress people, and argument proceeds by the use of anecdotes rather than by commonsense forms of logic. I recall a mountain man's description of the way a particular church group used the Bible. The group, he said, would take a verse here, one there, to build up its own case. The man, in very personal, anecdotal style, remarked that they were "making a saddle to fit their horse." Very plain and clear, yet very difficult to

[1] Harry Caudill, *Night Comes to the Cumberlands* (Boston: Little, Brown and Company, 1963), p. 25.

square with ideas of logic, math, or science. It is extremely difficult, for example, to keep any study or discussion group on the subject at hand or on the problem to be solved. The mountaineer is simply not interested in abstract ideas, or in intellectual fine points, or in learning for the sake of learning.

Reference-group life, with its impulsive approach to child rearing, its stress on action rather than routine, the competitive nature of its conversation (where several people may be talking at once), encourages a short attention span. This inability to concentrate for long periods, combined with the inability to see the value of learning that cannot be applied immediately, hinders the mountain child in his education. Certainly it is not lack of intelligence that makes him fall behind his city counterparts. Mountain children, like children everywhere, are quick to learn, but they are much quicker to catch feelings than ideas. The problem is that our educational system is based on ideas, not on feelings.

Much of the parents' laxness toward their children's education simply results from lack of experience on their part. How can a family know the value of a college education or trade-school training when they have seen so little evidence of its worth in their own lives or in their communities? In many a mountain community, the only college-educated person is the school teacher, and unfortunately he is so underpaid (a subtle evaluation of his presumed worth to the community), and often so little thought of, that his place in the world is no incentive to further education. It is to the credit of such teachers that so many of the young people who do go out to get education do so in the field of teaching. Yet how can parents in these isolated valleys know all about the possibilities for careers in aviation, law, business, art, music, engineering, or real estate? The chances are they have never even known anybody in these fields or perhaps don't even know that they exist. Indeed, many a mountain youth has never even seen a large factory, let alone known the kinds of jobs within them, until he leaves home to apply for work in one. It is incredible how immobile large segments of our mountain population can be, while living in the midst of the most mobile society that has ever existed. Mountain boys and girls simply must have experiences that will acquaint them with the "outside" world to which most of them will be forced to migrate—and the educational system must help provide these experiences.

For years, mountain-bred and mountain-taught teachers have been teaching mountain children. I admire tremendously those young people who break out of their home patterns to attend teachers colleges in their home state, and then return to teach near home. Their pay is low, and they have low status in the community, few supplies and books to work with, and multitudes of poorly equipped students in overcrowded rooms. There is real devotion in such a career.

Despite all this, my contention is that we are all more or less blind to our own culture. Mountain-bred and mountain-taught teachers find it too easy to perpetuate the ingrown and experienceless training characteristic of mountain schools. The Southern Appalachians desperately need teachers trained and reared in other cultures, with other experiences and often broader training. Perhaps even a teacher exchange, using mountain and city teachers, would be useful. Too often the mountain school system becomes a "closed shop," composed of a staff of teachers who have been trained in the same system, brought up in the same culture, and molded by the same forces as the children they seek to teach. Instead of challenging and stimulating the children, such a system simply perpetuates itself—and it cannot hope to prepare its youth for life in our American society. To be sure, it would be a mistake to go too far in the other direction. Public schools need both the direction and the understanding of the teacher who knows the feeling and the structure of the person-oriented reference-group society of the mountains as well as the outlook of persons from elsewhere who are not blind to the culture.

A broad educational program will probably not come about soon. Good teachers, wherever trained, can earn much better salaries in more stimulating surroundings than Southern Appalachia. Finally, many a mountain county school system is set up on a political basis, or a person-to-person hiring system. Persons wanting to come into the mountains to teach very often find it difficult to get in—especially in the school systems where outside help is most needed. (1965)

JIM WAYNE MILLER

As a teacher Jim Wayne Miller is concerned about the quality of education in the Southern mountain area, but unlike Jack Weller he proposes a somewhat different solution for the problem. For further comment on him see page 347.

A Mirror for Appalachia

Do yesterday's people have a future? Yes, the future of Appalachia can be bright if Appalachians can gain a sure appreciation of what is good about Appalachian life—our institutions and values—and if Appalachians realize what a tragic loss it would be to exchange their birthright for a mess of mainstream America.

There is no better time than now—when mainstream assumptions are being questioned—to begin promoting this appreciation among Appalachians. Mainstream America institutions are in trouble. Much that is shallow, superficial—and even sinister—in middle-class life is being exposed. Middle-class youth are modifying or altering their life-styles. Many people have concluded that Appalachia has something the rest of the country needs. The time is right for Appalachians

to realize that they, for once, are in a position to offer the
rest of the country something in return for the assistance
Appalachia undeniably needs. Now is the time for Appalachians to begin to move from under the shadow of the
dominant culture into the sunshine of pride in the region and
its way of life. Now is the time for Appalachians to move
toward recognition of their own self-worth. . . .

A mirror for Appalachia is needed, which will help Appalachians to become "aware of who we are and why, and be at
ease with this knowledge."[1] The record of the past suggests
that Appalachians cannot expect others to provide that mirror. It must be a mirror of our own making.

The proper place to begin promoting an appreciation of
Appalachian life is in the region's schools. We should start
with the understanding that the schools, though imperfect,
are still the most effective agency for the task. For there are
teachers in the region who understand both the mountain
culture and the mainstream culture. The main task of cultivating an appreciation for what is good in Appalachian life
will fall upon these teachers who have a knowledge and
understanding of two worlds—of Appalachia and mainstream America—and who can walk, like a plowman in
spring, with one foot in the plowed ground, the other in the
unbroken sod. They are teachers who, at a time when the
mainstream educational system is under particularly close
scrutiny for its inadequacies, can be independent and uncon-
ventional enough to be thankful that Appalachian schools
have not succeeded altogether in stirring Appalachia's children into the great educational melting pot.

There is nothing strange about the Appalachian mountaineer himself that has caused education in his region to be
less than successful. In fact, the mountaineer's resistance to
aspects of the education that has been available to him is as

[1] Loyal Jones, "What I would Like to See Happen to Our Land and
People," *Appalachian Heritage*, Vol. 1, No. 3, Summer, 1973, pp. 22–23.

much a tribute to his good sense as it is an indication of his backwardness. For the education he has experienced—and Jack Weller in *Yesterday's People* sees this clearly—has not been an expression of his own culture, but has been imposed from the outside. It is only natural that the mountaineer has been unable to see the use of much of it. "Education," Weller points out, "must have immediate and specific application before the mountain man counts it important or necessary." We are mistaken if we think this attitude is peculiar to Appalachians.

It is difficult for people anywhere to embrace enthusiastically twelve years of formal schooling based on values they don't fully share, reflecting a world they do not live in, a world difficult to connect to their own experience. Too often the schools say to Appalachian children, "If you stick it out and change a few of your peculiar ways all this can be of use to you someday." Alfred North Whitehead maintains, however, that "No more deadly harm can be done to young minds than the depreciation of the present." He recommends abandoning the notion of a "mythical far-off end to education," because students need regularly to enjoy some sense of accomplishment and some appreciation of the connection between what they are learning and what they already know and are. The result of educating children with one background only for life in another is inevitably felt by the mountaineer, and by anyone anywhere, as the "aimless accumulation of precise knowledge, inert and unutilised."

Educational theory which views the mind as an instrument to be sharpened first and used later is responsible, in part, for pointing all expectation into the future—to the detriment of the present. Whitehead calls this view of the mind "one of the most fatal, erroneous, and dangerous concepts ever introduced into education." The mind is not passive; it is not even an object; it is an activity receptive and responsive to stimulation. And the life of the mind cannot be postponed until the mind has been sharpened. This view of the mind as an instrument to be sharpened, or its variant, a vessel to be filled, is not implicit in mountain education alone. But surely its effect on the mountain child further intensifies the unreality of much mountain education.

Teachers in Appalachia need not consider students incorrigibly backward if they are not stimulated by the experience they get in the classroom. Instead, teachers need to examine that classroom experience. They need also to be appreciative of the strengths of mountain culture and mountaineer traits, and they need to build on these. Here Weller's *Yesterday's People* can be helpful. Weller points out, for instance, that Appalachian children "learn much more quickly to catch feelings than ideas. The problem is that our educational system is based on ideas, not feelings." That is the problem, but whose problem is it, ultimately? It is obviously the mountain child's immediate problem. But it need not always and inevitably be so. Could the system itself be inadequate? I am tempted to say in this instance: let the mountain come to Mohammed. And I urge teachers to avoid the assumption made by Weller that the educational system is to be accepted as it is, without critical examination.

There is wide agreement among critics of mainstream American education that a fundamental inadequacy of the educational experience is the divorce between thought and feeling, a divorce which results in our educating people who cannot feel what they know. We educate for a dreary, utilitarian, unimaginative sobriety, the "very kind of schooling needed," to use Weller's words, "in a technical society." It is a schooling which produces people who are "all up in their heads." William Butler Yeats had the result of such schooling in mind when he wrote: "God save me from the thoughts men think/ In the head alone."

If Appalachian children tend to learn "the feeling of words" quickly, teachers can learn to encourage this ability, to recognize it as a strength and asset. They can learn how to build on this and related assets. (After all, a feeling for words is a

subtlety of appreciation teachers everywhere want to cultivate in their students.) A related asset is the mode of discourse typically employed by Appalachians. Weller observes
that discussions in Appalachia are likely to proceed by the
use of anecdotes rather than by analytical exposition. He
gives the example of a man who described the way a particular church group used the Bible to justify their views by
saying: they make a saddle to fit their horse. Weller adds that
this is very plain and clear, yet very difficult to square with
the ideas of logic, math, and science.

Yet there is no necessity to square such usage with logic,
math, and science. Two modes of discourse exist and are
often interwoven: the discursive, or language in its literal use,
typified by expository prose; and the presentational mode,
which is the mode of symbol, metaphor, and image, the mode
used by the Appalachian to describe the church group. The
mountaineer's observation is not less but rather more vivid,
accurate and memorable than the prose in the textbooks his
children may be reading in school. I would further dispute
the notion that the presentational mode is inadequate for
dealing with ideas, concepts and abstractions. The literary
heritage of the western world is a record of the presentational
mode's being employed to deal with ideas and concepts.
Often, in fact, there are abstractions that cannot be evoked
through any means other than this presentational, or meta-
phorical mode typically encountered in the arts.

What discursive symbolism—language in its literal use—does for
our awareness of things about us and our relation to them, the
arts do for our awareness of subjective reality, feeling and emo-
tion; they give inward experiences form and thus make them
conceivable.[2]

I should not like to see Appalachians abandon their natural
tendency, so well described in the work of Cratis Williams,

[2] Susanne Langer, *Problems of Art.*

to employ figurative language. I don't think Appalachians are in any danger of doing so. But I do think we should decide to cultivate such usage rather than subtly discourage it in a thousand ways, not only in the mountain culture but throughout America. And because I agree with Weller that mountain children do develop a remarkable feeling for words, and because their language is characterized by liberal use of figurative language, mountain children will be most receptive to and will profit most readily from a teaching method that will make use of literary materials of a regional nature—materials that will permit students to see themselves mirrored in art. This experience will be preferable, especially in the earlier years, to books that show students only a world that is often foreign to them and that, after years of exposure to it, leaves them feeling vague, ill-defined, marginal person- alities who have been rather effectively cut off from much of their culture through a (however well-intentioned) melting pot theory of education. "First hand knowledge is the ultimate basis of intellectual life," Whitehead emphasizes. "Our goal is to see the immediate events of our lives as instances of our general ideas." Too often the teaching methods experienced by Appalachian children place a barrier between general ideas and immediate events in their lives.

I hope no one will gain the impression that I want to see a regional education which would produce individuals merely smug and blinkered in their provincialism. Nor do I have a wild-eyed vision of making "earth poets" out of every Appa- lachian child. I am aware, also, that different as the Appala- chian region is from most of America, the sub-culture and the dominant culture are bound to one another in innumera- ble ways. However, since not all is well in the dominant culture, and since not all is bad or irremedial in the sub-cul- ture, it makes sense to locate those potentially fruitful areas in Appalachian life and concentrate one's limited resources of time, manpower and money there, while at the same time being careful not to import uncritically from the dominant culture inappropriate or shoddy methods and materials under the guise of innovations.

A soft spot in mainstream American education is the neglect of artistic education, which is neglect to educate feeling. The arts, as Loyal Jones, Director of the Appalachian Center at Berea College, points out, are the last added to the school curriculum and the first sacrificed when a cutback is deemed necessary. In the mainstream schools, knowledgeable people assert, this neglect of the arts results in a kind of discrimination against creative children. Some observers maintain that creativity actually handicaps children in the public schools where the educational process is geared to producing quick success.

There are many reasons for the neglect of artistic education. Certainly a chief reason is that so many people, educators included, have the notion that feeling is essentially formless; they associate it with the animalistic, the wild, the violent, the chaotic. Thus the idea of educating feeling, of encouraging its scope and quality, seems not only odd to most people but downright absurd or even perverse to many. Yet many philosophers and educators are convinced that the education of feeling, through emphasis on the arts, is the very core of a personal education.

Another reason for the neglect is that our schools constitute a micro-society and reflect the values of our industrial society, which is taken to be the "real world." Thus our schools place a high premium on a certain kind of manipulative, exploitative intelligence—the kind of intelligence that has enabled us to gain greater but increasingly dubious control over our environment and to create the complicated world we live in. In so doing, the schools suppress and in many ways penalize the receptive, reflective, intuitive personality which seeks to "synthesize all the elements of its world into relevance."

A third reason why the arts are neglected or poorly taught is that society maintains an ambivalent attitude toward art and the artist, and the schools reflect this attitude. On the one hand, art, music and literature are looked upon with a certain uneasy tolerance. They are considered basically frivolous. They are to be indulged in, with moderation, of course, by people in pursuit of culture. But they are not to be confused with the "business" of life. Artists are at best decorators or clowns who may enjoy the privilege of dressing and behaving in eccentric ways. The other side of the ambivalence reveals the attitude that takes a serious, though negative view of art and the artist. The artist is often considered subversive. To the degree that a state is totalitarian, it will pay the artist the backhanded compliment of considering him potentially dangerous. Totalitarian states know that the artist reveals and creates reality; that he is the greatest educator, for he teaches us how to feel and how to experience the world. The artist's forms and symbols appeal to us at a level of common humanity, uniting us, linking us with the past, delighting and sustaining us in the present while giving us images of ourselves and intimations of the future. The artist is indispensable as a creator, revealer and shaper of the symbols, myths, and beliefs which define a culture.

Unfortunately, culture is too often thought of as certain bits of information, mannerisms, airs, refinements, polish. (Where culture is so conceived, a sub-culture such as Appalachia, living in the shadow of the dominant culture, will be measured by such superficial things and will always be found wanting.) This concept of culture influences the way we approach art in the schools. We try to acquaint the student with "the best that has been thought and felt and done," we teach "masterpieces" by "great authors." The student need only be passive and sponge-like to absorb this sort of culture. But if the student is normally healthy and active, he is frustrated by having always to extirpate the theme of a work, like ganglia from a corpse. But in order to justify giving attention to literary art—to make it as an example—we feel compelled to make it render up "meaning" and "significance." To do this, we too frequently undertake to translate the work out of its presentational mode back into the discursive mode, which is to ask of the work what it is least prepared to offer. It is no wonder students repeatedly ask, "Well, if that's what it means, then why didn't he just say that?" It is a perfectly sensible question, given the usual circumstances.

Students assimilate the accumulated goods of a culture—its literature, for instance—not for the pack-rat pleasure of acquiring them for some future use, but rather for the stimulation and illumination these works produced by other personalities give their own developing selves. Emerson valued books not for the information and knowledge he got from them (though he did not deny they contained information and knowledge) but rather for their power to stimulate the mind and spirit. . . .

Education in Appalachia could set itself no better goal than helping Appalachian children define who they are. Appalachian children especially need to see their lives and experiences mirrored in art, verified, corroborated, legitimized. They don't need what they so often get: subtle indications that their lives and experiences, their thoughts and feelings are different and don't really count for anything.

There are too few schools in Appalachia that know how or are even disposed to encourage students to value that which is unique in their background. Writing in *Mountain Life & Work*, Bill Best says the myth of the melting pot is responsible for the peculiar experience a mountain child so often gets in school. Children often find self-definition hard to attain because "those who controlled our material resources and educational institutions had already defined us." He goes on to describe his own experience as a third-grader in the hills of western North Carolina:

After drifting through two years of Dick and Jane, their dog Spot, and their fashionably thin mother and father who lived in a

fashionable house surrounded by a picket fence, I became very
excited about a story in my reader which depicted a life-style
similar to that which I was exposed to in my community and of
which I was a living part. It mattered little to me that the story
concerned a Laplander family in Finland. I had found a story
with which I could identify, and I read it and re-read it until the
pages were ready to fall out.[3]

What is the problem? you may ask. The materials provided
this third-grader did, after all, contain something he became
excited about. Yes, but this was the one memorable high point
in his early education! Finding materials that excited him
could and should have been a daily experience.

I grew up not far from Bill Best in those same western
North Carolina mountains. We are almost exactly the same
age. And although we never discussed this particular experience, we both came to write about it later. I dealt with it in a
story describing the feelings of a boy involved in a school
consolidation. It wasn't the consolidation, though, that gave
the boy difficulty. It was the image of the world he got from
the school texts:

The students already attending West Madison when we came
from Newfound were like those I had read about in the graded
readers. They ate hot lunches in the school cafeteria, had book
bags, pencil and crayon boxes, overshoes, raincoats, and little
umbrellas. Because they had all these things, I imagined that they
lived in the water-color world of the graded readers. The fathers
of these story children had dark wavy hair and wore suits. The
pretty blond mothers smiled and baked cookies. The boys flew
kites. The girls rolled hoops along the sidewalk. Every little girl
had a cat named Fluff; her brother had a dog named Muff. At
Thanksgiving the whole family went to the farm, where grandmother lived and baked pies. And if the children were ever ill,
they stayed home and watched birds eat suet on the window
sill, while the children themselves ate junket—whatever that was.

[3] *Mountain Life & Work*, November, 1970.

Of course no one living on Newfound Creek fitted into this world. We were queer: my father in his overalls and denim jacket; my mother, who wore resin-colored combs in her straight black hair; my little brother Eugene, with his large brown eyes, skinny arms and long face like a colt's. We lived at the end of a gravel road, far back where the creek was so small you stopped building bridges and just drove through it. There were few cars, anyway. The mailman came to the row of boxes at the turning place, and my father had a pick-up truck, but in the summer weeds grew out of the gravel in the center of the road, there were so few cars. On Thanksgiving Day my father and grandfather slaughtered hogs, if it was cold enough, or else they went pheasant hunting.

One of the best taught lessons in the schools of Appalachia is apt to be that Appalachians are imperfect versions of another kind of American; that to be different is to be diminished. So a greater emphasis on regional materials, and especially on regional art of all kinds, can validate the Appalachian child's experience by linking it to other lives, past and present. And it is this felt linkage that constitutes true culture, rather than the artificially applied polish or finish. A child is not a piece of dull furniture.

Increased use of regional materials in Appalachia is financially feasible. Literature, art and music in simple and popular forms can be presented without great strain on the resources of school systems. There is already available an abundance of mostly unutilized materials, including several magazines and periodicals that are excellent sources of ideas and materials for Appalachian teachers. The Council of Southern Mountains has an excellent list of books, magazines and records. (I wonder how many of the materials on that one list are available in abundance and easily accessible to teachers and students in Appalachian schools.)

In some instances, Appalachian materials are already being put to good use in the region. Elliot Wigginton at Rabun Gap, Georgia (the success of the Foxfire books is generally known) has been conspicuously effective in putting regional materials to use in the classroom and in showing students that all culture doesn't have to be imported, since they are living in one.

More needs to be done, however. First of all, we must communicate to teachers in the region the availability of materials and the advantages to be derived from putting these materials to use in the classroom. We need to conduct workshops and to disseminate the experience of teachers who have used regional materials successfully. We need to expand publishing facilities in Appalachia. We need to promote art and craft fairs, workshops and art festivals in the schools, by and for the students.

Many state colleges and universities in Appalachia are now being thought of and referred to as regional institutions. Progress is being made toward deepening the meaning of the term "regional university." These institutions need to be considered regional not only in the sense that they serve predominantly a particular region, but also in the sense that they play a role in promoting and preserving their region's sense of itself, of its traditions and cultural heritage. The activities of regional universities and of elementary and secondary schools that surround them need also to be more closely articulated.

If teachers can introduce materials into their classrooms that enable students to bring their own interests and experiences to bear in the learning process, then students can be reached where they are strongest, not where they are weakest. But how, precisely, should regional materials be introduced?

The development of Appalachian Studies programs appears to be one promising way. Such a program is preferable to the alternative of enriching or supplementing already existing classes, an approach that only reinforces the "fatal disconnection of subjects" and saps the vitality of instruction. Appalachian Studies programs allow the study of Appalachian life in all its manifestations, as a single entity, instead of breaking it down into distinct subjects or collections of disjointed scraps. Such programs can be implemented through Appalachian Studies curricula and through materials and resource lists.

An anthology or casebook of Appalachian documents can also be useful, and has the advantage of being adaptable to many different situations. Such a book ought to consist of contributions by historians, folklorists, linguists, sociologists, educators, poets, musicians, artists and craftsmen.

There are many different ways of introducing regional materials into Appalachia's classrooms. The particular strategy may not be important, ultimately. What matters is that these regional materials can be a mirror for Appalachia and Appalachia's children. (1974)

EARL F. SCHROCK, JR.

Earl F. Schrock, Jr., is a native Arkansan. In 1966 he earned the A.B. degree at Arkansas Polytechnic College, Russellville and in 1968 the M. A. degree at the University of Arkansas, Fayetteville where he was awarded with membership into Phi Beta Kappa, and where he is working toward the Ph.D. in English. A student of the English language and linguistics, and a former member of the English Department at East Tennessee State University, he has conducted extensive studies of the dialect of the Southern Appalachians. Professor Schrock's article is included because it transcends the study of dialect in Anne W. Armstrong's *This Day and Time*, being a systematic examination of Southern Appalachian language based in large part on actual field research.

An Examination of the Dialect in *This Day and Time*

This Day and Time,[1] a regional novel by Anne W. Armstrong, is set in the Big Creek section of Sullivan County, Tennessee, in the 1920's. A realistic novel portraying the struggle

[1] *This Day and Time* was originally published in 1930 and reprinted in 1970 by the Research Advisory Council of East Tennessee State University.

460

of Ivy Ingoldsby to endure in the face of numerous hardships, it was called by *Saturday Review* (August 23, 1930)
". . . a fine book, one which deserves to be read now and to
find its place on the shelf . . . beside such other novels as
Edna Ferber's *So Big* and Ellen Glasgow's *Barren Ground.*"
The novel is interesting not only in its presentation of the
life and customs of Upper East Tennessee in the 1920's, but
also in its reflection of the dialect of the area. The purpose of
this paper is to examine the validity of the author's representation of this dialect, specifically that of Sullivan County.
The statements that I have made about the exactness of Mrs.
Armstrong's dialect rendering are based upon a comparison
of the language of her novel and the results of a two-year
survey of Southern Appalachian speech which I have been
engaged in. The survey included making tape-recordings of
controlled and free speech, sending out written question-
naires, examining countless old documents and regional
novels, and a great deal of just plain listening. Since Mrs.
Armstrong's novel deals with uneducated speakers, the speech
described in this paper is, unless otherwise indicated, the
speech of the uneducated mountaineer.

One problem which presents itself in a study of this kind
is the length of time which has elapsed between the writing
of the novel and the beginning of my dialect survey. Language constantly changes and perhaps some of the forms
which the author records are no longer in existence. However,
vocabulary, rather than morphological patterns, idiomatic
expressions, or syntax, is the part of language which undergoes the most rapid change. The few items used by Mrs.
Armstrong which have not been recorded in the survey have
been accounted for in earlier writings on the dialect of East
Tennessee.

In her novel, Mrs. Armstrong has carefully captured some
of the flavor of the Southern Appalachian dialect in the
vocabulary that she uses in her dialogue. Sprinkled throughout the book, we find the terms *bait* (a large amount, "a bait

of 'em"), *balance* (remainder), *burying-ground, chimney shelf* (mantel), and *countenance* (composure). The archaic form *blackguard* (to abuse) appears along with the strange verb *hone* (to long, "Jim hones to see the mountains agin").[2] We find terms for wedding celebrations—*infare, shivaree* and *serenade. Grampus* is defined in *Webster's Seventh New Collegiate Dictionary* as a small cetacean such as the black-fish or killer whale. However, in the Appalachians a grampus is hardly a killer whale, but a particular type of fish bait (hellgrammite) found under rocks in streams and marshy places. *Whistle pig* is almost invariably the name the moun-taineers use for ground hog. The author is also accurate in calling a good penman *a good scribe* and steps, *a tread.*

Fistey (i.e., feisty) is used in the novel in its limited defini-tion meaning flirtatious or provocative. The noun (feist) from which the adjective comes originally meant breaking wind. Vance Randolph recorded the following definition of *feisty* in the Ozarks: "a feisty woman may not be fast, but she's a little too frisky to be nice."[3]

The phonetic spelling used in the book is, on the whole, fairly accurate in reflecting the pronunciations of the East Tennessee characters. We find the common excrescent "t" in words ending with the "s" sound (*acrost, chancet, clost, oncet,* and *twicet*) and the addition of "st" to common struc-ture words (*alongst, amongst,* and *whilst*). On the other hand, the lack of logic in language is shown by the form *agin* (against), which has dropped the final "st." The "s" ending on words that do not have it in Standard English (*somewheres, anywheres, face powders,* and *hairs* as in "bobbed her hairs") is prevalent among uneducated speak-

---

[2] In "Language of the Southern Highlanders," *PMLA*, Dec. 1931, p. 1307, Josiah Combs records *hone* in the sentence "Brice's jest a-honin (honeying?) to go." The questionable definition that he gives makes no sense. The word derives from Middle French *hoigner* and means to long.

[3] Vance Randolph and George P. Wilson, *Down in the Holler* (Norman, Oklahoma, 1953), p. 107.

ers of this dialect area. Also common are the Southern mountain suffixes "-er" and the alternate "y" for words ending
in schwa or "o" (*yaller, tater,* and *baccer: Californy, chiny,
extry, victroly, West Virginy,* and *idee* which is accompanied
by a stress change). Mrs. Armstrong also lists *widdy* and
grass-widdy man (divorced man). I have never recorded this
pronunciation, although the alternate *widder* is very common in this area.

One of the most striking, and immediately obvious, differences between the dialect of the Southern Appalachians and
some other dialect area is the pronunciation of the vowels.
Once again, Mrs. Armstrong's phonetic spelling stands witness to her sensitive ear. The spellings *fur* (far), *cheer*
(chair), *bedstid, afeared* (showing not only a vowel difference, but the reversal of the medial vowel and consonant),
pineys (peonies), *quair* (queer), *peert* (pert), *oneasy, deef,
crap* (crop) and *cowcumbers* show some of these vowel differences. The form *parbiled* (parboiled) is only one of a
whole group of words that have the "eye" sound instead of
the expected "oy." Others occurring in this dialect area are
jined (joined), *jinte* (joint), and *pizen* (poison). Most Americans, regardless of dialect areas, pronounce *roil* as *rile,* perhaps because most know this word only as an oral form and
have never seen it (or, at least, have never recognized it) on
the printed page.[4] The form *ketchin'* can be meant only for
the Northern ear because most Southerners, regardless of
educational level, pronounce the word in this way.

The spelling *ca'm* (calm) is a little confusing; the pronunciation that the author intends rhymes with *Sam.* This
form is almost extinct but can still be heard from a few of the
older speakers in this area. *Vomicked* is still fairly common.
Instead of the "t" expected in Standard English, we find a

---

[4] Alexander Pope used this pronunciation, which came about as a British
development of a French diphthong, in "An Essay On Criticism" (part I,
187–188): "In praise so just let every voice be joined,/ And fill the general
chorus of mankind."

"k," which reduces the word to two syllables instead of three. The spelling *mush-rats* reflects the "sh" variant of "sk" that is also found in *mushmellon* (muskmelon). *Flail* in the Southern mountain region almost invariably becomes *frail* as the author has recorded it.

The forms *ary* and *nary*, which have been accounted for historically as shortenings of *ever a* and *never a*, are still heard often from older speakers. The spelling *atter* (after), the medial consonant sound being the same as in *butter*, reflects a pronunciation that can be heard from old and young alike. Those people who consciously try, as a result of exposure to education and its usually narrow-minded approach to language, to rid their vocabularies of "vulgar" pronunciations usually find *atter* among the last to go, simply because emphasis is put on words that carry greater semantic significance rather than structure words.

The omission of "th-" in the spelling *'an* for than indicates either a glottal catch (when *'an* follows a word ending in a vowel) or elision (when *'an* follows a word ending in a consonant). Examples are "no more to me *'an* the dirt under my feet" and "A sight easier *'an* loggin'."

Whurr (for whether), which I have recorded on numerous occasions, differs from the standard form in the omission of the "th" sound, the vowel value, and the reduction of the word to one syllable.

Mrs. Armstrong falls back on the practice of other dialect writers for the form *allays* (always), a pronunciation which I have never heard. The form that is heard in this area could be represented by the spelling *allus*. Likewise, the spelling *sence* for since is neither necessary nor useful.

The use of *call* as a noun meaning reason seems limited mostly to older speakers, but is still very common. It occurs in the novel in "He hain't no call to brag!"

The pronunciation of *have* as *'a* (schwa) is found throughout all dialect areas of English and, as a matter of fact, has been around for centuries.[5] The use of *a-* before a present participle, however, is an entirely different thing (*a-carin'*, *a-comin'*, *a-fixin'*, and *a-talkin'*). This construction, very common in the South, is historically derived from the contraction of the Old English prefix *on-* preceding infinitives, e.g., *onhuntan* (a-hunting).[6]

The verb and the adjective seem to be the parts of speech that, more than any other, set off the dialect of the Southern Appalachians from other dialect regions. Some of the verbs used in the novel were representative of this dialect area when Mrs. Armstrong was writing, but are now dying out, probably because of the influence of radio and television and exposure to speakers from other dialect areas. For example, *beholden, fetch, mind* (remember, "I mind one winter"), *ride* (analogous to the deep Southern *carry* meaning take, "You-all kin jest ride me back to my place"), *pack* (take, "pack her along"). *Use*, a transitive verb, is found functioning intransitively in the novel: "There's a gang o' pa'tridges uses in our garden." I have never heard the word *youth* used as a verb, but Mrs. Armstrong records "the moon 'ull youth today" meaning that the new moon will appear today. The very descriptive verb *to big* ("he's bigged Pernie"), meaning to make pregnant, is not nearly so prevalent as it once was. One of the paradoxes of mountain speech is that expressions like the very earthy *to big* and the almost coy euphemism *in a family way* often roll off the same tongue.

The forms *reckon, suspicion* (suspect), *study* (think—"studied on hit"), and *swan* (a form of swear) are common throughout the South. *Name*, meaning to mention, can still be heard occasionally, and *a-lookin' for* (expecting) is of frequent occurrence.

[5] Margaret Paston in a letter to her husband, John, in 1443 wrote "I xulde a seyne yow er dys tyme" (I would like to have seen you before this time).

[6] The Second Quarto (1604) of *Hamlet* (III, iii, 73) reads "Now might I do it pat, now 'a is *a-praying*."

Mountaineers often apply animal terminology (especially sexual) to humans. For example, *ruttin'*, meaning mating, in "Ruttin'-time is over, Buck, fer varmints—but, by God, not fer you-all." The term *down*, meaning brought to bed in childbirth, in "I lowed you 'ud be down afore this," is used much as a farmer would use "The cow is down" (calving). White prejudice felt even by the poorest class comes through in the verb *niggerin'* (serving as domestic help, thus giving up part of one's independence). *Nasty*, an adjective in Standard English, is found as a verb in the mountain dialect: "don't you boys nasty your clothes." And *weather*, a noun, becomes a verb meaning to storm in "apt as not hit 'ull weather afore night." I have heard this form on numerous occasions on the local radio station.

Many verbs that are regular in other dialect areas are irregular in the Appalachian region, at least in the speech of the uneducated. They appear in abundance in the novel. *Writ* is the past tense of *write*: *wrote* is usually used as the past participle. *Went* is the past participle of *go*: "things 'twixt me an' her has went too fur. . . ." In "I taken the headache awhile back" (note also the use of the definite article in *the headache*), *taken* is used as the past tense. The paradigm of *take* is usually *take, taken, have took* in this area. Likewise in the verb *to see*, the past tense and past participle forms switch places: *see, seen (seed), have saw*.

Other examples in the novel of Standard regular verbs that appear as irregular forms in mountain dialect are *drug* (past tense of *drag*), *driv* (past and past participle of *drive*), *brung* (past and past participle of *bring*, which is often pronounced *brang*), *fit* (past tense of *fight*), *het* (past tense of *heat*), *growed* (past and past participle of *grow*), and *holp* (past tense of *help*). The form *et* (past tense of *eat*), although frowned upon by "cultured" Americans, reflects the accepted pronunciation in British English. *Heerd* and *heern* are used indiscriminately for the past tense and past participle forms of *hear*. Using this verb, the author records the interesting phrase, "Hain't you heerd no tell," a common variant of "I haven't heard tell of it."

Along with these irregular forms, we find a group of regular verbs with vowels that differ from the standard forms. *Wropped* appears for *wrapped, tech* for *touch,* and *skeert* and *skairt* for *scared.*

Wisht in "I wisht he hadn't 'a saw fit," at first glance, appears to be a past tense verb where a present tense is expected, but upon close examination we find that it is an assimilated form of *wish that.* It occurs only before a relative clause in which the relative has been omitted. I have recorded the forms *wisht* and *guessed* in this type of construction from the very well-educated as well as from the uneducated. The author records "retch me that spoon o' yourn." Here we find not only a peculiar pronunciation, but the verb is used imperatively, meaning *pass.* The verb *to smart* (to hurt) is ordinarily intransitive, but in the novel we find it used transitively in "hit hain't a-goin to smart ye more 'an a minute."

The adjective *rotten* frequently replaces the infinitive *rot* in the mountain dialect, resulting in the forms *rotten* (present) and *rottening* (present participle). "They 'ull rotten afore they ripens," and "I'ud sooner be a-rottenin' in the ground. . . ."

Right smart, an all-purpose modifier meaning a large amount, is used both as adjective and adverb phrase. For example, "a right smart time" and "You've growed a right smart." *A right smart piece* means a long way. The adverb *ever* occurs in positions where it would not occur in Standard English: "peertest old man . . . ever I seen," and "did ever ye see sech a sight o' rain?"

The area in which I find Mrs. Armstrong's rendering of the dialect poorest is in her handling of the verb *to be.* It seems that she indiscriminately chose to use the plural verb form with a singular noun and vice versa. It is true that this reversal is sometimes an accurate picture of this dialect, but it is by no means as regular as the author suggests in her dialogue. Josiah Combs says of the mountaineer's use of the verb, "The most common irregularity is perhaps the use of singular forms for plural forms. Use of plural for singular forms is not common."[7] However, I have a copy of a diary kept by an uneducated man in North Carolina from 1845 until his death in 1920 in which he consistently wrote the form *war* (were) with singular nouns and pronouns.

A verb phrase recorded often in the book is *have* (*has, had*) *obliged* instead of the expected *is* (*was, were*) *obliged*: ". . . a man has obliged to go away" and "I had obliged to come back."

One type of verb phrase one would expect to appear many times in the novel appeared infrequently. The example in the novel is *gone an' painted*: "His hairs is gray . . . but he's gone an' painted 'em." Other examples of this type of verb that I have recorded are *took and swept* (he took and swept the floor), *went and done* (he went and done it), and the similar *up and left* (he up and left). These verbs are peculiar in that they appear to be compound, but upon examining them semantically, one finds that the meaning is not that of a compound verb, each element being equal. On the contrary, the first part of the phrase (*went and, took and, up and*) seems to be a type of auxiliary verb. That is, the meaning of "he went and done it" is much closer to the emphatic "he did do it" than to "he went and he did it."

The mountaineer's love of the negative is matched only by his love of God. Typical of the uneducated of the area are the sentences, "I did*n't* aim to put up *no* bedstid tonight, *nohow*" and "Hai*n't no* use lightin' *no* lamp."

The adjective *common* is used in the novel with two meanings. It has the meaning of usual in "well as common" and the meaning of ordinary or not different in "she were nice an' common." *Sidlin'* is used to mean sloping: "Hit hain't much level, hit's right sidlin'." Synonyms that I have collected of

---

[7] Combs, p. 1318.

this word are *sigodlin, sigoglin, antigodlin* and *antisigodlin.*
Strange means overly nice, not frank: "A woman ortern't to
be strange afore her own daughters." *Terrible* is used as an
intensifier, as *terribly* is in Standard English, much to the
chagrin of many an English teacher: "I 'ull miss ye terrible."

The mountaineer is free with the comparative and superlative suffixes and often attaches them to almost any part of
speech. Examples from the novel are *free-hearteder,*
workin'est, tender-heartedest, precuriousent (?), *independ-*
entest-soundin', curiousest, beautifulest, and *beatin'est.*
Mrs. Armstrong does not overstate the use of the superlative
at all; a short time ago, I heard and recorded a word having
the *-est* suffix applied twice along with the use of *most* in the
statement, "he was the *most moaningestfullest* hound I ever
did see." The intensifier *a heap* is frequently used for much
or a great deal: "I'd a heap ruther . . .," and "Jim had a heap
o' manners."

The usual redundancy is found in the use of the personal
pronouns in examples such as "Lindsey, she. . . ." *Hisself, ye*
(especially in easily assimilated phrases like "did ye?"), and
you-uns are also common forms. The validity of the construction "who's him," however, is questionable. *Ourn* and *yourn*
are very common possessives in the predicative position, with
etymologies that go back to the Middle English period.

A few of the utterances that Mrs. Armstrong's characters
make tumble clumsily off the tongue as a result of her attempt
to present striking contrasts between the dialect she is recording and the Standard English utterance, instead of faithfully
rendering what she has actually heard. The one pronoun
that the author cannot handle well is the third person neuter
singular *hit.* The uneducated speaker, as well as a few of
the educated ones, of the mountain dialect does not use *hit*
consistently, but alternates between *hit* and *it.* He uses the
aspirated form *hit* in a stressed position in a sentence and *it*
in an unstressed position. *Hit* is usually the form used at the
beginning of a sentence. If *hit* is used within a sentence, it

will be preceded by a juncture (a strong pause), simply because the explosion of the "h" is so powerful it automatically makes the syllable in which it occurs a stressed one. The statements "No, hit's too soon," "Hit's a sight on earth," and "an' hit free of mortgage" are examples of good dialect rendering. But "Don't hit look natural" and "Glad I've got hit to give ye" are fakes, and "right at hit" is almost impossible to say. The same principle governs the use of *ain't* and *hain't*. In "ef hit hain't Mag an' Gid," Mrs. Armstrong is writing by formula and not by ear, a temptation which many dialect writers succumb to.

Molasses is considered plural by many speakers of the mountain dialect and serves as an antecedent for the plural pronoun, *they*: "fresh new molasses, an' them so good!" In the phrase "them molasses," we can make the usual observance of the noun's being considered plural, but more important is the use of the third person plural *personal* pronoun as a modifier instead of the singular *demonstrative* that we expect (i.e., that molasses). *Them* is almost always the form used in the plural demonstrative position in the sentence. Other singular nouns that are considered plural which I have collected are *cheese* (*them cheese*) and *lettuce* (*them lettuce*).

The strangest pronoun usage that the author records is *where* as a relative in the *which* or *who* position. Examples are ". . . my boys where's dead," "that old water where comes out of a fasset," and "from nobody where's treated me like Jim done." My first reaction, upon finding this form in the book, was one of amazement and incredulity. However, since that time, I have listened more carefully and have recorded the form on numerous occasions. Almost as interesting is the omission of the relative pronoun where it ordinarily would not be omitted: "She 'lows she won't have her no man cain't read."

The Appalachian area is rich in phrases of exclamation, many of which have been carried to the Ozarks and throughout the South. "The Lord help my time," "well, I do know," and " 'pon my honor" are very common. "This day an' time," the phrase which furnishes the title of the book, is used both as a statement of wonder and of disgust with things in the modern world. And "Law," alone and in phrases such as "Law, I reckon" and "Laws a mercy," is the mountaineer's most indispensable interjection.

Proverbs such as "trouble don't never come single" are common in mountain speech, as are roundabout ways of saying things: "He 'ud skin a flea fer hits hide an' tallow" meaning "he is miserly." I have heard this saying lengthened to "he would skin a flea for its hide and tallow and ruin a butcher-knife worth a dollar."

"Have your health" is a frequently heard phrase meaning healthy, as is "down in the bed" for bedfast and "parched for a drink" for thirsty. *Misery* is often used for pain or suffering: "Here, Leoly, hit 'ull draw the misery." Many older speakers of this area still use *miserying* or *punishing* for suffering; for example, "he is just a-layin' there miseryin'."

The phrase "a Wednesday" with the superfluous *a*, as in "I reckon you'll see me a Wednesday" is used by both educated and uneducated speakers. This *a* has the same etymology as the *a* in *a-hunting*. "Was a week" is a phrase used to mean a week ago: "Tuesday was a week." There is a very complicated method of expressing time in the mountain dialect. "Friday, was a week" and "Friday, a week ago" mean Friday in the week past, but "Friday week" means Friday in the week to come.

"Hide or hair," meaning "absolutely nothing," could have been more accurately recorded as "hide nor hair." The phrases "in any shape, form, or fashion" and "way, shape or fashion" are often habitually added to the ends of sentences in which they add no meaning.

The very confusing sentence, "I hain't never seed nothin' to town, me," at first glance, would make any grammarian tear his hair, but the sentence yields, besides three negatives, an interesting idiom *see to*, as in "I don't see anything to that" meaning I see nothing of importance in that.

Where the standard speaker would use *by*, Mrs. Armstrong records *aginst* (against) in the sentence "Have me a fire in the cook-stove aginst the time I git there." I have recorded this word in the form *'gin*, which shows both the dropping of the initial schwa and the final "-st," in the following sentences: "*'gin* I get home, my bread will be burned," and "*'gin* you go around the country looking for cows, they really cost you something."

"To get shed of" means to get rid of and occurs frequently in this dialect area. Frequently, the word *shed* is pronounced *shet*. "Go to" meaning intend to in the sentence "he didn't go to kill Godfrey" and "like to" meaning almost in "I like to forgot" are common. "Made theirselves" meaning produce is a striking idiom often heard in sentences like Mrs. Armstrong's "my taters has made theirselves good."

The old form *lief*, meaning prefer, crops up periodically in mountain speech, usually in the form *leave* with the final consonant voiced. It always occurs in the *as . . . as* construction: "I 'ud as leave to shoot the sorry old critter as no." The comparative for *liefer*, in the form *leaver*, is frequently used also in sentences like "I'd leaver to as not."

The phrases "what you might say" and "what's to say," although very similar, have completely different functions. The former is used to mean almost: "an' her naked, what you might say"; and the latter is used as an intensifier meaning something like really: "I cain't eat, what's to say eat." The phrase "to do no good" means well: "I cain't sew with mine to do no good."

"Laid off," to the working man, means to be temporarily suspended from his job. In the mountain dialect, however, it means planned to or intended to: "I've been a-layin' off . . . to get Doke to tie a broom for me" and "I've laid off to ketch me a eel."

This paper barely scratches the surface in the analysis of

the dialect found in the novel, but the task of examining all of it would be a monumental one. At times, we find that Mrs. Armstrong becomes so involved in accurately representing Appalachian speech that she sacrifices effectiveness to precision. The quantity of the dialect in the novel sometimes overshadows the quality, a mistake which many dialect writers make, notably the local color school led by Mary Noailles Murfree. There are few writers who, like William Faulkner in his presentation of the Mississippi dialect and Flannery O'Connor in the use of Georgia dialect, can sense the right proportion of dialect to include in their works. We may often wish, in reading *This Day and Time*, that Mrs. Armstrong had chosen to strike out a few of the more repetitious passages which consist mainly of stock phrases. However, it is true that such exchanges of "empty" conversation are commonplace in real life; and, in reproducing them in the quantity in which they actually occur, the author has given us a real slice of life. The novel, then, is like a photograph rather than like a painting, which depends upon distortion. Mrs. Armstrong's use of dialect helps to create her local color setting and to keep it always present in our minds. She is consistent in keeping the conversation of her mountain characters within the range of their dialect and experience. And, if we feel that she has at times overburdened us with the dialect of East Tennessee, we can still applaud her for what is, for the most part, a faithful reproduction of it. (1971)

JAMES ROBERT REESE

Assistant Professor of English at East Tennessee State University, James Robert Reese was born in St. Louis, Missouri, and received his B.A. in English from the University of Missouri, Columbia, in 1961. He attended the University of Guadalajara, Mexico, and later received an M.A. in Spanish and completed the course work for a Ph.D. in English at the University of Illinois, Urbana. He is presently writing his dissertation on dialectology at the University of Tennessee under the direction of Harold Orton, director of the Survey of English Dialects which was conducted at Leeds, England, and Nathalia Wright, Melville scholar and contributor to the study of English dialects. Professor Reese is doing a detailed investigation of the dialects of East Tennessee. His article not only summarizes a number of theories about the language of the Southern mountaineer but presents a new view as well.

The Myth of the Southern Appalachian Dialect as a Mirror of the Mountaineer

Linguists and literary scholars are as distinct as dolphins and whales. As such they seldom disagree on issues fundamental to their respective disciplines. Although they—recog-

474

nizing perhaps a certain natural kinship—swim in the same ocean of words, they are not acutely interested in or aware of the other's habits and skills; and unless they are ill-natured or hungry they rarely attack each other. Academic lore records that when the minotaur and unicorn yet wandered through the ivy covered labyrinths of research there existed a creature who was half dolphin, half whale: the philologist. However, the academic environment altered, causing the true American philologist (e.g., George Hempl, E. S. Sheldon) to become extinct and the great distance now separating the linguist and the literary scholar makes it unlikely that he will be bred anew.

The linguist is primarily a scientist. He gathers language information, analyzes it according to a linguistic theory, reaches generalizations and then re-examines his conclusions in light of more recently gathered data. He is objective; his concern is with language as it is spoken, regardless of whether it be aesthetically pleasing or socially acceptable. His goal is to discover the nature of a natural phenomenon, not to pass social or artistic judgment. After he has discovered and described the characteristics of a language he is unconcerned with such philosophical questions as to how they may reflect the nature of man or the universe. Conversely, literary scholars constantly seek that which linguists consider most nebulous—true meaning. Eternally diving in search of the deepest significance, the literary scholar feeds off the bottom of the ocean. He views the structure of a work of art as more important than that of the language which conveys it. Ultimately, the literati explore language to discover the nature of the characters who use it; the linguists use living informants to discover the nature of the language itself. In the modern age one of the few areas where these two distinct creatures yet feed together is the rather small but interesting discipline of dialectology.

The American dialectologist has traditionally been of

mixed scholarly parentage and often has suffered the disdain that comes with being an academic woodscolt. Partially because of this, in addition to dialectologists such as Hans Kurath, Harold B. Allen, and Raven I. McDavid, Jr., it has drawn to it not only whales, e.g., H. L. Mencken, who too often knew little about linguistics, and dolphins, e.g., George Knapp, who too often knew little about American dialects, but various other aquatic life such as creative writers, psychologists and educationalists who having fed upon its words, produced strange off-spring, especially about the language of the Southern Mountains. An attempt to classify some of these different types of academic research and to understand the theoretical perspectives which shaped them has been undertaken by JR,[1] but in such a brief essay as this there is space to address only two questions. First, is there a Southern Mountaineer dialect? Second, in his attempt at exploring the nature, mind and culture of the Southern Mountaineer, what is a linguistically reasonable manner for the literary scholar to approach the supposed mountain speech, whether it be recorded in word-lists, articles or fiction.[2]

Before one can discuss how the mountaineer's language reflects his character, which is assumed to be the product of a particular cultural heritage, one must answer two fundamental questions. In the world of the flesh, does such a creature exist, and if he lives, does he speak, as Cratis Williams

---

[1] See the University of Tennessee Ph.D. dissertation in English by the author, under the direction of Harold Orton and Nathalia Wright, which surveys American dialectology from 1889 to 1973, examines its philosophical tenets and reports the findings of a phonological survey of four East Tennessee counties.

[2] The periodicals which contain the most significant dialectal material of the Southern Appalachian area are *Dialect Notes, Publications of the American Dialect Society, American Speech,* and *Mountain Life and Work.* Numerous authors have used the supposed mountain dialect in their dialogue. A few of the most interesting are Anne Armstrong, Wilma Dykeman, Joel Chandler Harris, Mary Noailles Murfree, James Still, and Jesse Stuart.

and others seem to suggest,[3] one Southern Appalachian dialect? One notes that often the answer to these questions are peculiarly circular, i.e., the Southern Mountaineer can be recognized by his mountain dialect, the mountain dialect being that which the mountaineer speaks.

Although the language of the area has been referred to as Elizabethan English, Early English and American Anglo-Saxon, very little scientific investigation of it has been completed and published.[4] As a result, there are probably more misconceptions about the speech of this area than that of any other geographical region of the United States. Significantly, literary and pseudo-sociological conceptions of the hill-billy, the mountaineer or the Southern Highlander—depending on one's degree of prejudice or Jeffersonian romanticism—were current long before there was any meaningful linguistic evidence to support the belief that he might even possibly speak one distinct dialect. It is also important to realize that early proponents of the theory of a distinct mountain dialect were by training usually neither philologists nor dialectologists. In

[3] Cratis Williams, "The 'R' in Mountain Speech," *ML&W* (Spring, 1961), pp. 5–8; Lester V. Berrey, "Southern Mountain Dialect," *AS*, 15 (1940), pp. 45–54; Charles Carpenter, "Variations in the Southern Mountain Dialect," *AS*, 8 (1933), pp. 22–25.

[4] There are numerous ways to collect dialectal material scientifically, one of which is explained in Hans Kurath's *Handbook of the Linguistic Geography of New England* (Providence: Brown University, 1939). The three principal qualifications are: 1) the selection of compatible informants, 2) the eliciting of comparable dialectal information by use of a worksheet or questionnaire and 3) a systematic linguistical analysis of the information. Even the investigations of the Linguistic Atlas of the United States have not been completed or published for the mountainous regions of such states as Tennessee, Georgia, Alabama, Arkansas, Missouri, Kentucky and Illinois. The material for North Carolina and West Virginia is inconclusive. Joseph S. Hall's *The Phonetics of Great Smoky Mountain Speech* (New York: King's Crown Press, 1942) is an interesting work, but needs to be read cautiously in light of more recent dialectal theories. Tracey R. Miller's University of Tennessee Ph.D. dissertation "An Investigation of the Regional English of Unicoi County, Tennessee" (Knoxville, 1973) is scientifically executed but restricted to one Tennessee county.

reading the works of J. W. Carr, Josiah H. Combs, D. S. Crumb, L. R. Dingus, Horace Kephart, William O. Rice, Jay L. B. Taylor and later Vance Randolph, Cratis Williams and Joseph S. Hall,[5] it is quite evident that literary and quasi-sociological beliefs influenced their collection of dialectal material. One can be certain that a linguist, in the modern sense of the word, never wrote such statements as the following:

Brevity is the soul of the highlander's language. He prefers it to clearness and to grammatical accuracy.[6]

The truth is that sex is very rarely mentioned save in ribaldry, and is therefore excluded from all polite conversation between men and women. Moreover, this taboo is extended to include a great many words which have no real connection with sex and which are used quite freely in more enlightened sections of the United States. . . . Many mountain women never use the word 'stone'—the commoner term is rock, anyway. . . . So much for prudery in the . . . dialect. Perhaps a century or so of isolation is responsible for an abnormal development of this sort of thing, or it may be that the mountain people have simply retained a pecksniffian attitude once common to the whole country.[7]

As in the speech of primitive peoples generally, personification is inverted easily into powerful "beastification" in portraying alike man's most admirable traits of character and his bestiality.[8]

[5] See for example J. W. Carr, "A List of Words from Northwestern Arkansas," *DN*, 3 (1905–12), pp. 68–103, 124–65, 205–38; Josiah H. Combs, "Language of the Southern Highlanders," *PMLA*, 46 (1931), pp. 1302–22 and "Old, Early and Elizabethan English in the Southern Mountains," *DN*, 4 (1913–17), pp. 283–97; D. S. Crumb, "The Dialect of Southeastern Missouri," *DN*, 2 (1900–04), pp. 304–37; L. R. Dingus, "A Word-List from Virginia," *DN*, 4 (1913–17), pp. 177–93; Horace Kephart, "A Word-List from the North Carolina Mountains," *DN*, 4 (1913–17), pp. 407–19.

[6] Combs, "Language of the Southern Highlanders," p. 1302.

[7] Vance Randolph, "Verbal Modesty in the Ozarks," *DN*, 6 (1928–39), pp. 57–64.

[8] Cratis Williams, "Metaphor in Mountain Speech," *ML&W* (Winter, 1962), p. 9.

Early American philologists and leaders of the American Dialect Society, such as George Hempl, although believing that dialectal variation existed in the Southern mountains, did not accept the hypothesis that the mountainous area shared a common dialect.[9] In fact, they saw little in the reports of the speech of this area to justify its separation from Southern dialectal speech in general. Even after the earlier division of American speech (i.e., Northern, Southern and the mythical General American) was proven fallacious and a Midland speech area was found to exist, there seemed to be little reliable evidence to support the belief that the Appalachian mountains, or the Southern Appalachian in particular, was a distinct speech area.[10] Early American philologists, whose training and thought were closely related to European theoretical models of research,[11] believed that before accepting the existence of a geographical dialect[12] it must be established that the region shares a unified phonological system in addition to isolated lexical and set-phonological dialectal variants (i.e., words and their pronunciations in isolation). However, in the dialectal information supplied by Combs, Dingus, Carr and others such a unified system was not shown to exist. In fact, no qualified phonetician has ever published a complete, detailed, systematic, and unbiased phonological investigation of the area.

Furthermore, much of dialectal information presented to support the hypothesis of a distinct mountaineer dialect was neither scientifically nor consistently collected. Firstly, often

[9] George Hempl, "Grease and Greasy," *DN*, 1 (1890–96), pp. 438–44.

[10] Hempl, p. 438; even linguistic geographers divide the area into several sections. After reading Raven I. McDavid, Jr.'s "The Dialects of American English," in Nelson Francis, *The Structure of American English* (New York, 1958), 480–543, one notes that "Midland" refers not to a dialect but a dialect area.

[11] E. Bagby Atwood, "The Methods of American Dialectology," in H. B. Allen, ed., *Readings in American Dialectology* (Appleton: New York, 1971), p. 7.

[12] E. S. Sheldon, "What is a Dialect?" *DN*, 1 (1890–96), pp. 286–97.

even later collectors gathered information at random, believing that the items were necessarily compatible, i.e., from the same dialect, if they were collected in the same general geographical area and from people who appeared to be culturally similar. They were seemingly unaware that numerous dialects can exist in the same geographical area within the same socio-economic and cultural stratum. Secondly, the information reported was not elicited by means of a standardized instrument, such as the Orton-Wright *Questionnaire*,[13] nor was a large area of the Appalachian Mountains systematically investigated by the same investigators. Thirdly, little if any research on the informant's origin, education, age, occupation, exact place of birth and residence (or even if he was living in the area where he was overheard) was noted. Such information, which cannot be surmised by mere observation, is essential in ascertaining the reliability of an informant and serves as an indispensable indicator of whether or not one is interviewing persons who speak similar but distinct dialects. Fourthly, written sources —sometimes even the dialogue of regional novels—were drawn upon and such information equated with oral research, the latter often being collected under uncontrolled and curious conditions not conducive to accurate phonological transcription. Fifthly, many times one is uncertain if the corpus supplied contains exact quotations from one or several informants, or even if the sentences were not re-created by the author from memory to approximate what might have been said in a given situation.[14]

In addition, because different items were reported or the same item transcribed differently there was often no way to

[13] Harold Orton and Nathalia Wright, *Questionnaire for the Investigation Of American Regional English* (Knoxville: University of Tennessee, 1972).

[14] This is especially true in regards to the quotations used in the word-lists of *Dialect Notes* and the articles of *Mountain Life and Work* which contain extended conversations. The only accurate way to record such long passages would be with the use of a tape-recorder.

verify if what appeared in one area was spoken with the same meaning or pronunciation in another. Too many items of the supposed mountain dialect, such as the pronunciations indicated by the occasional spellings of *gin* (again I get home), *sich, ye, borry, jest, haint, hit, gin'rally, kem* (came), *fer* (far), *larnt, denamite* (dynamite), *rench* (rinse), *cheer* (chair) and hundreds of others, as well as morphological variants such as *housen, beastes, postes, nestes, waspers,* and even such phonological generalizations as the appearance of /t/ in final position in such words as *behind, end* and *shed* not only had been recorded as common in other areas of the country, but were spoken by persons who were neither socially nor culturally related to the mountaineer.[15]

It has long been recognized that in distinguishing dialects broad phonemic and lexical variation, the latter being the most fluid of all linguistic features, are seldom adequate.[16] Instead, the dialectologist needs compatible information consisting of fine segmental and suprasegmental phonetic features, such as the exact composition of vowels, diphthongs, consonants and intonation patterns in set syntactic environments as well as accurately recorded passages of free-speech which are sufficiently long to provide comparable syntactical information. Both in the collection and the presentation of dialectal information of the Southern Mountains it is precisely these kinds of features that have been most ignored. Pronunciation is generally presented, and probably originally noted, in occasional spelling (e.g., *fer* for *for, thar* for *there*), which masks all but the most glaring dialectal variations; and although great energy was expended on noting idioms, figures of speech and proverbs—which by themselves

[15] A comparison of the many word-lists contained in *Dialect Notes* from 1890–1939 confirms this fact.

[16] For a detailed investigation into the question of what constitutes a dialect and a summary of American dialectal theories concerning this question see chapter three of JR's dissertation.

are of little value in distinguishing dialects—little or no attention was given to important syntactical comparisons.

For most collectors of mountain speech the basic criterion for whether or not to note a particular speech form has been whether it varied from what the collector considered to be standard literary English and whether the person who spoke it fit the stereotype of a mountaineer living in the hollows and on the ridges of the area. The belief that such data was compatible was based upon the assumption that it was collected from a single homogeneous cultural and geographical community and that if these elements are present, the informants will speak the same dialect. Neither hypothesis has ever been proven to be true for American dialects. Without compatible data, no valid generalization can be drawn. By observing bits and pieces of speech Combs and others conjured a single dialect out of the parts of many various but similar dialects. Thus it would seem that what they identified as the dialect of the mountaineer is in reality a composite of many dialects, created in much the same way that a writer creates a composite character. Although all the individual features recorded may be spoken in the area, they by themselves in no way support the hypothesis that the Southern Appalachian mountaineer speaks a single dialect or that only one geographical dialect exists in the region.

It is unlikely that a dialectologist would question that today as well as in the past, much of the speech of the Southern Mountains significantly differs from that of other Southern regions; however, the hypothesis that there exists a Southern mountain dialect grows less convincing as more field research is undertaken. Recent research conducted on the dialects of East Tennessee by JR under the direction of Harold Orton and Nathalia Wright, and the independent research of Tracey Miller of Milligan College, as well as that of JR and Earl Schrock of the dialects of North Carolina, Virginia and East Tennessee suggests that several distinct dialects exist, and have existed, in the mountainous area for an extended period of time.[17] A large amount of information has been elicited from informants who by any standard would be classified as "Southern Mountaineers" (i.e., persons of similar socio-economic stratum in the rural, mountainous regions, all over sixty-five years of age with little or no formal education, born of parents native to the region, and who have traveled very few miles from their place of birth) which strongly suggests that what exists at present in the region is an interesting, though in no way unique, stage of linguistic development. The Appalachian region, although not possessing clearly distinguishable dialect areas, has—and in all probability has had for a long time—speakers of very distinct "mountain dialects." Although the speakers of these dialects and therefore the dialects themselves still exist, the small geographical pockets which previously isolated them have all but vanished. The speakers exist dispersed through the total mountainous region. Consequently, it may be appropriate to speak of the language of the Southern Highlander or Mountaineer—assuming that he is a cultural rather than a mythical reality—or even to speak of the dialectal elements in the speech of the area, but to talk of a Southern Appalachian dialect or the dialect of the Mountaineer is to create a generalization where none exists.

If the Southern Mountaineer does not share a common dialect, it therefore seems illogical to assume that dialectal information can be used to gain insights into his general nature. One wonders if the concept of an Appalachian dialect itself was not an unconscious desire on the part of those who seeing value in a culture that was different from what America was becoming, attempted to provide its language with historical linguistic respectability in an age when the only acceptable usage was that of the college educated. It was perhaps an

[17] JR and Earl Schrock conducted a two-year investigation (East Tennessee and Western North Carolina Dialect Study) into the speech of several counties of East Tennessee and western North Carolina. The results of this investigation have been tabulated but remain unpublished.

intuitive awareness of this that allowed such earlier scholars as Combs to attempt to distinguish between the language and the dialect of the mountaineer. Certainly, as the following quotation illustrates, Combs was aware that there was variation in the speech of his highlanders.

The Elizabethan English of these highlanders varies but little. In other respects their language varies greatly, most noticeably in the substitution of one vowel for another. This divergence in the use of the vowel does not confine itself necessarily to the different States. For example, the hillsman of the Cumberlands in Kentucky says *whut* and *gut*, while the pronunciation further west in the same State, but still in the hills, is *what* and *got*. . . . But in eastern Tennessee one hears *eent* (end), while the usual pronunciation is *eend*.[18]

Language must reveal some aspects of the people who use it; thus to say that the language or the dialects of the Appalachian mountains do not reflect the region's culture would be nonsense. If historical linguists can surmise aspects of the nature, origin and culture of the time-shrouded Indo-European, some meaningful cultural information must be obtainable from the speech of the mountaineer. However, to obtain it one must first determine which linguistic features are or are not culturally reflective. In determining this, certain principles and attitudes of modern linguistics must be understood. It must be remembered that the term *dialect* is a technical one, comparable in literary scholarship to such a term as *genre*, and therefore it is the linguist and dialectologist not the literati that must determine what constitutes a dialect and how one is distinguished.

Language and *dialect* are mutually dependent linguistic concepts referring to different levels of linguistic generalization. *Language* refers to a system of verbal habits employed

[18] Combs, "Old, Early, and Elizabethan English in the Southern Mountains," p. 283.

by a group of people to communicate. A language, being the total of all the rules and features of its speakers, contains many more rules and features than are possessed by any one speaker, any one dialect. *Dialect* is a relative conception existing between two extremes and refers to a complete, complex, homogeneous linguistic system shared by two or more speakers of the same language who usually have or have had significant cultural, social or geographical proximity. A natural dialect (as different from Dillard's consensus dialect[19]) is usually learned as a child and can be mastered afterwards only with considerable effort.

Numerous variations in the speech of the same language are recognizable. The rules or features peculiar to only one person are *idiolectal*. A speaker's idiolect consists of all the linguistic rules and features he possesses. All features of an idiolect are not idiolectal; only those which are not referable to a linguistic norm other than the personal system of the speaker are so classified. There is a level of linguistic generalization between idiolect and language, that of dialect.[20] A grammar of a dialect would be a comprehensive description of the grammatical, morpho-phonological, phonological and semantic systems shared by speakers of that dialect, along with a lexicon of all the items they use.

Linguistic rules and features shared by all speakers of a language are referred to as "languaged." Since all adult speakers of English employ the same structural positions to indicate the subject-verb-object relationship it is a languaged rule. Similarly, since all adult speakers of English possess the WH-transformational rule, it is a languaged rule. Rules and features peculiar to one speaker are termed "idiolectal."

[19] J. L. Dillard, "How to Tell the Bandits from the Good Guys: or, What Dialect to Teach," in *Contemporary English*, ed. David L. Shores (New York: Lippincott, 1972), p. 292.

[20] See for example Leonard Bloomfield, *Language* (New York: Holt, Rinehart and Winston, 1933), pp. 321–45; Edward Sapir, *Language* (New York: Harcourt, 1921); E. H. Sturtevant, *Linguistic Change*, 2nd ed. (1917; rpt. Chicago: The University of Chicago Press, 1965).

Those shared by two or more speakers, but not by all, are "dialectal."[21] Because the vocalic retroflex /r/ occurs in words such as *bird* and *third* in the speech of some Americans and not in that of others, it is a dialectal feature. One should understand that its presence, as well as its absence, is dialectal; the pronunciation / b ə^ d/ is just as dialectal as /b ə d/. Among some dialects of English there is a contrast between *might could* and *might be able to* as in the strings *I might could do it* and *I might be able to do it*. Since some of the speakers who use *might be able to* do not use *might could* and because some of those who use *might could* do not use *might be able to* both structures are dialectal.

Different dialects may share numerous dialectal rules and features. The presence or absence of vocalic retroflex /r/ in words such as *bird* and *third* in the speech of a number of persons does not prove that they are of the same dialect. Similarly, one cannot assume that if all speakers in a given geographical area employ the lexeme *diddies* but not *chicks* they speak the same dialect. One would only know that both *diddies* and *chicks* are dialectal rather than languaged lexemes and that they have a certain geographical distribution.

The above information should make it easier to understand and accept certain implications of various modern linguistic principles. Firstly, by realizing that everyone speaks a dialect, the fact that aspects of a dialect are indicated in print, however important it may be artistically, gives no primary

---

[21] Dialectal features and rules are of two kinds: indicative and non-indicative. An indicative dialectal feature is restricted to one dialect. Since it appears in the speech of all speakers of a particular dialect and does not appear in other dialects, its presence identifies beyond doubt a person's dialect. American dialectology has been relatively unsuccessful in isolating indicative dialectal features. Probably each dialect possesses such features, but as yet sufficient research has not been carried out to identify many American dialects by indicative features. A non-indicative dialectal feature is one shared by two or more dialects, e.g. *diddies* and *chicks*. A series of individual dialectal features that are non-indicative by themselves can form an indicative pattern which may be used to distinguish or identify dialects.

cultural information, even though it may be indicative of the culture to which the speaker belongs. Secondly, dialectal features even less than language does, cannot be accurately indicated by conventional and occasional spelling and though an author might use such, the dialect of the character cannot be identified through them.

Thirdly, since all dialects are complex, homogeneous systems of communication equally capable of conveying ideas —or expanding themselves to do so—in themselves their nature cannot heighten or retard a human's ability to perceive or to make conceptions. One cannot, therefore, relate either a person's ability or inability to express himself or his intelligence to the dialect he speaks. It cannot be assumed that because a person speaks a certain dialect he has certain mental or perceptional abilities or restrictions. Fourthly, social and aesthetic preference for any one dialect is an arbitrary judgment based on the prejudice of the hearer not upon any intrinsic linguistic superiority of one dialect over another. A person may or may not enjoy listening to one dialect, just as he may like or dislike cabbage; and although such attitudes reveal information concerning the hearer—his prejudice— they supply little regarding the speaker.

It is true, however, that a person who believes his culture inferior will usually consider its language also inferior. In regards to the speech of the mountaineer an interesting fact should be noted. Although it is not uncommon either in the recording of dialectal material or in fiction for a mountaineer to speak disparagingly of his speech, admitting it to be "untaught" and not the "best English," such admissions seldom have an apologetic or subservient tone to them. They are nothing more than an honest admission by the speaker that he has had little formal education and do not imply that he considers himself or his culture to be inferior; woe be unto the dialectologist who says: Oh well, perhaps your children will better themselves. On one tape recording that JR made, an elderly mountain man who was not formally educated readily admitted that he knew his speech was not "the bestest of English," but he quickly added that he had no trouble in saying what he meant and that 'to his mind' the midwestern farmer probably spoke "the bestest English in the country, he having finished some grade schooling" and not having been "over fattened on book reading." He did not consider his lack of formal education as a reflection on his intrinsic worth. "Learning and good words may improve a man's knowings but it haint nary made a body a better Christian person."

In considering the language of the mountaineer one must always be vigilant against pseudo-linguistic statements, eye-dialect and the mistaking of colloquial for dialectal features. Within all dialects there are distinct levels of usage employed by speakers in different social situations. The American, including the mountaineer, usually changes usage levels through the substitution of words or morphemes rather than, as do the British, by an alteration in pronunciation.

In deciding if an element is dialectal or colloquial one must discover if it appears in other dialects on the same level of usage and be careful not to compare it to formal, rhetorical English. For instance, if a character is depicted as saying "I hafta go," since all American speakers on the colloquial level will pronounce the unit *have to* in this syntactic position as /hæfta/, placing the open juncture after the last vowel rather than between the consonants /f/ and /t/, no dialectal variation is indicated. In addition, the consonant indicated by the grapheme "ve" will never be /v/ in this unit, and to pronounce it as such would be noticeably ungrammatical. The fact that the occasional spelling indicates the speaker to consider *have to* a unit is also not indicative of dialectal variation because, in reality, it must either be considered as one morpheme or one word since it appears in other environments (e.g., Do you have to?) with approximately the same meaning. Thus, not only is such a representation dialectally non-indicative, it cannot even be considered as "slovenly" or "careless" speech.

One must be careful not to infer cultural significance from purely structural differences among dialects. It is linguistically interesting that one speaker says *I hope how soon Sunday comes* and *I might could do it gin (again) the turning of the new ground* as opposed to *I hope Sunday comes soon* and *I might be able to do it before the plowing of the previously uncultivated land,* but in itself such a distinction is no more culturally reflective than the contrast between Spanish *yo tengo hambre* (I have hunger) and English *I am hungry.* Linguistic structure conveys meaning, but because it often offers no alternatives it cannot reflect the nature of the person who uses it. In the same manner, one should be careful about drawing cultural inferences from seeming linguistic redundancies such as *might could* or *rifle gun.* First, one does not know that they are not compound words in the mountaineer's speech and, therefore, not linguistically redundant. Second, redundancy is a natural linguistic feature of all speech, all dialects.

If, as argued above, a linguistic analysis of the dialects of the mountaineer reveals very little about his culture or his collective personality, other aspects of his language, especially his rhetoric, are most revealing. In any extended conversation one notices two striking features of his language. There is a retention both of older grammatical and phonological forms and a tendency to employ a vocabulary drawn from nature and common situations. Although extremely interesting, the retention of older grammatical and phonological rules and forms must be interpreted cautiously. Linguistic conservatism must never be equated with cultural conservatism. One must remember that American speech in general has retained many elements that have disappeared in British English, and yet one would be hard pressed to prove that Americans are more conservative than Britishers. Nevertheless, the retention of various lexical items lost in other parts of the country, especially if these items refer to occupational practices, may indicate that the mountaineer has continued certain modes of living after they were forsaken in other places. One notes in his vocabulary numerous names for wild plants and animals as well as words referring to older rural customs, crafts and home practices.

The qualities of the mountaineer's speech most interesting to the non-linguist, and probably most peculiar to his culture and heritage, however, are neither dialectal or languaged. They are rhetorical ones. In reading articles by Combs, Williams and others it is clearly evident that much of what they are carefully calling attention to are matters for rhetorical not linguistic analysis. Such an aspect of language is best understood and described by considering it in relation to the rules of classical rhetoric—for the mountaineer's speech is rhetorical in the classical sense, i.e., the art of beautiful speech and effective delivery. When one speaks of tropes, figures, metaphors, similes, idioms and tale-telling he has left the realm of pure linguistics and entered that of stylistics. It, as opposed to dialectal variation, is always a conscious manipulation of language and therefore is very reflective of the culture and the people who enjoy and use it.

Both Williams and Combs[22] note that many of the striking figures that seem original to the outsider are traditional ones in the mountains, having been handed down orally from one generation of good talkers to another. The mountaineer alters, adapts, recombines and uses anew old expressions with a freshness and creativity similar to that of the Beowulf poet who called upon his traditional poetic phrasing and word-horde to tell a tale. It is perhaps this large stock of traditional figures, adapted by each speaker in an original manner, that allows the mountaineer to make his everyday talk come alive. The fact that the figures are often based on natural and cultural events with which he is still familiar makes it possible for him to alter them to fit the proper occasion.

Oral rhetoric as an art form has a value to the mountaineer

[22] Combs, "Old, Early and Elizabethan English in the Southern Mountains," p. 283; Williams, "Metaphor in Mountain Speech," p. 9.

and his descendants that has been abandoned in most other areas of the country, if it ever existed. There is no doubt that he has retained the art of tale-telling, whether it be formal, i.e., the repetition of one that has been handed down (e.g., a Jack Tale) which usually contains older dialectal forms and set intonation patterns, or original, i.e., the relating of a personal event in a manner that enthralls his audience. This ability to tell a tale, to be articulate in the best sense of the word, is still extremely strong in the Appalachians. In recording dialectal free-speech JR has never yet encountered an older informant who lacked the ability to make the incidents of his life come alive by the use of rhetorical devices—figures, similes, tropes, metaphors and the use of the most effective image or pause at the perfect time. After an old mountain woman had related in a most vivid manner how she raised her "eleven younguns" on a six acre hill-side farm after her husband had "been kilt a-felling timber," JR asked her why she had never re-married. She paused and said: "Because I loved the sweat of his body and the dust of his feet more than ary other living man."

One of the favorite devices of this mountain art is the use of understatement to show humor. Sitting with two descendants of mountaineers one day, JR noted that one kept getting up and walking a few steps to a table upon which lay some of the largest green tomatoes ever grown. Too heavy to ripen on the vine, they had been picked and placed on a table to ripen. The man who had grown them kept picking one up, then another, but said nothing as he returned to his seat. His neighbor seemingly took no notice, but as he stood up to leave he said: "Carl, I'm plumb sorry your garden had such bad growings this year. Those are the sorriest looking melons I ever did see." Another time JR, having finished recording, was sitting with two neighbors, one of whom had given the other garden space after the latter had sold his best land. There was a noticeable difference in the amount of weeds in the garden; the one who owned the land had just finished hoeing his side. Pretty soon Sam, who had borrowed the garden space, got up, took a few steps toward the garden, looked long at it, turned and said: "You know I haint a-going to put out garden here again next year. That's two year following you given me the weedy ground and kept the clean for yourself."

It is, then, the way that the mountaineer uses his language —his rhetorical sources—not his dialect that those seeking to understand his culture and personality must study. There is little evidence that the dialects of the mountain area are disappearing.[23] Some morphological variants are being leveled and the vocabulary is changing as the referents for various items are no longer used by rural people; but the distinguishing characteristics of the dialects—fine phonetic features and intonational patterns—remain. The dialects are changing of course, but not dying. What may be passing is the art of oral rhetoric that has existed for so long in the Southern Appalachian Mountains and seemingly depends on three important qualities—the conscious belief that it is important, a closeness to the mountain land and time to sit and talk. The art is not yet dead, and hopefully it is not dying. (1974)

[23] For a fuller discussion of the state of Appalachian dialects see JR's University of Tennessee Ph.D. dissertation.

CRATIS WILLIAMS

Cratis Williams grew up in the Big Sandy Valley, referred to frequently as "Kentucky's last frontier." A descendant of Indian fighters, "long hunters," veterans of the American Revolution, Tories who had taken to the backwoods, refugees from the Whiskey Rebellion, and Kentucky mountain feudists, he thinks of himself as "a complete mountaineer." He attended Cumberland College and holds the B.A. and M.A. degrees from the University of Kentucky and the Ph.D. degree from New York University. His 1600-page dissertation on the Southern mountaineer constitutes the most authoritative work ever done in the field. Dean of the Graduate School at Appalachian State University, he is an active participant in several learned societies and is in popular demand as both a speaker and as a singer of American folk songs. "Who Are the Southern Mountaineers?" is a basic question that Dr. Williams attempts to answer on the basis of both his enormous knowledge and his varied experience.

Who Are the Southern Mountaineers?

The Southern Mountaineer appears not to have set himself apart from the borderer or frontiersman until during the Civil War. When one considers the whole movement called the

Westward Expansion and realizes that the mountain regions
of the South were really settled permanently rather late, he
does not find the fact that the mountaineer was discovered
late so odd, for permanent settlement did not average more
than three generations deep in the whole mountain area at
that time. True, the Valley of Virginia was being settled in
the 1730's, the valley of East Tennessee a generation later,
and favored spots in the Blue Ridge country of North Carolina by 1790, but such immense mountain areas as West
Virginia, Eastern Kentucky, the Cumberland Plateau region
in Tennessee, and the mountainous country of North Georgia
were not settled in any kind of permanent way until after
1800.[1] One hardly expects a people to acquire a distinguishing individuality sooner than from grandfather to grandson.

To assume that there was any mystery attached to the
settlement of Appalachia is to neglect the significant fact that,
once cleared of the threat of Indians, "its coves and creek
valleys were admirably fitted for the domestic economy of
hunter and frontier farms."[2] A frontier farmer in the mountains was no more isolated in reference to markets than the
settler in any other wilderness clearing. To expect the hill
farmer to foresee that future industrialization, with its railroads, steamboat navigation, and macadamized roads, would
pass his grandson by is "to read history backward with a
vengeance."[3] But retarded his descendants became. This "is
an outstanding fact in American life. When men of the same
type . . . settled elsewhere this retardation has not been
observed."[4]

Occasionally one finds references to mountain hamlets and

[1] John C. Campbell, *The Southern Highlander and His Homeland* (New
York, 1921), pp. 39–40.

[2] Rupert B. Vance, *Human Geography of the South* (Chapel Hill, North
Carolina, 1935), p. 244.

[3] *Ibid.*

[4] John P. Connell, "Retardation of the Appalachian Region," *Mountain
Life and Work* (April, 1922), 21–22.

villages of Civil War days. In 1860, Jackson, the seat of Breathitt County, Kentucky, "still had only a few houses. Its two stores, houses, jail, courthouse, and post office were all of logs."[5] This picture of a mountain county seat compares favorably with that of Jamestown, Tennessee, a generation earlier in *The Gilded Age*,[6] or of Chestatee, Georgia, about 1830. It would seem that such towns and pioneer homes had not attracted much notice, even by outsiders, until the industrial expansion that followed the Civil War afforded the economic conditions that enabled citizens of places that shared in that expansion to improve their own towns, after which they found an archaic flavor in the habitations of mountain people as well as in the speech and customs of the men and women their own age who were still speaking and viewing life much as they had remembered their own grandfathers doing. It was not until that time that we begin to find references to the residents of Appalachia as mountaineers. But they were not then called "hill-billies," a word used first in reference to the "poor-white" dwellers among the sand hills and piney woods of Alabama and Mississippi.[7] Only recently has "hill-billy" become a popular misnomer for mountaineer. Nor did they think of themselves as mountaineers. Today the cove-dwellers and ridge people do not think of themselves as mountaineers.

The Southern Highlands region, for strictly speaking much of the area is not mountainous and in the usual geological sense, begins with the Mason-Dixon Line on the north, follows just east of the Blue Ridge in a southwesterly direction into Georgia just north of Atlanta, turns westward to Birmingham to include northeastern Alabama, thence northward

---

[5] Federal Writers' Project, *Breathitt: A Guide to the Feud Country* (Northport, New York, 1941), p. 86.

[6] Mark Twain and Charles Dudley Warner, *The Gilded Age*, Harper and Brothers edition (New York, originally published in 1873), pp. 1–2. Jamestown is called Obedstown in the book.

[7] Shields McIlwaine, *The Southern Poor White from Lubberland to Tobacco Road* (Norman, Oklahoma, 1939), p. xv.

just west of the Cumberland Plateau through Tennessee and Kentucky to the Ohio River above Maysville, Kentucky. From that point it returns along the Ohio to the southwestern corner of Pennsylvania to complete a long ellipse which reaches like a finger for nearly eight hundred miles into the heart of the Old South. Including all of West Virginia, the mountain region spreads over parts of eight other contiguous states, covering an area, as Horace Kephart observed, "about the same as that of the Alps."[8] It makes up about one-third of the total area of these states and includes approximately one-third of their total population.[9]

To obtain a fairly representative notion of the population and its resources at a reasonably normal recent period in the mountains, one would probably do best to consider the decade from 1920 to 1930, a period marked by the boom following World War I and settled by the early years of the Great Depression. A study of maps furnished by the United States Department of Agriculture reveals the following picture of conditions in the mountain region for the decade under consideration: self-sufficient farms were more heavily concentrated here than in any other part of the United States. But the Cumberland-Allegheny region produced less milk than surrounding areas and marketed fewer than 50,000 beef cattle in 1930. Farming methods were still primitive, the value of implements and machinery per male worker being the least in the United States: less than $100. As would be expected, the acreage of cultivated land per male worker was under ten acres in an area of the heaviest concentration of part-time farms in the whole country. Outside the Valley of Virginia, not over $200,000 was spent for fertilizer in the whole mountain region. The number of farms decreased less than five per cent and the value of farm property was less in the mountains than in surrounding areas. Approximately twenty-five per cent of the population

[8] Horace Kephart, *Our Southern Highlanders* (New York, 1913), p. 14.
[9] Campbell, p. 19.

migrated from the mountain farms during that decade, but untold thousands returned to chink and repair abandoned cabins on the worn-out farms and to live off relief during the 1930's. It is not difficult to see that most of the mountain area was inhabited by a marginal economic group who made little money to spend and most of whose working efforts were exerted in merely subsisting from year to year.

Striking both to the sociologist and the novelist, the homogeneity of physical type found among the mountain people with their traits of blondness, rangy frame and spare flesh, "has proved a paradox when subjected to social interpretation."[10] Much futile controversy has marked the efforts to "explain" the biological stock of the mountaineer. Novelists, accepting the theory of origins of the highlander that best suited their fictional purposes, have sometimes presented him as Anglo-Saxon, sometimes as Scotch-Irish, and sometimes as Scotch. At times he is presented as disinherited gentry whose ancestors were victimized in Merry England or compromised in Bonnie Scotland. Again, he is frequently represented as the descendant of shiftless poor whites and ne'er-do-wells who trailed the vanguard of the pioneers and took up miserable abodes in the less desirable lands passed over in the Westward Movement. Placed against these views is the more tenable one that he was part and parcel of the whole Westward Movement and settled in the mountains because he sought fertile soil for his crops, good range land for his cattle, delicious drinking water from permanent springs, and coverts for the wildlife that would afford him the pleasures and profits derived from hunting.

Although the "retarded Anglo-Saxon of the highlands is no myth . . . and if there be such a thing as good stock, these highlanders have it,"[11] his isolation has left him stranded in an outmoded culture. But, though "proud, sensitive, self-reliant, untaught in the schools, often unchurched, untraveled,

10 Vance, p. 244.
11 Vance, p. 35.

he is not unlearned in the ways of the world, and when one chances to leave for the outside world before his personality has become set in the mold of his culture he is likely to climb far."[12] John C. Campbell found evidence of a falling away from culture among mountain people in the fact that many illiterate mountaineers possess copies of Greek and Latin classics bearing the names of ancestors and that given names of mountain children reflect a knowledge of the classics on the part of the ancestors.[13]

One would think mountaineers themselves could help solve the problem of their origin. Such, however, is not the case. When questioned on the subject of their racial stock and ancestry, they usually know nothing more than that certain ancestors came from North Car'liny or Ole Virginny or occasionally Pennsylvany and that they "reckon" they had come from the "old country across the waters" and were English, Scotch, Irish—any of which might mean Scotch-Irish—or Dutch, which usually means German.

Much has been done in an effort to determine proportionate racial stocks in the mountains through a study of family names. Because so many names may be either English, Scottish, or Irish, because many names have become corrupted, and because translations of names from German or French have added to the confusion, the conclusions arrived at through such studies are not sufficiently reliable to be of much help.

An analysis of the whole pioneering movement into the Piedmont and upland region of Virginia and the Carolinas yields more conclusive proof in determining who the present day mountaineer is racially than any other known approach to the problem. The Valley of Virginia, with few inhabitants

[12] *Ibid.*

[13] Campbell, p. 50. Ella Enslow (pseud. for Murray) and Alvin F. Harlow point out that the petition of the Watauga Settlements to North Carolina in 1776 was signed by one hundred and thirteen men, perhaps all in the colony, but only two had to make their marks. *Schoolhouse in the Foothills* (New York, 1935), pp. 9–10.

in 1730, was well-populated in 1750.[14] By 1765 Governor Tryon could report that over a thousand immigrant wagons had passed through Salisbury, North Carolina, in one year.[15] That the Scotch-Irish outnumbered by far any other racial group can hardly be doubted. "From the year 1720 to 1776 this people came on the average of 12,000 a year, or 600,000 people before the Revolution."[16]

A study of the list of over four thousand names attached to the petitions of the early inhabitants of Kentucky to the General Assembly of Virginia from 1769 to 1792 shows "a decided preponderance of Scotch and Scotch-Irish names with a large number of English and a few German, Dutch, and French. The number of English increases in the later petitions. The large number of religious names indicated the non-conformist character of much of the population."[17] That the Scotch-Irish predominated in the migrations westward to 1800 is to be inferred; that they were also more numerous than any other groups in the settlements made to the same date in the mountain regions is logically assumed.

The most significant single trait to mark all mountain communities is the essential non-conformist quality of their religious views. In the very beginning of the settling of the mountains, the Valley of Virginia afforded homes for Lutheran, German Reformed, Quaker, Mennonite, Dunkard, and Presbyterian. "Between the ramparts of the mountains, these descendants of persecution dwelt in peace with one another."[18] With the flooding migration of the Scotch-Irish, even the Great Valley became a stronghold of Presbyterianism that stood out in sharp contrast, frequently in sharp

[14] *Ibid.*, p. 25.
[15] *Ibid.*
[16] See footnote, Campbell, p. 23.
[17] *Petitions of the Early Inhabitants of Kentucky to the General Assembly of Virginia, 1769 to 1792*, Filson Club Publication No. 27 (Louisville, n.d.), pp. 31–32. Quoted by Campbell, pp. 60–61.
[18] Julia Davis, *The Shenandoah* (New York, 1945), p. 36.

antagonism, to the Anglicanism of Tidewater Virginia.[19] The mountaineers, a pious people, were largely Presbyterian to begin with, but they "lost their pastors and took up with Baptists of three sects and with Campbellite leaders."[20] Since no schools were provided for them during the early days and they found themselves unable to provide their own until recently, "they came to think education a superfluity, if not an evil."[21] The most permeating influence in their lives remained an essentially unintellectual and basically Calvinistic religion kept alive by the energy of fire-eating and untrained ministers.

The question of the origin of mountaineers from the indentured servants of colonial times is fraught with confusion. To many writers who have seen mountaineers as the descendants of the boundmen, the implications are that they are therefore of the depraved origin ascribed to the poor whites of the Tidewater country and the Deep South. Other writers, noting essential differences between the character of the two groups, hasten to deny that the mountain people descend from those wretched souls described by William Byrd in his *History of the Dividing Line* (1729) as lolling their days away in shiftless ease on the back fences of Lubberland. As a matter of fact, it would seem that even most of the Scotch-Irish came as indentured servants, first to the eastern counties of Pennsylvania, "but when their terms of service expired, they found lands in Pennsylvania too expensive and some of them were settled by Lord Fairfax on his holdings between the Rappahannock and the Potomac."[22] The traditions of some of the mountain families certainly indicate that

[19] Evarts Boutell Greene, *Provincial America* (New York and London, 1905), p. 236.
[20] Julian Ralph, "Our Appalachian Americans," *Harper's*, CVII (June, 1903), 236.
[21] *Ibid.*
[22] Thomas Perkins Abernethy, *Three Virginia Frontiers* (Baton Rouge, Louisiana, 1940), pp. 38–39.

many of the ancestors were bound boys who earned money to pay for their passage before they became their own men.

In general, efforts to link the rank and file of mountain families with the Tidewater poor whites have certainly failed, but that some of these people found their way into the mountains can hardly be doubted. And that much of the fiction portraying life among the mountaineers deals with a branch-water variety of mountaineer whose moral and cultural standards are equivalent to those of the poor whites who appear in the novels of Erskine Caldwell and William Faulkner is well known.

Historians have been generous in their praise of mountaineers as soldiers. The Scotch-Irish disseminated among the older population at the time of the Revolution have been credited with holding the colonies together, for whereas the older population knew certain loyalties both to King and their own colony, the recently arrived Scotch-Irishmen, 600,000 strong, knew no loyalty to a colonial government yet and carried with them a grudge of long standing against the King. Their resistance to the injustices of British policy exhibited itself in strong measures even before the Revolution began.

But to enroll all mountain men in the lists of the Sons of the American Revolution would certainly be rash, for there is excellent evidence that many of the early mountaineers were Tories. Too, many of the mountain families especially those in the higher echelons socially and culturally, preserve traditions in their families of having descended from Tories who came to the mountains during the Revolution to escape the wrath of the revolutionists in their home communities. Even the Scotch-Irish in the Carolinas were not the unalloyed anti-British men that most writers have tended to make them. As late as 1779 there were so many Tories in Burke County, one of the western counties of the state, that British officers recruited men there who were so numerous that they planned to kill all the patriots in that region. These Scotch-Irish mountaineers pitched their support with the wealthy planters of the Tidewater section in acting against rebellion. When one considers that this whole area of North Carolina was a nursery for the advance phalanxes of the Westward Movement, he must make some reservations in regard to the patriotism of both the pioneer ancestors of the people of the Mississippi Valley and of the Appalachian mountaineers.

Evidence indicates, then, that the Southern mountaineer, though mainly of Scotch-Irish ancestry, of dissenting religious convictions, and of Whig descent, is not necessarily any of these things. He turns out to be a rather complex individual when we examine him closely. Hence, sweeping statements, stereotyped presentations, and generalizations as to his essential character are not to be relied upon as adequate interpretation of mountain life and character.

In arriving at a concept of the Southern mountaineer along sociological and economic lines, it is important that we consider what his ancestors were like before they moved into the hills from the Carolina Piedmont Reservoir. The Piedmont pioneers were a peculiar people made up of like-minded groups from several nationalities rather than a distinct racial type. Because of the remarkable qualities they possessed before they became mountaineers, environment and isolation do not sufficiently account for much of the same qualities found among them today, for their pioneer peculiarities "have curiously survived, in spite of the weathering of time."[23]

Not only did the mountain people become isolated as a geographical unit after about 1850,[24] but they became more and more isolated from one another. As William Goodell Frost observed in 1899, the double isolation resulted in "marked variations in social conditions." The moving out or death of leading families in one valley may mark a decline in the social state that leads to collapse and awful degrada-

[23] James Watt Raine, *The Land of Saddle-Bags* (New York, 1924), p. 39.
[24] Campbell, p. 24.

tion, while in the adjoining valley heirlooms and traditions "witness a self-respect and character that are unmistakable."[25] Because the better type of mountaineer was conscious, by 1900, of his stranded condition, and knew that he was "behind relatively as well as absolutely," his character was affected. His pride became vehement. He developed a shy, sensitive, and undemonstrative personality. Aware now of the scorn from the lowlands, his old predilection toward Presbyterian fatalism led him to struggle but feebly with his destiny.

As a result of isolation, economic depravity, struggles, hardships and common interests, the sons of the mountain pioneers of from five to eight generations back are by now blended into a somewhat homogeneous people[26] who in eastern Kentucky have more in common with their kind in northern Georgia than they have with their fellow Kentuckians in the Bluegrass Region, or who in western North Carolina share more points of view with their neighbors across the state line in Tennessee than they share with their fellow

[25] William Goodell Frost, "Our Contemporary Ancestors in the Southern Mountains," *Atlantic*, LXXXIII (March, 1899), 315.

[26] Arthur H. Estabrook in *Eugenical News* (September, 1927) announced the results of a painstaking study which concluded that the southern Appalachian area does not contain a truly homogeneous population. Nathaniel D. M. Hirsch, a professor of psychology at Duke University, studied school children in three eastern Kentucky counties in the 1920's, and came to the conclusion that the Kentucky mountaineers are "one of the purest strains in the world, yet they possess physical traits which reveal that the compounding and inter-mixture of racial strains has not yet after six generations of intermarriage proceeded to the extent of blending the component elements." ("An Experimental Study of East Kentucky Mountaineers," *Genetic Psychology Monographs*, III, March, 1928, 229).

John F. Day said in 1941, "During the 100 years and more between settlement and arrival of the machine age the hills bred a distinctive people. It is an exaggeration to say, 'Mountaineers look like this—Their traits of character are thus and so—Under certain conditions they will react in this manner.' Even so, similar ancestry, inbreeding, a common fight against poverty, and a century and a half of isolation in an unusual environment have given Kentucky mountaineers characteristics common to the majority." (*Bloody Ground* [Garden City, New York, 1941], p. 21.)

North Carolinians and remote kinsmen in Charlotte and Greensboro.

Rupert B. Vance has noted that in the great Appalachian Valley "society has developed as a checkerboard in accordance with topography." A slow process of social differentiation took place, resulting in the plantation culture in the fertile limestone valleys and the marginal cabin culture among the less energetic who were pushed into the shale hills and chert ridges. But Professor Vance does not presume to ascribe a different ancestry to the dwellers in the mansion and the cabin. It is a matter of population pressure that results in the division of fertile fields among heirs until the time comes when fields are too small to offer subsistence and "young sons have pushed out beyond the mountain rim; others have retreated back up the slopes to the shelter of a cabin and a cleared patch."[27]

But overcrowding, though the principal problem, is not the whole answer to the poverty that came to exist among most of the mountain people. As William Bradley pointed out in 1918, the extinction of game and the exhaustion of the soil contributed immeasurably. On Troublesome Creek in Kentucky it was discovered that "every creek at all capable of growing corn (the one staple crop) had a population far in excess of its power to support, and that many of these people . . . were crowded into one and two room cabins, sometimes without windows." On one branch three miles long "thirteen houses, with a total of ninety-six people, of whom sixty-seven were children," were found.[28]

It must be remembered that this heavily increasing population is of the original mountain stock. Only about two per cent of the mountain people are of foreign birth,[29] and these are concentrated in the mining areas of the Cumberland-Allegheny Belt where they had exerted little influence on

[27] Vance, p. 243.
[28] "The Women on Troublesome," *Scribner's*, LXIII (March, 1918), 320.
[29] Campbell, p. 363.

the native stock up to 1920.[30] With an increasing density in population and the consequent further division of family lands (for two-thirds of mountain men own land), it is easy to see that struggles and hardships would increase.

But it must be remembered that although a homogeneity of the ethical and ethnic character of the mountain people may more or less exist, there is no homogeneity of social and economic status. Mountaineers, socially and economically, fall roughly into three groups:

(1) Town and city dwellers. Nearly two million live in incorporated places of 1000 or more. They are mostly of native stock, descended from the same people as their rural cousins, and either grew up with the town or have been dwellers in the town but a generation or so. Having risen but recently from what they regard as the more odious aspects of mountain life, they are sensitive on the score of labels and resent being called mountaineers.

(2) Valley farmers. These people are the largest of the three groups. They live along river valleys, near the mouths of creeks, or on main highways, and are more or less prosperous rural folk. Their problems are likely to be more or less identical with those of people living anywhere in the country. But they, like their neighbors in the towns, reveal the ethical and ethnic homogeneity of the whole mountain population. Only in material things and social living with the consequent polish that comes from the enjoyment of their prerogatives are they different from the mountaineers of the third class.

(3) Branchwater mountaineers. These, fewer in number than those belonging to the second class, live for the most part up the branches, in the coves, on the ridges, and in the inaccessible parts of the mountain region. They are the small holders of usually poor land, or tenants, or squatters who move from abandoned tract to abandoned tract. It is the

[30] *Ibid.*, p. 75.

mountaineer of this third type, closely akin to the "poor white" if not exactly the same, that became the mountaineer of fiction.

Ironically, mountaineers of the third type do not think of themselves as mountaineers either: they are just people. Hence, no one admits to being a mountaineer. The resentment against fictional interpretations of mountain life and character arises largely from the town and valley folk, who rebel against "the exaggeration of the weaknesses and the virtues of individuals in the third group, and from presenting as typical the picturesque, exceptional, or distressing conditions under which some of them live," for, "through lack of qualifications they are, by inference, pictured as living under such conditions."[31]

Understandably, the general attitude of the mountain people is not one conducive to progress, for they have been victimized through exploitation of the natural resources around them and quaint journalism "until they resent anything said about them or offered for them."[32]

Unforgiving of writers that exposed their peculiarities, the mountaineers of Clay County, Kentucky, escorted the reporters who came to cover the Howard-Baker feuds at the beginning of this century out of the county and warned them not to return.[33] Horace Kephart discovered that the mountain people are provoked at being called mountaineers. He thought the provocation stems from the fact that the word is not in their vocabulary, a "furrin" word, which they take as a term of reproach. Anything strange is regarded with suspicion; hence, anyone writing about these people runs the risk of offending them.[34] (1973)

---

[31] *Ibid.*, p. 89.
[32] Day, p. 323.
[33] Ralph, "Our Appalachian Americans," *Harper's*, CVII (June, 1903), 33
[34] Kephart, pp. 206–207.

LOYAL JONES

Born in 1928, Loyal Jones grew up on a mountain farm in western North Carolina. He graduated from Berea College in 1954 and received his Master's degree from the University of North Carolina in 1961. He is author of numerous articles on Appalachian culture and is presently director of the Appalachian Center at Berea College. His essay on Appalachian values is a compendium of the best qualities of the Appalachian people.

Appalachian Values

We mountain people are a product of our history and the beliefs of our forefathers. They came mostly from England, Scotland and Wales, some from Germany, France and Africa, and of course many married Indians who were already here. Most came seeking freedom—freedom from religious and economic restraints and freedom to do much as they pleased. They were unfriendly to the institutions of the day, both religious and secular. The patterns of their settlement show that they were seeking space and solitude. Although considerable numbers of them were literate—as evident in their signed public documents and personal books—they abandoned formal education when they took to the woods. This was a choice of profound significance for mountaineers. They chose freedom and solitude and mainly rejected the accoutrements of civilization. Perhaps the choice was both their strength and their undoing.

Our origins, our history, and our experience have made us Southern Mountaineers different in many ways from most other Americans. The Appalachian value system that influences attitudes and behavior is different from that which is held by our fellow countrymen, although it seems clear that it is similar to the value system of an earlier America.

Religion—Mountain people are religious. This does not necessarily mean that we all go to church regularly, but we are religious in the sense that most of our values and the meaning we see in life spring from religious sources. One must understand the religion of mountaineers before he can begin to understand mountaineers. Formally organized churches that the early settlers were a part of required an educated clergy and centralized organization, impractical requirements in the wilderness, and so locally autonomous sects sprang up. These individualistic churches stressed the fundamentals of the faith and depended on local resources and leadership.

The home mission boards of the mainline denominations have usually looked on our local sect churches as something that we must be saved from. Many social reformers also view the local sect churches as a hindrance to social progress. What they fail to see is that this religion has helped to sustain us and made life worth living in grim situations. Religion shaped our lives, but at the same time we shaped our religion, since culture and religion are always intertwined. Life on the frontier did not allow for an optimistic social gospel. Hard work did not always bring a sure reward, and one was lucky if he endured. Therefore, the religion became fatalistic and stressed rewards in another life. The important thing was to get religion—get saved—which meant accepting Jesus as one's personal savior. It is a realistic religion, so far as the human condition is concerned. It is based on belief in the Original Sin, that man is fallible, that he will fail, does fail. Someone said that man was made at the end of the week when God was tired. We mountaineers readily see that the human tragedy is this, that man sees so clearly what he should be and what he should do and yet he fails consistently. Not only does he fail, but he is presumptuous, pretending to be what he is not. But in spite of his failings and presumptions, man is still saved if he has accepted Jesus Christ, who has already died for him. This is the Good News!

Individualism, Self-Reliance and Pride—Several years ago there came a great snowfall in western North Carolina, and many people were snowed in for weeks. The Red Cross came to help. Two workers heard of an old lady way back in the mountains, living alone, and they set out to see about her, in a jeep. They finally slipped and skidded down into her cove, got out and knocked on the door. When she appeared at the door one of the men said,

"Hello, we're from the Red Cross." But before he could say anything further the old lady replied,

"Well, I don't believe I'm a going to be able to help you'ns any this year. It's been a right hard winter."

Individualism, self-reliance and pride are perhaps the most obvious characteristics of mountain people, as mentioned by John C. Campbell and others. Our forebears were individualistic from the beginning, else they would not have gone to such trouble and danger to get away from encroachments on their freedom. Individualism and self-reliance were traits to be admired on the frontier. The person who could not look after himself and his family was to be pitied. There is a lesson in the mountaineer's all-out search for freedom. He worked so hard to gain it, that eventually he lost it. The mountaineer withdrew from the doings of the larger society, and it passed him by, but not before it bought up the resources around him. The industrial system was interested in the mountaineer as long as it needed his muscle to extract the resources. When it no longer needed muscle, it cast him aside. This once-free man became a captive of circumstances beyond his control. But his belief in independence and self-reliance is still strong whether or not he is truly independent and self-reliant. We value solitude, whether or not we can always find a place to be alone. We want to do things for ourselves, whether or not it is practical—like make a dress, a chair, build a house, repair an automobile, or play the banjo. There is satisfaction in that, in this age when people hire other people to do most of their work and supply their entertainment.

The pride of the mountaineer is mostly a feeling of not wanting to be beholden to other people. We are inclined to try to do everything ourselves, find our own way when we are lost on the road, or suffer through when we are in great need. We don't like to ask others for help. The value of self-reliance is often stronger than the desire to get help.

Neighborliness and Hospitality—The mountaineer's independence is tempered somewhat by his basic neighborliness and hospitality. It was necessary to survival for everyone to be hospitable on the frontier, to help each other build houses and barns and to take people in when night caught them on the road. No greater compliment could be paid a mountain family than that they were "clever," that is that they were hospitable, quick to invite you in and generous with the food. My father told of eating at a neighbor's home where the only food they had was corn bread and sorghum, but the host said hospitably, "Just reach and get anything you want."

We who were brought up on this value, will always have the urge to invite those who visit to stay for a meal or to spend the night, even though this is not the custom over much of America now, unless a formal invitation is sent out, well in advance.

Familism—Appalachian people are family centered. As Jack Weller has pointed out in *Yesterday's People*, the mountain person wants to please his family, and he is more truly himself when he is within the family circle. Loyalty runs deep between family members, and a sense of responsibility for one another may extend to cousins, nephews, nieces, uncles and aunts and in-laws. Family members gather when there is sickness or death or other disaster. Many supervisors in northern industry have often been perplexed when employees from Appalachia have been absent from jobs because of funerals of cousins or other distant relatives. Appalachian families often take in relatives for extended visits. For example, one of the biggest problems authorities in the cities *think* they have is overcrowding as Appalachian migrants take in relatives until they can get jobs and places of their own. In James Still's beautiful novel, *River of Earth*, the father takes in relatives even though there isn't enough food for everyone. The mother in desperation burns the house down and moves the family into the tiny smokehouse in order to get rid of the relatives whom her husband could not ask to leave. Blood is very thick in Appalachia. Two mountaineers were talking about one of their kinfolks. One said, "You know he is a real S.O.B." The other replied, "Yeah, but he's our S.O.B."

Personalism—Jack Weller has also pointed out that one of the main aims in life of Appalachians is to relate well with other persons. We will go to great lengths to keep from offending others, even sometimes appearing to agree with them when we in fact do not. It is more important to us to get along and have a good relationship with other persons than it is to make our true feelings known. Mountaineers will give the appearance of agreeing to attend all sorts of meetings that they have no intention of going to, just because they want to be polite. Of course, this personalism is one of the reasons that those who work for confrontation politics often fail in Appalachia. We are extremely reluctant to confront anyone and alienate him, if we can get out of it. If, however, the issues are important enough, we will take a stand. The Widow Combs, Dan Gibson, and Jink Ray confronted and stopped strip miners when they came onto their land. But mountain people place a high value on their relations with others and it takes something mighty important to cause us to jeopardize these relationships.

Appalachians respect others and are quite tolerant of their differences. We allow others to be themselves, whatever that is, as long as they are not infringing on our right to be ourselves. Mountaineers, even as far south as northern Alabama and Georgia, were anti-slavery in sentiment and fought for the Union in the Civil War, and although Reconstruction Legislatures imposed anti-Negro laws, thus training us in segregation, Appalachians have not been saddled with the same prejudices about black people that people of the Deep South have. We have our prejudices, but we have not made a crusading cause out of them. My great-grandparents took in a black orphan to rear in North Carolina in the late eighteen hundreds, and all of the children slept in the same bed. Indians, whom we fought bitterly, are accepted in Appalachian culture, as contrasted with attitudes in the Southwest. Mountain people tend to accept persons as they are. We may not always like other persons, but we are able to tolerate them. We usually judge others on a personal basis rather than on how they look or what their credentials or accomplishments are.

Love of Place—One of the first questions a stranger is asked in the mountains is, "Where you from?" We are oriented around places. We never forget our native places, and we go back as often as possible. A lot of us think of going back for good, perhaps to the Nolichucky, Big Sandy, Kanawha, or Oconoluftee, or to Drip Rock, Hanging Dog, Shooting Creek, Decoy, Stinking Creek, Sweetwater, or Sandy Mush. Our place is always close on our minds. One fellow said that he came from so far back in the mountains the sun set between his house and the road. Our folksongs tell of our regard for the land where we were born. It is one of the unifying values of mountain people, this attachment to one's place, and it is a great problem to those who urge mountaineers to find their destiny outside the mountains.

Modesty—Several years ago my phone rang and when I answered it a rather brusk voice demanded, "Whozis?" Somewhat offended, I answered stiffly, "With whom did you wish to speak?" There was a long pause, and finally the voice came back softly but with great reproach, "Well, I c'n tell by the way your a talkin' you're not who I'uz a wantin'." That should have taught me a good lesson, but it didn't. A few weeks later the phone rang again. I answered. A voice said, "Who's this?" I answered, "With whom did you wish to speak?" The voice came back, "You, you stuffy bastard." It was a college friend who came from my part of the mountains.

We mountaineers believe that we are as good as anybody else, but no better. We believe we should not put on airs, not boast nor try to get above our raising. A mountaineer does not usually extoll his own virtues; there is little competition among mountaineers, except perhaps in basketball or in who has the best dog. Persons who are really accomplished, such as in playing or singing, will be reluctant to perform and will preface a performance with disparaging words about themselves or their musical instruments. The mountain preacher will talk of his unworthiness for the task at hand and hint of many others who are far more able. Of course, when these formalities have been dispensed with, the preacher or musician will probably cut loose with a great deal of vigor.

My feeling is that we mountaineers have a pretty realistic view of ourselves, and we don't take ourselves too seriously. We never believed that man could be perfect. We don't become as cynical as others may when men fail. When they do not fail we are pleasantly surprised. These beliefs make us somewhat at peace with ourselves. We don't pretend we are something that we are not.

Sense of Beauty—We mountaineers have a sense of beauty,

and we have many art forms, even though some may seem somewhat crude to those outside the culture. These artistic expressions are often tied to functional necessities. Great pride was taken in the past in good craftsmanship—in the design, quality and beauty of wood in a chair, the inlay and carving on a rifle, the stitchery, design and variety of color in a quilt, the vegetable dyes in a woven piece. Much time was put into making household utensils attractive. There was fine exceptional craftsmanship in items which were beyond necessities, such as in the banjos, fiddles, and dulcimers which were played with great skill. Appalachian people have perpetuated or created some of the most beautiful songs in the field of folk music. We have preserved some of the great ballads of English literature and passed on old old tales, with great attention to the dramatic effect. We have also been the masters of the simile and metaphor in song and in speech. Such as, "He'd cross hell on a rotten rail to get a drink of likker." Or, "She's cold as a kraut crock." Or, "He looks like the hind wheels of hard times." Those are statements that involve the imagination.

Sense of Humor—We have a good sense of humor, although we may sometimes appear to others to be somewhat dour. Humor has sustained us in hard times. We tend to laugh at ourselves a good deal, saying self-deprecating things like, "I was hiding behind the door when the looks were passed out." Our humor is tied up in our concept of man and the human condition. We see humor in man's pretensions to power and perfection and in his inevitable failures. We may poke a great deal of fun at pompous people and may scheme to "get their goat" by playing a "rusty" on them. We may say, for example, of those who aspire to learning, "preachers and lawyers and buzzard eggs—there's more hatched than ever come to perfection."

Sometimes the humor reflects hard times, like when the woman went to the governor to ask him to pardon her husband who was in the penitentiary. "What's he in for?" the

Governor asked. "For stealing a ham." "Is he a good man?" "No, he's a mean old man." "Is he a hard worker?" "No, he won't hardly work at all." "Well, why would you want a man like that pardoned?" "Well, Governor, we're out of ham."

Patriotism—Appalachians have held a special feeling about the flag of the United States. This is a land that gave them freedom to be themselves, and when this freedom was threatened they led in seeking independence. It was mountaineers who defeated a British army in the important battle of King's Mountain. Many areas of the mountains were settled by Revolutionary War soldiers who were given land in lieu of money after the war, and they and their descendants retained intense feelings for the U.S. Great areas of Appalachia remained loyal to the Union in the Civil War. West Virginia seceded from Virginia and became a Union State. Kentucky was split, and many mountain counties were behind the Union. East Tennessee was a hotbed of Union sympathizers. North Georgia and Northern Alabama had pro-Union counties.

Mountaineers have turned out with enthusiasm for all of our national wars except for the Vietnam Conflict. It is a much noted fact that draft quotas in Appalachia have often been filled by volunteers.

We have an abiding interest in politics. Contrary to popular myth we do turn out in significant numbers to vote. In fact it has been a problem in some counties to keep people from voting several times. We tend to relate personally to politicians who catch our fancy and appear trustworthy. FDR won over great numbers of formerly Republican counties with his personal charm. Eastern Kentucky, all of Kentucky, was able to switch very readily from Alben Barkley, a Democrat, to John Sherman Cooper, a Republican, as Favorite Son, quite aside from political parties. We mountaineers are more closely tied to the national government than we are to the South or to our local and state governments, and we are generally supportive of national policies, even though these policies have often been fickle, so far as the mountains are concerned. . . .

I have written mainly of the values which I think are good, that I take some pride in knowing are held by my people. Some of these values and beliefs however, are a disadvantage to us, sometimes keeping us from putting our best foot forward, sometimes keeping us from putting either foot forward. Our fatalistic religious attitudes often cause us to adopt a "what will be will be" approach to social problems. Our Original Sin orientation inhibits us from trying to change the nature or practices of people. Our individualism keeps us from getting involved, from creating a sense of community and cooperation and causes us to shy away from those who want to involve us in social causes. Our love of place sometimes keeps us in places where there is no hope of maintaining decent lives. We have been so involved with persons that we have not taken proper notice of ideas and organizations which are important to us in today's society. We have been hospitable and neighborly to strangers who have deceived us over and over again. We have been modest and retiring, and thus have let others from the outside do the jobs we should have been doing ourselves, only to find that usually they have not done what we wanted done. Finally, we have been so close to the frontier with its exploitive mentality, that we have seen our resources squandered, and we have seen our neighbors exploited without our giving these acts much thought. Our sense of freedom has bordered on license, and we have thrown our trash and allowed our neighbors to throw their trash all over the mountains and into our streams, adding to the pollution from strip mining and industrial waste. In our modest way, we have watched, have not accepted responsibility, and problems have closed in on us.

There are many strengths in the culture, however, strengths which have been lost in much of America. The strengthening qualities must be preserved and nurtured, as we attempt to change the qualities which diminish the chance for a better life. All work in Appalachia must be based on the genuine needs as expressed by mountain people themselves. Whatever work is done must be done with the recognition that Appalachian culture is real and functioning. This implies that change will not come easily and will not come at all unless the reasons for change are sound and are desired by mountain people. (1973)

HARRY M. CAUDILL

Harry M. Caudill was born at Whitesburg, Letcher County, Kentucky, near the headwaters of the Kentucky River. Other than years spent away at school and in military service, his entire life has been spent in this area, where his ancestors were among the early settlers. Since receiving his law degree from the University of Kentucky, he has practiced law in Whitesburg, served in the State Legislature, and consistently taken a strong lead in conservation of natural resources. He is author of the nonfiction works *Night Comes to the Cumberlands* and *My Land Is Dying* and a recent novel, *The Senator from Slaughter County*. Over the years he has been a voice for values and sanity for all of Appalachia. He has received numerous awards and honors including the National Honor Award for Soil Conservation Service. His essay "O, Appalachia!" may be regarded as a final lament or else a challenge for change. It was published in the April, 1973 issue of *Intellectual Digest*.

O, Appalachia!

The Appalachian mountain range is the least understood and the most maligned part of America. In the last decade alone it has been the subject of scores of economic and sociological studies. Lyndon Johnson's Great Society made it a principal battlefield in the War on Poverty. And, yet, despite this there persists a monumental unwillingness to recognize the harsh realities of the Appalachian paradox.

"Paradoxical" is the adjective most applicable to that vast region embracing western Pennsylvania, western Virginia, eastern Kentucky, northeastern Tennessee, nearly all of West Virginia, northern Alabama, and bits of Maryland, North Carolina and Georgia. The very name of the region has become synonymous with poverty and backwardness. Arnold Toynbee sees its people and culture as serious internal threats to Western civilization. "The Appalachians," he wrote, "present the melancholy spectacle of a people who have acquired civilization and then lost it." As he sees them, our southern highlanders have reverted to barbarism and are the "Riffs, Albanians, Kurds, Pathans and hairy Ainu" of the New World.

But the land itself is rich in every respect that an ambitious people would find necessary for greatness. To assert that the Appalachian land is poor is to display the same ignorance so often imputed to the mountaineers themselves.

Appalachia is rich. Its heartland is a mere 480 miles from Washington, D. C., and is within easy reach of the populous eastern third of the nation. This huge, sparsely populated region thus lies close to the heart of the most highly industrialized continent in the world.

Its forest—the finest expression of the eastern deciduous—is the most varied and splendid of the globe's temperate zones. Fifty million years old, it contains almost every plant the glaciers shoved down from the north and many that later seeded up from the south. More than 2,000 seed-bearing plants are native to West Virginia alone. Although this forest still covers Appalachia like the folds of a mighty carpet, human greed has reduced it in many places to thickets and stands of new growth.

The bottomlands produce excellent potatoes, grains, berries, grapes and fruit, and a survey by the President's Appalachian Regional Commission disclosed that there are 9.5 million acres suitable for pasturage.

After a century of mining, Appalachia's coal veins still contain 250 billion tons of the world's best coal. Economists have declared one of its coal beds to be the most valuable mineral deposit on the globe. The first petroleum wells gushed there; its oil and gas resources still boom. And in addition the region ships out limestone, talc, cement rock, iron ore, clays, gneiss, gibbsite and grahamite.

Appalachia has beauty. The ancient crags, timber-cloaked slopes, rhododendron and laurel thickets, beds of ferns and flowers, and creeks and rushing rivers make it a land of stunning loveliness. The Great Smokies is the most visited of all U.S. parks, and it is not mere coincidence that two of the nation's greatest aggregations of scientific minds have been brought together within the shadows of the Appalachian hills at Huntsville and Oak Ridge.

Little credence is due the notion that the troubles of the mountaineers stem from the mountainous character of their habitat. Mountains and poverty do not automatically go together, as the little Republic of Switzerland so dramatically proves.

Nor does the mountaineers' failure stem from any genetic deficiency or some ill fortune at the beginning. The settlers—whose descendants are a majority today—were English, Scotch, German and Scotch-Irish, with a virility and toughness legendary on the frontier. In 1780 at Kings Mountain, South Carolina, an army of 30-day volunteers administered to a larger British force the most unequivocal defeat in the history of the empire. Of 907 British and Tory soldiers engaged, all were killed, wounded or captured. These backwoodsmen proclaimed American independence and liberty at Mecklenburg Courthouse a year before July 4, 1776. Tough, sturdy stock had a promising beginning in a labyrinth stuffed with riches and bright with promise.

How, then, did it happen that more than a century ago the descendants of Kings Mountain were already so poor and ignorant they had become a matter of grave concern to President Abraham Lincoln and his friend, O. O. Howard, head of the Freedmen and the Refugees Bureau? The essential trouble lay in this reality: from the beginning Appalachian people nurtured a profound distrust of government, sought to elude its influence and consistently refused to use it as a tool for social and economic enhancement.

Appalachia's population was drawn almost entirely from the frontier of the revolutionary war era. The same qualities that made the frontiersmen effective Indian fighters and revolutionaries doomed them and their descendants as social builders. What Toynbee has described as a retreat to barbarism is actually a persistence of the backwoods culture and mores into an age of cybernetics and rockets—nearly two centuries after the frontier itself rolled westward and passed into history.

The Europeans whose descendants filtered into Appalachia were poor. They were landless younger sons, people swept from the farms by landlords, indigents who swarmed into the cities in search of work, disbanded soldiers and Ulstermen pauperized by parliamentary acts designed to protect the English wool trade. Many came as indentured servants too poor to pay a shipmaster for their passage. The quest for land took them to the backwoods. They shared a tenacious hatred of the English rulers whose policies had brought them only toil and bitterness. They soon shared another sentiment —disdain for the copper-skinned aborigines who presumptuously claimed to own the virgin lands the newcomers coveted. In their struggles to preserve their ancient domain, the Indians fought skillfully against the interlopers and through much of the struggle were supported by the crown.

In 1763 His Majesty's government proclaimed the Appalachian crest as the settlement line beyond which no British subject could lawfully build a cabin. Thus, reasoned the King's counselors, peace with the natives would be preserved until they could be civilized and turned into good servants of the crown, the fur trade would be stabilized, and the whites would turn the land east of the line into a vast expanse of orderly, English-style farms. The Proclamation caused the fast-breeding backwoodsmen to pile up on the border and provided the stock for a massive wave of settlers when the revolution shattered English power.

The Indian wars lasted more than 40 fiery years until Anthony Wayne's victory at Fallen Timbers in 1794. Raid and counter-raid, scalped corpses, burned crops, slaughtered livestock, stratagems, counter-stratagems and a perpetual all-pervading unease—these were the elements that etched into the backwoods culture an acceptance of bloodshed as a normal part of life. With no effective government to protect them, the settlers became supremely self-reliant, loyal only to the helpful clans who moved westward as they did. They learned, though, from the enemy; and Cherokee corn bread, parched corn and fondness for the hunt mixed with lively Old World fiddle tunes as part of the burgeoning culture.

Many settlers stayed abreast of the frontier, forming the keen cutting edge of the scythe that reached Oregon a mere 80 years after the Mecklenburg Resolves. But most were absorbed by the Appalachian maze. They stayed, steeping in the backwoods behavioral patterns with their quick violence, subsistence farming, hunting, antipathy to government and, after the revivalist movement of 1800, old-time Baptist religion. All the later migrants—Germans, Poles, Jews, Italians, Scandinavians—went westward without touching the hill people. Until the railroads began to reach out for the coal and timber, they simmered undisturbed, acquiring the characteristics that have led to the present plight.

Having no one else to learn from, they learned from their

forebears, repeating the techniques and perpetuating the aspirations of their frontier past. They evolved a traditionalism that ruled out everything unsanctioned by time. The patriarchs cautioned against the untried, and the mountaineer became a conspicuous anachronism.

Like someone of a Swiss Family Robinson within his fold of the mountains and surrounded by foes real or imagined, the mountaineer was crankily individualistic. He tenaciously defended the ideals and freedoms that made his bizarre individualism possible. He became a loner to whom cooperative efforts were distasteful and strange.

The sun began setting long ago for the highlander. His fields eroded and he had to clear new ground, which became barren for the same reasons. The labor of clearing exhausted him, and his unremunerative cropping bound him to subsistence levels except in a few broad and fertile valleys. New waves of out-migration drained off the strong and energetic. The primitive economy generated little money for schools and the traditionalism did not encourage them. E. O. Guerrant, a Presbyterian evangelist, wrote that during the Civil War he crossed the mountains many times without seeing a schoolhouse or a church. The roads remained little better than the ancient buffalo traces. The simplest manifestations of government advanced with glacial slowness. For example, in 1799 all of eastern Kentucky was organized into a new county called Floyd. Sixteen years elapsed before the fathers could complete a log courthouse 22 feet square. And promptly after it was finished someone burned it to the ground.

Ignorant, disorganized, old-fashioned and poor, the people were perfect victims for the mineral and land buyers who came after the Civil War. The buyers knew from their geologists what was in the land. The mountaineers knew nothing and sold everything at prices ranging from a dime to a few dollars per acre. The already precarious plight of the highlanders then became desperate, because the deeds gave to industrialists in New York, Philadelphia and London the legal title to "all mineral and metallic substances." And with the ownership of the mineral reserves passed, also, the political mastery of the region.

Thus, as the West Virginia Tax Commission warned in its 1884 report, "the history of West Virginia will be as sad as that of Poland and Ireland." And indeed all the elements of the Irish famine were present: inadequate agriculture, absentee ownership of the landed wealth, incapacity to generate and follow wise leaders. With the Great Depression and post-war mechanization of the mines, the Appalachian social order collapsed, and large-scale death by famine was prevented only by the largesse of the federal government and the most massive out-migration in U.S. history. If contemporary Appalachia has viable symbols, they are the public assistance check, the food stamp and the ancient sedan wheezing its uncertain way toward Detroit.

Thus two Appalachias grew up in the same domain, side by side and yet strangers to each other. One, the Appalachia of Power and Wealth, consists of huge land, coal, oil, gas, timber and quarry companies that "recover" the minerals from the earth; rail, barge and pipeline companies that convey the minerals to markets; and steel, refining, chemical and utility firms that convert the minerals to marketable products. This Appalachia, headquartered in New York and Philadelphia, is allied to mighty banks and insurance companies. It is exemplified by Edward B. Leisenring, Jr., now president of Penn Virginia Corporation, who boasted (*Dun's Review and Modern Industry*, April 1965), that his company netted 61 percent of gross income.

The second Appalachia is a land devastated by decades of quarrying, drilling, tunneling and strip-mining. Five thousand miles of its streams are silted and poisoned beyond any present capacity to restore them, and as many more are being reduced to the same dismal state. Its people are the old, the young who are planning to leave and the legions of crippled and sick. Its lawyers thrive on lawsuits engendered by an ultrahazardous environment.

Government has never pretended to serve both Appalachias impartially. Appalachia One routinely raises money to persuade and bribe Appalachia Two to elect candidates acceptable to wealth and power. Until recent stirrings of revolt, Appalachia Two invariably elected "bighearted country boys" beholden only to the corporate overlords who financed their campaigns. Invariably, they gave a bit more welfare to the poor and enlarged the privileges and exemptions of the rich. The poor sank into apathy and the rich, all curbs removed from their arrogance, wantonly triggered such calamities as the destruction of towns on Buffalo Creek, West Virginia. On February 26, 1972, a total of 124 people perished after a mountain of mining wastes collapsed.

In 1862, Abraham Lincoln became the first president to pledge aid to the impoverished Appalachians. The war and John Wilkes Booth kept him from acting on his promise. Seventy years later Franklin D. Roosevelt rediscovered them in an even worse situation.

The New Deal spent hundreds of millions of dollars on relief projects. Some of the ugliest schools and courthouses the human mind has ever contrived sprang up as destitute men chipped, hammered and sawed on relief works. The Civilian Conservation Corps and an expanding army and navy lifted thousands of benumbed youths out of idleness and away from moonshine stills. National Youth Administration jobs kept threadbare students in school so that they could graduate into World War II. On the eve of that conflict the New Deal formulated plans to resettle a million highlanders, a goal the postwar coal depression accomplished with dispatch.

It is doubtful that FDR could have done more even if he had wanted to. There were ranks of senators dutifully determined to protect Appalachia One even if Appalachia Two starved to death, and a Supreme Court determined to hold unconstitutional anything that tampered with the vested rights of the Mellons, Rockefellers, Pews and Insulls. A firm commitment to Appalachia Two might have aimed at a TVA-like program designed to use Appalachia's bountiful resources in a job-generating cycle within the region. The Tennessee Valley Authority pioneered in an area with few rich vested interests to offend while the equally destitute hill people were never considered for a federally mandated Appalachian Mountain Authority.

When John Kennedy ran for the White House in 1960 he overruled the advice of his aides and challenged Hubert Humphrey in West Virginia's primary. To the amazement of the nation, he won and went on to the White House. In the mountain state, the young president had seen two million people within the ruinous grip of the Appalachian culture. To do something, Kennedy appointed PARC—the President's Appalachian Regional Commission—to study the paradox of Appalachian poverty in what John Kenneth Galbraith was pleased to call the "affluent society." PARC was chaired by another Roosevelt, FDR, Jr., who, whatever his father's feelings may have been, displayed little comprehension of his task and learned little at his carefully staged "hearings."

In the bleak autumn of 1963 Homer Bigart of the *New York Times* came to eastern Kentucky and wrote about children so hungry they were eating mud from between chimney rocks, of people living in collapsing shacks, of a society that offered no alternative to the dole. The story roused the lethargic PARC to action. John Kennedy was in his grave when the pallid report went to the president's desk and the recommendations entered the U.S. Code in 1965. Lyndon Johnson signed it in a little ceremony in the White House Rose Garden, made it a part of his Great Society, and in a typical example of rhetorical overkill, declared that in Appalachia "the dole is dead."

The dole remains very much alive, and there is nothing in

the much touted Appalachian Regional Development Act that can ever bring it to an end. ARDA was written to please —or at least avoid conflict with—Appalachia One. One of Kennedy's requirements was that it be tailored to gain the support of governors whose states had counties in the region. These ranged from George Wallace to Nelson Rockefeller, and a more safely square, establishmentarian bunch of non-reformers can scarcely be imagined. They tucked in a clincher that allowed a governor to veto for his state any proposal he found offensive. Thus the Appalachia of Wealth was formally secured in its capacity to strike down federal efforts to lift the Appalachia of Poverty.

The initial authorization for LBJ's project to eradicate poverty in a diverse territory as big as Great Britain was by no means so bloated as to alarm fiscal conservatives— $1,092,400,000. And if the financing was modest, the plans, too, were calculated to stir few objections in the most cautious soul.

In America roads are beloved of all men from Paul Mellon's globe-girdling corporations to the humblest welfare recipient in a floorless cabin at the head of Powderhorn Creek. And, since roads are so favored, the governors, FDR, Jr., and Congress agreed that more than 75 percent of the money—$840 million—should be spent to build new highways.

But these were not highways of the first quality like the Interstates then beginning to lace the country together. The governors and their highway commissioners decreed 1950-style two-lane affairs, with a third or "passing" lane at intervals. The roads that emerged as a result of this saddle Appalachia with an archaic transportation system of continuing obsolescence.

And though the new highways would be rammed through the endless string of towns that shelter Appalachia Two, the bill provided no homes for the dispossessed. Hundreds of men and women—most of them old and sick, and some helpless from senility—were handed small sums and told to clear out. They did, generally into house trailers strewn about the landscape like huge, oblong dice. And the roads were scarcely completed when immense and immensely over-loaded coal trucks began pounding them to pieces. In some instances the last guardrails were not even in place when highway departments started calculating the cost of resur-facing.

Then the lawmakers prepared a small Band-Aid for the stag-gering devastation inflicted by the strip-mining of coal. They appropriated $36.5 million to patch up some of the worst eyesores. Next they acknowledged that long exploitation had ravaged the hardwood forests and that the owners of small tracts could be helped if their timber stands were improved. Five million dollars went into this task!

The mammoth erosion that was shaving mountains to the bedrock and choking streams in hundreds of counties was combated with $17 million. A study of water resources was financed with another $5 million. Sewage treatment facilities and vocational schools drew $6 million. Demonstration health facilities were financed with $69 million. Vocational schools received $16 million.

Finally, the Act provided for support to local development districts—but only after their "genuineness" had been certi-fied by the governors.

In due time the rest of the Great Society programs were impaled on the horns of the same dilemma: How to aid the region's poor without distressing its rich? It could not be done and the efforts broke down in frustration and failure.

Transferred from the Peace Corps to head the Office of Economic Opportunity, Sargent Shriver sent platoons of young, idealistic VISTA (Volunteers in Service to America) workers into Appalachia. They started "community action" enterprises, summoning the poor to countless meetings and exhorting them to organize. For what? No one had told the volunteers the answer to that or even informed them about the existence of Appalachia One. They promptly perceived the outlines of the truth, however, and began telling audiences about them, whereupon a lively time in the hills ensued. Boards of education were beset by people demanding better schools.

It was all entertaining and encouraging while it lasted. But sleeping dogs were aroused at last and telephones began ringing in the offices of congressmen and senators. VISTA was decried as Communist and un-American. A few of the volunteers were jailed on charges ranging from reckless driving to criminal syndicalism. The Great Society withdrew its soldiers from the War on Poverty, and Appalachia One settled back to digest the region undisturbed.

Henceforth federal funds came down through safe, orthodox channels where the control was well established and the people involved knew how to play the game without causing discontent in powerful quarters. With Richard Nixon came even further routinization of procedures and approaches. All told, billions have been spent on Appalachian renewal in the last 12 years and only a gimlet eye can tell any difference in the homes and lives of that numerous citizenry I have referred to as Appalachia Two.

Except in Kentucky, where a severance tax was imposed in 1972, the endless outflow of natural resources goes almost untaxed to the markets of the world. The flow is so great that as many as 25,000 railroad cars of coal have piled up at Hampton Roads, Virginia, awaiting ships for Europe and Japan. Strip-mining shatters the ancient ecology, and "reclamation" is a sorry joke. The out-migration continues, and new vocational schools supply plumbers and typists to many cities in other states. Silt from mine spoils is ruining lakes the Corps of Engineers has built at enormous costs. After a decade of much publicized "anti-poverty" efforts in the Appalachians, relief rolls have swollen ominously—in some counties to support 65 percent of the population. A whole new generation has come to maturity as public assistance recipients struggle to qualify for a continuance of the grants for the rest of their lives. In growing numbers of families no one has held a job in three generations.

In September 1972, ARDA issued its annual economic report. Within the tenacious hold of the old culture of poverty and of the great corporations that own its wealth and shape its destiny, Appalachia Two reflected the following interesting facts:

(a) Eleven percent of the residents of Central Appalachia had departed in the 1960s.

(b) Thirty-four percent of the homes lacked essential indoor plumbing.

(c) A third of the work force may be jobless.

On August 28, 1972, *Barron's National Business and Financial Weekly* characterized the entire Appalachian Poverty Program as a "costly failure."

The modern Appalachian welfare reservation makes few demands on its inhabitants. They are left alone in their crumbling coal camps and along their littered creeks to follow lives almost as individualistic, as backward looking and tradition ridden, as fatalistic and resigned as in those days three or four wars ago before the welfare check replaced the grubbing hoe and shovel as pot fillers. Then a man needed to know the seasons and the vagaries of the bossman if he were to eat. But new skills are required in an age when government is gigantic, when a few men with giant machines can drag from the ground all the fuel a nation can consume, and when the poor are of little use to the well-to-do. It pays to sense winners and vote for them—and to let them know of one's intention in advance. And one must recognize that there are powers that cannot be overturned or defied, and so one does not resist. Once these concessions are made it is generally possible to enjoy many of the freedoms and prerogatives of the nineteenth century without its toils and dangers. Perhaps Toynbee's "barbarism" is actually a preview of the twenty-first century, when the rich will be truly secure and the poor will not work, aspire or starve. Appalachia was the nation's first frontier. Now it may be foretelling America's final form. (1973)

Acknowledgments

James Agee. From *A Death in the Family* by James Agee. Copyright © 1957 by the James Agee Trust. Reprinted by permission of Grosset & Dunlap, Inc.

Sherwood Anderson. "A Jury Case," from *Death in the Woods*. Reprinted by permission of Harold Ober Associates Incorporated. Copyright 1927 by American Mercury, Inc. Copyright renewed 1954 by Eleanor Copenhaver Anderson.

Harriette Arnow. Chapter 21, *The Dollmaker*. Reprinted with permission of Macmillan Publishing Co., Inc. from *The Dollmaker* by Harriette Simpson Arnow. Copyright 1954 by Harriette Simpson Arnow.

Walter Blair. "Six Davy Crocketts," from *The Southwest Review*, XXV (1940). Reprinted by permission of Southern Methodist University Press and the author. Another version of this forms Chapter II of the author's book, *Horse Sense in American Humor* (New York: Russell & Russell, 1962).

John G. Burnett. Printed by kind permission of the Museum of the Cherokee Indian, Cherokee, North Carolina.

Harry Caudill. "O, Appalachia!" from *Intellectual Digest*, April 1973. Copyright © 1973 by Communications/Research/Machines, Inc. Reprinted by kind permission of the author.

Beulah R. Childers. "Sairy and the Young'uns." Reprinted from *Story*, 1935, by the kind permission of the author.

Donald Davidson. "Sanctuary," from *Poems, 1922–1961*. University of Minnesota Press, Mpls. © 1966 by Donald Davidson.

Wilma Dykeman. Chapter 3 from *Return the Innocent Earth* by Wilma Dykeman. Copyright © 1973 by Wilma Dykeman. Reprinted by permission of Holt, Rinehart and Winston, Inc.

Mildred Haun. "Melungeon-Colored," from *The Hawk's Done Gone*. Vanderbilt University Press, 1968. Reprinted by kind permission of Professor Herschel E. Gower, Trustee of the Mildred Haun Literary Estate.

Marion Hodge. "Cole's First Song." Printed by kind permission of the author.

Loyal Jones. "Appalachian Values," from *Twigs* X/1, pp. 82–94, Fall, 1973. Reprinted by kind permission of Dr. Leonard Roberts, Editor, *Twigs*.

David McClellan. "The Ballad of the Captain's Scars" and "East Side Manhattan Brooklyn Resurrection Vision" from *Leaves from the Legend of Luther Lamp*. Reprinted by kind permission of the author.

Louise McNeill. "Scotch Irish," "Appalachian Mountaineer," and "Overheard on a Bus (Miner's Wife)" reprinted from *Paradox Hill* by kind permission of the author and Robert F. Munn, Director of Libraries, West Virginia University. "Jacob Marlin," "Katchie Verner's Harvest," "Mountain Corn Song," "Faldang," and "Jeemes MacElmain" reprinted from *Gauley Mountain* by kind permission of the author.

H. L. Mencken. "The Hills of Zion," copyright 1926 by Alfred A. Knopf, Inc. and renewed 1954 by H. L. Mencken. Reprinted from *The Vintage Mencken*, gathered by Alistair Cooke, by permission of the publisher.

Jim Wayne Miller. "For SFS," "Family Reunion," and "The Bee Woman," from *Dialogue With a Dead Man*. Reprinted by permission of The University of Georgia Press, 1974. "Small Farms Disappearing in Tennessee" reprinted by kind permission of the author and in agreement with the *Appalachian Journal*. "Mirror for Appalachia" reprinted by kind permission of the author.

Lee Pennington. "Poet of the Soil," "The Singer of W-Hollow," "Man With A Dream," "Robert Williams Sings His Song," "Poet of the Flowers," and "In the Field." Reprinted from *Scenes from a Southern Road* by kind permission of the author.

James R. Reese. "The Myth of the Southern Appalachian Dialect as a Mirror of the Mountaineer." Printed by kind permission of the author.

Earl Schrock. "An Examination of the Dialect in *This Day and Time*," from *Tennessee Folklore Society Bulletin*, June 1971. Reprinted by kind permission of the author and The Tennessee Folklore Society.

Randall Stewart. "Tidewater and Frontier," from *The Georgia Re-*

view, volume XIII, Number 3, pp. 296–307, 1959. Reprinted by permission of *The Georgia Review* and Mrs. Randall Stewart.

James Still. "A Master Time," from *The Atlantic*, vol. 183, pp. 43–46, 1949. Reprinted by permission of International Famous Agency. Copyright © 1948 by The Atlantic Monthly Company, Boston, Mass. Reprinted with permission.

Jane Stuart. "Where Stuarts Lie," "Song of the Blackbirds," "Corn Shuck Dolls," "Roots," and "Eyes of the Mole," from *Eyes of the Mole*. Reprinted by kind permission of the author.

Jesse Stuart. "Vacation in Hell" reprinted by kind permission of the author. The following poems are reprinted by kind permission of the author: "Spring in Kentucky hills," and "Autumn is coming now" from *Man With a Bull-Tongue Plow*; "Robert Diesel," "Anannis Tabor," "Issiac Splinters," and "Lonnie Biggers," from *Album of Destiny*; and "Builders of Destiny," "Modernity," and "These Hills I Love," from *Kentucky Is My Land*.

Arnold J. Toynbee. "Scotland, Ulster and Appalachia," from *A Study of History, Volume 2: The Geneses of Civilizations*, by Arnold J. Toynbee. Oxford University Press, 1934, 1935. Reprinted by permission.

Robert Penn Warren. "Some Don'ts for Literary Regionalists," from *American Review*, VIII, pp. 142–150, 1936. Reprinted by kind permission of the author.

Jack Weller. "The Mountaineer and the Outside World," from *Yesterday's People* by Jack Weller. Reprinted by permission of the University Press of Kentucky, Lexington, Kentucky.

Billy Edd Wheeler. "An Old Man," "Mountain Fertility Rite," "Christmas in Coaltown," "The Craft Shop," and "Goliath" from *Song of a Woods Colt*, copyright 1969. Used by permission of the author Billy Edd Wheeler and Droke House Publishers, Inc. "Coal Tattoo" reprinted by permission of the author. Copyright 1963, Quartet Music, Inc. Bexhill Music Corporation, 1619 Broadway, New York, N.Y. International rights secured. Used by permission.

Cratis Williams. "Who Is the Southern Mountaineer?" from *Appalachian Journal*, 1973. Reprinted by kind permission of the author and *Appalachian Journal*.

Samuel Cole Williams. *Early Travels in The Tennessee Country 1540–1800*, copyright, 1928 by Watauga Press. Excerpts reprinted by kind permission of Mrs. Robert R. Miller and Mrs. Gordon Brown.

Edmund Wilson. "Poisoned!" from *The New Yorker*, XXXI, pp. 150–154, 1955. © 1955 The New Yorker Magazine, Inc. Reprinted with

Selected Bibliography

FICTION AND POETRY

Agee, James. *A Death in the Family*. McDowell, Obolensky, 1957. Reprinted by Grosset & Dunlap, 1972.

Anderson, Sherwood. *Death in the Woods*. Liveright, 1933.

Armstrong, Anne W. *This Day and Time*. Knopf, 1930. Reprinted by the Research Advisory Council, East Tennessee State University, 1970.

Arnow, Harriette. *The Dollmaker*. Macmillan, 1954.

———. *Hunter's Horn*. Macmillan, 1949.

———. *Kentucky Trace*. Knopf, 1974.

———. *Mountain Path*. Council of the Southern Mountains Publishers, 1963.

Caudill, Harry. *The Senator from Slaughter County*. Little, Brown, 1974.

Davidson, Donald. *Poems, 1922–1961*. University of Minnesota Press, 1966.

Dykeman, Wilma. *Return the Innocent Earth*. Holt, Rinehart and Winston, 1973.

———. *The Far Family*. Holt, Rinehart and Winston, 1966.

———. *The Tall Woman*. Holt, Rinehart and Winston, 1962.

Edwards, Lawrence. *Gravel in My Shoe*. Times Printing Company, 1963.

Ehle, John. *The Journey of August King*. Harper & Row, 1971.

———. *The Land Breakers*. Harper & Row, 1964.

———. *The Road*. Harper & Row, 1967.

Fox, John, Jr. *The Trail of the Lonesome Pine*. Scribner's, 1909.

Harben, William N. *Northern Georgia Sketches.* Books for Libraries Press, 1970.

Harris, George Washington. *Sut Lovingood's Yarns.* 1867. Reprinted by College and University Press, 1963.

Harris, Joel Chandler. *Tales of the Home Folks in Peace and War.* Reprinted by Books for Libraries Press, 1969.

Haun, Mildred. *The Hawk's Done Gone.* Vanderbilt University Press, 1968.

Marius, Richard. *The Coming of Rain.* Knopf, 1969.

McCarthy, Cormac. *The Orchard Keeper.* Random House, 1965.

McNeill, Louise. *Gauley Mountain.* Harcourt Brace, 1939.

————. *Paradox Hill.* West Virginia University Library, 1972.

Miller, Jim Wayne. *Dialogue with a Dead Man.* University of Georgia Press, 1974.

Murfree, Mary N. *In the Tennessee Mountains.* University of Tennessee Press, 1970.

Pennington, Lee. *Scenes from a Southern Road.* JRD Publishing Company, Inc., 1969.

Roberts, Elizabeth M. *The Great Meadow.* Viking Press, 1930.

————. *The Time of Man.* Viking Press, 1945.

Roberts, Leonard. *Up Cutshin and Down Greasy.* University of Kentucky Press, 1959.

Still, James. *Hounds on the Mountain.* Viking Press, 1937.

————. *On Troublesome Creek.* Viking Press, 1940.

————. *River of Earth.* Viking Press, 1940.

Stuart, Jane. *Eyes of the Mole.* Stanton & Lee Publishers, 1967.

————. *Yellowhawk.* McGraw-Hill, 1973.

Stuart, Jesse. *Album of Destiny.* Dutton, 1944.

————. *Jesse Stuart Reader.* McGraw-Hill, 1963.

————. *Kentucky Is My Land.* Dutton, 1952.

————. *Man with a Bull-Tongue Plow.* Dutton, 1959.

————. *Taps for Private Tussie.* Dutton, 1943.

————. *Trees of Heaven.* Dutton, 1940.

Tarleton, Fiswoode. *Bloody Ground.* Dial Press, 1929.

Wheeler, Billy Edd. *Song of a Woods Colt.* Droke House Publishers, distributed by Grosset & Dunlap, 1969.

Wolfe, Thomas. *Look Homeward, Angel.* Scribner's, 1929.

————. *The Hills Beyond.* Harper & Row, 1935.

NON-FICTION

Arnow, Harriette. *Flowering of the Cumberland.* Macmillan, 1963.

————. *Seedtime on the Cumberland.* Macmillan, 1960.

Blair, Walter. *Horse Sense in American Humor.* Russell & Russell, 1962.

————. *Native American Humor.* Chandler Publishing Company, 1960.

Boatright, Mody C. *Folk Laughter on the American Frontier.* Peter Smith, 1971.

Burton, Thomas G. and Ambrose N. Manning. *Folklore: Folksongs.* Research Advisory Council, East Tennessee State University, 1967.

———. *Folksongs II.* Research Advisory Council, East Tennessee State University, 1969.

Campbell, John C. *The Southern Highlander and His Homeland.* Russell Sage Foundation, 1921.

Caruso, John A. *Appalachian Frontier.* Bobbs-Merrill, 1959.

Cash, W. J. *The Mind of the South.* Knopf, 1941.

Caudill, Harry. *My Land Is Dying.* Dutton, 1971.

———. *Night Comes to the Cumberlands.* Little, Brown, 1962.

Clark, Thomas D. *Travels in the Old South,* A Bibliography. University of Oklahoma Press, 1956.

Coles, Robert. *Migrants, Sharecroppers, and Mountaineers.* Little, Brown, 1972.

Crockett, David. *A Narrative of the Life of David Crockett of the State of Tennessee.* Tennesseana edition. University of Tennessee Press, 1973.

Dargan, Olive Tilford. *From My Highest Hill.* Lippincott, 1941.

Draper, Lyman C. *King's Mountain and Its Heroes: History of the Battle of King's Mountain.* 1881. Reprinted by Blue and Gray Press, 1971.

Dykeman, Wilma. *The French Broad—A Rivers of America Book.* Holt, Rinehart and Winston, 1955; University of Tennessee Press, 1965.

Eckert, Allen W. *The Frontiersman.* Little, Brown, 1967.

Flint, Timothy. *Biographical Memoir of Daniel Boone.* Edited by James K. Folsom. College and University Press, 1967.

Frome, Michael. *Strangers in High Places.* Doubleday, 1966.

Gazaway, Rena. *The Longest Mile.* Doubleday, 1969.

James, Bessie. *Anne Royall's U.S.A.* Rutgers University Press, 1972.

Jolley, Harley E. *The Blue Ridge Parkway.* University of Tennessee Press, 1969.

Kephart, Horace. *Our Southern Highlanders.* Macmillan, 1922.

Kincaid, Robert L. *The Wilderness Road.* Bobbs-Merrill, 1947. Reprinted 1966.

Matthiessen, F. O, *The American Renaissance.* Oxford University Press, 1941.

O'Connor, Flannery. *Mystery and Manners.* Farrar, Straus & Giroux, 1969.

Rice, Otis K. *The Allegheny Frontier.* University of Kentucky Press, 1970.

Roosevelt, Theodore. *The Winning of the West.* Review of Reviews Co., 1889.

Royall, Anne. *Letters from Alabama, 1817–1822.* University of Alabama Press, 1969.

Scarborough, Dorothy. *A Song Catcher in the Southern Mountains.* Columbia University Press, 1937.

Sharp, Cecil and Dorothy Karpeles. *Eighty English Folk Songs from the Southern Appalachians.* MIT Press, 1968.

Starkey, Marion L. *Cherokee Nation.* Knopf, 1946.

Stewart, Randall. *Regionalism and Beyond.* Vanderbilt University Press, 1968.

Stuart, Jesse. *The Thread That Runs So True.* Scribner's, 1949.

Thornburgh, Laura. *The Great Smoky Mountains.* Thomas Y. Crowell, 1942.

Turner, Frederick J. *The Significance of the Frontier in American History.* Annual Report of the American Historical Association, 1893.

Weller, Jack E. *Yesterday's People.* University of Kentucky Press, 1971.

White, Helen and Redding S. Sugg. *From the Mountain.* Memphis State University Press, 1972.

Wigginton, Eliot (editor). *The Foxfire Book.* Doubleday, 1972.

Wilkins, Thurman. *Cherokee Tragedy.* Macmillan, 1970.

Williams, Cratis D. *The Southern Mountaineer in Fact and Fiction.* New York University dissertation, 1961.

Williams, Samuel Cole (editor). *Early Travels in the Tennessee Country, 1540–1800.* Watauga Press, 1928.

————. *Lt. Henry Timberlake's Memoirs.* Watauga Press, 1927.

Wilson, Edmund. *Patriotic Gore.* Oxford University Press, 1962.